Young Conquerors

ALSO BY
CHRISTOPHER COSMOS

Once We Were Here

Young Conquerors

A Novel of **HEPHAESTION** *and* **ALEXANDROS**

CHRISTOPHER COSMOS

PENINSULA

Copyright © 2024 Christopher Cosmos

All rights reserved. No part of this book may be reproduced or used in any manner without the prior written permission of the copyright owner, except for the use of brief quotations in a book review.

Hardcover: ISBN 979-8-9894134-0-9

Library of Congress Control Number: TXU002397238

First Edition

Cover design by Laura Klynstra.
Interior design by William Overbeeke.

CHAPTER ONE

I WAS BORN A PRINCE, though I'm the only prince I know that was born without a kingdom. A young boy could have easily thought of that as a curse, and for a time I did, too, but it instead ended up being a gift for me. My father died when I was six years old, and since I was too young to take his place, the kingdom that he ruled on the jagged and rugged coast north of Greece near where the Ionian and Adriatic waters mix went to my uncle, Kleon, to safeguard until I came of age to rule in my uncle's place. But in the world and kingdom into which I was born, men don't easily or willingly relinquish thrones upon which they sit, and so I'd always known, since I was very young, that the path that I'd make—or, conversely, the one that I wouldn't—would have to be my own; I'd always known that in the rugged and harsh world into which I was born, I'd be whatever I was strong enough or had it in myself to become. And so for a prince born without a father, and without a kingdom, that would be enough. That would be more than enough, because that's what the world and the future is, isn't it? At least that's the world and future that I know, and I'm not sure what any other looks or feels like, and I'm not sure I want to, either. The thing I didn't expect, however, was for my future to come as quickly as it did; I expected to be a boy for just a little longer, but that's also something that isn't often allowed in the harsh corner of the world where I was born and made.

The change comes the week of my fifteenth birthday.

It's still night and dark outside with only a sliver of light from the northern moon that's always wild and restless when my mother comes to my room with fear and tears in her eyes and tells me what my future will be, and that it won't be in Illyria, at least not for some years after this moment. I'm asleep when she wakes me with the news and I'm embarrassed because she's my mother and I have no clothes on under the lion-skin blanket that covers and protects me from the chill that comes during the night, the biting and cold temperatures that roll down from the high and sharp-peaked mountains above where we live. It's still two days before my birthday, and a year before the birthday in which I'll become a man, but she tells me it's already time—that it's better to be early than late, in a matter such as this, in a matter such as succession, which is of course also a matter of life and death—and so I have to leave. She doesn't want to give my uncle Kleon any excuses or reasons to see me, his nephew, as a man, or anything other than just a harmless and unthreatening child, and so we had planned for this moment, and what would need to be done.

And now the moment is here.

She turns away as I get out of bed and quickly dress.

When I'm finished and clothed, cinching my leather belt tight across my waist where it holds my dark-colored riding chiton in place over my torso and upper-thighs, she turns back and looks at me, up and down, up and down. I'm taller than she is now, by more than a few inches, which is something that has only happened in the last year, or maybe even the last month. I look back at her and wonder what she might be thinking. I look back at her, into her deep and blue-flecked eyes that are set against her dark northern mountain features and wonder what it must be like to give to the world your son, your oldest son, and to give him for nothing in return. Then there's no more time for wonder, or anything else.

"Let's go," she whispers, very quietly.

I wait for another moment, looking back at her, then I nod, and we begin to leave, together.

We head towards the door and before we get there, I take my broadsword from where it always leans against the wall, near my bed, ready for anything that might come in the night or otherwise, and we walk out. I softly close the door behind us as we quietly go down the mosaic-tiled hallway, the ancient stone under our feet worn from generations before us, and the color that was painted on the stone faded from weather and time and shuffling feet. My mother wants to take me straight to the stables and the horse that she'd gifted me for the birthday before this one, but I insist on stopping at my brother's room first. I can hear her breathe nervously when I tell her this, because someone in the palace might wake and see us and know what we're doing in the darkness, in the black Illyrian night. But even though she breathes sharply and disapproves, she won't stop me. We go further down the hallway, and then come to his room, and I go inside. I quietly move towards his bed where I kneel and shake him awake, and when he opens his eyes and returns from sleep and back to his body, I tell him with hushed and urgent words what's happening and what I, his brother, must now do.

I see him frown, wrinkling his nose, blinking his still sleep-filled eyes.

"Why?" he asks, his voice soft, the voice of a child.

He will still have to live here, in Salona, in Illyria, in the mountains that are our mountains and by the great seas that mix off our coast that are our seas, where we were both born and made, and I don't want him to live in fear, so I don't answer; I just tell him my exile won't be forever, and that one day soon I'll see him again. I hope my words are truth, even as I speak them, and that I'll have the strength to be able to make them so. I tell him to watch over our mother, and when he practices with his sword and spear to keep them both held high and above the guard of his opponent. I tell him all the things our father told me, and would have told him, too, had he still been there to raise us, his sons, because I know that since the day he died I haven't been just a brother, but a father, also, in so many ways, and now I'm a father and brother that has to leave.

I embrace him, longer than I ever have before.

Then after another moment holding him, lingering, remembering, looking down into his young and questioning eyes that are my eyes, too, I turn and I go.

THE STABLES ARE QUIET when we get there, and it's still dark.

I adjust my chiton and feel the pommel of the broad-sword that I carry in my hand, clenching and unclenching my fingers around it, then my mother comes and hands me a new chlamys that she's knitted for me to wear as I ride. I see that there's a hood attached to it that can be pulled over the head and around the face, which is unusual for a chlamys; the hood is for the cold, I know, the chill that will come in the high-peaked and snow-covered mountains where I'll be riding, but it's also for something else, too. Disguise. There will be men that will come looking for me. I feel the sword that's in my hand again, my fingers still wrapped around the handle, still clenching and unclenching, and even more now, harder, firmer, knuckles turning white, and part of me wishes that when the men come looking, they'll find me. It's what I've been trained to feel, and want, and so I do. It's normal. It's what all young men in Illyria are trained to feel and want, even if they shouldn't.

Will it be different elsewhere?

Do boys in Macedon train the same way, and feel the same things, and what about further south, and the other Greeks?

I don't know.

But perhaps I'll soon find out.

"Get to Pella," my mother tells me, with hushed and whispered words. "Pledge yourself to Philippos and make sure that he accepts your service, because even Kleon won't be able to touch you there. Even Kleon wouldn't dare harm one of Macedon's wards."

"I will," I nod.

"I love you," she whispers, her words carried to me on the cold wind.

I look back at her.

I wish I could do more.

I wish I could stay, I wish I could fight, I wish I could do something to prevent what's now happening and what's happened, both to me, and to my family, but I know that I can't.

At least not yet.

"This isn't forever," I tell her. "One day, when I'm strong enough, I'll come back and I'll take again what's ours. For all of us."

"I know you will, my son," she breathes in return, and I can see the tears that are on her cheeks again. "But until that day, know that wherever you go, wherever you travel, wherever the gods and the winds and your spirit takes you . . . know that those same winds and spirit will bring my love along with you, also."

"Mother—"

There are more tears.

They're mine now, though.

I try to blink them away, but I can't.

I don't want them to come, and she's my mother, so she knows this, too, and pretends like she doesn't see. "Hurry now," she whispers instead, pushing me towards the horse.

I look back at her, one more time, and for one more moment.

I finally unclench my hands and sling my broad-sword up and across my back, fastening it there with the leather strap that's attached to the hilt, before I jump up and onto my horse, a practiced and familiar movement that a boy growing in these hills and mountains has done and practiced more than one million times.

I look down at her.

I look down at her as she stands there and watches me in the darkness and this is strength, I realize, and it's also perhaps strength of a type I will never know. But there's one thing of which I'm certain: if I'm going to grow, and if I'm going to find out all that I will know, and all that I can be, and the different type of strength I've been given, then I need to leave, and it can't wait any longer.

There are more tears.

I don't hide them this time or try to, because I can't, and I don't wipe at them, or blink, either. I simply nod, one more time, then turn my horse and head towards the gate. The horse walks at first, quietly, then I squeeze my thighs to pick up the pace and go faster, out of the courtyard, and my horse's hooves make a gentle clacking on the worn and cold stone beneath us as he starts to trot, then gallop, but no one in the palace wakes and no one comes. I don't look back; I can't. I keep riding, away from the palace and through the city, and after I leave the town and place where I was born and where I was raised, I still keep going, on and towards the snow-capped mountains in the distance and the still-dark future that waits on the other side of them. I'm soon alone with the peaks and horizon and the path that leads towards future, and destiny, and whatever fate will now come for a young and ambitious prinkipas that was born without a kingdom. I keep riding, galloping even faster now, hooves pounding dirt and grass as I head towards the pass that rises sharply through the mountains and away from my people and home and all that I know. I still don't look back. I want to, but I don't. I just keep riding.

I'VE RIDDEN FOR SEVERAL HOURS when the sun finally begins to rise and crest in the distance, and the light that comes spreads across both my path, and also all else there is, reflecting sharply off the whiteness of the snow that's fallen and accumulated in greater amounts the higher I've gotten into the mountains. Then not long after the sun and first light comes, I hear something behind me. I turn from my place on my horse to see a group of startled birds fly from a branch where they'd been sitting. My eyes tilt up and I look at them as they head into the cloudless mountain sky. Then my eyes turn back down, towards the path, the one I've just travelled, and I see two other riders. They're there in the distance still, but galloping through the snow, towards me, following the same path as the tracks I've already and just made. There's only one reason they'd be galloping, I know, and it can mean only one thing.

Kleon's men.

And they've found me.

How did they gain on me so quickly?

They must have heard me leave; they must have known somehow.

I turn and look to the east and weigh my options: I could continue to gallop and ride, too, and just as I know that I'm a gifted swordsman, I'm a gifted rider, also, and I could out-distance them, at least for a time. But there are still several hours between these mountains and Pella, and I can't risk them finding me when I have to stop, or catching up to me when I'm unawares, or perhaps most importantly, I can't risk them knowing where I've gone.

I have to fight them, or do something else.

They've seen me, they've found my tracks, and so there's no other way.

I reach around to my back and unsling my broad-sword that's there and then turn towards them and wait as they approach.

I wait.

I wait.

They get closer.

They start to slow as they get near, riding through snow that's on the ground and snow that begins to fall now again, too, around us, from the clouds above, and as they get closer, riding through the flakes that fall harder and harder, more and more, they stop galloping.

They come even closer still, walking now, even slower.

I recognize them as soldiers I've seen in the city before, and in the palace.

I try to control my breathing, and work to keep myself calm.

Then they pull their horses to a halt across from me.

I've practiced with my broad-sword since I was little more than a child, which means I've practiced with it since before I can remember, and since I was a prince raised without a kingdom, and a father, I've put everything into my training that I could put into it, knowing I would have to make my own way in the world.

But that had all been just that.

Training.

This is now real.

More snow begins to fall, brighter and larger flakes drifting down from the clouds. "What do you want?" I finally call to them, towards where they've pulled their horses to a halt across from me.

"We're here to take you back to Salona, Hephaestion," the first soldier responds.

"Why?"

"Because your uncle wishes to speak with you," it's the second that answers this time.

I take note of their weapons: they each carry a short, double-sided xiphos, the type of sword favored by the Illyrians, the southern Greeks, and the northern ones, too, the Macedonians who are on the other side of these mountains. But my weapon is unique. My broad-sword was made in a different way, and is from even further south, from the islands, and was fashioned for me by a travelling blacksmith from Kriti. It's heavier, a relic from an older and more ancient world even than ours, and it's more difficult to wield. But it also has a much greater reach and strength, which I've trained the muscles in my arms and chest and shoulders to bear, and which will give me an advantage over them.

If I can exploit it.

"Were my uncle's orders to bring me to him alive?" I call back to them.

"He didn't say," the first soldier responds again. "So I suppose either way works just as well."

I raise my eyebrows.

I wasn't expecting such honesty.

It goes against everything that's in me, everything that I want and that I know and feel, but it's the best plan, and so I decide to match their honesty with my own. "Then tell him that," I call back to them.

"Tell him what?"

"Tell him that I died here. Tell him that we fought, and that you killed me."

"Why would we do that?"

"Because it's easier, and then you won't have to lose your lives."

They look at each other, and then to me again, and they smile.

"What makes you think we'd lose?" the second soldier laughs as he calls back.

But I'm ready.

I'm ready for this question, and it's what I've wanted them to ask.

"Do you know what my job was, ever since I was born?" I ask them.

They shrug.

No.

"It was to learn how to use this," I tell them, patting the great broadsword I hold in front of me. "What were your jobs, before you were soldiers? Were you farmers? Fisherman? Something else perhaps?"

I know this about them, and that they haven't always been warriors; they were hired to fight for Illyria in the war my great-uncle fought against Macedon, and lost, then they'd stayed soldiers after we'd been defeated because they made more gold and worked less than they had in their previous lives. Being a soldier was an easy job in Salona, when there was no fighting and no war. But now they're faced with both, because they face me.

I see them hesitate.

I'm young, but they've heard of my reputation, I can see, and perhaps have even seen me practicing in the palace courtyard, too, with the armsmaster, and I know they can see the great and unfamiliar broad-sword that's in my hand.

"And why would we do that?" the second one speaks again, slowly this time, and without laughing now. "Why would we leave you alive and risk Kleon's wrath by lying?"

I reach to my waist and take the pouch that's there, the one that holds my gold coins, the ones that are made for the royal family, embossed with the head of my great-grandfather Bardylis who brought our tribe together with the other tribes of the northern mountains and ruled over them all. I hold it out in front of me so they can see it, too. "Show this pouch and these coins to my uncle, and he'll know where it's from, and he'll believe your story," I tell them. "And you can keep and split the rest of the coins between you, that you don't show him."

They look at each other again.

"We never took you for a coward, Hephaestion-prinkipas," the first soldier speaks now, turning back to me. "But first you run from Salona, in the night, and now this?"

I could win.

I know that I could win, in a fight against them; I could spill their blood, red and bright and fresh across this white snow.

But I have my reasons for doing this.

It pains me, but I have my reasons.

"What will it be?" I ask them, instead.

The soldiers hesitate, for a moment, both of them.

Then finally they each nod, one after the other, the second and then the first, and when they do, I toss the pouch to them through the falling snow. It twists in the air as it flies, and then the first one catches it with a soft clink of metal. He opens it, takes one of the coins out to inspect the gold, and what's embossed on it, and after he does, he nods. He tucks the pouch away into the chlamys he wears then turns and with one more look, kicks his horse to a trot and starts to head back the way he came, the second soldier doing the same next to him. I watch as they go, to make sure they'll keep their word and that they'll actually leave and won't come back and they'll let me continue in peace. They do, and I watch until they're finally gone, out of eye-sight and back down the path and mountains, and then when they are, I turn, too, and once again continue heading east.

I ride.

I think about what they said.

It's not that I'm a coward, as they called me, it's that if I'd killed them, as I knew I would have, then Kleon would know I was alive, and well, and exactly where I'd gone. I think of my mother and brother, because it will be a great blow to them when they hear, but it will be more useful if Kleon thinks I'm dead because there will be no assassins in the night, there will be no poison slipped into my breakfast, when I least suspect it, or an entire youth and childhood spent looking over my shoulder for whatever other evil might come or that he might send. This is hard for me. This is hard for a boy who would think of himself as a man, and a warrior, and who has trained his whole life to be both of those things.

But it's right.

The snow begins to lessen, and then finally stops altogether.

I soon come down out of the mountains, too, and I ride towards the foothills that are beyond them. This is the point where the high, sharp, and rugged peaks of Illyria give way to the wide and endless rolling hills of Macedon, and as I gallop across the fields and between the rocky slopes, I crest one of the low hills, and when I do, I pause, because I see a city beneath me, at the edge of a wide and long and golden plain.

It's a great city, I see, an ancient and bustling capital.

Pella.

I look down and I see the palace, first, then I look and make out the great temples to gods I don't yet know. I see the gymnasium, and what must be the barracks, and I see the rest of the city spread all around, also, and between those things, the larger stone houses near the palace that are two and three and four stories tall, and then the smaller ones with just wood and thatched roofs that are only a single story, further south, and built much closer together, too, in the lower parts of the city.

I breathe in, deeply.

I let my chest settle, and then I breathe again.

I look up at the sky, which on this southern and eastern side of the mountains seems to go on and on in a way that it doesn't in Illyria, and the north, with no interrupting peaks or clouds or anything else for as far as I can see. Then I turn from the sky and look back down at the city again, and I wonder about it, and what it will hold; I wonder a great many things about fate, and family, and fortune, but most of all, I wonder what my future will now be. There's only one way to find out, though, and so I slowly exhale, letting out the breath I've been holding, squeeze my legs to bring my horse to a gallop again, and then ride down and towards the strange and unfamiliar place that I hope will now be my new home.

CHAPTER TWO

I STAND IN FRONT OF PHILIPPOS, the basileus of Macedon. He's a relatively short man—this basileus and warrior we've all heard so much about—but he's also very broad of shoulder and has a thick, black beard below a scar that begins at the top of his scalp and extends down and across his right eye which is squinted shut by the rough tissue that has formed and grown over the lid. Philippos' reputation as a soldier has been the subject of song and legend, both in Macedon and beyond, but his reputation was built when he was a young man. He's older now, I see, and the years have begun to take a toll; when he walks, he does so with a slight limp, and when I look at the sagging muscles in his arms, I'm sure he doesn't swing a sword in the same way he used to, either. His body has changed, it's clear, after many decades of war and conquering, but I can also tell the state of his body has done nothing to change his mind, the alertness of it, or his temper, which seems very close to the surface. Well, time has done nothing to his temper except perhaps to sharpen and hone it, even further than what it was when he was a young man, and having only just taken his throne.

"And why should I welcome you into my home?" he asks me, as he stares across the room with his one still-good eye that's colored a deep and speckled grey. He stands in front of the great desk that dominates most of the room we're in, his office, where he takes meetings both military and civil, and I'm across from him. We're alone except for a young guard that waits quietly behind us near the door.

I look back at him, at this great and famous man, and I meet his gaze.

"I've heard that you've brought the sons of all the noble families here," I say, very slowly, choosing my words with as much precision and specificity as I can. "I've heard you've brought all those sons here to live in your house, so that they can train until they're of age to serve you, and Macedon, and fight."

"That's right," he nods. "I have."

"I'd ask to be able to take a place among them, too, as one of your wards, and I'd train here also, to serve you."

"No."

"Why?"

"Because there's a difference between you and them."

"What difference?"

"I've brought the sons of the noble families in my kingdom to train here. Which means they're all sons of *Macedonian* families. We don't train foreigners in our court, with our swords and shields and strategies, eating our food and sleeping under our roofs. Your uncle is no friend of mine, and for the type of hospitality you ask, you might have better luck if you continue further south and to the other Greeks that are there, the softer ones," he says dismissively, waving his arm in that general direction, and then turns back to his desk.

I stand there, looking at him.

He's been trained, and I have, too; we've both been trained to never give up.

"But you're ruler of more than just Macedon now, Philippos-basileus," I say, calling him by his title. "You're also ruler of Illyria, where I'm from, and which you've conquered, and Thrace, and Epirus, and even more kingdoms and tribes, too."

He doesn't speak.

He shuffles through items I can't see, pushing them both here and there, back and forth. "I am," he finally says. "But what of it?"

"The world becomes smaller every day, or at least all the rest of the world, but your kingdom becomes larger."

"That's right. It does."

"So perhaps it's time to expand the sons that you bring here to serve you, too. Perhaps it's time for you to expand that, as well, to represent *all* the kingdoms and tribes that you rule, and not just Macedon."

"But I have peace with the Illyrians. I've conquered them, as you've said, and in return they give me tribute and soldiers and gold and leave my northern border alone. Why should I risk that?"

"What would be the risk?"

He finally looks back up at me.

I see his eye again; his one good, grey eye.

"I thought you were clever, Hephaestion of Salona, when you first walked in here. I suppose even a basileus as successful as I am can still be wrong."

"You're worried about Kleon. My uncle."

"He rules Illyria and the tribes, doesn't he? You don't think it would offend him if I offered sanctuary and blessing to the boy who the throne was supposed to go to before him, the boy who is the greatest threat to his power and rule?"

"He thinks I'm dead."

"And so what if he finds out you're not?"

"He won't be basileus of Illyria forever."

"No one is basileus forever, not even me. But he's basileus *right now*."

"He won't be for long. I swear it."

The words just come.

I don't know where they come from, they just do.

Philippos stares back at me, his single eye narrowing. "Why?" he asks. "Because *you* will be?"

"Yes," I nod.

My eyes.

I feel them blaze and flash as I say this, and Philippos must see this, too, what I feel and believe, because the look in his own eye begins to change as he stares back at me. And when I see this, I remain stoic and try to stand a little bit taller. I try to play the part, to be the part. I try to look strong, to look like a young and confident prinkipas who will one day be a great and strong and wise basileus, just as I've said I would be. Philippos doesn't answer, though.

I wonder if I've gone too far.

I may have, but it doesn't matter, because I swore to myself a long time ago that too far is the mistake I'd always make if a mistake had to be made, and not the opposite of that; I swore to myself, as a young boy, by a stream in the mountains above where I'm from, that I'd always err by pushing too much, by asking for too much, by reaching for the sun and moon and stars and anything else there is in this world to reach for.

"You could have continued on south, to Athens, Corinth, Thebes, wherever, and where you know they're more hospitable," Philippos speaks slowly, his eye still staring back at mine, sizing me up.

"Yes."

"But you came here, and you're still here. Why?"

"Because Macedon is the future."

"They've said that of those other places, once, too. Some even still do."

"They're not. We both know that."

"How?"

"Because soon all of Greece will be yours."

"You sound very sure of that."

"I am, as I know you are, too, and if you give me sanctuary now, and allow me to grow here, in your city, and kingdom, and away from my uncle, then I swear to you that Illyria will be yours when my time comes and I promise it will *always* be yours, which is certainly more than Kleon can promise. He'll stab you in the back, the first chance he gets. You know him, so you know that, just the same as I do."

Philippos thinks about that, weighing my words.

"And if I don't accept?" he asks.

"I don't know what the future holds, the same as you don't. But I do know that you'll have insulted the basileus that will one day sit on the throne of the kingdom at your northern border, the one you wish to keep secure and peaceful, as you've said."

Philippos still stares back at me.

I can't read his eye anymore, or his look.

He comes towards me, standing even closer now. Then I'm surprised when he reaches out and touches me. He touches my chest, feeling it with his worn and scarred hand, letting his touch linger, and I find this strange. I can smell him now, too. He smells of horses and dirt, and I find this strange, also, because there aren't many rulers like Philippos of Macedon; there aren't many basileus left in this world like the ancient ones of myth and legend, the ones who were first into battle, the ones who were the best with a sword, and shield, the bravest and strongest and wildest and boldest, and the world is a worse place without leaders who do these things they ask their men to do.

But this one does.

And that's why he's Philippos.

I watch him and I can still smell him as he touches my chest, then he takes his hand away and turns to look at the guard, who waits near the door. Philippos' gaze rests there for one more moment, his eye connected with the guard's clear blue eyes, as if they're communicating and speaking in a way that I don't know and don't understand. Then Philippos turns back to me. He reaches up and uses his hand to turn my face to the side, as if he's inspecting me.

I wait.

I hold my breath and I wonder what he'll do.

Finally, he takes his hand away again.

His skin no longer touches my skin.

"I was also a son that was to inherit nothing, a son that was born without a kingdom and that had to earn and take all that I now have and rule," he speaks low and slow, like the rulers even further south of

Athens and Corinth, the warrior-basileus' that rule the Peloponnese. "I felt the same way when I was your age," he continues, "and I want no boys around my family or in my kingdom who don't feel similarly, or as deeply. You will swear your allegiance to me, for the rest of your life?"

"I swear allegiance to Illyria," I tell him, and I don't hesitate with my answer, because when it's what we feel in our heart then there isn't time for calculation, only truth. "I swear allegiance first to my people, the same as you would, and then I swear to you second. You have my word."

There's another moment.

Philippos stares back at me.

Then, very strangely, his lips start to part into a smile, a very small smile, and he laughs, a loud and barking noise that interrupts the seriousness and gravity that's been in the room. "Your dead father was an honest man, too," he tells me, still smiling, "and he would be proud of you," Philippos says, then his eyes flick again towards the door and the guard that's standing there. "Go and find him a room with the others."

The guard nods.

I bow my head in thanks and then turn towards the door, to follow after the guard, as the basileus has said, and I'm almost there and gone when I hear Philippos, once more, from behind me, near his great desk again. "Why does your uncle think you're dead?" he asks.

I pause. I turn back.

"Because it's what I want him to think," I say, when I meet his eye.

Philippos waits, for another moment, looking back at me.

Then he slowly nods.

"You might just go some distance in this world, Hephaestion of Salona," he tells me. "You just might."

I nod, once more, and so does he.

Then I turn and leave.

I WALK THROUGH THE CITY with Philippos' bodyguard who tells me his name is Pausanius, and when he does, I turn and look at him again: he's tall and has dark hair, similar to my own, but his eyes are clear and blue, like the eyes of those not born in the mountains; they're the eyes of one born carrying the sea in them, and I also realize, now that I've seen him in the light, and thus really *seen* him, that he might be the most good-looking man I've ever met. I wonder about this, as we keep walking, but then I turn my eyes from him, and to the city around us, the city I know now will be my new home, as I've hoped. We go past the stables first, as we walk together, which are large, larger than any I've seen in Salona or Illyria, and then we continue on, and beyond them. We come to the barracks next, where there are men outside, both young and old, and they train with the short xiphos swords like the ones that soldiers use in Illyria, and here in Greece, too, as well as the men I faced in the mountains, but didn't fight. We go past houses, built two and three and four stories into the air, something I've never seen before, and fashioned out of pale-colored stone that must be mined and quarried from somewhere near here, I realize, where the stone is also pale, and then we pass what Pausanius tells me is the Temple of Dionysus. It's tall and large with massive carved columns that reach up towards the blue and endless sky, above even the four-story-houses, and there's a beautiful, mosaic-tiled floor beneath the columns, fashioned into an intricate geometric pattern of inter-connected diamonds and squares. I smell incense, coming from between the pillars, wafting in great clouds of aromatic smoke, and as I look, I also see the temple is big, bigger than any I've ever seen before in my life, big enough to take my breath away, and then the next breath after that one, too.

We don't have things like this in Illyria.

We don't have things like this in Illyria at all.

"It is beautiful, isn't it?"

I turn to look at Pausanius now, who's still next to me, and he closes his eyes as he inhales, smelling the incense, also. Then he opens his eyes again and looks at me. I take him in, and see that he does the same to me, and as I look at him further, this is what I find: we're both about the same height, and with the same build, but that's where the physical similarities between us end. I can't read his eyes, which aren't open, as I know mine are, or his intentions, and there's nothing else about him that seems or feels familiar. He's also much better looking than I am, as I've already noticed, the proportions of his face absolutely perfect, a strand of hair never out of place, a smile that goes on and on and doesn't seem to ever end.

"It's unlike anything I've ever seen," I finally tell him.

"I thought the same thing, too, when I first came to the capital."

"Where did you come from? Where did you grow up, before this?"

"Orestis," he says, and then frowns slightly at the name of his city. "So I come from the mountains, too, like you do," he finishes, and then the frown turns back into his smile, his beautiful smile, his endless smile which I also see now is a seductive smile and a smile of many secrets. I've been wrong about him, I realize. I was wrong about his blue eyes, and what they meant, and I was wrong about where he was from. I'll need to be careful here; it isn't like it is in Salona, where men and women are what they seem. Here, at least so far, with him, the opposite has proven to be true.

Then he gestures with his hand, down the road. "This way," he tells me, and we keep going.

We keep walking through the city.

We go past more houses, which are large and high and must belong to more of the wealthy and noble families that live in Pella, and then soon after these houses, we come to the gymnasium.

We go inside.

The doorway's wide and large, and so is the ceiling and room that's beyond the doorway, and that we walk into after we leave the cobblestone street. Once we do, and go inside, we're immediately greeted by the familiar smell of sweat mixed with sand and also all the similarly familiar sounds and noises that go along with any gymnasium, and training, and exercise. We walk a few more paces and go beyond a couple more pillars, and then the building opens into the large and main room, and that's when I see them: they're all young men of my own age that are training long, muscular, and summer-dark bodies which are tanned from their time outside in the sun which shines stronger and more clear and uninterrupted here than it does in Illyria, here under the large, endless, and mostly cloudless Macedonian sky. And so even though it's not summer, their skin still looks like it, and I watch as two of the boys wrestle, gripping their limbs, moving and pushing for better positions, trying to unbalance and throw the other. Some of the other boys watch them, too, waiting to take the place of the loser, and then some of the others yet run short but intense sprints off to the side, or box against each other with cloth pads wrapped over their hands, or push large and heavy stones across a short distance as they strain the muscles in their legs and thighs to lift and roll the rocks and then turn around to do it over again. They do all this, along with many other exercises, too, to build their stamina and endurance in any way that they can. These young men aren't soldiers, I can see, not yet, the same as I'm not a soldier yet. But they soon will be, the same as I also soon will be, and they will be fearsome and strong, since it's clear their whole purpose, life, and existence is dedicated to this singular and all-consuming reason and goal.

One of the boys turns and sees us, where we stand, and then the others do, too.

They look over at us first, as they pause, and what I'll soon learn is that while these boys may have been brought here from all corners of the kingdom, these aren't the favored ones; these are the boys who are the second and third and fourth sons of noble families and provincial rulers, and these are the ones who are the cast-offs, the extras, the spares who have been given less love, less attention, less responsibility, less everything. So they've had to take all those things for themselves, as I also have. They stop their exercises when they see me, the new boy that's now amongst them—the new cast-off, I know that they think—and do they recognize a kindred spirit in me, as I perhaps can recognize in them? I don't know, but then there's no more time for thoughts or questions, as they start to come over and stand in a line in front of me, and Pausanias introduces each of them.

Ptolemaios.
Kassandros.
Philotas.
Perdiccas.
Nearchos.
Leonnatos.
I will remember their names.

I nod my head in greeting, a shallow but respectful nod, and they do nothing in return, they just stare back at me. Then Pausanias motions to me with his hand and we keep going, past them and through the gymnasium. We keep walking, over and around the sand where they train, and as we do, I can feel them watching us as we go—watching *me*, of course, really—and while I can't hear what they whisper behind their hands, whether they recognize my kindred spirit as the same as their spirit, or not, I know what they feel, and what they call me, because it's what I've felt and been called all my life.

Barbarian.
Mountain-dweller.
Not-Greek.

Pausanias takes me down another sparse and mosaic-tiled hallway on the far side of the gymnasium, and there are chambers on each side of us, on each side of the hallway, and in them I can see low and small beds pushed against the walls and not much else. These are beds made only for a single person, cots really, made for soldiers or those training to be soldiers. We keep walking then finally come to an empty chamber at the far end of the hall which we enter and Pausanias tells me that this room is the one that will be mine. There's an un-made bed without sheets or blankets that's small and only made for one person, just like all the others, and there's a bowl for washing. There's nothing else, and nor will there be, because I carry with me the only thing that I own, and it's the broad-sword that's strapped across my back.

"Wake before the sun rises tomorrow," Pausanias tells me, "and join the others."

I nod.

That's how it'll begin.

Pausanius doesn't leave, though, as I expect him to, at least not immediately, and he stands there and looks at me for one more moment. Then he does more than look and takes a step forward and comes closer. He stands in front of me, in the same way that Philippos did earlier, and he reaches out and touches my chest, too, in nearly the exact same way. His hand isn't cold, but I feel a distinct chill when he touches me, his hand on my chest, then he moves it underneath my chiton, and I don't know if the chill comes from cooled flesh, or something else. His hand rests there, not moving, feeling, or doing anything else, and he stares back at me. I hold his eyes with my own as I breathe; evenly, strongly, and I don't smile, I don't swallow, I don't flinch, I don't do anything.

For a moment, he doesn't do anything either.

"I hope you'll be comfortable here, Hephaestion of Salona," he finally says, and smiles again, his seductive smile, his secret and wide smile that reaches up and past his cheeks, and then he nods his head, turns, and leaves. When he's gone, I wonder what's just happened, and what it was about, but I won't wonder for too long. I don't have time to wonder. There are other things. There are so many other things.

I look around.

I look at the room, the one that will now be mine.

It's small and sparse, and there isn't much else to see or do here, and I haven't yet seen much of Pella, or even the rest of the gymnasium, I realize, and so I turn and I leave, too. I go out and walk further down the hallway—in the opposite direction than we just came, though, away from the sand and the training area—and the hallway leads me outside, turning into a cloister that runs alongside an enclosed courtyard where there's a small but regularly-tended garden. The sun is higher and brighter now, later in the day, and when I look towards the garden, I see there's another boy who's laying in the grass and reading from a worn collection of bound papyrus that he holds propped open and above him, propped up and towards the light. I haven't seen him before; he wasn't with the others. I pause, and I look at him, and where he lays. The sun's bright and so I can't make out his features very well, and then he lowers the papyrus, and he sees me standing there, in the cloisters, watching him.

He looks back at me and cocks his head up and to the side.

Then his eyebrows raise in question.

"Who are *you*?" he asks, and places an unusual emphasis on the last word of his question.

I look around and see that there's no one else in the garden; there's just me, and him. I slowly walk forward and towards where he now stands and rises from the grass, setting the collection of papyrus down on a bench that's next to him, and then I'm there, and in front of him. I take him in, across from me. He's shorter than I am, and he has a fair and light complexion with blonde hair flecked with shades of red that he pushes back from his forehead.

And, when he does, I see his eyes.

Once I see them, they're what I end up noticing most about him, more than anything else, because they're eyes unlike any I've ever seen before, ever in my whole life. They're two different colors, which is something I've never even heard of, much less known was possible: the right one is a deep shade of blue, not unlike Pausanias' eyes, and the left is a dark grey, not unlike Philippos' good eye.

I look back at him, across from me.

Not only is he short, but he's fairly skinny, also, and so I can see that he's not as strong as I am, either.

"My name's Hephaestion," I finally say.

"And where are you from, Hephaestion?"

"Salona. In Illyria."

"Ah, the old basileus' son, it must be. And what are you doing here in Pella, Hephaestion of Salona?"

"I've come to offer my services to Philippos," I tell him. "I've come to live and learn at his court here, and to serve him."

He takes that in. His expression doesn't change.

"How old are you?" he asks, looking me up and down now.

"Nearly fifteen."

"You're strong."

"Sometimes."

He frowns at that.

"I'm nearly fifteen, too," he tells me, after a moment. "Which I suppose means that soon we'll both be men."

"Yes."

"It also means that your uncle Kleon would see you in the same way, wouldn't it?"

I look back at this boy in front of me.

He might be smaller than me, and skinnier, and less strong, but he's clever; I can see that, too. He knows who I am, and my father, and my uncle, and I'd bet that he knows all the rest of the leaders and ruling families of this peninsula, and maybe even beyond, too. I look closer and take in more of his features: I see his strong and defined nose, his narrow and pursed lips, his ears that are uneven and proportioned in a manner that makes them seem just slightly-too-large for his face and there's no hint of stubble or hair on his chin or his cheeks, like there is on mine.

He's not handsome.

Is he a second or third or fourth son, too?

Is he a cast-off, like the others I've already met?

He looks back at me, also.

Then I see that what he's really doing is looking *past* me, over my shoulder and at the weapon that's still slung to my back. "Is that the type of sword your people use?" he asks, then begins to walk closer before I answer, to inspect what he's just seen and found.

"No," I shake my head.

"No?"

"It's the type of sword that *I* use," and I emphasize the word, the same way I heard him do, when I first came to the garden.

"I see," he says. "May I hold it?"

He's next to me now.

I unsling the broad-sword from my back and I hand it to him.

He takes it and looks down at it, studying the blade with his strange and unique hetero-chromatic eyes, feeling the very specific weight of it, the peculiar balance, the perfect heft, and he does so with a practiced and near-expert touch and feel which surprises me because of his stature and the way that I found him, in a garden, and with a book. "Where'd you get it?" he finally asks, his eyes still studying the metal, the craftsmanship, the strangeness of the blade, at least to his eye.

I wait for a moment, as he continues to look at the weapon.

Then I tell him.

"A traveling blacksmith from Kriti made it for me," I finally say, and move closer and point to the sword, as I explain, even though I'm fairly sure he can already tell everything I'm about to say. "With a more full weight, it can be harder to swing and maneuver in close quarters, but once you train with it and get used to the weight, in single-combat it provides an advantage with its length and heaviness over the traditional xiphos that every other soldier in Illyria uses."

"In Illyria *and* in Greece."

"That's right."

"When a xiphos and this sword swing and meet, this sword wins."

"Yes," I nod. "It does."

"And when you swing and the swords don't meet, it's because yours has met flesh or armor, because of the length at which you can strike your opponent."

"Exactly."

"What about on a horse?"

"If you're strong enough to wield it, it works the same way on a horse, or anywhere else, too. But more than being stronger, and longer, it's also something else."

"And what's that?"

"Unexpected."

He looks at me as I say this, and he holds my eyes for a moment: it seems like he's judging something, or making a determination. Then his eyes flick back down to my sword that he still holds and he looks at it, too, for another moment, calculating, his eyes moving back and forth, up and down the blade, up and down, up and down, taking in every detail, every nuance, every single thing that's new and that he hasn't seen or felt before, and committing it to his memory.

    He looks up, and back at me again. "Where were you going?" he asks.

    "When?"

    "When you came to the garden here."

    "I only just arrived, so I was going to see the city. I haven't been to Pella before, or any city of this size."

    "I'll show you Pella if we can stop at the blacksmith on the way."

    "Do you know the city well?"

    "Yes, I know it well."

    "How?"

    "I live here."

    "Have you lived here for a long time?"

    "Yes," he nods. "I've lived here for a long time."

    "What's your name?" I finally ask him.

    He pauses as he looks back at me, with both of his different colored eyes—the light one, and the dark, too—both of them looking again into my own, looking deep into my own. And then his lips finally begin to split, part, turning up and into the very smallest of smiles. "My name is Alexandros," he tells me.

CHAPTER THREE

WE LEAVE THE GARDEN and the courtyard that's attached to the gymnasium and walk through the city together. We go back past the great Temple of Dionysus, and as we do, Alexandros tells me how there are other temples in the city, but it's no mistake that it's the temple to Dionysus that's the largest because if there is one god that's worshipped in Macedon above all others, then it's him: the god of wine, the god of fertility, the god of pleasure and ecstasy. These are all very important things to Macedonians, Alexandros tells me, speaking with an even and measured tone, seemingly not excited, interested, or embarrassed by anything he says, but perhaps judging my reaction with quick and measured glances as we walk, to see if I am.

What does my face and lips tell him? What do my eyes give away?

"How about Ares?" I ask, wondering about the god of war, and his place in all this, because surely it's one of prominence, also, from all that I've seen so far, and all that I know about Macedon and the Argeads that rule this kingdom.

"Ares is worshipped here, too, of course," Alexandros responds, but it seems to be an afterthought for him. It's certainly not for his father, though, I know. The whole world knows of Philippos, and his strength and taste for war and expansion.

We keep walking.

We're lower in the city now, the palace above and behind us.

We go past smaller temples that are dedicated to other things, and other gods—familial love, wisdom, temperance, and virtue—but these temples aren't built with large, carved columns, or ornate and expansive mosaic-tiling beneath them. Macedonians don't make offerings to virtue; citizens of Pella don't worship and pray for temperance. We keep going, and then we finally turn a corner and come to the blacksmith, our destination. Alexandros carries his book of papyrus with him, the one that he was reading in the garden and that he set on the bench when I came near. I glance at it, as we duck our heads to go under the narrow stone doorway of the blacksmith, and I wonder about it. I don't see the title, or what it is, though, so I just wonder.

Why was he reading, while all the others trained?

What was he reading, while all the others trained?

I don't know, and I don't ask, I don't know him that well; in fact, as I think about it, I don't know him at all.

We go inside the building.

Once we're inside, and after my eyes adjust to the semi-darkness, I see the blacksmith himself. He's small and with lighter skin and darker features than the others I've seen here, and there's a haze in the air between us, coming from the ash and soot that billows and swirls and catches in our lungs, the ash and soot from the fires that are always kept burning, no matter the hour, the day, the month, the year, the generation. And when the blacksmith sees Alexandros through the semi-darkness and soot-filled haze that he's used to, and we're not, he comes over and bows his head. I look at all the weapons displayed on racks behind him, as he bows, and I see there are forged and crafted weapons everywhere, too, some on tables, some on the walls, some half-made and still being hammered and shaped and perfected and even to my young eye, and even though the weapons aren't all yet assembled, I can tell this blacksmith is a man that knows his craft and is gifted with his hands.

I wonder where he's from. But, again, I don't ask.

Instead, Alexandros turns and asks me to show him my sword, and so I take it from where I carry it strapped across my back. The blacksmith holds it after I give it to him, feeling the unusual weight of the blade in his worn and calloused palms; he feels the heft, the unfamiliar but perfect balance.

"Can you make one?" Alexandros asks him, young eyebrows raised again in question and hope.

The blacksmith feels the sword a bit longer, turning it over and over in his hand—first once, and then again, and slower—studying the craftsmanship and making calculations in his head. Then he finally nods.

"Yes," he says. "I think I can."

"Good," Alexandros answers. "I'll need seven of them."

"Seven?" the blacksmith's eyebrows raise now, too.

"As quickly as possible," Alexandros says. "I'll pay whatever you need."

"Of course," the blacksmith answers as he nods, and takes the sword to his desk and places it on an unrolled piece of parchment. He sketches the outline of it: the size and shape of the blade, the hilt, the handle, making notes on what he sees and how it all fits together. Then after he makes a few more markings in the margins and around the sides, he places the sword on a small scale that's next to the desk. He jots further notes in the margins of the sketch, figures that relate to weight and balance, I know. Then he finishes and hands the sword back to me.

I take it.

"I won't rest until they're completed," he tells us.

"Thank you," Alexandros says and takes out a purse not unlike the one I used to carry, the one I gave to the men that my uncle sent to kill me, and instead of counting out specific coins, he just hands the entire thing to the blacksmith. I understand. He's overpaying, of course he is, that much is obvious, by the look on the blacksmith's face, but I know why he's doing it; for young men in Greece a good sword is literally life and death, and so there's no amount of money that can be exchanged for what a skilled tradesperson such as this one can do for young warriors like me and Alexandros. I also see that he knows this blacksmith, and for those closest to Alexandros, his default is always generosity and loyalty, which of course isn't always the case for all prinkipas' and sons of basileus', whether they're first-born, like I am, or second-born, like he is.

We leave the blacksmith, and I expect to go back to the gymnasium, myself, and Alexandros to the palace, where he lives, but he says that he'll show me the rest of the city. We walk together and go past the other trade-shops that are near the blacksmith, and he points to each of them, telling me what they are and what they sell, and then we continue further on and into the even lower parts of Pella. The houses are smaller here, where we now walk, the doorways narrower, the single-story ceilings lower, and there are certainly less great temples near us, and perhaps not any at all, I realize, as I look around. There are shrines, though; there are small altars to even smaller gods in the streets where we walk, the lesser gods that are worshipped here, the gods of individual families and individual lives, and sacrifices, and stories, and these are the forgotten ones, the forgotten gods who live amongst the forgotten people and bless these forgotten lives. And while there aren't as many great temples here, there are more people, the people that *build* the temples in the other parts of the city, and they smile as they walk past us, and Alexandros smiles back at them, and he nods and waves, and they do the same in return. He stops to talk to a few here, and more there, of all different ages and stations. He seems to know them, and they seem to know him, too.

How?

He's a prinkipas, isn't he?

He's the second son of the basileus of this city, and he lives in the palace, right?

I wonder how they know him, and I wonder why he's doing this, why he's taking time out of his day to show me, a complete stranger, around the city, but he is, and then after we've seen much of the city, we begin to return, the same way that we came. We continue to walk together, and as we do, I see it's the stables that he leads us towards now. We reach them and then go inside. There are stalls on one side, and stalls on the other, too, and horses that are kept in all of them. He tells me to wait there amongst the stalls and horses, who all watch me curiously, a stranger now amongst them, also, and then he comes back from one of the stalls near where I stand and leads out the most magnificent black stallion I've ever seen: the stallion must be at least twenty hands, with thick and defined muscles gathered around the legs, chest, and haunches, and with a distinct and piercingly white marking on its forehead.

"He's beautiful," I tell Alexandros, as I look him over, up and down, up and down, nose to tail to hoof.

"Yes, he is," Alexandros nods, then points to all the other horses, the ones that still watch me. "You can choose whichever you'd like," he says. "Whichever you think will most suit you."

I look at him, for another moment.

Then I nod and turn to look at the rest of them, but instead of choosing a Macedonian horse, as he's said, I walk to the brown that I rode here on from Illyria, that my mother gave me, and that I grew up riding there in the mountains. I take reins from a hook next to the stall and fasten them around the brown's nose and head, and Alexandros does the same to his black horse, next to me, and I see that he doesn't use a bit, and so I don't now either. Then when we're ready, we both leap up and onto their backs with practiced and familiar motions, with trained and muscled legs and thighs, and we sit there comfortably.

We leave the stables, and Alexandros leads us through the city.

I follow after him.

I wonder what we're doing, and where we're going, as we ride, and I see that I'm not alone. People look at us as we pass: the young and fair-haired prinkipas, who they're used to seeing walk and ride in these streets, I know, but now he's with a foreign and unfamiliar friend with pale skin and dark features that rides next to him. *Who is that, with our prinkipas*, I'm sure they ask. *Who is that young and foreign mountain boy, with the great sword strapped across his back, and why does he ride with Alexandros?*

They won't know.

The truth is, I'm not sure I do, either.

We keep riding, though, and we eventually make it back to the palace, which I recognize, and where the guards that stand outside bow and nod to Alexandros. And then I'm surprised when we don't stop, but we keep going, further, and past the palace.

We leave the city.

Alexandros rides towards the countryside, and I still follow after him.

The smell of the city begins to fade as everything freshens around us, and the sounds of the city begin to fade, too; there are no voices here, out in the country, in the wide and long fields, no yelling or bartering or trading or fighting, and then when we're some distance from Pella, Alexandros kicks his great horse to a gallop. I look at him, for a moment, in front of me, and then I do the same, to try to keep pace and continue to ride next to him. I catch up, and we ride together, through and over the rolling and grass-filled hills north of the city that are so different than the rocky and steep mountains of my youth, and where I grew, and then we begin to climb. The hills become steeper. We go up, higher and higher, gradual at first, and then more. We keep riding and then finally come to a river, and we cross it, together, swimming our horses in the fast-moving current. The river is deep and wide and the water comes up to the point where it reaches the bottom of the chitons that we both wear and that fall to a length that's halfway between our knees and our thighs.

I look behind us, and then I look up.

The sky is blue.

The sky is wide, and the sky is huge.

Then I look down from the sky, and I can see the outline of Pella below us, just a speck in the distance now. Alexandros smiles as he sees me take it all in: the vantage, the view, all that's beneath us. "It's just a little further," he says. "Just a little further yet to go."

"What's further?" I ask, as I turn back to look at him.

"What I want to show you," he tells me, very simply.

He pushes his great black horse forward and leaves me to squeeze my thighs and push my brown forward, too, and follow after them as we climb more steep hills. There aren't any roads or paths here, just Alexandros and his stallion, leading us, and me and the brown, following, and then we finally crest the mountain and reach the peak and I see the great, long, and wide lake that's there. The water is blue, completely still and clear, as if it hasn't ever been touched, and it looks very, very cold. We ride towards the lake and then dismount from our horses, when we're to it, and I go to tie my brown to a nearby tree, but Alexandros tells me I don't need to.

"He doesn't know the mountains here," I explain. "He could run. He could try to get back home."

"He won't."

"You don't think?"

"He'll stay with Bucephalus."

"How do you know?"

"Because I do. Because they all do."

"They all do what?"

"They all stay with him."

"And what about Bucephalus?"

"Bucephalus stays with me," he smiles.

I stare back at him, across from me, and even though I'm still young, we both are still young, I also know in this moment that he's unlike anyone I've ever met, or likely ever will meet again.

He seems to not notice me staring at him.

The sun is high above us, and it's hot, so instead he leads Bucephalus a few feet into the lake, to cool him off, and then reaches up and unties his chiton. He unties it where the cloth meets at the shoulder, and then uncinches his belt, too, and lifts the chiton up and takes it off so that he's naked. He bends down and rinses the chiton in the fresh lake water, to clean sweat and dirt from it, I assume, then he turns and drapes the wet piece of clothing across the length of Bucephalus' back, in order to dry, along with his belt. The horse eats some of the seaweed that's there, in the shallows of the lake, near the small rocks, quietly walking and eating while the chiton dries on its back and Alexandros goes further into the lake and dives into the water and then comes back up again.

I look at them.

I look at them both, for another moment, as they stand there and Alexandros shakes the water from his hair.

Then I do the same thing.

I walk into the lake with the brown following behind me and I'm surprised to find it's not as cold as I thought it would be. I go in up to my ankles, and then keep going after that, too, and once the water's to my knees, and the brown's, I untie my chiton and take my belt off, rinse the sweat from the chiton in the lake, the same as Alexandros did, then ring it out and drape it over the brown's back, along with my belt, and the brown stays there and next to Bucephalus, just like Alexandros said he would.

Then I turn.

I see Alexandros looking at me, at my skin, at my body, up and down, taking it all in. "What is it?" I ask him.

"Nothing."

"Tell me."

"You're so pale."

"The sun's different in the north, in the mountains."

"Different how?"

"There's less of it."

"Be careful in the sun here, then. Because it's bright, and there's not many clouds."

I nod and I keep walking, and then I'm next to Alexandros, too, further into the lake. The water is nearly up to our chests, in the place where we stand together, but we're not there in the water for very long as it's just to rinse off and cool. The sun here is hot and strong, as he's said, and while I might be pale, I look at him and his body and see that the sun has made his skin the color of dark honey; lighter than the skin of the others I saw in the gymnasium, but still darker than mine.

I wonder how many times he's done this.

I wonder how many times he's come here, and with who.

Why do I wonder this?

I don't know.

He turns and begins to walk out of the lake.

He walks past me, on his way to the shore, and he does so in a way that our shoulders gently brush as he passes, and then once he's past me, I turn and follow after him. I walk out of the lake where he walks, first into the shallows, and then up and onto the bank, and I follow him away from the water and towards the bluff and that's where he sits under the bright and strong sun to dry off, and I sit next to him. I look at him again, as I sit down—at his mis-colored eyes, and his dark honey skin—but he doesn't look back at me. His eyes are forward now, and in front of us, and so I turn mine there, too, and when I do, I look and see what he sees, and this is what it is: I see what must be the whole of Macedon spread out before us, spread out *below* us. It's a stunning sight, from this vantage, and from this height. I take it all in, this place which is now my new home and which is so different from my old home, and from what I've grown with, and what I've known, and I also take in this new boy next to me, who is now my friend here, my only friend. We sit together for a few more moments, in silence, then he finally turns his head and looks at *me* now, as I look out at all that's before us. He cocks his head slightly, to the side, in the same way he did when he first saw me in the garden, so that he almost looks *up* when he looks at me, up and towards the clouds, too, up and towards the sun, up and towards the moon and the stars and the gods, those both known and unknown, those both worshipped here, and also those that are not.

"It is something, isn't it," he finally says. "All that you can see from up here?"

"Yes," I nod, agreeing. "It is."

"It's my favorite place," he tells me, then turns and goes back to looking, but not at me anymore, instead just out and in front of us again. "It's my favorite place, in all the entirety of my father's kingdom."

"Not the barracks, or the gymnasium?"

He smiles, gently. "No," he says.

"Not the Temple of Dionysus?"

"It's here."

I smile, too.

As he continues to stare out at all that's spread before us, it's my turn to look at him now, in the same way he did with me. I look at his eyes, first, the same as I do with everyone when I first meet them, which is something my mother taught me, and as I look at his unique and monochromatic eyes again, it's the first time I see it; it's the first time I see what the sight of the never-ending horizon does to him, and the change that it brings. I see the great promise of the unknown that's reflected there, in his mis-colored irises and pupils, the promise of the unconquered, the unexplored, the always rising sun, out of reach, out of reach, always and just right there and out of reach. Eyes are how we see soul, and that's what I see. Soul. Pure, unfiltered soul. I'm sure of it. I wait for a moment, when I see this; I wait for one more moment, and then I wait for another, and then after the second moment passes I gesture with my head and eyes back towards where the horses graze on the grass that's behind us, near the lake, together. "That's the most beautiful horse I've ever seen," I tell him, my eyes taking in his stallion again. "And we have beautiful horses in Illyria."

"Bucephalus is the most beautiful horse in the world."

"Where did you find him?"

"I didn't. He found me."

"I don't understand."

"I didn't either."

"But you do now?"

"Yes."

"So how did he find you?"

Alexandros is silent for a moment, still looking out, in front of us, still looking at the wide and endless horizon. I don't think he's going to answer me, or my question; I think he's going to let it hang between us.

But then, after a moment, he does.

"My father has been trying to change our cavalry and the way they fight," he speaks slowly, measured, with thought and purpose. "He's been buying Thracian horses because they're bigger, and they'll scare the southerners, he says, with their size. One of the merchants from Perinthos that he does business with came to Pella with a horse that was the biggest and most beautiful of any I'd ever seen, but no one could ride him. He would let no one that was there onto his back. My father dismissed the horse as unridable, and asked why he or anyone else would buy an unridable horse, even as big and beautiful as this one was, but as soon as I saw him . . ." I watch Alexandros as his voice and words trail off and he still looks out at the horizon; I can see his eyes flash, too, and again, turning bright once more as he talks about this, as he tells me this story that seems like a legend already, or at least it seems like one to him.

"Then what happened, when you saw him?" I ask.

"I knew that we shared a destiny," Alexandros whispers, still calm and measured, but even more quiet now, as if it's a secret, a secret that only we two now share. "I knew in that instant that our fates were to be forever and irrevocably intertwined," he says, and then swallows the lump that's grown in his throat before he turns back and looks at me. "Does that sound stupid to you?"

I look back at him.

His eyes are wide and I look at his blue eye first, and then I continue, and I look at his grey one. I now see, also, that he looks embarrassed, the first time I've seen that during this whole day we've spent together, and I don't know why.

"No," I finally say, softly, as I shake my head. "It doesn't sound stupid at all."

"I could see that the trainer was hurting him," he continues, speaking louder now, and faster, his words closer together. "They were pulling too hard, to try to control him, and so I told them to get away, all of them. I heard later that some of the trainers and the others that were there said he was scared of his shadow, and that I turned him away from the light so he wouldn't see it, but that's not what happened. The truth is, I've always been good with animals, and more than that, he was Bucephalus, and I was Alexandros, and I think perhaps it was that simple. I think perhaps it was something that had already been decided, and written, long before the merchant ever came west with his horse to try to sell to my father."

"Written where?"

"The stars," he says, and then nods above us, as if it's the most obvious thing. "Where else?"

I take that in.

I think about what it all means, and how Alexandros is different than all the other boys like him that I knew in Illyria, and that I'll know here in Macedon, too; the ones I've already met, his Companions, and the ones who would be mine, also, if they'll have me, and if they'll accept me.

"And so your father bought him for you?"

"He had to. He couldn't lose face in front of his generals and the other merchants and trainers after that, so he bought the horse. My father's strategos Parmenion said it was a good thing that we were going south to conquer the rest of Greece soon, because clearly Macedon wasn't big enough for Philippos' son Alexandros, and after Parmenion said that, my father had to buy him for me."

"That's quite a story."

"It's just what happened. They even heard about it as far as Athens, or some version of it."

"How do you know?"

"Because the orator Demosthenes sent my father a toy horse, carved from wood, after he'd heard the story told."

"Really?"

"Yes."

"He'd send a toy all that way, just to call you a child and give you a child's gift?"

"No, but he would to call and give my father one."

I pause when I hear that and as I look back at Alexandros I realize for the first time just how far ahead of the rest of us he thinks, and how much he understands of people; their ambitions, whether hidden or un-hidden, and their desires, the deepest and darkest and most-obscured corners of that which dwells within us and makes us who and what we are. I suppose for one born short and small of stature, skills such as his are imperative if ambition burns in him the same way it does in the rest of us.

"I'm glad that you told me."

He's quiet for another moment.

My words linger, and then fade, and we stay like that, for some time, in silence. Then he speaks again, still looking out at the horizon, still looking out at all that's in front of us. "After they were all gone," he says, very quietly, "and it was just me, my father, and the horse, I thought he would be proud."

"He wasn't?"

"He looked at me from head to toe then told me if I ever embarrassed him like that again in front of his generals, or his men, then he'd kill me himself."

"I don't understand. Embarrass him?"

"What don't you understand? He's basileus and couldn't ride the horse, and said that no one could. Then someone did. There is nothing else."

"Not even the basileus' son?"

"*Especially* not the basileus' son."

I look back at Alexandros.

He knows I don't understand, and so he explains further.

"There have been twenty-four Argead rulers of Macedon," he tells me. "There have been twenty four basileus born of the same line and not a single one became basileus by peacefully following their father onto the throne. Philippos was never meant to rule Macedon. He was appointed regent for my six year old cousin, Amyntas, when Amyntas' father Perdiccas died, and Philippos didn't even wait a year before stepping over his dead brother's body and his young nephew to declare himself basileus instead."

"Really?"

"Yes. He had the support of the army, which is all that matters here, and the nobles, too, so when Philippos can't ride a horse and someone else can, even when it's his own son, it's something that he takes very seriously, as he should."

"Where's Amyntas now?"

"He's still here, in Pella."

"And your father hasn't declared an heir?"

"No, and he won't."

"Why?"

"Declaring an heir is giving them power he doesn't want to give, and doing a disservice to the kingdom by promising it to one who might not deserve it. I did ask him once, though, who he would want his kingdom to go to, if he were to die the next day."

"What did he say?"

Alexandros pauses for a moment, still staring at the horizon, as we sit there, alone, together.

"*To kratisto*," he finally whispers, to the wind, and to me, and then he smiles.

To the strongest.

I hear the words, and I feel them, too, as they echo through the ancient hills and mountains where we sit.

"My father died when I was young, also," I tell him, softly, "and my uncle took the throne from me."

"Yes, and now you spend every waking moment of your life training and growing stronger, so that one day you can kill him and take back your father's throne."

"Is it that obvious?"

He nods towards my body and the large and defined muscles of my shoulders, back, arms, chest. "That doesn't just happen overnight, does it? It comes with a lot of training."

"Before I started training, I looked like you," I tell him.

I've begun to speak easily as I sit there with him, which I'll soon learn is one of his gifts, for people to open up to him, for people to trust him, to believe in him, but this is the first time for me, and even as I say the words, I wish I could take them back. I look at him, at his skinny body, his shorter body, everything about him less developed: it's the body of a warrior, sure, but not a great one, and surely not one trained to use a broad-sword from Kriti instead of a xiphos. I'm worried he'll be offended, but I quickly see I don't have to be worried, and that he still smiles, but just for me now. "I'm sure you did," he says, "and I'm sure that you trained a lot. Which is why we're here because we'll start tomorrow, together, and you'll show *all* of us how to train in the same way and to use the swords that the blacksmith will make for us. And you'll also show us how to shape our bodies so that the broad-swords feel in our hands as light and maneuverable and advantageous as they do in yours."

"All of the others?" I ask, and I frown now.

"Yes," he nods. "And me, too."

"You weren't training with them before."

"I train in the morning, before we break for ariston. And then, after we eat, I leave and they continue."

I take that in.

I look back at his body, but closer now, and more analytically, and we sit there for another moment, my eyes still on him, his thin and narrow waist and stomach, and how his shallow chest moves up and down as he breathes, a bead of sweat running from the indentation in his sternum down towards his navel where the sweat stops, and then gathers, and rests. I look at it. He looks into the distance, away from me. I see now that he always does that when he's thinking and feeling deeply, his head cocked up and towards the sky, and perhaps towards the gods and the future, too. Then after another moment, he stretches his arms, first, and then his legs, and he begins to stand. I watch as his limbs uncoil and move, and then I do the same, and I stand, too, next to him.

We're close to each other, next to each other.

Our shoulders brush against each other again, very slightly, just as they did in the lake when he walked past me. It's just a moment, just the very briefest of moments, then he turns and starts back towards where the horses graze. Our skin is dry now, and so our chitons must be, too, and he walks slowly, and I do, also, and I look around, because I don't want this moment and afternoon to end, I realize. We soon get to where the horses shorten the medium-length grass with their blunt and strong teeth, and I take my chiton from the back of the brown, and I feel it, the fabric.

"Dry?" I hear him ask, next to me.

I look over at him.

I feel that the fabric *is* dry, from the time it's been there in the sun.

"Yes," I nod.

"Good," he nods, too.

I throw one of the cloth-ends across my left shoulder and then wrap the other around my waist before bringing it up and over my right shoulder, in the much-practiced move of how I've gotten dressed every morning of my life, and then let the rest of the chiton fall down and across my body, covering it, the hem resting on my thigh just above the knees. I take my belt from the brown's back, also, and I cinch it at my waist to hold the chiton in place.

Next to me, Alexandros does the same.

He spreads and ties and cinches his belt, too, after he lets his chiton fall across his body, and down to his upper-thighs. And then, once we're both dressed again, our clothing dried by the same sun and the same mountain breeze, we each jump back up and onto our horses. We're about to leave, together, again, but I have one more question; I have one more question for him, and I want to ask it here.

"Why don't you train with the others after ariston?" I ask him.

He turns to look at me.

"What?"

"You were in the courtyard, with your book, when I saw you."

"I was."

"And you said that you leave them after ariston, and they continue to train, while you go to do something else."

"Yes."

"Why?"

"Because they're just warriors, so strength and war are the only things they practice, or need to. But being a warrior is only half a basileus."

"And the other things that are needed, to become a basileus, those things can be found in a book?"

"Everything can be found in a book. Or, at least, it can be found in the *right* book."

"And which one is the right one?"

He looks at me for another moment, cocking his head slightly up and to the side, once more, his own personal acknowledgement of the gods, I think, and perhaps the role they've played in all that's happened today. I think again that he's not going to answer me, and this time, I'm right. He nods to the setting sun, instead, getting lower in front of us, the light starting to change, and then disappear.

"It's time to go back down," he tells me.

So I nod, and then we turn, together, and we do.

NEITHER OF US SPEAKS the entire way down to Pella, and then once we reach the stables again, in the middle of the city, we gently pull the reins of our horses and they come to a stop outside. We swing our legs and jump off their backs to land on the uneven cobblestone street of pale and worn stone, where we then lead the two animals inside the stables, on foot, and each put them away, back into the stalls where they came from.

Then we go back out and onto the street once more.

We stand there.

We face each other, and we're each silent, for a moment, looking at the other. I try to read the look on his face, in his eyes, as people walk past us, but I realize I'm not clever enough. I wasn't born to read men, or trained for it; I was born and trained for something else, the same that his Companions train for every day, in the morning, before ariston, and then after, too.

But Alexandros?

What was he born for?

What has he trained for, if he's trained with more than a sword, if he's trained with books and stories and words, as well?

"I'll see you in the morning, at the gymnasium," he finally says. "To begin the new exercises you'll show us."

"Yes," I nod.

"Good," he nods, too.

There's one more look, one more moment.

I open my mouth again, but then Alexandros turns and leaves.

He walks a few paces, back up towards the palace, and then pauses. He stands there for a moment, and then he turns back, he turns back to me. The outline of his body is silhouetted by the burnt oranges and bright yellows of the strong and now-sinking Macedonian sun, and for a moment, he doesn't look like himself. For a moment, he looks like something else entirely, something more, something of a world both different and bigger than this one. "I'm glad that you came here, to Pella," he finally tells me. "I know that you didn't want to, and that you'd rather be with your own people, but I'm glad that you did."

I wait, and then I nod.

It's all that I can do.

"I am, too," I whisper.

It's not what I was going to say before, but it's what I say now.

Then with no more words, he turns again and continues on and back towards the palace, and I watch him as he goes. I watch as he gets smaller and smaller in the street, and as he begins to shrink and disappear into the distance. He walks between and amongst the men and women and children who pass and nod to him, bowing their heads, and he does the same to them, bowing his head, acknowledging them as they go by. He's one of them, and of their world, but he's also not, too. Then when he's completely gone, swallowed by the city and the last of the light and dying sun, the same men and women pass by me, also, and so do their children.

Do they know what it is they've just witnessed?

Do I?

Do they know that the world has just shifted, moved, changed, and it was because of us, and what happened today, and what will now begin?

I shake my head.

I don't know.

I don't know how much the world knows, and I don't know how much I know, either, and so I do the only thing I can and I turn and start to walk back towards the gymnasium and my room there. I find my way down through the ordered and planned streets of the city, past the great, majestic, and mosaic-floored Temple of Dionysus, and the great and tall houses, and then soon I'm there. I go inside, and when I do, I hear noises, laughter, even some loud shouting, and I realize what the others must be doing: the evenings, after their meal, are for drinking wine and chasing women, and that's what they're consumed with, when the sun disappears and darkness comes. They aren't burdened with what Alexandros is burdened with; they have the gift of thinking in terms of a single and present moment, which is to say they think in terms of pleasure, and strength, and little else.

I frown.

I don't join them.

I don't know why I don't, because I feel like yesterday or perhaps even earlier this morning I would have, and I certainly would have joined them if I was still in Salona. But something's different now; something's changed, inside me, in what I value, and what I look towards, and also what pleasure might mean to me, I realize. So, instead, I continue on and down the sparse hall and to my own small room with just the single bed and the simple washing basin in it, and then when I'm there, I strip my chiton off again and I lay down on the bed. It's still hot, and it stays hot at night here, too, unlike in the mountains when it cools, and so I spread my limbs as wide as I can. I spread them as far as they will spread, to try to cool down, so that none of my skin will touch any other bit of skin. It'll be difficult to sleep, I know, and I'm not able to at first, so I just lay there. I just lay there, and I think of the last hours, and all that's happened. I think of the prinkipas that decided to spend his day with me. A prinkipas, yes, but one in name only, and not in rank or stature, another who like me doesn't yet have a kingdom, doesn't yet have anything to inherit, and again, I wonder why. I think once more about how we met, and how we've now been brought together by circumstance and time and I think of how Alexandros so often cocks his head up and towards the sun. We're two young men, both born without kingdoms to inherit, but perhaps two young men at the beginning of everything and who both still have kingdoms to gain.

Perhaps.

I don't know.

I think of his eyes again.

I think of his eyes and of the two different colors in them—something that I've never seen before, not in anyone I've ever met, in my whole life—and I think of what else besides just color I saw when we sat there together and the sun dried our skin and we looked out and at the horizon, at all that was in front of us: at all that was there, and also all that wasn't.

More.

That's what I felt, and I realize that now.

I felt that there was more, so much more, more even than what we could see in front of us, even from the great height at which we sat together and looked.

My eyes.

His eyes.

I've met Alexandros' father, and so I know where the left eye that's grey has come from, and where it was inherited, so surely that must mean the right eye, the one that's clear and that's blue—as blue as the place where the Adriatic and Ionian Seas mix, near the place where I was born—surely that must be from his mother, right? I haven't met her, but I've heard stories of Philippos' basileia, stories that have reached even as far as Illyria and Salona. She's from the mountains just south of us, in Epirus, and so she's closer to being Illyrian, like I am, than Greek like they are. And the rest of the stories? Who knows. I'm sure they're exaggerated, like everything else, and I'm sure they'll soon say the same things about me, too, if they haven't already.

I can still hear the Companions, louder now, no signs of bed or sleep.
I breathe.
I hold my breath, and close my eyes.
His eyes.
I can't stop thinking of them, and what they seem to mean: one foreign and barbarian, one sophisticated and Greek; one born of the high peaks and wild mountains, one of the rolling hills and great plains; one bred of measured discipline and reason, the other of virtue and rage. What does it mean, to have so many opposing things, all gathered together in one young man? What does it mean, to have so many things all gathered together in Alexandros?

Where could it take him? How *far* could it take him?
I think of all this, as I close my eyes, and wait for sleep.
I think of all that it could be, and then I think of it again.
I exhale.
I don't open my eyes.
I once thought that I was the only prinkipas that was born without a kingdom, but now, I know that I was wrong, because now . . .
Now, I know that I've met another.
I exhale again, even more.
Now, I know that I've met another, just like me.

CHAPTER FOUR

THE NEXT DAY, I rise before the sun, as I always do, and I take my chiton from near the bed where I left it the night before and put it back on. I throw it over my shoulders and tie the ends and cinch the belt tightly across my waist to hold it in place. Then I take my broad-sword from where it rests near my bed, the same as it did in my room in Salona, and I strap it across my back; it's too big to wear at my waist, like the shorter xiphos swords of the Greeks—it's too long, and too heavy—so I have to wear it between my shoulders. When I'm dressed and ready, I leave my chamber and go out into the hallway. I walk towards the gymnasium, and when I get there, I see that Alexandros is already waiting. He's already there, and so are all the others, too. I've heard them, the other Companions, up late and deep into the night, as I tried to sleep, so the first thing I do is search their eyes for signs of hangover, or tiredness, but I find none. I smile wryly.

Dionysus.

They worship and make sacrifices to their god, and their god shows them favor in return.

So it will be.

So it will always be.

"I didn't know you slept so late," Alexandros says, as he looks back at me, up and down, up and down, the Companions gathered around him, too, behind him, and at his side, all their young eyes trained on my own young eyes across from them. I notice a change in Alexandros' tone, and in his words: he speaks different here than he did when we were alone. I notice it, and know why, so I don't say anything further. This is how he is with the others, and as one who would be a leader of these others, and many more besides just them, too; a leader of all of us.

"The sun's not even up yet," I finally say.

"We don't need the sun to train," his response is curt. "So let's begin. We've already wasted too much time."

I nod once more and then slip my broad-sword from where I carry it. They watch as I do, my movement practiced and measured and familiar. They've never seen someone carry their sword like this, though, I know, which is why they watch, and why they're here, to learn about it from me.

"It's heavier than what you're used to," I tell them.

They nod, as if that much is obvious.

Then I hold the broad-sword out to them.

Ptolemaios comes forward first and takes it, holds it, feeling the heft and weight, and then passes it to Perdiccas, who does the same, and then Perdiccas passes it on, too, to Kassandros, until they all have handled it, felt the differences in shape, and balance, the same as Alexandros did yesterday. And I watch as they all do it. I watch each of them as they take it, their muscles straining to hold it in a way they're not used to when holding a sword. Alexandros tells them that he's ordered one from the blacksmith for each of them, and so he wants them to know what the weight feels like before we begin the training that will help them be able to handle their own blades when they come.

They nod.

They understand, and I see that they listen when Alexandros speaks.

Then Alexandros tells me a story that they already know, but I don't: he tells me about how his father, Philippos, had been held as a captive in Thebes during his youth, and when he'd returned to Macedon after his years of captivity, he brought with him the idea for a new weapon. The new weapon he thought of was the sarissa, which is a twenty foot long spear that Philippos made and had given to every member of his pezhetairoi phalanx to learn and train with, and just as the sarissa was designed to revolutionize and set apart the Macedonian infantry, because with a sarissa they'd be able to reach their enemies at a greater length when they fought—a length in which their enemies wouldn't be able to strike them back, in return—so was this new sword similarly revolutionary in both concept and execution. The sarissa was Philippos' military revolution. This, Alexandros tells us, will be ours. The pezhetairoi will still use the short xiphos that are more maneuverable at close quarters, but Alexandros and his Companions are training to be hetairoi cavalry, and this new sword will give them that same advantage of length and distance, while they sit their charging horses; it will give them that same revolutionary advantage of greater reach.

The Companions take this in, all that he's told them.

Then I watch as they all nod.

They agree, they all agree with Alexandros, and they understand.

And so, then, the training begins.

WHILE THE PREVIOUS EXERCISES they had done had been to build endurance and stamina, the new ones that I show them—the ones I designed and practiced myself, in Salona, and in the Illyrian mountains—they're made for one thing, and that's to build strength. They need to be bigger through the arms, through the chest and shoulders, just as I am, and that Alexandros saw when we stripped our chitons off and went into the mountain lake above the city, if they want to be able to hold and carry the Kritin broad-swords that will come. So, instead of pushing boulders, like they used to do, I have them pick the boulders up and carry them. I show them how to grip the rock and do it, and they have to work at it at first, but they grunt and strain and then are finally able to go a short distance with them. They'll go further tomorrow, I know, and then they'll go even further the day after that. I show them how to climb a tree, next, and they think we'll only do it once, as they've done before, just for fun, as boys do when they're young, but then I show them how to do it ten times in quick succession using nothing but arms and chest and the muscles there and not giving the body or muscles any time to rest between sets of climbing, which is important and different from what they've done before. After that, I show them how to lie on the ground and use their own bodyweight as resistance to push off the ground many times in rapid succession to strengthen chests, and backs, and shoulders, and core. Then I show them how to do it with a rock or partner sitting on their back, and weighing them down. They take to it quickly, all of them, even Alexandros, who is smaller than they are and has to work twice as hard to keep up with how they lift, climb, throw, and carry.

But he does. He always does.

We fall into a routine.

We wake early in the mornings, earlier than I woke on the first day we trained, and we go through the exercises I've shown them, again and again, each time pushing ourselves a little bit further than we did the day before. They all give me strange looks, at first, when I push them like this, but then they look at Alexandros, and after they look at him, they do what I ask. And the looks aren't just because of the exercises, I know, because these boys, these young, fit, athletic boys in this city and in this country that were born with the strength to lead—though not the order of birth to do so—they take to these exercises I show them as naturally as everything else they've ever done in their still-short lives. The looks aren't because of that, and because of the difficulty, they're because of *me*: the stranger and interloper that's here in Pella, and amongst them now, and who has become friends with Alexandros, their leader.

It's normal, for them to be jealous.

I know this because every time I'm in his presence, and he's with them, I find myself wanting to be closer to him, too; waiting for a look, a touch, an acknowledgement or kind word and wanting to be closer to him myself, in any way that I can. Some people have this gift, the undefinable gift of magnetism and appeal, and so I understand what they feel, and why they feel it, because I feel it, too.

The new broad-swords eventually arrive.

And then, once they do, we begin to train with them, as well.

Ptolemaios tells me the new swords don't feel as heavy in his grip as mine did, when he first held it, on the first morning of our new training, even just a few short weeks ago, and Alexandros smiles and nods as his lips part and the smile tells us both the same thing: that the exercises I've designed are working. The truth is, though, even before Ptolemaios' words and discovery in holding the new sword, I can already see the changes in their bodies, as they've all started to become bigger, stronger, muscles expanding and growing and filling out inside their chitons.

So we continue to train together, every morning, from before the sun rises, until it's high and bright, at ariston.

And then, after ariston, Alexandros leaves.

At first, he goes by himself, and I stay with the other Companions to continue to train more after we eat. But then, one day, I decide to leave with Alexandros, and he doesn't say anything, either in acknowledgement or protest: he simply just walks next to me, and accepts what I've done. I don't know if he's glad, or indifferent, or how he feels at all, because he doesn't tell me. This is normally the time he goes to the garden to read, the same as when I met him, and at first that's what he does, and so it's what we do together. But a few days after I've begun to join him, he suggests that we do something else.

"What?" I ask him.

He doesn't answer, he just does the exact same thing he did before, on that first day that I met him, and walks to the stables. And just the same as *I'd* done before, I follow after him. He goes inside the stables when we get there, and then I do, too, and he silently ties the reins around Bucephalus' face and nose as next to him I do the same with the brown. Then we leave, and go through the city, and when we're through the streets and past the palace, we kick the horses to a gallop and head back towards the hills. We do this same thing, repeating the first day that we met over and over, day after day, for several weeks; after our morning training sessions, we leave the city together and ride across the fields, across the river where the water reaches up to the hem of our chitons, to our upper-thighs, and then we *rise, rise, rise*, going up until we finally come to the now-familiar lake. We take our chitons off when we get there, and rinse the sweat and dirt from them in the calm and translucent mountain water and then we lay them on the backs of our horses, to dry, as we swim for a few minutes, ourselves, to cool off, then walk out of the lake and go to sit together on the bluff and look out at all there is below and in front as our skin dries.

And also, that's when we begin to talk.

We grow closer, with all that we talk about, and all that we share.

He tells me about his father, and how it is Philippos' great dream to go south, and conquer Greece, and unify all the Hellenic people under one single basileus, and that's also when Philippos would then finally turn his attention east, and to the liberation of the Greek cities and people of Asia Minor that are currently under Persian control, and bring those Greeks under his rule, too. Alexandros tells me how in Athens they call his father *Philippos-barbaros*—Phillip the Barbarian—which is something his father once took great pride in, but it also now poses a great problem, too, because for a proud democracy like Athens and all the other city-states of the south, a barbarian basileus is the most substantial threat to their existence and values that could possibly be dreamed or imagined. So the southern resistance of Macedonian hegemony over all of Greece has thus far been fierce, and not only has it been fierce, but it will also continue to be so because they think that their very souls, their very essence, the very fibers of the dreams and life that are within them and makes them who they are depends on it. Are they right? I don't know, and neither does Alexandros, he tells me. Will Philippos succeed? Only the gods know the answer to such things. The only thing I know for sure is that when Alexandros speaks of his father, and Athens, and the great cities of the south, his eyes always drift there, away from the mountains, and away from Macedon and his home and towards those distant places. They're places that we haven't yet seen or been—only heard stories upon stories upon stories—but we hope that one day soon we might.

Will we?

I don't know.

So we hope.

And as we do, we talk of other things, too, besides just the horizon.

We talk of the Companions, and how Philotas, the youngest and smallest, is the son of Parmenion, Philippos' strategos, and he's inherited his father's intelligence and military wit, and we talk of how Ptolemaios, the oldest and strongest amongst them, is in love with Alexandros' sister Cleopatra. They think it's a secret, Alexandros tells me, with a smile, and a small laugh, but then again there's not much in Pella that's secret from him.

"How?" I ask, wondering the way in which he knows so much.

"My mother," he tells me.

And when he does, and when he mentions her, the bright look that's on his face and the laughter that's in his eyes and on his lips fades. Then it disappears altogether.

Olympias.

I ask him about her, and when I do, he just stares out at all that's in front of us, and this time, he doesn't answer. So I change the subject, and I ask him about the other Companions. "Who do they love?" I ask him, and when I do, he laughs, and when he does, I'm glad again.

"They love so many," he tells me. "And so often."

Then I laugh, too, and with him.

"I hear them, at night."

"I'm sure you do. Does it keep you up?"

"Sometimes."

"I can imagine. I wouldn't be happy."

"It's fine."

"You can tell them if it's not."

"I know."

"They'll listen to you."

"Do you think so?"

"Yes, because I listen to you."

I hesitate. There's another question that I want to ask, but do I dare? I think of my life, and all that's happened, and brought me here, and

I realize that life is too short to be lived in such a way, and so I do. I hesitate, and I swallow, wondering if this is too bold, even as the words come, but I'll still ask.

"And what about you?"

"What about me?"

"Who does Alexandros love?" I ask him, and I'm surprised when I hear my own words, and how softly I speak them.

He's not offended, though.

I'm glad when I see that he's not upset, and then he tells me about the girl named Aria that lives in the lower part of the city, and how he sleeps there when he needs to get out of the palace, which lately has been more and more often. She had married young, he tells me, but her husband was killed fighting against the Thracians, the year before last, and so she's only eighteen but already a widow and with a child, too. I'm surprised by his honesty when he tells me this, but at this point, perhaps, I shouldn't be, I realize. "So that's me," he says. "But what about you, Hephaestion of Salona, and of the wild northern mountains, as long as we're sharing secrets of the bed and the heart."

"What about me?"

"Have you been with a woman?"

"Yes," I nod.

"When?"

"In Salona," I say.

I tell him about the girl there who I used to know, the one who lived down by the docks. I tell him about how I met her, about how her mother worked in the palace and how I saw them together on the street one day and recognized her and spoke to them and then how things grew from there, and what we did, and where, and how, in the mountains, and near the streams, and the lakes, and that when I left, I wasn't able to say goodbye because of how I had to leave.

He's silent when I tell him.

He's still looking south, and then I watch as he turns and looks east.

He stays like that for a moment, and I stay watching him, wondering if what I've just said is something that I perhaps shouldn't have told him, because what has it done and what has it caused?

Silence.

Silence.

I have to know.

"What are you thinking?" I finally ask him.

"I'm wondering why my father wants to stop," he says, very slowly, and I realize he hasn't been thinking about me, or what I said, and the girl that I once knew at all. "They say that Macedon is small," he continues, "and that Persia is large, and so it's no use to even try to look in that direction, but what is size, really, Hephaestion? It's nothing. Or at least it's nothing compared to heart, and skill, and ambition. If size was important, then Ajax would have been Achilleus, and Achilleus would have been nothing at all, just a common soldier."

"That's true," I nod, slowly. "I never thought of it that way."

"I have," he says, still looking east. "So why just stop at Asia Minor? I've said it to the others before and they just laughed and said that Greece was plenty large enough for all of us, and so why would we need more? But there's *a whole other world* out there, Hephaestion," he tells me. "There's a whole other new and exciting world that's just waiting to be explored, to be travelled, to be discovered, and . . ." he begins to trail off.

"And what?"

"To be *conquered*," he finally finishes.

I think about how he pronounces this last word, and how he says it differently than the others. He pauses for a moment, still staring east at the rolling hills that are there and in the distance. Then his eyes shift. He slowly turns, and his eyes turn, too, back to me now; he looks into my own eyes, deep into them, and even through them, perhaps, and into my soul.

"I just need to become basileus first," he finally says.

"You will."

"How do you know?"

"Because I'll make sure of it, and so will the others."

He keeps looking at me for another moment, and I look back at him, too, and he moves closer so that we're touching again now; he moves so that the skin of my shoulder is pressed against the skin of his shoulder, hot and sticky, my pale complexion pressed and touching against his that's honey-dark. And I feel something, when we touch, too. It's like a current, or perhaps something else that I can't quite describe, because it's something I've never felt before. He lays his head on my shoulder, which is something he's never done. His head rests near my neck and the curve made by my jaw and cheek, and when he does this, I can feel him breathing. I feel his chest, rising and falling, rising and falling, breath after breath. We sit there like that, together, as the sun goes down in front of us, and this time we stay there even past when the sun goes down; we still sit there, longer than the time when we normally leave. We sit there like that for many hours, as light turns to dark, and day and sun turn to moon and stars, because that's what's now between us and these new things and secrets which, like all secrets, when they're shared, begin to grow and expand and surround and take hold in the grass, in the rocks, in the hills and mountains, and in us. We feel that. I know that we do, that we both feel that, and we let ourselves. We let ourselves feel it, and feel it deeply. Then when it's all finally there and between us and grown in an unmoveable, unshakeable, indestructible way, we finally stand and go back to our horses and head down through the near-darkness and towards the city. Alexandros will one day be basileus of Macedon, of that I no longer have any doubt.

But what of me, I wonder?

Just a few short weeks ago I was sure that my destiny lay to the north, and the west, in Illyria and in Salona, in the land of my people, and my home, but now? Now, I don't know. Because now, I find my eyes drifting, the same as Alexandros' twice-colored eyes drift; now, I find my eyes turning south, and towards the great cities that are there; now, I find my eyes turning east, and towards the horizon, and the rising sun; now, I find my eyes turning, always turning, towards the unknown and the unconquered, just as often and as frequently as Alexandros' do, too.

CHAPTER FIVE

THREE WEEKS LATER we receive word from Philippos and the palace that a delegation of Persians will be coming to Pella, and they'll be coming soon. They're making the journey west and to Macedon to hold what they call *peace talks* with the basileus, and after the talks conclude, there will be the traditional lion hunt in the mountains that accompanies the visit of any foreign dignitary that visits the capital. Alexandros asks me to join him when the Persians come—both on the hunt, and then at the feast, that will be held after—which is something not usually allowed for wards of the basileus or any others outside of the extended royal family. But Alexandros doesn't care about what's allowed, and if he doesn't care, then I won't, either. So I nod when he asks, and I tell him that I'll be glad to accept his invitation, and honored to join them.

The day before the hunt, the Persians arrive.

I stand in the courtyard to watch when they come.

It's afternoon and I wait in front of the palace where all the other people of the city are gathered, too, all the others who want a glimpse of these famous and ancient enemies from the east, and we don't take our eyes from them as they ride towards us, towards where Alexandros and his family stand outside the palace entrance to greet and receive them. They get closer, and as they do, the first thing I notice is the way they dress. It stands out, even from a distance. All the clothes we wear in both Illyria and Macedon are muted in color and simple in design, as most of our clothing is just the chitons we tie around our shoulders and let hang to cover our bodies and which are made of a light, linen-type fabric and usually bleached white. The clothes that the Persians wear, however, cover the entire spectrum of color and their clothes also cover more of themselves and their skin than ours do, too; their billowy and loose tunics have long sleeves that reach the length of their arms (which must make it harder to swing a sword, I think, as I frown, my mind always turning to the practical), and their trousers have legs that don't stop at their thighs, like our chitons do, but rather extend all the way to their feet and the stitched leather boots they wear instead of sandals.

Are they hot?

Isn't it uncomfortable with that much cloth covering their body, as if it's winter all the time, even in the middle of their vast, desert kingdom, which is surely hotter even than it is here in the summer?

Is there a reason?

There must be.

I don't know, but I'll find out.

The second thing I notice are their weapons.

I see that each rider carries a sword that's sheathed at their waist, and I see that these Persian swords are longer than a traditional xiphos, though they're still not as long as my broad-sword. The other distinct feature of these Persian weapons is that they're *curved*, and while the curvature is subtle, it's still there, and unmistakable, and which also makes them unlike any other sword I've seen, all of which have edges and lines and angles that are completely straight.

I wonder about this.

Does it make them easier to wield in battle? What advantage does it give their holder?

They're an ancient civilization, too, and one that's conquered and held all of Asia, so there must be a reason. We'll need to find out what it is, if we want to defeat them, unless Alexandros or someone already knows. I glance at him now and where he stands across the courtyard from me, next to his family, and I can't tell what he's thinking, his face and mis-colored eyes blank and impossible to read again, like they are when he's with the Companions, and not like they are when he's with me. He's doing this because the men in the courtyard are enemies, I know, but I also know it doesn't matter that his eyes are blank because we'll discuss everything later, we'll *all* discuss this later; me, and Alexandros, and the rest of the Companions, too, the next time we train at the gymnasium with our broad-swords and discuss all that we've each seen.

So we need to take in as much as we can.

My eyes flick back to the Persians.

I look them over once more, searching for every last detail I can find and committing it all to memory. I see that they hold no shields, and besides their curved swords, the only other weapon they carry is a short-bow that's slung across the backs of some. A bow is of course a weapon no Greek or Illyrian would carry publicly on an occasion such as this, as bows—and anything meant to bring death from afar, to bring death without honor—are weapons for cowards, and for the weak. Bows are Paris' weapon, the honorless son of Priamos that killed Achilleus.

I smile wryly.

Years and generations have passed, and yet they're still the same, aren't they?

Yes.

And so are we.

The Persians dismount and my eyes flick back to Alexandros, again, to where he stands across the courtyard from where I stand. He's with his father, and next to Philippos are his generals, Parmenion and Antipater, his childhood friends, along with the basileus' three wives. I look at the generals, first, and Parmenion stands out because he's clean-shaven, which is most unusual in our world, either in the east or west. Then my eyes continue to Philippos' wives, and when I see them, my eyes are drawn to one who's taller than the rest, with bright blue eyes and red-tinged hair, and it's not hard for me to tell that this is Alexandros' mother. I see the other wives, too, the ones that are shorter, with darker hair, and from different places and kingdoms. Alexandros has told me about them, and where they come from, but not with much interest. Then my eyes continue, and I see the girl who must be Alexandros' sister, Cleopatra, next to him, and she's still small, like he is, and still young, too, younger than we are, but she already has the same prominent and distinct features as Alexandros—the same large nose, and the same widely-shaped ears—and while neither feature does anything to make her more beautiful, she's still a prinkipissa, and so she'll be desirable to a great many suitors, anyways, and for that reason. I see Thessalonike, Alexandros' older half-sister by his father's marriage to his Thessalian wife, and his other half-sister, Cynane, by his father's marriage to Audata of Dardania, which is a place not very far from Salona and my own people. They stand further back, behind Alexandros and Cleopatra, and the rest of the family. I frown. It's strange to learn about his family like this, and see them for the first time in such a way. But here we are, and then after I see Alexandros' sisters, I see his half-brother, Philippos Arrhidaeus, too: he stands at a place behind the others, so I don't get a good look at him, but he's large, I see, much larger than Alexandros, and larger even than I am. He seems to hide, Philippos' oldest son and namesake, moving closer to a pillar, trying his best to stay out of sight and completely invisible. I suppose he's probably been told to do this. I'd asked Perdiccas about Arrhidaeus once, as he's commonly called, when we were training, and out of earshot of Alexandros. I'd wondered why he didn't train with us, or why I never saw him in the city, and Perdiccas told me that he was simple, and that he didn't often leave the palace.

"Simple?" I'd asked him.

"Touched by the gods," Perdiccas had answered, and pointed to his head, at his temple, and then I'd understood.

I see him for the first time now, the great and large son that should have brought pride to a basileus and father, and while he stands behind the royal family, I see that the one he stands closest to is Alexandros, and then after I see this, my eyes continue, and standing further to the side, the furthest away, is one last member of the family of Argeads: it's Amyntas, I realize, Alexandros' cousin and the one who was to be basileus before Philippos took the throne from him. I look at him. I look at him, for the first time. His face is blank, unreadable, also, and I wonder what he's thinking. I wonder what Amyntas is thinking both right now, and every other time he's had to stand behind his uncle during ceremonies like this. A muscle flickers in his cheek, a spasm he can't control. I wonder what he's feeling, for one more moment, and then I don't, because I know what it is that he's feeling, because I feel it, too, so it's something that he can't hide, not from me. And I know it's something that I can't hide, either, but that's alright, because I don't want to, and here ... here, in this place that I've come, I don't have to.

 The Persians reach the courtyard, and then they dismount.

 The leader of the delegation hands the reins of his horse to a servant, and then comes forward, himself, with soldiers behind him, who carry gifts to lay at Philippos' feet. Philippos nods as he glances down at them, and then Pausanius comes forward, from behind Philippos, and he brings the Persians gifts in return, laying the Macedonian offerings at their feet, too, and in the exact same way.

 Lips move, and words are exchanged.

 I can't hear what they say, though; I'm too far away.

 Then with the ceremony of greeting over, they all turn and go into the palace. Philippos goes first, with Pausanius falling in at his side, closer to him than any other, even his family, and then Olympias and the wives follow after, and then the children after that. My eyes flick to Alexandros, as Arrhidaeus leaves, hurrying inside as quickly as he can, and then Cleopatra goes after him, but I see Alexandros hesitate, just for a moment. He looks out, and through the gathered crowd, his eyes scanning and searching.

 What is he searching for?

I watch him, and then he finds me.

Of course.

My eyes. His eyes.

He stands there, looking at me, as the others all walk past him, and many walk past me, too, as the crowd begins to disperse and thin and leave. The space between where he stands and where I stand is obscured and blocked by all these moving bodies, coming and going, but our eyes remain, and it's as if in finding me he's also found something else, something he's going to need during all of this. This isn't easy for him, I know, these times with his family are never easy for him. But this is another moment. We both can feel it. I know that we can both feel it, even though I'm not exactly sure what *it* is, but I know this more than I know anything. The moment builds, stronger, consuming, heat rising in my cheeks, and in his, too.

I breathe.

He breathes, also, and I can see him exhale.

Then his sister Cleopatra comes and takes him by the hand and the moment's gone, as she pulls him along with her, back towards the palace, towards the entrance, towards the others and the rest of their family and the newly-arrived Persian guests. He gives me one more look, over his shoulder, and it's that look that she sees, that she catches, and she's a sister who knows her brother and so she follows his eyes and that's when she sees me, too, for the first time. She looks at me, and I look at her, and then she turns and whispers into his ear and pulls him along with even more strength, and finally they pass through the entrance to the palace, and then they're gone.

The crowd thins, even more, almost completely dispersed now.

There's nothing left to see with the basileus and the Persian guests all inside, but I stay there, in the courtyard, until everyone else has left, too; I stay there, looking at the place where the Argeads and the Persians had just stood, which is now empty, and I wonder what it means, I wonder what it all means and what our places are.

I breathe once more, deeply.

I breathe again.

Then I turn, and I finally leave, too.

THE NEXT DAY, the hunt begins before dawn.

I meet Alexandros at the stables, like we normally do later, after training in the morning, and he silently readies Bucephalus, while I do the same with the brown, next to him. We don't speak. It's too early, even for Alexandros. Once the horses are saddled and ready, we jump up onto them and ride through the city to meet the rest of the hunting party near the palace. I see Philippos when I arrive in the courtyard, already seated on the back of a grey stallion, and I wonder about him, and getting up this early, and then as I look at him, I realize he hasn't gotten up at all, because he hasn't yet been to sleep.

I smile, and shake my head.

Dionysus.

We join the group of other Macedonians that are already there, too, and near the basileus, and when Alexandros and I ride up together, Philippos' eyes flick to us, once, noticing this, but he doesn't say anything. Then the Persians come, and when we're all gathered, we depart. We leave the city and head west into the mountains that are there. We don't go north, where Alexandros and I normally go, but *west*, towards the sharper and more rugged and harsh peaks that I crossed to come here some months ago. We ride together, everyone in complete silence, which the dawn and stillness seems to demand.

We come to the forest.

It's still very early, so along with the quiet, it means that the mist rises, swirling through and between the spaced trees, and the humid air around us smells of fresh pine. My broad-sword is strapped across my back, like it always is, but I won't use it; not today, and not for the hunt. Instead, I carry a long sarissa in my right hand, while my left holds the reins of the brown, and next to me, Alexandros does the same, except he just has a sarissa, and he didn't bring his broad-sword.

We continue to ride, no sounds from us, just snorts from the horses. Then as a soft breeze comes, the dogs catch a scent.

They bark and the sudden and harsh noise breaks the silence of the morning, and the dogs throw their heads back and go bounding off and into the distance, continuing to bark and bark as they run, creating an even greater noise now as more of them pick up the scent and most of them sprint in the same direction, along the path we've been following. But there are two dogs that hesitate. The main hunting party with Philippos and Pausanius and Amyntas and all the Persians gallop after the main pack of dogs, in a flurry of hooves and displaced earth and human shouting now, too, as they yell and urge their horses on, wanting to be first, wanting to be the one that gets the kill, but Alexandros remains. He looks at me, then nods towards the two dogs that are different, the ones that lift their noses and smell the wind in another way, and I nod to him, too, and we watch them.

We sit our horses, and we wait, and we watch.

The dogs sniff, judging the changing of the winds and the scent that the new breeze brings.

Then they finally bark, too.

They begin to run, also, but instead of bounding down the path in front of us, the one that the others have followed, they go in a different direction. Alexandros silently reaches out and touches my leg and I know what he's telling me and so we kick our horses to a gallop, together, and we follow after the two dogs and in the opposite direction as the others. Alexandros rides in front, down the narrow path between the pines, on Bucephalus, a horse which no other horse could possibly match strides with or catch, and so it's Alexandros that comes to the clearing first, on his great black stallion, and it's him that sees it first and pulls his horse to a halt. I pull back on the reins as hard as I can, and I'm sorry that the rope will cut into the brown's cheeks, but if I don't, we'll crash into the back of them.

Why did they stop?

Then I see it, too, and I know.

In the clearing in front of us there's a full-grown lion, crouched and with powerful legs and muscles coiled underneath its body, ready to pounce and strike.

I raise my sarissa, getting it ready.

"*No*," Alexandros whispers.

Why, I want to ask, though I don't.

He gives me a look, and I wonder if he can hear my unspoken question, because I hear his voice again, even though he doesn't speak; I hear once more what he told me, back in the hills above Pella. *I've always been good with animals.*

Is he?

We'll soon find out, I know, or else it will be the end of us, the end of both of us, here, and together.

I hesitate.

He gestures to me again and more urgently, and so I sigh, and then slowly begin to lower my sarissa, as he's told me, because I trust him, and so I can't help it; it's his gift, and it's my blessing.

Next to me, he does the same thing.

I'm confused, though.

Isn't it lion that we're hunting?

He slowly dismounts, never taking his eyes off the crouched animal, and then I slowly and carefully do the same, and climb down off the brown and to the ground.

I don't know why, but I do.

The lion doesn't move as we dismount, it just stays where it's at, in its crouch, its golden and not-blinking eyes never leaving us, and our own eyes.

We stand there, all three of us.

I hold my breath.

I think the animal is about to pounce; I think it's about to spring, uncoiling great muscles and leaping and bounding after us with teeth and claws that will rip and tear our flesh but, instead, it starts to gradually relax.

I exhale. I breathe.

Then we all do, all three of us, together.

We stand there, looking at each other, and the lion blinks now, slowly.

I don't know how much times passes, but eventually I see the great muscles in its chest and legs relax even more, then it turns, and we watch as it begins to silently pad away, and back into the forest. It goes, then looks over its shoulder, just once—back at Alexandros, I realize, and not back at me, the one that had my hand raised and poised to strike—and then it finally returns, back to nature, and is gone.

Alexandros still stares at the spot where the lion disappeared, between the trees.

"I thought this hunt was for them?" I finally ask him.

"It is."

"Then why did you stop me?"

"It chased a boar into these bushes," he says, then nods towards the dense thicket that's in front of us, telling me what he saw before I arrived. "You go around the other side and flush it out, and I'll take it when it runs. Lions are killed for no reason, for their skin and pelts and teeth to be used as trophies. They're killed simply because our fathers killed them, and their fathers before that, which is of course no reason at all. If we kill this boar, though, then it'll feed the entire palace."

I wait a minute, looking at him.

There's more than this. I know that there's more than this.

But instead of asking again, I just nod.

"Alright," I tell him, and I go to the other side of the thicket, as he's told me to do, and once I'm there, I look back across at Alexandros. Then he nods, too, giving me the signal to begin and I start to yell and shout and wave my arms while using my sarissa to rustle the bushes as much as I can.

It doesn't take much, and then the boar breaks from its cover.

It happens in a blur, in less than an instant.

The animal's body is low to the ground, tusks curved and yellow and deadly, and when it runs from the thicket—a powerful brown mass, streaking wildly through the forest—it runs straight towards Alexandros, and where he stands, and holds his sarissa ready, just as we had planned, but then—

It changes course.

It swerves away from him, right at the last moment.

The boar runs in a different direction now, and towards the forest, towards where it thinks there will be escape and safety, but there won't be. Not this morning, and not with us hunting. Alexandros brings his arm back quickly, taking aim, and then grunts as his muscles uncoil and he throws the sarissa with all his strength. The weapon whistles and spins through the heavy, damp, and still mist-filled air, and then—*thump*—it plunges into the boar, at the front shoulder, and the animal stumbles.

It stumbles, but it doesn't fall.

Instead, it turns.

It looks back at Alexandros, who has just done this, as it takes a breath, and then it starts to run again. It rushes back towards him now, away from the forest and safety, and Alexandros is defenseless with his sarissa sticking from the boar's side, and I see this, so I begin to run, too, and I yell. "*Alexandros!*" I call, but my words will do nothing, I know. My words won't be able to save him. Only I'll be able to do that.

And so I push myself.

I push myself and run as fast as I can, as fast as my well-muscled and well-trained legs will carry me, around the thicket, and towards where the boar charges at my friend.

The boar.

Me.

Streaks and blurs in the forest.

We're both almost to him.

We're both going to make it there, right at the same time.

No, we're not, I then see, and I think the boar might make it there first, and in front of me I watch as Alexandros bends his legs, getting ready, armed with nothing but his hands, and I make my own calculations, and then I dive. I throw myself forward and down, onto my knees, in a lunging and skidding motion, and as I do, I also plant the butt-end of my sarissa into the ground, just as the charging boar is about to reach us.

The animal runs even faster.

His powerful legs churn dirt beneath him.

Then he's upon us, and that's what I've been counting on as I use the force created by the animal's charge to impale it on the sharpened end of the long sarissa.

Squeal.

The boar lets out a great noise as its body flips up and into the air.

I brace myself, but the force and weight is too much, and it knocks me over and off my feet, and into a heap.

Blood splatters across my face, though whose blood, I'm not sure.

Then the animal's body falls, too, and the massive beast lands heavily on both me and Alexandros, knocking the wind from us and pinning us to the ground.

There's one more squeal from the animal, lower, a death rattle, a final sound.

Then there's silence.

Silence and mist and forest.

My arm feels bruised, maybe broken.

There's blood from the boar leaking out and across us, and we're covered in dirt now, too, and our breath returns and so we breathe, together, in and out, in and out, we breathe.

"Are you alright?" I finally ask him, quietly.

"Yes," he says, and I think I feel him nod next to me, his chin pressed against my shoulder.

We're about to try to lift the massive beast off us, and that's when I see it, in the distance: more fur, more stout and powerful legs, more sharpened and deadly tusks.

Another boar.

There had been two that had gone into the thicket.

And now this one begins to charge, too.

It begins to charge towards us and we both see it and then strain our muscles and the heavy corpse that's on top of us begins to move, little by little, but it's too late, and anything we do now won't be enough.

The second boar keeps charging.

Then it's to us, on us, only a body-length away.

The giant tusks are lowered, ready to gore us where we lay with the body of its mate draped across our own bodies and pinning us, completely defenseless, together, the easiest of targets and the easiest of revenges, and just then as death is only moments and seconds away—

There's a whizzing in the air, and another squeal of pain.

Then it happens again. Another whizzing.

There's another squeal, a final one, and a great cloud of dust.

The boar stumbles and falls right as it gets to where we're trapped, crashing into us in a second great shower of earth, and blood, and we both cry out in pain again as the body slams into ours, but it's just pain from the impact, and not death from the sharp tusks.

The dust clears.

The earth settles, and the forest is quiet again.

And when it does, and my vision and breath begin to return, I see there are two feathered arrows that protrude from deep within the boar's stomach, and blood leaks from the punctures that the arrows have created and mixes with our own blood that's already there in the dirt, as well as the blood of the first boar.

I strain and flex.

We both do.

We grimace and use all the strength we have left and finally push the carcass off our bodies, and to the side, and that's when we look above us and see that our savior is a Persian who sits astride a great Arabian horse, and he holds the bow that he's taken from where he normally carries it on his back.

Of course.

A bow.

I smile, the irony not lost on me.

There's silence.

We look at each other, all three of us. I recognize him as one of the leaders of the delegation.

"Thank you," Alexandros finally says, breaking the silence.

The Persian just stares back at us, with his dark eyes that are two black spots above his thin and neatly-trimmed beard, and then his lips part, finally, into a smile.

There's another moment.

Then the Persian lifts his hand and presses two fingers to his lips, before bringing them to his forehead, in what must be a sign of respect in his culture, and where he's from. Then he turns, and just as quickly as he's come, he's gone again, back through the pines and the mist and towards the rest of the main hunting party.

Silence again.

Nothing but silence, and mist, rising, rising, rising.

Alexandros and I are alone.

We turn.

We look at each other.

We'll go through much together, in our lives, of that I'm now sure, but if I had to try to find one moment when everything changed, then this moment would be it. I know this, even as it's happening; I know it's one of those times in our lives that will remain, one of those blessed and important times that will live between us and in us long after this day. He didn't bring his broad-sword. Why wouldn't he do that? He normally brings it everywhere, just as I do. I look up, at where the stars are when darkness comes, wondering what's been written there and in them. I don't know. But I'm excited to find out, because we're two boys—we're just two boys, really, with everything in front of us—who have now faced certain death together, and lived. What does that mean? And if we've done it once, who's to say how many more times we could do the same thing?

A hundred?

A thousand?

More than that?

And what else could we do?

I don't know, because even in my short and young life, I've already learned it's not worth wondering, because there are certain things that we come upon, certain things such as this, to which only the gods know the answer.

WE DON'T GO to the feast together that night.

When we return from the hunt, separate from the rest of the party, and later than them, too, though they send no one to look for us, Alexandros goes back to the palace, and I head down into the city and return to my small room next to the gymnasium. The rest of the Companions hadn't been invited on the hunting trip, but they *have* been invited to the feast—to which all noble families are invited—so they're already getting ready by drinking, as they normally do, when I get back. And I'd guess by how much it seems they've drunk, they've been at it for some time, also. Since mid-day? Maybe even earlier? I don't know. But they look up as I walk in, and they see me covered in dirt, blood, sweat, my skin torn and bruised, my eyes exhausted and spent, my chiton ripped and hanging loose across my chest and their own eyes go wide when they see this and they ask me what happened.

I don't tell them.

I simply walk past them, and towards my room.

They stand and follow me down the hallway, but when I get to my room, I go in, and I close the door, and then they don't follow anymore. I don't want to talk about it. Not yet. Not when it's still so fresh, and when it's still just mine; just mine, and his. I want to live with it, for a moment more, for a little while longer. I lean against the wall. I can feel my heart. I can feel it in my chest, the way it beats only when there are important things that have been done, and seen, and felt, and when there's a world that has somehow shifted and been made to be less big, as the world should always shift. I take another moment, to gather myself, and to let myself feel as much as I can feel. And then, once I have,

I slowly untie and peel off my dirty and ruined chiton, and I let it fall to the floor. I stand there, naked. The stones are cold on my feet as I walk to the washing basin and take the cloth and scrub my body with both the cloth and fresh water that's in the basin. Once I'm done, and my skin is clean—or as clean as I'll be able to get it, before I can find a proper bath in a river, or the lake—I get ready as quickly as I can, finding a new chiton in the chest that sits in the corner of the room. I wrap it up and over my shoulders and then cinch a new leather belt at my waist so that the chiton stays in place and falls and hangs as it should. By the time I'm dressed, then leave my room again, I see that the others have already gone, up to the palace, I presume, and so I leave, and I go up to the palace, too, but I go alone.

When I get there, the feast has already begun.

I walk into the large hall where the light's dim and getting dimmer, and everywhere I look there are men reclined on low and comfortable-looking couches; laughing, talking, drinking. There are servant-boys and servant-girls that walk between them, wearing only loin clothes, thin strips of fabric, barely anything at all, and they refill plates of food and held-out cups that wait for more strong and undiluted Macedonian wine.

I understand now.

Dionysus.

For the first time, perhaps, I truly understand.

I see the other Companions across the room and I walk towards an empty couch near them and I sit down. As soon as I do, I'm handed a cup of wine by a servant, a young-looking boy. I take a sip, noticing how strong and potent it is, and then I look towards the front of the room and I see Alexandros there: he's with a woman who looks to be a few years older than we are, and who must be the girl he's told me about that lives in the city, and that he sees occasionally, and that he sleeps with.

Aria.

That's what he told me her name was, right?

Yes, I remember.

I look at her, and I study her more closely.

She has fair hair and skin, like he does, and gentle curves to her body that are amplified by the way she lays next to him, one hip sharply in the air, the other anchored on the couch and lightly pressing against his narrower and smaller hips.

I frown. I don't know why, but I do.

Then I find myself wondering: what do they talk about?

Is it the same things that we talk about, or is it different things?

I hear a great laugh and my eyes travel past Alexandros until they find Philippos, still surrounded by his many wives, and the beautiful bodyguard, Pausanius, who is there with and amongst the wives, too. As I watch them, Philippos makes a waving signal with his hand, and when he does, all the wives stand and bow to him, and then they leave. I think Olympias is going to be the last to bow, and the last to leave, but she's actually the first gone, and when she goes, which it seems she's very eager to do, I see that she's the only one that doesn't actually bow at all, she just stands and turns and walks out.

Philippos pretends not to notice.

But I've met him, the basileus, and I know that he does, because I know that he doesn't miss anything; even with just one good eye, he sees everything, and that's why he is who he is.

Then as soon as the royal wives leave, and are gone, all the rest of the women that are gathered take the same cue, and they leave, too. The exception, though, is the servant-girls that carry the wine and bring the drinks to the men that are on the couches.

They will stay; they will stay for wine, and for pleasure.

Half the oil-fueled lamps are extinguished.

The light in the room becomes even lower, even dimmer.

I look at the Persians who lounge near Philippos and Alexandros, at the head of the room, and near Amyntas, too, and I also look at the young Macedonian boys that wear next to nothing and refill their cups: the Persians never drink undiluted wine, like the Illyrians and Macedonians drink, which I can tell by the glassy sheen that's come to their eyes and the languid and less-than-calculated movements of their bodies and limbs. The effect can also be seen in the apparent lack of inhibition and modesty that's crept into their arms, their hands, their fingers that reach, and search, and touch, and caress. One of the Persians has his colorful tunic off, pulled up and over his head, and his hair-covered chest is bare and exposed in the hall. Another of the Persians touches one of the young Macedonian serving-boys, and then pulls him closer, down and onto his couch where they both lay together, limbs intertwined, skin pressed against skin, lips finding lips.

Dionysus.

The largest temple.

The largest temple, and most worshipped god, in all of Pella.

I frown again.

This is my home, and has been for some time now.

So if Dionysus is the god that's worshipped, and the god that all the others feel, and is strongest here, then why don't I feel him, too?

If he's the god that speaks to them, why don't I hear his words?

I look past the Companions, and to Alexandros again, towards where he sits amongst his family, the Argeads, and next to his father, and cousin, and brother, and he surveys all that's happening. Philippos is with Pausanius, whispering into his ear, his scarred and calloused hand on the young guard's thigh. Amytnas is with a serving-girl, and so is Arrhidaeus, his massive body dwarfing the smaller one that's next to him, touching him also, running her fingers through his hair as he closes his eyes in pleasure.

Alexandros is alone, though, now that Aria is gone.

I look at him, for another moment, but he doesn't see me, and so I turn and look at the Companions next to where I sit, all gathered on their couches alongside where I'm on mine, too. I look at the girls that they've set their eyes on. The Companions take big gulps of wine before holding out cups to have them refilled, and then try to make small talk when the girls come back around. Some of them stay, and lay with them. Some of them don't. It's unappealing to me. It's all so very unappealing to me, and I don't know why, because there was a time when it would have been. This should be everything, right? This should be everything that a young man could ever want. This should be every need, every desire, all rolled into a single room, into a single evening, into a single god and feast, desire fuelled and then re-fuelled until it's fulfilled, and yet here I am, and it's not.

It's not for me.

I want more; I want something else.

But what?

My kingdom, my birthright, my revenge.

That's all I think of, and the only thing that can calm my soul, my thoughts of Illyria, and Salona, and my uncle, and all that was taken from me, and as I think of this, and let it consume me again, I stand and go outside for some of the air that's more fresh and not perfumed with lust and wine and sweat. I walk out, and when I do, I see a man and a boy that are already there; I see the brightly-colored tunic and full-legged trousers of the Persian, first, juxtaposed next to the fair and light-complected skin of the Macedonian serving-boy who's wearing much less. I look at the boy, first, and then I look at the Persian, and I recognize him; he's the same man that was on his horse, from earlier, in the forest, on the hunt, the same man that saved our lives with his bow. He sees me, too, and when he does, he whispers into the boy's ear and the boy waits there where they stand, closer towards the garden, as the Persian begins to walk until he's in front of me.

He looks at me, up and down, taking me in.

"Thank you," I finally say, trying to motion with my hands so that he'll understand the unfamiliar Greek words. "For earlier," I point to the west, back towards the mountains, and the forest, and the pines. "With the boar," I say, trying to imitate tusks with my hands.

"It was my pleasure," he responds, in perfect Greek.

I raise my eyebrows in surprise. "You speak our language?" I ask him.

He doesn't have even the slightest hint or trace of a foreign accent, which makes me more than curious.

"Of course."

"How?"

"Because I'm Greek."

I don't understand.

I look at his clothes again, his dark beard, the way that he's dressed and acts, like a Persian, like all the others he rides with, and I can tell that he knows what I'm thinking and so he answers the question I haven't yet asked. "I was born on Rhodos," he tells me.

"The island?"

"Yes, the one that's very far from here."

"If you were born on Rhodos, how did you end up in Persia?"

"I'm a warrior who fights for the highest bidder, and the Persians have the most gold, don't they?" he says, and then sees my look, the questions that are still in my eyes, and so he smiles, and continues. "I travelled to Anatolia, when I was very young, and which is very close to my island," he tells me, "and when I did, I met and married the daughter of the satrap in Sardeis, and stayed there with her, in her father's house, and so now I serve at the pleasure of both him and the shahansha."

"Shahansha?" I frown, the word unfamiliar to me.

"*Basileus-basileon*," he smiles wider. "The King of Kings."

"He's not king here."

"No, but he rules over a great many kings there, a great many in Asia, that serve beneath him, and at his pleasure, and so that's what they call him."

"You look like them," I say, still not understanding.

"It's because I've been there in Sardeis for a long time, since I was younger even than you are now."

"I've heard of your city."

"Yes. It's a very beautiful city."

"But it's not Greek."

"No, it's not."

"And you've never wanted to come back?"

"Come back where?"

"Here. To your own people."

He looks at me, and I look back at his dark eyes, and then I realize that they're *made* to be dark by make-up that he's painted on or had a servant paint on for him. He waits for another moment, looking back at me, and then another moment after that one comes and passes, too. Then he finally smiles, and turns to walk away, back towards the boy that waits for him, in the darkness, in the garden, in the shadows of the courtyard and the palace, but I have one more question.

"What's your name?" I ask him, as he leaves.

He hears my words, and he pauses.

He stands there, for a moment, halfway between us, halfway between me and the servant-boy he'll take to his room to be his pleasure, and then he turns back. His eyes seem less dark when I see them now. "Memnon," he tells me.

"Memnon of Sardeis," I repeat, nodding.

"Memnon of *Rhodos*," he says, and he smiles again.

"Why did you save our lives today, Memnon of Rhodos?" I ask him, the thing that I've really wanted to ask, all this time, since it happened. "You might have been born Greek, but you serve them now, and he's the son of your shahansha's greatest threat and adversary."

"Yes, he is."

"So why did you do it?"

"And what are you?"

"What do you mean?"

"You said that he's the son of Philippos. And so what are you?"

"I'm his friend."

Memnon stands there, for another moment, looking back at me.

Then he finally smiles again, and he spreads his arms.

"In this great world and grand scheme of gods and stars, and all their plans that have been written and recorded, what is just one boy and his friend?"

There's another moment between us.

We look at each other, there in darkness.

I think there might be more words, but there's not, and so after one last moment and one last look he turns and walks away, away from me and back to the boy that waits for him in the night. When he reaches him, he takes the boy by the hand and leads him away and I watch as they walk together, and then they're both gone, and once they are, I'm alone again with nothing but my thoughts, the way I usually am.

I look back inside the palace, at the feast.

The light is even lower now than it was before, more of the oil-fueled lamps having been extinguished and there's less clothing that's worn, too, less cloth that's covering skin. I hear voices, drunken voices, and I see Philippos, in the middle of it all. He's pulled Pausanius down and towards him—even closer than he was before—hands on skin, flesh pressed against flesh, and then I see that Philippos has pulled the bodyguard's chiton off, too, so that Pausanius of Orestis is completely naked, in front of everyone. I wonder if Pausanius wants this. I wonder if there's any pleasure in it for him. I think back to the way he touched my chest, when we were alone, in my chamber.

Of course. Of course.

Then I watch as Philippos takes his own chiton off, too, and he moves behind Pausanius, and when he does, he starts thrusting. I'm surprised and shocked to see that he does this right there, on the couches, in public and in front of everyone that's still in the hall and gathered in the drunken half-light.

No one seems to mind.

No one even watches, or pays attention to them.

This is normal, I realize.

Dionysus.

In the distance, somewhere outside the palace, the low sound of a drum-beat begins. It's soft at first, and then it grows, faster, louder, and so that it's more.

Louder.

Louder, louder, louder.

Faster.

Dionysus.
Dionysus.
He's here, he's amongst them, he must be.

I see the Companions—all of them except Ptolemaios, I realize—and they're on their couches which are pushed together now, and I see that there are three servant-girls that have remained between the five of them. The Companions all take their chitons off, too, and the girls have removed what little they'd been wearing before, so that there's nothing that's between any of them except skin and dim-flickering candlelight, and the soft sounds of love and pleasure.

The drums pick up.

Louder, louder.

So does the beat, the rhythm, it begins to go faster, too.

I look around, and I only search for one person, but I don't find him; he must have left earlier, he must have gone to Aria's, after she left along with the other women. He told me that he stays at her house sometimes, in the lower part of the city, when he wants to escape the palace. I smile, low and dim, just like the flickering light. What night could possibly be better to escape than this one? He feels the same as I do, and so that's where he's gone.

I look through the darkness, one more time.

The basileus and his beautiful guard are in a different position now.

The Companions all move and contort and subtly compete for the attention of the prettiest of the girls who have stayed, the best-looking of the ones who are there between them, on the couches that they've pushed together so that it's really just one couch now, one long and flat and comfortable surface.

More lamps are extinguished.

More skin presses against skin, beaded sweat mixing in the hot night.

I don't see how it ends, though, because I turn and leave.

Their god doesn't speak to me in the way he speaks and calls to them, and so I walk away, from the hall, and the palace. I walk out and through the courtyard, and as I do, there's a breeze that picks up and the breeze is welcome, it's very welcome, as it's cooling and fresh in the humid air. I'm going to take the long way back, I decide, because I'm not quite ready for sleep yet, and the path I choose brings me to the far side of the palace where there are no lamps, just shadows and moonlight and a cluster of olive groves before the hills and fields begin. My thoughts are elsewhere, so I'm not really paying attention to my path, or where I go, but then in front of me, out of the corner of an eye, I see the shadows move. My body tenses at first, alert and ready, and then I look closer and see that it's just two bodies that hold each other, softly, gently, tenderly, and I stop walking. I hear hushed, whispered voices. Then I see the first shadow move, and dress, and leave, heading back towards the palace and the feast and I recognize the young face in front of me when the light catches and criss-crosses his distinct features.

Ptolemaios.

There's a smile on his lips, and in his eyes, the type of smile that only comes from one thing.

Love.

Pure, requited love.

And he also wears a twisted and broken twig from one of the olive branches behind his ear.

I watch him from the place where I stand, and then after a moment, when he's gone, and everything is still again, I see a second shadow move, too. It heads back the same way, back up towards the palace and the feast, and I recognize this young face, also, that follows after Ptolemaios.

Cleopatra.

Alexandros' sister.

She doesn't see me.

I smile as I watch her go, and I don't realize my lips have turned, and moved, but they have, and then when I search myself, and my feelings, I realize why: it's because this is love, pure and plain and simple, and it's different than the type I've seen at the feast, which is of course not really love at all. I feel happiness for them. This could be the god that speaks to me, I realize, because I feel an intense and consuming happiness for them and what they've found, with each other. But then, as soon as I feel this, I then feel a rush of sadness, too. I wonder why, and then that answer comes, also, because is there a place for them in this world? Is there a place for the type of love that they have, pure and real and between a very common boy and a very uncommon prinkipissa?

I don't know.

I hope so, but I don't know.

I keep walking.

I see no more movement or shadows as I continue from the palace, and then soon I'm to the ancient cobblestone streets of the city, and I go past the great Temple of Dionysus, and then the stables where Bucephalus and the brown surely sleep in their stalls, and then soon I'm back to the gymnasium. I go inside and I see that it's empty. I go past the common areas, and the pits of sand, and then I go down the hallway and to my chamber. I walk into my room and shut the door behind me, and even though I've already washed myself, before I went to the feast, I unwrap the chiton from around my body, let it fall to the ground, and then I go to the basin and wash myself again. I use the cloth and fresh water that's there to cleanse myself of the feast, of the lamps, of the hall, of the god that doesn't speak to me and all his work I've just seen.

When I'm done, I go to my bed.

The breeze I felt when I left the palace picks up and it cools my still-wet skin as I lay down and the temperature begins to drop outside, too. My thoughts drift and wander, just like the wind that cools me. I think about the day, and all that's happened; I think about Alexandros, and the hunt, and the man that saved us that I thought was Persian, when we were in the forest, but now I know is actually Greek.

Or is he, I wonder?

Are we simply what we're born, or are we something else, something that we choose and find within ourselves?

I don't know. I don't know.

I think of his eyes, and the dark eastern make-up that he wears.

Perhaps in this world we are what we choose to be, and perhaps we can become something different than what we were born, and that is carried within us, in our blood, rushing and pumping through our veins, our bodies, our souls, our hearts and our spirits.

Soul.

Heart.

Spirit.

When I think of those things, I think of only one now, one in particular above all others that I know.

Alexandros.

I'm glad that I've come here and that I've found him, or perhaps it's him that's found me, I realize, and those are the last thoughts I have before I smile and close my eyes and then sleep comes.

There's nothing for a moment.

Darkness. Rest. The night.

Then I'm woken.

I don't know what time it is.

I hear a noise, a rustling, and I realize there's someone else that's there, a shadow that's entered my room.

Panic and adrenaline rushes through my body as my limbs tense and I jump up and grab my broad-sword from the place where it rests near my bed.

Persians?

I swing it around, so that it's ready, in the darkness.

"It's alright, it's me."

I recognize the voice.

Then I see him, through the darkness and shadows.

It's not the Persians, I see, because it's Alexandros, standing by the washing basin, and I lower my sword when I recognize him and relax my muscles as he crosses the small room and comes closer to me.

"What are you doing down here?" I ask, my voice hushed, barely more than a whisper that vibrates in my throat.

"I couldn't sleep," he tells me, and when he speaks, I hear that his voice is just a whisper, too.

"Where were you?"

"In the city."

"And you left?"

"Yes."

"Why?"

"I told you. Because I couldn't sleep."

"What's the matter?" I ask, with concern in my voice now. "Why couldn't you sleep?"

He looks back at me, and he doesn't answer at first, so I put the broad-sword back to where it rests against the wall and then sit down on my bed. He comes closer and I motion for him to sit, too, and he does, but not on the bed; he sits on the floor, *next* to the bed. He sits there on the cool stone, and then once he does, he moves his body so that it comes closer and leans against my legs, his head near my knees, gently touching and pressing against my thigh and his hair tickling my skin.

The breeze picks up, even stronger.

There's still the faint sound of drums in the distance, coming from the hills near the palace, rhythmic, pulsing.

"Were you scared today?" Alexandros finally asks me from his place on the floor and against my leg. I can't see his eyes, but I know they search for mine, in the darkness, and I know mine do the same in return; they look down, and they search, they search, in the most human and meaningful of ways, they both search.

"No," I finally tell him, shaking my head.

"We could have died."

"We could have. But we would have died together."

Silence.

Have I gone too far?

My eyes adjust, and they find his.

And then, when they do, I'm relieved at what I see, and I breathe in, deeply, and as I do my body is flooded with the relief that comes when you know that someone shares the same feelings and the same depth and degree of them, too; I feel the relief and pleasure of knowing that someone else feels something that's so important and that they feel it in the exact same way as I feel it. How many times does that happen? How many times does that feeling come, how many times in our lives? Maybe once. Maybe never. "You were at Aria's?" I finally ask him, my voice still a whisper.

Silence.

More drums, in the distance.

Closer.

Louder.

"Why did you come here?" he finally asks, and he still whispers, too.

I frown.

I don't understand.

"It's my room," I tell him. "I know what the others are doing, up at the palace, but I have no taste for—"

"No," he cuts me off, shaking his head in its place pressed against my thigh, his skin against my skin. "What brought you *here*," he says, and he emphasizes the word differently, the same as the first time we met, in the garden not very far from where we now sit.

"I don't know."

"Yes, you do."

I think, then I answer.

"The same thing that brought that rider to the clearing today, I suppose," I finally tell him.

"See?" he asks.

"See what?"

"I told you that you knew."

"Yes," I nod. "I guess I do."

"Yes," he says, also.

Silence.

I feel him against me, his pulse, his breath, both of them quickening. "It's bigger than us, Hephaestion," his voice is even lower now, softer, even more quiet.

"What is?"

"My father dreams of going south, and conquering all of Greece, and everyone calls him a visionary for it. But fathers so rarely change the world, and do you know why? Fathers so rarely change the world, because it's their sons who do that."

I think of Alexandros' mis-colored eyes.

I think of where they turn, and where they look, where they always look.

The horizon.

The unconquered, and the unknown. The rising sun.

If there's no room for the type of love that Ptolemaios and Cleopatra have in this world, then is there room for this? Is there room for us?

I don't know.

Maybe not in this world, I think.

But another?

One that we could make, together?

"Wherever you go, Alexandros," I finally tell him, not knowing where the words come from, only that they're truth, and they're not mine, but they also are. "Wherever you go, I will go with you."

"I know."

What god is this?

What god is this, that now speaks?

Because this is him. This is my god.

Next to me, Alexandros moves and shifts and unties his chiton, and then he takes it off, letting it fall to the floor in a puddle of cloth near where he sits, and I think he's going to stand, but he doesn't. Instead, he turns and pushes the chiton into a pile to use as a pillow and then lays on the stone floor because the breeze has stopped and the stone is cool in the still-warm night. We keep talking for a few more moments, about this and that, as we lay there, things that are less important than gods and dreams and fathers and fate, and then eventually the drums in the distance soften, and the breeze dies and disappears, too, and at some point, we both finally stop talking and go to sleep, me on my bed, him on the floor, next to me, on the stone.

But before we do, I remember the last thing that I say to him, before sleep and darkness comes.

"Why didn't you kill the lion?" I ask him.

"What?" he whispers, his eyes half-closed.

"The lion, in the forest today," I say again. "Why didn't you kill him, or want me to?"

My question is no more than a whisper.

My words are no stronger than the dying breeze that drifts through the window and between us and past our young and salty and sweat-soaked skin.

He's silent, for a moment.

Then he looks up, from his place on the floor.

"Because it would have been like killing myself," he finally says.

Then he rolls over, and closes his eyes, and there is nothing more.

Some time in the night I half-wake and feel him next to me, on the bed, where he's climbed from his place on the floor. His skin touches and presses against my skin, just barely, and I smell the scent of his hair next to my hair, near my nose, on my lips, and spread across my pillow. It's only a moment, though, and I soon go back to sleep, and then when I wake again, in the morning, I look over and see the place where he was is now empty, and that he's already gone.

CHAPTER SIX

WE TRAIN THE NEXT MORNING with all the Companions, as we usually do, and then, when we finish at Lariston, Alexandros and I leave, as we also usually do. We saddle our horses together at the stables and then ride out of the city, up to the lake at the top of the mountains. We talk as we ride, but we don't talk about any of the important things we talked about the night before, when there were drums and stars and wind and gods between us; instead, we talk about things that we normally talk about. We talk about who has progressed the most during training, and in what areas, and who hasn't and needs to be pushed harder and in what way we might be able to push them. We talk about strengths and weaknesses, tactics for new training, and plans for when we've become what we aim to become. We soon reach the top of the mountain and strip off our chitons, as we go to the lake, and then into it, and once we're cool and cleaned, we leave and come back to sit in the sun and dry, on the bluff, on our bluff, the horses grazing peacefully nearby with our also-drying chitons resting on their backs. As we sit there, Alexandros tells me about the Persians he spoke to during the feast. He tells me the questions he asked them, and all he learned about who they are, and what they do, and the shape and geography of their great and wide empire. He asked them about roads and distances, he tells me, governors and satraps, cities and tribes and the differences between them all and they were too eager to share everything he asked, and it's all new and important and vital information for us both.

I smile when I hear it.

"Undiluted wine," I tell him in return.

"Exactly," he nods, smiling, too. "One of the most clever things my father ever thought of, many years ago. They think there are no rules or consequences, outside their borders, and so now I hear they fight amongst themselves over who gets to come to Pella as part of the delegations. They think of it as a vacation, a sojourn amongst one-eyed Philippos and his loyal and wild barbarians."

Arrogance.

There's an unmistakable Persian pride that's grown and festered as their empire has become larger and larger, and more prosperous by the day, and their pride and arrogance has been allowed to metastasize into a type of laziness and complacency that we know nothing about here in our mountains and amongst our low hills and angry tribes. These Persians think they're invincible—or invincible, at least, from anyone besides themselves and the destruction they can bring to each other—and they think this because they have been for so many years and generations, and perhaps Alexandros is right: Greece is small, and Persia is large, but if there's one thing that all the stories we've ever heard are clear about, it's that such hubris is always, always, *always* punished by the gods, no matter whose gods they might be, east or west, high or low, Greek or Persian.

Our skin soon dries, and the sun begins to sink.

We stand and go to our horses and our chitons that are also now dry on their backs. We reach for them, and take them, and then tie them at the shoulders and cinch our leather belts at our waists, the same as we always do. Then after we're done, we climb back onto our horses and begin our ride down the mountain. We ride together and soon return to the city and stables. We get there and dismount and put the two horses away, each back into their stalls, next to the other, the same as every other afternoon we ride together, but then when we turn to leave, that's when he stops me. This is normally the time I go in one direction, back towards the gymnasium, and my room at the end of the hallway that's opposite where we train, and he goes in the other, up towards the palace, and his room, but today he places his hand on my shoulder, and he makes me pause.

I look down at his hand, resting there.

Then my eyes turn back, and I look at him, across from me.

There's a look on his face that I'm not sure how to read. "What is it?" I ask, frowning and wrinkling my nose. He hesitates. I've never seen him hesitate before. "Is something wrong?"

"No," he says quickly.

He's nervous.

Why is he nervous?

"Then what is it?"

"I don't want you to be mad."

"I'm sure I won't be."

"Good."

"So what's happened?"

"I had them bring your things up to the palace," he finally tells me, and then swallows.

I look back at him. That certainly isn't what I was expecting.

His eyes search mine, looking for something, anything, my reaction, pleasure or displeasure, or perhaps something else, I realize. What is there? What is there in my eyes?

Perhaps even I don't know.

"Are you angry?" he finally asks me.

"Angry?" I frown again.

"Yes."

I look back at him, as he swallows one more time, and my eyes give away nothing, I know, but that's not what I feel. That's not what I feel at all.

"There's not much to bring, but... do you think they got everything?"

"They said they'd be careful, and that they would. I made sure of it."

A moment.

I think of what this means, I think of all the possible things this could mean and that might now come next. I'll be closer to him. That's what I want, when I think about it, and it's clearly what he wants, too.

So I nod. "I suppose we should go to the palace, then," I tell him.

He nods, too.

We wait there, for one more moment, feeling the world shift and change around us once more, and then we turn, and we go, towards the palace, together.

I HAVEN'T YET BEEN to the part of the palace where he lives, but we go there now, and he shows me. We walk through the part that I *am* familiar with, first, the mosaic-tailed hallway and then the door that leads to what I remember as the basileus' office, where I first met Philippos and where I pledged myself to him just as I told my mother I would, and in return he told me I could stay in Pella and train with both his son and the second and third and fourth sons of the other noble families that trained there and with him. I wonder if he realizes the implications of that decision; I wonder if he regrets it, or if he's glad, or if he even thinks about it at all. We get closer to the door and I see again the guard that stands there, outside of it, Pausanius of Orestis. I've seen more of him now, though, then I had before, during the last time I was here; I've seen more of him at the feast, after the hunt, and I know more about his relationship with Philippos, too, which of course Alexandros already knows, as well. He's not much older than we are, but he seems different. He seems very different than both me and Alexandros, and even in this short time I've been here, in Pella, he seems to have changed.

"Alexandros," he says when he sees us, and nods. "Hephaestion."

But Alexandros doesn't say anything in return. He just keeps walking.

He doesn't look at Pausanius, doesn't acknowledge him, doesn't respond or anything else. I do, though. I nod to him as we pass, towards his blue eyes that I know now are mountain eyes, not eyes from the sea, and then we're gone, and beyond him.

We keep walking.

We go across another black-and-white tiled mosaic floor that's fashioned into an intricate and different design beneath our feet, some type of extended hunting scene, I see, and this hallway leads to open-air colonnades and a trimmed and well-kept garden. We continue through the cloisters next to the garden, and then go back inside again, into a different wing of the palace now, and down another hallway yet and towards the far north and eastern end of the building. I look around and realize that this is the wing that's occupied by the royal family; Philippos, his wives, and all of his children.

Alexandros comes to a wooden door that's next to a few others.

Then he pushes the door open, and shows me his room.

It's small and decorated similarly to the one I was given off the gymnasium, except there's a window at the far end that's larger than the window in my room was, as well as a basin for washing that's larger, too. I see his trunk that's there, in the corner, that contains all his clothes, I assume, and then in the corner opposite his trunk, I see mine. There are also now two equal-sized beds that are positioned on each side of the room, with some distance between them. I can feel him watching me as I look at it, as I take it all in, how everything is set up and configured and what our future here will be and look like. "Is this alright?" he asks.

I nod.

I don't need to, but I do. "Of course," I tell him.

"Good."

"So what now?"

"Do you . . . want to see the rest of the palace?"

It'll be my new home, and so I nod again, and then we leave.

We go back out into the hallway, and then down it, in the other direction, opposite the way we just came. He shows me the rest of the palace, as he's said, all of the places and rooms and hallways I haven't seen. It's a modest palace, by the standards of the different kingdoms of our world, but it's massive to a boy from Salona, a boy who hasn't really travelled further than where he was born and where he's at right now at this exact moment.

This moment won't be forever, though, will it?

No, it won't. We both know that.

The sun begins to sink, and then disappear.

We turn to go back to his room that's now our room, and he stops in the kitchen on the way and takes two jugs of wine from the shelf where he shows me they're kept, and so that I know, too, and when we get back, we drink the first one together, undiluted, like at the feast. And then, when we finish the first jug, I'm surprised he reaches for the second, and we drink more, and we finish that one, too. I suppose it feels like a celebration, or an occasion. I didn't even know he drank wine, or at least I didn't know he drank so much, and then I realize: he does drink, and he likes to, very much, he just doesn't in front of the others.

Control.

It's all about control, I realize, and never wanting to lose it.

But he does drink in front of me.

What does that mean?

We stay up late, and we drink even more, and this time and this night we talk of many unimportant things, and that feels good to do, too. We keep drinking, and we keep talking, and I don't remember going to sleep, the first night that I'm there, with my friend, in my new home, and in our new room, but we eventually do.

THE NEXT MORNING, I wake before he does.

I look around and I don't recognize where I am, at first, and there's panic and confusion, and then I see Alexandros, sleeping on his bed across from mine, and then I remember. It's still dark, like it always is when we wake to begin our training, before the hot Macedonian sun rises, and I stare at him in the bed where he sleeps. I watch as his chest rises and falls. He sleeps with no clothes, and I see the affect the new exercises have had on his body: it's grown, expanded, become larger and stronger and now looks even more like the body of a man and young warrior. There's a hint of light that then comes, too, just a sliver, from the larger window and through the darkness, and it dances across his skin in beautiful and symmetric patterns, and then finally rests there.

His eyes flutter, when it does.

Then he opens them.

"Is everything alright?" he asks, when he looks over and sees me watching him, rubbing the sleep from his eyes as he comes back to his body and the world.

"That's the third time you've asked me that."

"Well?" he smiles now. "Is it?"

I smile, too, and tell him I've just woken, and that everything's fine, and then we both get up and go to the washing basin that's there in the corner. We stand side-by-side in front of it, and we both wash the sleep from our eyes, first, and then the sweat from our bodies that's come in the night, next, and then when I normally begin to dress, I pause, because he doesn't yet. Instead, he takes a piece of copper that's been neatly carved and sharpened into a blade and after splashing some more water on his face, he begins to run it across his cheek. I watch as he shaves his upper-cheek first, on the right side, and then makes his way down to his chin, and as I look closer, I see the faintest hints of stubble being peeled away. I hadn't noticed it before and thought only that he couldn't yet grow any facial hair, not that he could, but had decided to trim it away every morning. I watch as he finishes with his right cheek, and his chin, and then his left cheek, too, and his neck. When he's done and washed his face clean with water once more, soothing any irritation and cleaning any stray hairs from sticking to it, he then turns and hands the blade to me.

I look down at it, and then back up at him.

"I don't know how," I tell him, very honestly.

He smiles and takes the blade back from my hand. "Splash some water on your face," he says.

I do.

I splash the water from the basin and feel it drip down my cheeks, towards my chin, and he comes closer. He moves his head next to mine so that he can see better, and then he brings the blade up and uses it to start trimming the short beard I've managed to grow, just below the ear first, on my right side, and cutting back down and towards the chin, and lip, and then finally even further and down onto my neck, in the same pattern I watched him do on his own face. I expect it to hurt—the copper blade running across my skin and trimming soft and new hair—but it doesn't. I expect it to knick and cut my cheeks and neck, but his hands are steady and the blade glides smooth. When he's finally done, he splashes more water on my face, like he did to himself, and then splashes some on my chest, too, as a joke, and I smile and look in the mirror. It's been some years since I've been completely clean-shaven, and I realize it might take some time for me to get used to it; to how I now look, and how it feels when I run my hand over my chin.

"Well?" I hear him ask, and then turn to see him still smiling.

"You do this every morning?"

"Yes."

"Why? It seems like a lot of work."

"It's something Parmenion taught me," he says. "He told me that the first time you see a soldier grab another soldier's beard in battle, and use it to gain leverage and end his life, then it'll be the last time you aren't clean-shaven."

I take that in, looking back at him and thinking of the clean-shaven Parmenion that I saw in the courtyard when the Persians arrived, and I now know why. I think of it for a little longer, and it seems to make sense to me, and will be a part of my new life here, I suppose, at the palace, and with Alexandros, and then I nod and we both turn and silently dress together, pulling chitons up and around our shoulders and tying them, letting them drop down and across our bodies, to our thighs, then cinching belts tightly at our waists.

I look at him, once more, and he looks back at me.

A new routine has been established.

Then we both nod again, accepting it, and leave the room together, the same way that we came.

WE GO BACK OUT into the hallway, and it's completely quiet, completely still, the entire palace asleep and no one awake this early. We walk across the mosaic-tiled floor, and then keep going, out of the palace, through the courtyard, and into the not-yet morning. We walk through the city, next to each other, and there's more activity here. We go down past the Temple of Dionysus, and the stables, and all the merchants and vendors from both this city and beyond who pass us with their wagons, and horses pulling them, their wares inside that they're getting ready to sell at the agora. Then we finally get to the gymnasium, and all the rest of the Companions are awake and there, waiting for us, and when they see us enter, together, they pause, and they're silent. They would have seen my empty room, of course, and they would have also seen the servants that had come to move my things up to the palace. But this is the first time I've seen them since it's happened. They look at me, all of them. Normally, they look at him, but today . . . today, they look at me.

I feel them, all their eyes on me, and of course Alexandros does, too.

I'm now living at the palace with him, and I'm clean-shaven, like he is.

"Well?" Alexandros asks, meeting each of their eyes in turn. "Does anyone have something they want to say?"

They all stand there, looking back at us.

Some of them look at each other, too, and then Ptolemaios speaks. "No," he finally says, shaking his head.

"So what are we waiting for, then?" Alexandros asks them.

Silence.

Another moment of silence.

"Nothing," Philotas answers.

"Good," Alexander nods, and then goes to the stones to begin training.

The rest follow after him, and we all begin our normal exercises.

I decide that I'll wrestle to start, and I go against Kassandros in my first match, and I win. Then I face Perdiccas, and then Philotas after that, who are the two that are usually best at wrestling, out of all the Companions, besides myself. They give a little bit extra today, to try to beat me, to try to beat this foreign interloper that has come to their home and upended their lives and changed everything by taking their place with Alexandros. I know that these reasons and more are why they try harder than they normally do and would, but it doesn't matter, and I still win; I still beat every single one of them, waiting and finding my opening as they attack, attack, attack, and then throwing them through the air when I find that opening and pinning them against the sand where they land. On the other side of the gymnasium, away from where we grapple, Alexandros practices with his broad-sword against Leonnatos. He's pretended like he hasn't been watching us, as he practices, but when I see him smile—his small, secret smile that only he smiles—I know he has.

And also, I of course know why.

When we're done with our training, we go back to the palace, just the two of us. This is normally the time when we'd go riding, but today we don't. He tells me that he's going to read, instead, and when we get to our room, he walks to his bed and takes a collection of papyrus from underneath his pillow—the same book I saw him reading before, in the garden, near the gymnasium, the first day we met, that I still don't know what it is—and he tells me he'll be back later, and then he leaves.

I'm alone.

I'm alone in our room.

I look around for a moment, unsure of what to do, or what I *should* do, and so I decide to leave, too, and that I'll go see more of the palace, and what happens in it when people are awake and during a normal day. I walk down the mosaic-tiled hallway again, and then instead of going outside and towards the cloisters and the garden, I take a new corner and walk down another hallway. There's more mosaic here, on the floor, and on the walls as decoration, a great scene of gods and men and mountains and sea. We have nothing like this in Salona, or Illyria, and I marvel at it. And this is only Pella, too, only Macedon. What are their hallways like in Athens? In Thebes? In Corinth, or in Sparta? What do their mosaics look like, their palaces, their sculptures and their great temples? And who are their temples built for? Are they built for and dedicated to gods that will speak to me, and the ones that perhaps watch over me, whichever ones those might be?

I smile, small and to myself.

And I smile because while I don't yet know, I suppose, one day, I might find out.

I keep walking and the hallway I'm in then opens into a different area of cloisters, and there's another garden that's there, one I haven't yet seen that's smaller, and then I hear something: it's the soft, beautiful, melodic sound of an instrument being played, and not just being played, but being *expertly* played. I look between the olive trees planted in the garden and I see the two women that are there.

A lyre.

The instrument that's between them.

That's what it's called.

I recognize the prominent and familiar features of Cleopatra, Alexandros' sister, and the older woman she's with must be her instructor, I realize. I slowly walk towards them and when Cleopatra looks up from the strings, and sees me, she looks at me for a moment, sort of strangely, and with a look I can't read, and then motions for her teacher to leave and the other woman stands and does as she's been told. The instructor walks past me, and as she goes, I nod, and smile to her, as kindly as

I can, and then Cleopatra and I are alone amongst the olive trees and the not-yet-ripe fruit that hangs above and creates the fractured and uneven patterns of light and darkness that dive and twist and spread between us.

I stand there.

She studies me, and I study her, too.

She has Alexandros' eyes, I realize, the shape of them, but the color? No.

They're grey, I see, which means her eyes are the piece of them they received from their father. She doesn't have the blue, too, like Alexandros does, from their mother, and she smells of mint and thyme, the perfume she must be wearing and also the scents that signify the virtues I'll learn are the ones that define her. "You must be the boy from Salona," she finally says.

I look back at her.

"Yes," I finally say. "Hephaestion."

"My brother's told me a great deal about you, Hephaestion," she says, still looking at me, up and down. "And now here you are, living with him in the palace, living with him here in his room that's been his room since he was just a little boy."

"Yes, I am."

"Do you love him?"

I open my mouth, but then I pause.

No one's asked me that before, and in such blunt terms, and it catches me off guard. I think about the question, and what I should say to her in response, but I don't need to think about it for very long, though; she's used one of the three different Greek words for love—$ἀγάπη$—which is the strongest type of love, the longest, the most true and noble and very highest and most pure form. It's not lust, or physical. This type of love is soul-love, which makes it very easy for me to answer.

"Yes," I tell her. "I do love him."

"Good," she says, and then finally warms, slightly, and she smiles. "I also love my brother, which I suppose means that I'll love you, too."

I hear her words, and I'm glad of them.

I feel the relief, and I smile, also. "I hope so," I tell her.

Then she stands and walks closer to me, and I smell the mint and thyme even more now, as she takes my cheeks in her hands. She holds them for a moment, looking into my eyes, then she leans forward and kisses me, once on each of my freshly-shaven cheeks. She stands and looks at me again, after she does this, still looking into my eyes, studying them, searching for soul and for truth, I suspect.

Does she find it?

"You are beautiful, too, aren't you?" she finally says.

I keep looking back at her.

"I don't think of myself in that way," I say, even though it's something I've been told before, especially as I've grown and become older.

"So what do you think of yourself as?"

"I don't know."

"A warrior?"

"Yes."

"The barracks and gymnasium are for warriors, but the palace isn't, is it? So be careful who you trust here, Hephaestion of Salona, now that you live here and amongst those of us who must make our way in this world with something other than strength and steel. Perhaps even something stronger, too, and more deadly."

"A warning?"

"Yes."

"Of whom?" I frown. "Who should I be wary of?"

She stands there, for one more moment, looking back at me, into my eyes, into my soul.

She smiles again, as she leans forward.

"Everyone," she whispers.

Then she picks up her lyre, and begins to walk away.

I watch as she leaves, out of the garden, through the cloisters and back towards the palace, but I stay for another moment, looking around, then up and at the ancient and gnarled branches of the olive trees that are above me.

What have they seen?

What conversations have they heard, over time and years and generations, and what other Argeads have stood and spoken here under their crooked limbs?

What will now come next?

I start to walk again.

I leave the garden and see more of the palace, all the rest of it that there is to see, and when I pass servants in the hallway they nod and bow their heads to me. Do they do this to everyone? No, I realize, because they didn't before, when I first came; they didn't when I was just and only a foreign boy from across the mountains to the north and west who wished to be a ward of the basileus.

But now, I'm more than that.

Or at least, I am to them, because I am to Alexandros.

I keep walking.

I've allowed my thoughts to collect and gather and I think for a moment I might be lost because I haven't been watching where I've been going with my head in both future and past, but then I see a statue I recognize where two hallways meet, and I turn the other way, the way I know leads back to Alexandros' room.

No, I catch myself. *Our* room.

I walk down the hallway I recognize, the one that passes the door to Philippos' office, and there's a different guard that stands there now. I look at him curiously. I've never seen him before, and he's never seen me, and he seems to be even younger than Pausanius, and then the door opens and Philippos comes out. He's with three other men and I recognize them as Parmenion, his clean-shaven strategos, as well as Antipater, another childhood friend, and Attalus, a nobleman from an ancient family that controls all of Lower Macedon, the provinces that are south and east of the capital and near the sea. I try to move so they don't see me, but there's nowhere to hide, and it's too late, and they do.

Philippos calls for me to come to them, and I walk over. He looks at me, up and down, taking me in.

"What are you doing here in the palace?" he finally asks.

I search his words and tone for anything I might find in them, but his words are neutral, without anger or accusation, or anything else, or at least nothing that I can sense, and so is his tone.

I feel blood coming to my cheeks, though, with the four men and the boy watching me.

I don't want it to, but it does.

"Alexandros didn't tell you?" I finally manage, with all five staring at me.

"Tell me what?"

"That he had my things brought up."

"Here?"

"Yes."

"Where?"

I pause. "His room," I finally say, and then swallow.

Philippos pauses at that, too, as he looks back at me through his one still-good eye, a fierce and blazing dot above his thick and jet-black beard and his harsh and strong warrior features. "You've certainly managed to ingratiate yourself rather quickly, haven't you, Hephaestion of Salona?" he says, and I don't know how to respond. "You're even beginning to look like him," he continues, "though of course you're much better looking."

That's not what I've done, and that's not who I am.

I've just been me, while I've been here, as best I know how.

But can I say that? Can I say that to the basileus, and to Alexandros' father?

Philippos still stares at me, still takes me in, looking up and down, critically, every inch of my body. "My son has gotten bigger, since you arrived," he finally says, his still-good eye meeting mine now, "and Parmenion's told me he saw him disarm Ptolemaios twice in a row." Philippos pauses in his speech, and I'm left with wonder at what words will be next. "Keep pushing him," he says. "Keep pushing him, as you've pushed yourself, and maybe he won't die in the first battle he sees after all."

Pausanius and Antipater don't react, but I watch Attalus smirk at this comment. Then the basileus turns, and he keeps walking, and his friends continue with him.

I watch as they go.

When they're gone, I turn and go back to our room.

After I get there and walk in, I see that Alexandros has already returned, and is waiting. We don't speak, as I enter and see him, we don't say anything to each other at all. I go to my trunk and change my chiton for something fresh and more simple, just a cloth that I tie around my waist and between my legs, and then we sit and eat some of the food that's been brought and left for us, crusted bread that was baked in an open fire with honey and smashed dates spread across it. We chew, together, and then I turn to look at him, and he sees my eyes. "What is it?" he asks, raising an eyebrow as he eats.

"Why didn't you tell your father?"

"Tell him what?"

"That you had me move into the palace, and into your room."

He doesn't answer at first, he just keeps chewing, and then after a moment he stands and walks to his bed. He takes the worn papyrus book from underneath his pillow, and I look at it, held so gently in his hands; the pages frayed, stained, bent and worn from so much use and reading. I finally see the title. I almost laugh. Of course. And then I watch as he opens the pages to the most worn part, the part that's very clearly been the most-read, and I'm surprised at what part of the story it is, at first, and what he reads to me. And then, after I'm surprised, I'm not.

But one more thing.
A last request; grant it, please,
Never bury my bones apart from yours, Achilleus;
Let them always, lie together, always,
Just as we grew up together, in your great house.

CHAPTER SEVEN

The next time we go to the gymnasium for training, when we get there, the Companions are already awake and ready, as they usually are, but this time we see something else, too: we see that they're all clean-shaven, in the same way that Alexandros and I now both are. We notice this as we enter and Alexandros doesn't say anything; he just smiles, and then we begin our exercises. More weeks pass and our routine at the palace stays the same, and then once again, not long after I move into Alexandros' room with him, our whole world changes. And when it changes this time, it does so in a most unexpected and unusual way. I'm in our room when Alexandros returns from a long meeting in his father's office, which is something that doesn't happen very often, and when he comes back and walks past the door, he tells me that Philippos has arranged for a tutor for him. "A tutor?" I ask, looking as he goes past me and to the basin to splash water on his cheeks and wash his face.

"Yes," he says.

"I don't understand," I frown, looking at his back as he washes, wondering what this will now mean. "I thought you were beyond tutors."

"I thought so, too."

"So who is this, then, that your father would have you learn from?"

"His name is Aristoteles."

"I've never heard of him," I say, not recognizing the name; I'm a warrior, and I only know warriors.

"I hadn't heard of him either," Alexandros says, "but apparently he was Plato's most famous student, at his Akademia in Athens, until he had a falling out with his teacher. My father knows him somehow from when they were young."

"Your father is friends with a *philosopher*?" I ask, and I'm even more confused now, thinking of Philippos and what he told me about the change in Alexandros' body and the change that Parmenion had noticed in his fighting skill, too, which are the things that Philippos values. "Since when has your father cared for philosophy or tutors or anything even remotely close to that?"

"Since the orator Demosthenes in Athens repeatedly calls him a barbarian at their ekklesia."

"The one that sent the toy horse?"

"Yes, the same. And Philippos apparently wishes to demonstrate to him and all the rest of them that he's *not* what he actually is, which is why he's chosen to hire this philosopher to come here from Athens and tutor his son."

"Tutor his son? Not the basileus himself?"

"Can you see him with a philosopher?" Alexandros asks, and then we both laugh at the thought. "It won't be him, so he'll show the southerners his intent by making me do it, his son, the next best thing, as I suppose they don't know how little regard he actually has for that same son. In Athens, even though I was born second, they probably still think I'm part of his pride and joy, a happy and loving family."

"So when does this Aristoteles arrive?'"

"He already has. He's gone to Mieza, west of here, and begun to set up a new Akademia there. It's nearly finished, and so we're to leave tomorrow."

"*We?*"

I'm surprised. I thought I was going to have to fight to go with him.

"Yes, all of us," he nods. "Me, you, Ptolemaios, Philotas, Kassandros, Perdiccas, Nearchos, Leonnatos. I told my father that if Amyntas were invited, I wouldn't go. It was supposed to be just me, but I told Philippos the only condition under which I went willingly was if everyone else went with me, too."

I take that in, what he's just told me.

It's smart.

It keeps us together, his friends and Companions, all the others that are the sons of important Macedonian families and allies that Alexandros will eventually need if he wants to sit on the throne in Pella. They're second and third and fourth sons, of course, but they're still sons. I nod and start to move towards the chest where I keep my clothes and what little possessions I have, to pack, and as I do, I glance at him, out of the corner of my eye, and I see him hesitate.

"What is it?" I ask him.

"There's one more thing."

His voice is smaller now, I realize.

"What's that?" I ask.

"My mother wants to see you before we go."

"*Me?*"

"Yes."

"Why?"

I look back at him, and he doesn't answer, which is of course his answer. I haven't spoken to Olympias, I've only just seen her, from a distance, and she terrifies me. She seems to terrify Alexandros, also, the only thing in all of Pella, in all of Macedon, in all the world that seems to even remotely have that affect on him. I've heard him speak warmly of her at times, especially when he speaks of moments when he was young, and she was still favored amongst the royal wives, but she's not now, and there's no way to escape this, I know. She's Alexandros' mother, and I live with her son, in the palace, and in his room, so I'll go to see her. I'll go to see her, for him, as he's asked.

I MEET HER AT AN ANCIENT SHRINE south of the city. It's where she asked to meet, and as I walk and then come to the place she described in the letter she sent to our room, I find it tucked between the soft hills, where they just begin to thin and the land starts to become more flat before it gets to the sea. There are groves of olive trees that are here, scattered throughout the uneven countryside, before the marshy and shallow lake I see in the distance, and standing in the largest of the groves are worn and carved statues of gods and goddesses formed into a semi-circle under the shadow of the ancient branches. The air is more damp here, too, and tastes saltier, with the Aegean not very far, and the weather has taken its toll on the stone, I can see, as I get closer; it's taken its toll on the rock that the statues are carved from, wearing it smooth, and changing the color. I see these statues, as I get even closer, and then I see her, amongst them.

Her back is to me when I arrive.

She walks through this outdoor shrine, between the carved gods, and I watch for a moment before I go any closer as she stops at the bust of one here, and another there, gently touching them. I take a deep breath. I wonder what it is she says to them, and to which god it is that she prays. But when I get closer, I see that all the statues are statues of the same god, and then I don't wonder anymore.

Of course.

Dionysus.

"Do you speak to him?" she says, without turning around.

I look behind me.

There's no one else that's there with us, and so I realize she's not praying, or speaking to the statues at all; she's speaking to me. "I try to," I answer.

"You try to, or you do?"

"I try to."

"When?"

"As often as I can, I suppose. As often as I feel I should."

"Come closer."

I look around again.

There's no one else here but me, so I do as she says and walk further into the grove and towards her so I stand amongst the statues, too, instead of outside of them, the branches now above us, above both of us. She still looks at them, at the carved busts and figures of these gods that are our gods, and her back is to me so I can't tell what's in her eyes, whether it's pleasure or contentment, whether it's approval or disapproval, whether it's joy, or pain, or something else entirely.

Then she finally turns, and she looks at me.

Blue.

Her eyes are so blue, so strikingly and piercingly blue, just like the blue of the water in the place where the seas mix near where I was born and near where she was born, too, I know, in the western mountains of Epirus.

"You've been to a feast now," she speaks slowly.

"I have."

"So you've seen for yourself."

"Seen what?" I ask, knowing I need to be careful.

"How Philippos and his friends make a mockery of him," she practically spits, and then turns back to the statues and reaches out and touches one, and then moves and touches another. "You've seen how they all make a mockery of him. Philippos, Antipater, Parmenion, Attalus. All of them except my son. They all think he's the most important god, too, even though they make a mockery of him. Is he the most important god to you?"

"I don't know."

"Yes, you do. He's the god of longing, desire, passion, ecstasy, and he's also the god of love, too, isn't he? And you know these things, don't you, Hephaestion?"

I see her closely, for the first time.

Disgust.

It's what's there in her eyes, and in her heart.

Not for me, though. Of that I'm fairly sure.

I look closer and study her features and see her red hair that's not unlike Alexandros' sometimes-red hair; I see her angular features, also, her thin and high and defined cheek-bones, set like twin pillars guarding her handsome and strong and mountain-born face, the type that I recognize, the type that I'm used to, the type that I know. She doesn't remind me of home, though, I realize, because my own mother reminds me of that, and this woman is nothing like my mother. I search for Alexandros there, in the features that I see. I search for him beyond hair color and the one blue eye he's inherited from her and from the mountains. I search and search and search, but I'm surprised when I don't find him; I'm surprised when I don't find any of him, at all, because I thought I would.

"Well?" she finally asks, as I continue to study her. "Do you have nothing to say?"

"You risk the displeasure of Aphrodite with your words," I finally answer.

"Why would my words displeasure Aphrodite?"

"Because she's the goddess of love. Not Dionysus."

"Yes, she is *a* goddess of love, no doubt," Olympias speaks softly, and then smiles, a half-smile, the left side of her mouth turning up. Ah, there he is; there's Alexandros, after all, or at least a small part of him. How small? I don't know. "But she's the goddess of a *different* type of love than the love of which I speak, isn't she?"

"I don't know."

"You say that often."

"I say it if it's truth."

"I think it isn't. I think you *do* know."

I'm silent.

She looks back at me.

She studies *my* face now, looking at my features, taking them in, trying to read my intentions, my emotions, my desires.

"You love my son," she says, and it's not a question.

I open my mouth, but then I stop, because of what I was going to say.

She smiles.

"It's alright," she says. "I already know that you do."

"How?"

"You told my daughter. And does he love you in return?"

"I don't know."

"You don't know *again*?"

"I think so."

"You *think* so?"

"Yes."

"That's it?"

"Yes, that's it. And it's enough."

I look back at her; I've been wondering since I've arrived if she will be friend or enemy, and now I have my answer, beyond any shadow or hesitation or doubt. Some are dismayed when they make a new enemy, but I'm a warrior, and so I'm only dismayed when I don't know who my enemies are. "Do you love him in the way you should, or do you love him, just like all the others, because of who he is, and what he can do for you?"

"What do you mean?" I'm emotionless now, as I speak, as I've trained myself to be in the presence of enemies. "What is it that you think he can do for me?"

"He's the son of the basileus."

"Being the son of the basileus means nothing here, as you know."

"Is that what you think?"

"Amyntas was the son of the basileus once, too, wasn't he? And now what is he? Nothing. I'm the son of a basileus, also, and yet here I am. So I'll ask you again . . . what do you mean?"

"Good."

"Good what?"

"I was hoping you were clever," she says, and then moves closer.

She reaches out.

She slips the corner of my chiton off one shoulder so that it falls and my chest is bare. Then she reaches towards me and touches my chest.

Her touch is cool against my skin that's warm and always hot. It's my blood, my warrior's blood, the blood of the north. She rubs her hand across my now-tanned and muscled shoulders, and then down, stopping just above my heart, her eyes never leaving my own eyes, even as her hands move. I look back at her, wondering what her goal and purpose is. This is his mother, I think to myself. I think of that once, and then tell myself again. *This is his mother.*

"Stop," I finally say, as I brush her hand away.

"Why?"

"You're another man's wife, and you're my best friend's mother."

"You sleep together, and you say that he's just your *best friend*?"

"You know what I mean. We are what we are."

"I don't know why he loves you, Hephaestion of Salona, but he does, and he listens to you, unlike any of his other Companions that he grew with, who he doesn't listen to at all. Maybe it's the barbarian blood that he has, and that you have, too, the blood of Achilleus that I've given him. Do you know that story?"

"Yes," I nod. "I know it."

"Make sure he remembers it, and make sure that you remember it, too. Make sure he remembers his ancestor, Achilleus, and what his destiny was, and where it took him."

"And where was that?"

"*East.*"

I look back at her.

I look at her eyes, the way that they change when she says that word, the way that the fire comes again and even stronger as her eyes flick to the horizon.

I now know where he gets that from, also.

"It's not even certain he'll be basileus."

"He will be basileus," she says. "I will make certain of it, and then when he is, it will be your job to make sure he doesn't follow the path set by his father, a man who dreams too small and too narrow. But that's because his father is Philippos, and Alexandros is Alexandros. So make sure that he never forgets that, what I've told you here today. Make sure that he never forgets who he is and what he's meant to be, even at his darkest moments and at his times of greatest weakness and doubt, because for men that are of the type that my son will be, the ones that are touched by the gods and carry the gods within them, there will be a great deal of light, of course there will be, but there will also most certainly be a very great deal of darkness, too. That's how it always is inside such men, because there are both gods of light and darkness, and they each have their purpose, and so that's what will always be there. Make sure that he remembers the horizon, Hephaestion, and his destiny that lies at the end of it. Make sure he remembers the end of the world, and not just the end of this peninsula. If you do all of this, as I ask, then I will support you and be your friend. If you don't, then I will be your enemy. Do you understand?"

She looks into my eyes again, searching them.

"I understand," I nod.

"Good. Now tell me, what is it like when you sleep with him?"

I stand there and I look back at her.

I don't know what else to say, and so I don't, I just shake my head and then I turn and I leave. I can feel her watching me, as I go, as I walk away, away from the gods and the ancient shrine, into the distance, back towards the city and the palace, and I can feel her smiling, too, and maybe even laughing. I can feel it, even though I don't turn around to look, I simply concentrate on putting one foot in front of the other, counting every step I take and then once I'm gone, and out of her presence, I let my thoughts wander. I let them wander, and drift, and wonder, as I get closer back to the city, and think more and more about this very strange and foreign and dangerous place I've come to.

WHEN I FINALLY GET BACK to our room, the sun is going down, and Alexandros is on his bed and waiting for me. He reads from his worn papyrus copy of the Iliad, and he looks up when I come in. When he sees me and the look that's on my face, he sets the book aside, and studies my eyes. I look back at him and I'm surprised to see he's wearing his nicest chiton, one that's been freshly bleached and cleaned.

"How was it?" he finally asks, his eyes still searching mine.

"It's over."

"What did she ask?"

I stand there and look back at him. I don't want to lie to him, and it's his mother, after all, so I have to say something, but what do I say? "Not too much," I finally manage and settle on.

"That doesn't sound like my mother."

"She wanted to know why I live here with you."

"That's more like it," he smiles. "And what else?"

"Her plans for you, and the future. Where are you going?"

"What?"

It's my turn to nod this time, towards his chiton and the way he's dressed. He looks down and sees it, and when he does, it's almost as if he's forgotten, and is embarrassed. "Oh," he says. "I'm going to Aria's house tonight, in the city. It's the last time I'll be able to see her before we go, and I don't know how long we'll be gone, so I told her I'd come."

"Oh."

He hasn't been to Aria's since I moved to the palace.

"I wanted to see you before I went, though," he says.

"Why?"

"To make sure you were alright."

I look back at him.

I hear his words, I hear all of them, and I feel myself nod, but it's Olympias I still think of. If she wanted to kill me, she could, I know: a hired knife, a paid arrow in the darkness, the smallest drop of poison from one of the snakes they say she worships and keeps in her bedchamber. I know she resents me because of my place next to her son—the most precious thing in the world to her—but would she dare? Would she dare risk his displeasure, and would she dare risk his wrath? His eyes still search mine. I know what it is that they search for, but he won't find it, because it's not there. "Enjoy yourself," I tell him instead. "I'll see you tomorrow."

He waits for a moment, then he nods, and walks to the door.

When he gets there, though, he doesn't open the door right away, but instead looks over his shoulder, one more time, back at me, sitting on my bed. Nothing's changed. Surely he knows that, and surely he can see that, and feel it, too, because I will be here, and I will wait for him. I will always wait for him. If he didn't know it before, then I'm sure he does now, because I feel it, and so I know that he must feel it, then, too. He waits for another moment. Why? Then his lips begin to turn and there's his half-smile again, the one that I know now is also his mother's half-smile, and he nods, once more, before he finally pushes the door open and walks out into the night.

CHAPTER EIGHT

I RISE EARLY THE NEXT MORNING, and after I shave and dress, I leave the room that we share. Alexandros hasn't returned yet and so I go out and down the hallway and towards the courtyard on my own. When I get there, I see that Alexandros is already waiting, in the courtyard, with the rest of the Companions, and the whole royal family is gathered, too, to see us off. He must have come straight from the city, and from her bed, I realize. Our horses are brought from the stables and I walk towards the others, and join them, and I climb up and onto the brown next to where the Companions all sit their horses, too. Alexandros doesn't go to Bucephalus, though. First, he goes forward and closer to his family. He hugs his sister Cleopatra, when he reaches them, and when he does, and holds her, she holds onto him for too long, and from where I sit on the brown, I can see the tears that are there on her cheek. I wonder if she holds him simply because she loves her brother, or if she's imagining that he's another, and if the tears she sheds aren't for him, but for Ptolemaios. I don't know. I watch as she moves away from Alexandros, and as she does, I entertain the possibility that her tears might be for both, and I do not envy her or her place, in any regard; not her place in the palace, or her place in her family, or her place in this world in which we all live.

But what else is there?

Alexandros goes to his mother next.

He hugs Olympias, and she whispers something into his ear, also, but I'm too far away to hear what she says, and it's too soft for any of the others to hear what she says, either. They wonder about her words, though, the ones that are just for him, her son; I know that they wonder, the same as I do, and worry about this woman who brings fear to all of us and I study Alexandros' face. I try to read his eyes. I know his body, his limbs, his movements, and I can see them stiffen when she touches him. I might not know what she's said, but I know what it's done to him and what it's made him feel because I can see and feel it, too. Will her words echo in Alexandros' dreams, the way they echo in mine? I don't know, but they must. She is his mother, so they must.

He moves away from Olympias and goes to his father.

He stands in front of Philippos.

They're the same height now though the father is still bigger, thicker, heavier, even with all the muscle that Alexandros has gained in the last months. "In Athens they call me *Philippos-barbaros*," he says, and speaks loudly so that all who are gathered can hear, and not just his son. "Make sure that you learn all that Aristoteles has to teach you so that Demosthenes and the other *orators* and *politicians* can eat their words before we all go south and rip their cursed and forked tongues from their mouths."

Alexandros bows his head.

"Yes, Father," he says.

"What?"

"I will," he speaks louder, as Philippos has asked.

"You will what?"

A pause. A muscle flickers in his cheek. "I will do as you say."

"Good," Philippos nods.

I still study Alexandros' movements as he goes through this, his body, his limbs, his eyes. He glances at the large Arrhidaeus, who's behind Philippos, and then Amyntas, who's across the courtyard and away from us. Neither are Alexandros, but they will both be left behind, in Pella, at Alexandros' request.

Is that wise?

Is it prudent to leave the two most likely heirs to the throne in the capital and with the army while Alexandros leaves and goes somewhere else for an indeterminate amount of time? Arrhidaeus is first-born, but he's simple, and so not a real threat. But the other? His cousin? The oldest son of an Argead basileus?

Alexandros' gaze lingers on Amyntas.

I know he's thinking the same thing as I'm thinking, but there's nothing to be done about it, so after one more look, Alexandros turns and comes towards where the servant holds Bucephalus for him. They're near to where I sit on the brown, now, next to the others, and Alexandros jumps up and onto Bucephalus' back. I look over at him, next to me now, too, next to us. Alexandros is shorter than I am, by nearly a full head, but when he's on Bucephalus he sits taller than I do by the same amount; when he's astride his great horse, he sits taller than all of us, I realize, for the very first time.

I smile.

It's as it should be. And perhaps, even, it's all as it should be.

Reins are tugged and young and well-muscled thighs squeeze against equine ribs, and with the familiar click of hooves on ancient cobblestone, we begin to ride. We leave the courtyard and then once we're out and into the city, and away from the palace, we start to ride quicker, together, past all the vendors and people going about their day and their business and some of them wave as we ride past, and we wave in return. Do they know why we leave, and what we go to do? I don't know. We get to the edge of the city, and then instead of stopping, we go even further, past all that we know, and we begin to head west. We ride across the great expanse of grass and then soon get to a full gallop on our horses, going even faster, heading into the distance and towards where the landscape begins to change and there are less rolling hills and more sharp, craggy outcroppings. I look next to me and see Alexandros smile and his smile widens the further and further we get from his family and from Pella. He holds Bucephalus' mane and then leans down on the horse's neck and whispers into his ear and I'm surprised when Bucephalus seems to listen, and go even faster, and we follow after them, or at least we try to. We follow after Alexandros and Bucephalus and we leave behind the hills that we know and the ones that we've explored, and we leave them behind in search of something else, and something new. Hooves pound upon grass in a torrent of muffled sound and dirt. We ride quickly, all of us experts on a horse, and none of us look back, not a single one of us; we've trained our whole lives not to.

A QUARTER OF A DAY'S RIDE from Pella, we slow our horses and let them drink from a shallow river that cuts across the road we follow. We walk them down to a place near the base of a stone bridge that spans the river, and we wait as they drink and cool their hooves in the water. The sun is beginning to rise now, higher, and there are beads of sweat on our brows and underneath our chitons, so I know the horses must be hot, too, and after they finish drinking, we cross the river, over the small bridge, and as we do, I look around and see that the countryside is even more rocky here, the further west of Pella we get; the ground is more dry and arid, a place that hasn't had enough rain, and there's less grass, too. It's beautiful, in the way that all the land where we live is beautiful, but it has a beauty that's different than Pella's. It's more rugged and harsh here, and strong-featured, which perhaps makes it more like the mountains and land where I'm from.

There are bits of conversation around me.

Ahead of where I ride with Alexandros, I can hear Perdiccas and Philotas arguing over how far we have left to go until we reach Mieza, while Kassandros and Ptolemaios discuss what lessons they think we'll learn, and how lenient or strict our new tutor might be.

"What are you thinking?"

These words don't come from Perdiccas or Philotas or Kassandros or Ptolemaios, though; these words come from next to me, and from Alexandros. I don't answer him, at least not at first. Then I turn to look at him, and at his eyes. "Nothing," I finally say, and shake my head, not wanting to talk about my home, and my family, and what I feel when I think of them.

"That's not true," he smiles.

"How do you know?"

"Because I know."

"And what is it exactly that you know?"

"That you're always thinking of something, and that I want to know what it is."

We keep riding.

Our bodies move up and down, with the bouncing rhythm of the young and strong horses beneath us.

"There are no secrets between us, Hephaestion," he says.

"What fun is that?"

"Tell me."

"What is it like, when you sleep with her?" I finally ask, very quickly. I say it calmly, and softly, and I think I'll take him off guard, or perhaps maybe make him upset or suspicious, but when I risk a small glance at him next to me, I see that he's not any of those things. Instead, he smiles even wider. His eyes don't leave mine, and he continues to smile, all the way to his eyes. "What's it like with Aria?" he asks, his eyebrows raised now. "That's what you want to know?"

"Yes."

"I thought you said you'd done it before?"

"I have. I asked what it was like for you."

"It's not why I go to her house, or why I see her."

"I didn't ask that either."

We keep riding and Alexandros seems to retreat inside himself again, just a little bit, the way he does before something important comes, and as I watch him, he seems to wrestle with something deep inside. I've known him for many months, at this point, and we've shared a room—shared the sun and the moon and the stars, shared everything that we could possibly share and have become as close as we could possibly become—but there's still more; there's always still more to him, I've learned, still more depths, more layers and secrets to be unpeeled and uncovered and discovered. "It feels like something mortals do," he finally says.

I look back at him.

I don't understand.

He still looks ahead, at the sun that reaches its peak and shines down on the distant place in front of us that we now travel to, together. We continue to ride, and what I realize is that of everyone I know, everyone I've ever met, I somehow seem to know Alexandros both most and least, all at the same time. It's confusing. I shake my head. "And so what are we?" I finally ask, frowning.

"What do you mean?"

"What are we, if not mortals?"

"It's not what we are, Hephaestion, I don't care about what we are. It's what we *strive to be* that's important. That's what matters in this world. In fact, it's *all* that matters in this world, because that's where the gods live, isn't it? And that's the reason they are gods, too, don't you think?"

I make note of the words he chooses to emphasize, and how he says them, how he feels them. We've touched on something, I realize, and it's something that he believes with all his heart and all his soul and blessed companion that I am, I also realize that I believe it, too, and I believe all of it in the exact same way that he does. And that's his gift, I realize. He still sits high on Bucephalus' back, next to me; he sits high on his great black stallion, higher than all of us that are around him and that ride with him, despite the way that we were all born. Because sometimes we can defy that, can't we? Because sometimes how we're born isn't what defines us, and that's what he's known and the truth he's given to me and to all of us who follow him. It's what we do in the world that matters, and also what we *strive* to do. That's who we are, and who we'll be. The light from above shines down and it lands on his now-golden hair, dancing in beautiful and ancient geometric patterns and reflecting in his twice-colored eyes.

We're fortunate, his Companions.

I smiled, once before, in the courtyard, at Pella, and I smile again now, realizing who it is that I ride next to, and who it is that the mountains and the stars and the gods have brought me to.

WE SOON COME TO MIEZA, which it turns out is only a full-day's ride from Pella, and we arrive just as the sun's going down and it begins to become cooler. We approach the place on our horses, and then we're to it, and that's also when we meet Aristoteles for the first time. He comes from the building that's being constructed in an L-shape around a nearby fresh-water spring and next to a grove of gnarled and ancient olives that grow underneath an outcropping of jagged rock above. The landscape doesn't look like this in Pella, or in Illyria, either; Mieza has a unique look all to its own, I realize, as I glance around, taking it in for the first time. And as I do, the rest of the Companions do, also, and that's when Aristoteles comes forward from the building and we all look at him, this famous man. He stands in front of us, and our horses, as we approach, and then we dismount. Alexandros goes in front of us once he's off Bucephalus and stands across from the philosopher. Then another comes from the building behind him, to stand next to Aristoteles, too; one who looks younger, near the same age as we are.

"You must be Aristoteles," Alexandros finally says, when he reaches them, both of them.

"Yes," the philosopher nods. "I am."

"I'm Alexandros."

"Greetings, Alexandros," Aristoteles tells him, as I look on and watch from my place behind him, from my place at his shoulder. Aristoteles is short, I see, shorter than Alexandros even, I calculate, and he's skinny. His eyes are small and dark, too, unlike so many of the other Greeks from the south whose eyes are wide and blue, and his hair is thinning on the top and in the back, though it's still thick around the sides and hasn't yet begun to lose any of its color. He has a beard, too, unlike us, but it's trimmed neat and close to his cheeks and not left to grow wild or long. Aristoteles' eyes rest on Alexandros for a moment, and then they move behind him, to his waiting and freshly-shaved Companions, and Alexandros introduces each of us by name.

Ptolemaios.

Kassandros.

Philotas.

Perdiccas.

Nearchos.

Leonnatos, and—

Hephaestion.

He introduces me last, and I watch Aristoteles' eyes as they flick between each of us, as he takes in our faces, then our names, committing them to memory, and I can tell that being told once will be enough and that he won't forget them. This is a mind that's in front of us: he'll be told something once, we'll all soon realize, and then it'll be forever. "Let me show you inside," he finally says, and then walks towards the building he's been constructing as his new Akademia, and we follow after him. We all go inside together, and when we do, we see the near-finished rooms and the small and rustic bed-chambers that are being constructed and where we'll sleep. Each of us has their own bed-chamber that's been readied and prepared and assigned; each of us, except for me and Alexandros. A servant goes with the other Companions to show them which room will belong to each of them, and where to put their things, while Aristoteles leads me and Alexandros to a room at the end of the hallway that's set up exactly like the one where we lived in the palace at Pella. I look inside. It's the same size as all the other rooms, I see, which will be alright, even with two of us sharing it, we'll just be physically closer than we were in Pella. I turn to look at Aristoteles, to try to read what he might be thinking, and also wondering what he's heard—what he knows, or what he thinks he might know—but his eyes give nothing away, and instead he tells us that everything being built at the Akademia will be finished in seven days, and in the meantime, we're free to do as we wish, until the building is finished.

We nod. So we will.

We each settle into our rooms, me and Alexandros in one, and the others each where they've been assigned, and while the building is still being worked on, we fall into a routine similar to the one we had in Pella. We wake early in the morning, before the sun, and we continue our strength and weapons training together. We each have the heavy broad-swords that we practice with and that we've brought with us, and we find new boulders in the hills outside the Akademia to carry and throw. We wrestle and box with our fists, on the grass that's shorter in Mieza, and more wiry and firm, too, rather than the sand of the gymnasium, and we run sprints across the few open fields that we can find, which tire us more quickly on the rocky and uneven ground. It's cooler here, too, and there's more shade, which is different than the constant heat and sun of Pella and eastern Macedon. Aristoteles watches all this as we train, from a distance, his small eyes missing nothing, and with a week free to do whatever we please, after we're done training, we decide we should explore more of this new place that we've come to, out in the countryside, and away from the Akademia. When this discussion happens, though, I see Aristoteles begin to walk towards us and then when he reaches us, he says that he, too, will come with us to the countryside to explore as he, too, is also new here. He didn't hear the conversation we had, he couldn't possibly have heard from the distance where he stood, but he already knew what it was, and what it was about.

We all nod.

He's our teacher, and so we can't do anything else but nod.

He leaves behind the young man who was with him when we first arrived, who we also meet and learn is called Callisthenes, and is Aristoteles' nephew, and he leaves Callisthenes to oversee the completion of the Akademia and the final stages of building, which is strange to me because Callisthenes seems to be the same age as we are. He's an apprentice here in Mieza, too, though he's an apprentice in a different way: he serves his uncle and studies medicine and philosophy and history, which are different than the things that we've studied.

We all leave Mieza, together.

Callisthenes watches us go, then he turns back to the Akademia.

Why did we come here, before it was finished? Why weren't we told to arrive later?

I shake my head. I don't know.

So, instead, we ride towards a tall peak in the distance.

Aristoteles is terrible on a horse and looks uneasy and uncomfortable as he rides, which makes us all smile—all of us who are as comfortable on the back of a horse as we are on our own feet—but he tries his best, and from the place next to us, where he sits unevenly on his small horse, he points towards the peak that's there in front of us and tells us that he's discovered from the locals it's called Vermio, and it's what marks the boundary of Macedon from Epirus, which begins on the western side of the mountains.

Epirus.

The land ruled by the descendants of Achilleus, and the land of Alexandros, too, through the blood of his mother, Olympias, descended from Neoptolemus and Mollosus.

We haven't been there, to Epirus, either of us.

Perhaps we will?

I don't know.

We keep riding.

We get closer to the mountains, and then when we do, and are into the foothills, we stop. We rest for a moment under the branches of another grove of ancient olives that we find, and that's where Aristoteles points up and shows us how the fruit that the olives grow here is larger and more green than the olives that grow on the trees around Pella.

"Why?" Leonnatos asks.

Aristoteles smiles.

Leonnatos has just discovered the philosopher's favorite word, we'll soon learn.

So Aristoteles answers, and he tells us.

He explains to us how the olives are different here because of the climate and rocky soil, unlike the dark and smooth olives that grow further east, where it's warmer and the soil is different, and less dry, because it's closer to the sea and the breeze that comes off the water and carries with it moisture and salt. We nod. We take that in. We'd never thought of the sea before, and its influence on the plants and trees and what they grow and what we eat from them. We climb back onto our horses, and continue, and we soon get hungry, as we ride, as we so often do, and so we stop again and Aristoteles shows us the type of berries that grow wild here that we can pick to eat. We've only ever thought about tracking and hunting and what we could kill, which is how we'd been raised, so berries are new. Aristoteles doesn't eat meat, though, so he shows us these alternatives. There is no judgment in his voice or tone as he tells us this; he simply gives knowledge, and then once its been given, he retreats and watches. It's his way. It's his way, and it's made him who he is.

We keep riding, again, further through the countryside.

We cross a small river that winds between the foothills of the mountains, and as soon as we do, and start to ride up the other bank, we come upon a lioness, not unlike the lion that Alexandros and I came across in the forest, only this lioness has cubs. Perdiccas has crossed the river first, in front of the rest of us, and his horse rears when it sees the lioness that hisses to protect its cubs and the horse throws Perdiccas from its back to where he lands heavily in the shallows of the river. The lioness quickly runs away, towards the mountains, with her cubs running close behind her, but when Perdiccas stands again, from the water, I see the arm he used to brace his fall hanging limp at his side. The skin on the arm is scraped and bloody, and the bone clearly broken. Normally, this means it's time to return home, but not with Aristoteles; for him, this means it's time for another lesson.

Aristoteles gets off his horse and comes forward.

He takes Perdiccas' arm and holds it still to keep any further structural damage from happening, and then shows us how to clean the wound, with water from the river that he boils over a fire that he has Ptolemaios gather wood and make with Kassandros. Then once the wound has been cleaned with the sterilized water, he shows us how to line and reset the bone and bind it in place, with two pieces of wood on either side, and strips of cloth that he tears from the bottom of his chiton to tie around it and hold it in place. It hurts, when he has to manipulate the bone so that it lines flush again, but it will be worth it, he tells us, as he shows us the final details on how to make the wooden brace. "Now it'll heal," he tells Perdiccas, and all of us. "Now the bone will grow back and hold firm again, in the same way it was before."

"In the exact same way?"

"Yes," Aristoteles nods, "and perhaps even stronger, too."

"So I'll still be able to hold my shield?" Perdiccas asks, worry in his eyes; it's his left arm that's been broken.

"Of course," Aristoteles smiles. "Though maybe not for a month or two."

"Thank you," Perdiccas tells him, gratefully.

"It's my pleasure," the philosopher responds, "and I'm sure being young warriors and young men, it's not the first broken bone amongst you, which means it won't be the last, either. So now you know what to do, and how to make it so that an injury doesn't have to be permanent or debilitating, but will instead grow back, and heal, just as strong as it was before."

"Or stronger," Perdiccas nods, determination in his eyes.

"That's right," Aristoteles looks at him, and smiles. "Or stronger."

We decide to stay there that night.

We make our camp in the foothills and next to the fire that we've already built to boil the water to clean the wound on Perdiccas' arm. It gets cold when the sun goes down here, so we all gather closer to the fire. Kassandros passes around travelling skins filled with undiluted wine, and as we drink from them, and then pass them on to the Companion next to us, Aristoteles points above and towards the sky and tells us about the constellations that are there: he tells us of some that we already know, and he tells us of many that we don't, too, and the stories about them, and what they are.

I look at the stars, for a moment.

Then my eyes turn down, and they look at Alexandros.

He listens with rapt attention as he always does when he hears stories of gods and heroes and faraway lands, and when Aristoteles finishes, I ask the philosopher about where he's from, before he came to Mieza. He looks at me first, and Alexandros next, and then the rest of the Companions, and he tells us. He tells us about Stagira, and the Halkidiki peninsulas, and the sparse and rural beauty of the place where he grew near the sea, even further north than we are now or when we're in Pella, and he tells us that he just grew there, though, and that he didn't stay.

"Why not?" Alexandros asks, frowning. "Didn't you like it?"

"I did," Aristoteles tells us, nodding. "I loved it. It's very beautiful, and it's my home, the land and people that made me, which is all at once both indefinable and irreplaceable, and also unescapable, for all of us."

"So why did you leave?" Alexandros asks.

"Because while my home was my home, the world lay elsewhere," he says, and then he's quiet, and I see Alexandros' eyes flash and shine when he hears this and recognizes another soul that's like his soul, and perhaps like mine, too, I don't know, and so then we ask him what we really want to know, which is about Athens, and the great cities of the south, and he tells us. Instead of stars and gods, he now tells us about poleis, and democracy, and the epic and nearly thirty year war that raged between Athens and Sparta, and what that war cost. He tells us about philosophy, and his teacher, Plato, and the famous Akademia there that he was once part of, but is now run by Speusippus, a lesser man than him, and he tells us this not as opinion, but as fact. Speusippus was a nephew of Plato, he explains, and blood is still blood in Athens, which is something that's foreign to us here because things aren't given in such ways in the north; in the north, things such as succession have to be earned and achieved.

Is this what Athens and the other great poleis have become?

If it is, then they will be conquered, I know. They will be conquered, and it will be soon.

Aristoteles continues and tells us about medicine, and Hippocrates, the man who found and discovered all the knowledge and techniques that he knows and has used to heal Perdiccas' arm, and he tells us about the oath that all physicians in Athens and the Hellenic world make to Hippocrates when they begin to practice what he's taught them. We listen with rapt attention as he speaks, even about these topics that are uninteresting to most of us, who see ourselves as warriors, and not men of science or medicine, and that's his gift, I realize: his gift is to make the un-interesting sound interesting, and to make the ordinary appear as if it's extra-ordinary and the most important thing in the world when he speaks of it. It soon becomes late, and one by one we begin to drift to sleep, around the fire as it burns lower and lower and lower, down to just dull embers, but before we do, I have one last thought. I think again of the incomplete Akademia, as I did before, and why we were brought here before it was finished, and I realize that this is it. I realize that this has all been orchestrated and choreographed for our teacher to be able to watch us first, to be able to observe us as we naturally are, on our own and together, and I also realize that even though the classrooms aren't yet complete, and neither is his new Akademia, our lessons with Aristoteles of Stagira have already begun.

CHAPTER NINE

A YEAR PASSES IN MIEZA LIKE A DAY, and during that time, we're happy at the Akademia, the place that soon becomes our new home. The days and evenings are slower than they were in Pella, without any others around and without a palace, and the rest of the goings on that occur at and in a capital of that size, and I realize during these slow days, even as I'm living them, that these are the days I'll look back on and return to many times in my memories and in the future. Perhaps that's wisdom, or a gift, having the foreknowledge and awareness to know and understand that, even as the experience is still being lived, but perhaps it's also not, too, as I've never thought of myself as wise, so perhaps it's something else. Maybe it's even a curse, or a burden, I don't know. I just know it's the first time in my life it's happened to me, and the first time I'm not always looking forward to some distant and just-out-of-reach goal and moment. I could ask Aristoteles about this, and he'd have an answer, I know—of that I'm sure, because it does seem that he has an answer for everything, or at least a question that leads to an answer—but I won't, because another lesson I've learned during my time in Mieza is that sometimes things are best left exactly as they are; sometimes, I've found, things are best left exactly as we feel them, as we believe them, and as we shape them in our own minds without the influence or prejudices or perceptions of another.

Our mornings, during our time in Mieza, all still begin in the same way, even after the Akademia is completed and our formal lessons begin. I'm not sure that will ever change for as long as we're all alive and together. We continue to rise early, before the sun, and we train with our broad-swords and the exercises I've devised, and we all continue to grow even bigger, and stronger, and then after ariston, we go to the classrooms with Aristoteles. Our bodies begin to change, even more than they already have, while we're here, as we grow older, day-by-day, and they fill out and expand, with more muscle through the arms, the chest, the back and the thighs. That's what happens during this time in a young man's life, great change in ways both physical and in ways that are more than that, too; before this time, we all had the *promise* of being warriors about us, as something that we would soon become. Now we're all beginning to look the part, and we're actually becoming warriors, too, in every single way but one.

Blood.

We've never faced combat, real combat, but we all know, also, that will soon change, as well.

Do I want it to?

Or do I want to remain as I am, as we all are, as we always could be?

In the mornings, I continue to wake even earlier than Alexandros, and I watch for a few moments as he sleeps on his cot at the far side of our room before he then wakes, too. Philippos and the Macedonian army have gone east during our time in Mieza, to fight against the last remaining Thracian and Scythian tribes that claim independence there and then, once all of Thrace and Scythia bow before Philippos and pay tribute to the Argead Star, the whole world knows where Philippos will turn his attention next.

The rest of Greece.

Athens, Thebes, and all the other southern city-states.

We wait for news of battles, and while we wait, the Companions also naturally divide while we're here, the same as we divided in Pella, after

I first arrived. I find myself with Alexandros on one side of things, and perhaps with Aristoteles and Callisthenes now, too, as all the rest soon grow bored with the afternoon lessons and start to not come to them. They grow more and more anxious and restless with the stories and news and rumors that reach Mieza, and they wait for only one thing now.

War.

And to take their place in it.

Alexandros and I continue our lessons with Aristoteles, though, as Alexandros sees them as imperative and so we go to see the philosopher every day, together, while the others instead go into town. Aristoteles doesn't punish them, when they stop coming, and neither does Alexandros. There are girls there in town, we find out—not many, but a few—because they tell us about them when they return. They start to come back later and later each night, and the stories they tell become more wild and far-fetched than those from the night or week or month before, and I'm not sure I believe them, or at least all of them. What I do believe, though, is that they begin to drink more, even more than they did in Pella, and they start to become slower in the mornings when we train, and have to rub sleep and left-over wine from their eyes.

Dionysus.

It's always Dionysus, here in the north, and while he blesses them—he definitely blesses them more than so many of the other less strong, less handsome, less attractive and less athletic boys—he doesn't bless them this much.

I watch as Alexandros looks at them with contempt.

He's good at disguising his feelings, though, so they don't recognize what it is that he thinks of them. But I do. I recognize it, and I'm able to because I know him in a way that they don't; I know his eyes, and his heart. I don't feel it the same as he does, though, the contempt for them. I don't see or feel anything as I look at their hungover limbs and sleepless eyes, except perhaps an advantage. There's one among us that trains to be a basileus, I think, and there are others that are training to *serve* a basileus, so perhaps it's good, and it's as it should be and is just as simple as that. Yes, I nod, to myself. Perhaps it's good, and simple, and as it needs to be. There is one more Companion, though; there is one more Companion, and I find myself wondering, more and more...

Which group do I belong to?

I was born a prinkipas, the same as Alexandros was born, but am I a prinkipas that's meant to train and fight to eventually become a basileus, or am I meant to train and fight *for* a basileus? I ask for an answer, from both gods and stars, but there's no answer that comes, so I keep wondering. I wonder, and I stay awake at night in the room that we share, and I ask the same question, over and over, again and again. I think perhaps it's something that I'll keep wondering, that I'll keep asking, and that I'll keep searching for, maybe even for the rest of my life.

IT'S LATE AND CANDLES BURN LOW, but Alexandros and I are still together in Aristoteles' study finishing our last lesson when Callisthenes enters with a message he's just received. We all look up from the astrological chart that Aristoteles has been showing us, and Callisthenes comes forward, and then begins to read the note from the piece of papyrus that he holds. It's news of Philippos' latest victory. He's already defeated the Thracians, earlier in the summer, but instead of resting and consolidating his kingdom and what he's already conquered, he's carried on further north, and defeated the Scythians on the banks of the great Istros River. The victory was total and complete, and Philippos has even found a new city there that will bear his name, a new Macedonian city in the middle of the Thracian kingdom that is to be called Philippopolis. Then Philippos continued on even further, and while he'd been fighting there—north of the Istros River, and amongst the wild Triballi—he'd taken a spear in the leg that had passed completely through his flesh and into the horse that he was riding. The spear had killed the horse, but Philippos was still alive, and despite the great and serious wound, he was expected to make a recovery back to some semblance of health and mobility, but the recovery would take significant time, and it was during that period, while he was recovering there, north of the Istros, that he'd grown bored and decided to take a new Thracian wife. She was from Odessos, on the banks of the Pontos Axeinos, and her name was Meda, the letter says, and he'd married her in a traditional ceremony on the beach: to bind the locals to him and Macedon for good, he'd explained, though I watch Alexandros roll his eyes at this. No matter what the reason, though, Philippos would now bring this new girl back to Pella with him as his sixth bride, as soon as he was well enough to travel. The message is then finished, and Callisthenes stops reading as he re-folds the piece of papyrus and tucks it back away, and into the folds of his loose-fitting chiton, and then we all stand there and look at each other.

This is significant, we all know that.

But just how significant? That's what will remain to be seen.

"Well," Aristoteles begins, turning and speaking to Alexandros. "Your father's kingdom is now twice as large as it was when you first came here to Mieza."

"Yes, it is."

"But?" Aristoteles asks, as he can always tell when there's something further on Alexandros' mind.

"What is it compared to other kingdoms?"

"Which ones?"

"Persia."

"In size?"

"Yes."

"It's still very small."

Silence.

"Can I ask you something?"

"Of course. That's why you're here."

"And you won't be upset?"

"No."

"Are you sure?"

"Reasonably," Aristoteles answers, and then smiles.

"You were born here in the north," Alexandros says. "Like we were, right?"

"Yes."

"But Stagira isn't a kingdom, like Macedon, it's a democracy."

"That's correct."

"And after you left, you went south, and lived in Athens, and you loved the city, and you love democracy both there and here, and speak of it so often."

"That's also true. Have you asked your question?"

"It's no secret that my father plans to march south, and conquer the city that you love, and threaten the very thing that both you and they hold so dear, so why would you help us?" Alexandros looks back at him. "That's my question. We're Greek, but we don't believe in democracy, like you and the other Greeks do, so why would you agree to come here, to Macedon, and to my father, to teach his son and his friends?"

Aristoteles sits up in his chair.

He looks at Alexandros more closely now, because this is important, and significant, too. "After all this time . . . you're just now wondering this?" he asks, still smiling.

"No," Alexandros shakes his head. "I wondered it before I came, and so did Hephaestion. I'm just now *asking*."

"Be more specific."

"What?"

"Be more specific about what it is that you want to ask."

Alexandros pauses now.

I could watch and listen to them talk forever, the way the conversation between them glides and twists and all the great things and ideas that are behind their words and thoughts. I look at Callisthenes, next to me. I can tell that he feels the same way, or at least he does about Aristoteles. How does he feel about Alexandros? How do they *both* feel about him? Do they think he can be great, too, like his teacher? I look back as Alexandros gathers himself, searching for and then finding the right words; the exact, specific, and most appropriate ones to be used, just as Aristoteles has taught us about the power of words when used appropriately and correctly. "All of your lessons, especially the lessons you've given lately, have been about Greece, and democracy, about philosophy, and free thought. They've all been about the strength and importance of the polis, and the people that exist and live within the polis. Yet you've agreed to educate the son of the basileus of Macedon, and that basileus, while Greek, is the man who is now on the very doorstep of invading and conquering everything that you've taught us about and that you seem to hold so very dear."

"That's right," Aristoteles nods. "I do feel that way, and I have agreed to do that."

"Why?"

The philosopher looks back at Alexandros with his small and dark eyes, which flick to Callisthenes, for a moment, and then to me, and finally back to Alexandros.

He inhales.

He takes a deep, deep breath.

Then he begins.

"The Persians came here a hundred years ago, and they were defeated once, against all odds, and then they came back, and they were defeated again. They are our enemy, our one true enemy, or at least their shahansha is, and he rules a very large and very powerful empire, as we've said, but still we were able to defeat them because even though we're small, we've made ourselves great in many other ways, which are all the ways I've endeavored to teach to both you and your Companions."

"Yes," Alexandros nods. "And you have."

"But then what happened?"

"What do you mean? We're still here."

"No. What happened after the Persians were defeated?" Aristoteles asks.

"The Peloponnesian War."

"That's right," Aristoteles nods now. "The small minds of very greedy and power-hungry men overtook the great cities of Greece, and we all so quickly forgot the threat to the east, the great threat to all that we'd done and accomplished and our democratic way of life, and we entered into a hundred years of war between Athens and Sparta. And as you know, that war weakened Greece to a degree that we wouldn't be able to defeat the Persians for a third time, if they raised another army to come and invade again. Pride in Athens says I should be whipped and punished for speaking these words, but they're truth. They're truth, and it's also how empires fall, when men search for power, no matter the cost, no matter the moral price, or the desire to mislead and misinform the polis. So now, the only way that we'll be able to stop the Persians, or anyone else that would come, is if we band together, *all* Hellenic people, all people and tribes that are on this peninsula, fighting together, as one unit, and under one ruler, and the reason that I'm here, in Mieza, is that I believe the basileus of Macedon to be the best suited to unite us in such a way."

"So you do believe in Philippos, and what he's doing."

"Language is important, Alexandros, as I've taught you. Who did I say?"

"The basileus of Macedon."

"That's right."

I watch him as his mind turns, and he takes that in, what our teacher has just told us. I'm silent, as I watch them, and so is Callisthenes; I couldn't summon the right words to speak in this moment, I know, even if I'd wanted to. I brought the sword and the exercises and the other tools to turn him into a warrior, I realize, but Aristoteles? This is what he's brought. This is how many steps ahead he's been, and is, and I'm in awe.

"Why me?" Alexandros breathes, finally understanding.

"I've watched you, longer than you know, and have heard a great deal of reports about Philippos' middle child, even before I came to Macedon, or Pella, or Mieza. I know that Philippos believes a son of his is the least likely person to follow him onto the throne, no matter when or how that son is born, and he has acted accordingly, but I don't share his sentiment. So that's why I'm here."

"Why not his oldest child, though, who you could control? Or why not Amyntas?"

"Anyone can believe in first-born sons," Aristoteles smiles. "But I believe in those who are born with something to prove, the ones that are born with something only they can see in the stars, in *their* stars, and something only they can feel in their hearts and souls. And I believe in the sons that won't be able to rest until they make all that come true, no matter where it takes them, no matter how far or wide, and no matter what stands in the way because they've already overcome it before, simply because of the way and order in which they were born."

Alexandros is alive.

Every inch of him is alive: his eyes, his skin, the small blonde hairs that run the length of his arms and legs.

And I am, also.

I'm alive, too, along with Alexandros.

Aristoteles turns and walks to his desk where he picks up a book that sits there, then comes back, to stand in front of us, in front of Alexandros. He hands the book to him. It's thick and well-bound, in immaculately-kept condition, the words written in fresh, bright ink, and on untarnished and unworn pages of papyrus of which none are missing. Alexandros stands there and holds the book gently, reverantly. He opens it and flips through it, and I move closer and look over his shoulder to see what it is Aristoteles has given him, and I read the first words:

Sing, Goddess, it begins . . .

I smile.

Of course.

"I'd heard that you slept with a copy underneath your pillow," Aristoteles tells us, with a casual shrug. "I'm not sure if that was true or not, or just a story, but I saw your copy when you arrived and it looked like you could use a new one. I know there aren't many books here, this far north, so I sent for it from Athens."

Alexandros looks down at it, holding it in his hands like it's the most important thing in the world.

Silence.

Silence.

"It's a great history of our people and what we are, and who we could be again, too, if given the chance," Aristoteles continues. "So I hope that you read it, a great many more times than you already have, and that Hephaestion does, as well," he says, with a wink towards me, to let me know he hasn't forgotten I'm still there. "And while it's a history of our people, your history, the one that will soon come, Alexandros... unless I'm very profoundly mistaken, your history might perhaps even be more and greater still. That's the answer to your question, and the answer to why I've come here. I've come to shape and mold the mind of the one who would shape and mold and bring together the rest of the world, both for our time, and perhaps for all the rest of time, too, and to teach him the things I think are important and that he should know and have respect for, which includes democracy, and Athens, and all the rest we've discussed."

Silence.

More silence.

I see Alexandros shaking, so I reach out and touch him, and then hold his arm so that he too knows that I'm still here.

"Thank you," Alexandros finally whispers, though not to me.

Then he looks up, and I see the tears that are in his eyes, coming down his cheeks now, and he doesn't bother to hide or push them away as he whispers the same thing, one more time.

"Thank you."

THE REST OF THE SUMMER PASSES, and then in July, I turn sixteen first, and then Alexandros does, and for the first time in too many days, when my birthday passes, I wonder about my mother, and Illyria. I wonder about my brother, too, and what's happened there during the time I've been gone. I haven't heard anything from Salona, since I've left, as I've still managed to maintain the illusion of death, both for my safety and theirs, though I know it won't be an illusion that will remain forever.

I know that. I know it in my heart.

But it won't be yet, because there's still more left to do first; wisdom to gain, strength to build and temper, tribes to conquer and armies to lead. And then, after all those things are done, it will be time to fulfill my oath, with my friend at my side.

He'll like Illyria, I think.

He'll like anything that's wild and ancient, I know, and then I smile, because the other thing I know is that he'll like anything that I like.

Recently, Alexandros has been spending more time by himself, though.

As I've thought before, it often seems that I know him both more and less than anyone else I've ever met, all at the same time, and I feel that again now as he retreats into his mind and thoughts, as he retreats even from me, around the time of his birthday. He's stayed in our room more often, either to read or study, and he's gone to Aristoteles' office at all hours of both day and night to ask him questions about the south—distances between cities, differences between people, and tribes, and philosophies—and then he'll leave again, once he has the answers, just as abruptly as he's come. I know what he's doing, and I know where his thoughts are, making strategic and important notes in his mind that he'll need and use one day soon. He only has so much time left here, in Mieza, and he's going to try to receive and learn as much as he can and all the philosopher has to teach, all that Alexandros will be able to have and keep and call upon, for all the rest of his life.

And what a time it is: what a time in my life, to be able to watch them.

People already recognize Aristoteles' mind, of course they do.

But they don't recognize Alexandros' yet, not his mind, or his heart, or his spirit, or anything else, not like I do. But they will. One day... I know that they will.

And what does it mean?

I wonder sometimes, late at night.

What does it mean that these two great minds were brought together like this, and that they were able to meet and that we were able to learn from one such as Aristoteles? I think about stars again, and I think about gods, too. I don't have anyone else to talk to while Alexandros is thinking, or withdrawn, or gone, and so I ask Callisthenes about this one day after dinner and he tells me very simply that he agrees that the gods and stars always work in mysterious ways, but while their ways might be mysterious, they're also ordered, and it's not our job to understand them, just to accept them, and the universe and the world in which we live, and how it conspires to help us continue. I'm surprised at that. I thought a man of science and reason and fact—a man such as the philosopher's nephew, who was training to be a doctor, and a historian, and philosopher himself, in his own right—I assumed a man such as that would have no need for gods, or for stars, or for destiny and fate and all the rest. And besides having no need of such things, I thought someone like him would perhaps even think of them with contempt, as superstitions reserved for peasants and soldiers, and when I tell him of my surprise, he laughs and says that men of science still have need of the gods, too, and perhaps even have need of the gods more than any other.

"Even more than a soldier?" I ask him.

"Even more than a soldier," he smiles.

I'm surprised again, when I first hear this, and what he thinks.

But then, when I think about it more, and further, I then find that I'm not.

WHEN ALEXANDROS RETREATS into himself, I spend more time with the other Companions, and one afternoon when most of them have gone into town to drink, or chase girls, or both, I go with Ptolemaios to the small river that cuts through the rocky hills just south of the Akademia. Ptolemaios doesn't go with the others very often, and he has even less in recent days, and I of course know why: it's because he loves and spends his days thinking of another. Being away from her must be hard, but being away from her and not being able to talk about it, because he thinks no one knows?

That must be even harder.

We get to the river, and it's hot, so we take our chitons off and go into the water and swim. Once we've cooled off, we climb back out and sit on the bank, in the shade underneath the branch of an olive, and we drink some chilled and fresh grape juice mixed with honey that we've brought. We sit there and pass the skin back and forth as we talk. "So . . . what do you think's going to happen, in the coming months?" Ptolemaios asks me, and I of course know what he's asking about, and why.

"I think we're going to leave."

"And then what?"

"Then we're going to fight."

"You think we'll finally be allowed to?"

"Alexandros is sixteen now, and so is Nearchos, and you, and me, and the rest will be in the next few months."

"So it'll be south, then?" he asks, drinking again. "And into the heart of Greece?"

"It seems so."

"When do you think we'll go?"

"Whenever Philippos is healthy enough, I suppose, and returns from Thrace."

"You don't think he'll want to spend time in Pella with his new bride?"

"No," I tell him, thinking of Pausanius, who stands outside his door. "I think he'll want to keep going, and I think he'll want to fight."

"I think so, too," Ptolemaios says, and then we sit there in silence as the sun begins its descent in front of us. Perhaps this is the last bit of peace that we'll know, for the immediate future; perhaps this is the last bit of peace that we'll know, for all the rest of our lives. We're never sure, are we? We're never really sure, and so the sun continues, as it always does, behind the great peaks in the distance, the peaks just before the ones that are my own, and that's now what I think of again.

Illyria.

Salona.

My home is so close I can almost taste the wind that comes from the place where the seas mix and where I was born. The future is so close now, too, so close that I can almost feel what it will be like to stand over my uncle and watch as my father's kingdom is returned to me, his oldest son.

"What is it like when you're with him?" Ptolemaios finally asks, from his place next to me.

I turn and look at him.

"Who?" I ask, still thinking of my uncle and my father.

"Alexandros."

"I'm not sure what you mean."

"I've always wanted to be closer to him, but I never could be. He never let me in."

"You're one of his Companions."

"Yes."

"So you're as close to him as anyone."

"No," he says, then shakes his head. "Not like you."

He turns and looks back at me now, too, and I study his eyes as they look into my own, and I find nothing there that I'm searching for: I find no jealousy, or discontent, or hate, or judgment. I just find curiosity. The sun sinks even lower now, in front of us, almost gone. The mountains are painted in brilliant and vivid tones of orange and yellow, with long trailing shadows spread across them. "I was strong, before I came here," I finally tell him, my words coming slowly in these slow hills outside the city. "But when I'm with him, I'm even stronger than I was before, and better. We all are."

"I think so, too. But why?"

"I don't know."

"What is it about him? Why is he different, and why is he what he is? He's not the best warrior, or soldier, or athlete, or anything else."

I've thought about this. I've thought about this many, many times, since I first met him. "I've stopped asking why a long time ago," I tell him.

"Some people in this world are just simply bigger than it, aren't they?"

"Perhaps."

"I think so."

"I think so, too."

"I'll follow him."

"So will I."

"I'll follow him anywhere," he says, as the sun sinks even further, and then finally disappears altogether, and Ptolemaios turns to me again. "I'll follow him, Hephaestion, wherever he leads us," he continues, the disappearing sun changing the color of his coal-dark eyes. "I'll follow him, even if it's to the ends of the earth."

WHEN I RETURN TO OUR ROOM, I find Alexandros sitting on his bed with a letter in hand, and I see the seal on the letter: it's the familiar and multi-pointed Argead Star. "From your mother?" I ask, wondering if she's written to tell him what he already knows, about his father's new child-bride from the north, and that they both will return soon to Pella.

"No," he shakes his head.

"Who?"

"Cleopatra."

"What does she say?"

He puts the letter down and then looks up at me. "She says that Amyntas has grown three inches since we've been gone, and that she's heard the men talking about his strength in battle and what he did fighting against the Thracians in the north. She says they think he's the best swordsman for his age they've ever seen."

"That's because they haven't seen me."

He tries to stay stoic and look grim, and serious, but he can't, and shakes his head, trying to hide what he can't hide.

A smile.

It's just a flash of one, though, just a suggestion.

Because this is still very serious business, of course it is.

"I will impress them," Alexandros says, looking back down at the letter again, holding it in his hand, running his fingers over and across the royal seal.

"Yes," I nod. "You will."

"You've never understood this part of me, and who we are here in Macedon."

"What part?"

"You called me prinkipas, when you first arrived, and you still do sometimes."

"Do I?"

"You know that you do, but we don't use that word here, because to us here in Philippos' kingdom, being the son of the basileus is the same as being the son of anyone else. It means nothing to him, or to us. Not in the way it does in Illyria, or Epirus, or Persia, and not in the way it does in the south, either."

"You're wrong."

"How?"

"It *does* mean something," I tell him. "It means that the sons of all the noble and important families who *will* choose the next basileus are your friends and Companions, and living here with you, in Mieza, the same as they did in Pella, too."

"*Sons*, Hephaestion. Not their fathers."

"And what is a son's job, no matter the order of their birth, but to be better than their father? There is no other job for a child. And we will be, Alexandros, and we'll replace them. We'll do it, for you, and with you, and they support you now and they will then, too, and because they do, their families will all support you, as well."

"*They*?" he asks, and then looks up at me.

He knows what I mean; I'm Illyrian, and have a kingdom of my own there to worry about, in the north, a kingdom that one day I'll return to.

There's silence between us.

"Arrhidaeus will support you," I finally tell him. "For the Argeads."

"Maybe."

"You've been kind to him, all your life, while Amyntas and the others have been cruel and tortured him."

"It's not why I did it."

"No, but it'll help. I've heard that your mother has been cruel to him, too. You should tell her to stop."

"It's not that easy with her."

"What isn't?"

"You don't just tell her things and have her listen."

"You should try."

"Is your mother the same?"

"No, my mother's kind."

"What else is she?"

I pause at that question and think back: I see her face, I see it in front of me, I see it when I'm young, and when she is, too, and then I see it when I'm older, and she's older, and I see the look that was in her eyes the night I left my home. I glance at my trunk and the chlamys that's there, the one that she made for me. I wonder, how long did it take to make? I wonder, what were her thoughts when she knit it, piece-by-piece, twisted thread connected to twisted thread? Because I know her thoughts and love are twisted and held within that thread, too. "She's a mother," I finally tell him, knowing no better description.

It's simple, but it's also truth.

"Perhaps she would be mine, too?" he asks.

"Of course she will be," I say, as I go to my bed on the other side of the room and sit down, and I'm surprised when he stands and follows after me and sits on my bed, also. He sits next to me, our elbows touching, gently pressing against each other. "Tell me about her," he says, from his place next to me now. "Tell me about her, Hephaestion, and your brother, and how you grew."

Images, memories, they come flooding back.

I think of a day together on a boat; a picnic by a stream, all three of us, the sun coming from behind a cloud; the way she runs her hand through my hair, straightening it; how she looks at me when I've done something wrong, challenging me to be better, the only person in my life that was able to do that.

I breathe in.

Then I smile again, remembering it all, and with all that I know and have learned of Alexandros' own childhood and upbringing, I realize just how much of a blessing my memories and family are. I smile when I think of them and the way that I grew, and the mother and brother who grew with me, and who are still there, at my home, and who still love me. It's always something that's felt small to me, and inevitable, but now, I realize, for the first time . . . now, I realize that perhaps it's not.

So I tell him about it, as he's asked.

I tell him about how my mother used to sit on my bed and sing to me, how she used to sing our dark and sad Illyrian mountain songs, which I still hear at night, sometimes, just before we pass into sleep, next to each other, and so if he listens close enough, perhaps he might hear them, too. I tell him about how tall she was, about how so many of the mountain women are tall, and I tell him about how when I was little she used to walk in front of me and I thought I'd never be able to keep up with her long strides and how fast she went. I once thought I'd never reach her height, or have as long of legs and stride, or be able to walk as fast, and I tell him about my brother, too. I tell him about how I taught him to ride a horse, and to keep his heels pushed down when he does, because that's what good horsemen do and everyone that comes from where we come from is a good horseman. It's a birthright, I'd told him, and it was *our* birthright, as sons of our father and boys of the mountains. "I wish I'd had that," Alexandros whispers. "I wish I'd had a brother like that."

"You're my brother, so he's your brother, too, and you do."

Alexandros smiles again when I say that, and then I tell him about the mornings we used to spend out on the sea, and how I taught him to fish, in the same way our father would have taught both of us, if he'd still been alive, and I tell him about how I saved money I'd earn from the fish that I'd caught to buy him his first small sword, and how I'd begun to teach him how to use it; to always start with it held high, above the height of his opponent's weapon, and how it gave him an advantage to strike from there. I'm about to continue and tell him even more, but when I look over again, I see that Alexandros' eyes have drooped and closed, and his breathing is now rhythmic and steady.

He's asleep.

I look at him, sadly, knowing what the anxiety of being here in Mieza and not in Pella and with the army has done to him. So I move closer and I lay down, too, next to him, and I look up at the ceiling. My life has been one thing, ever since I've come to Macedon, and now it's going to change. I can feel it, just as I know that he can feel it, too, and that's why we've been speaking tonight in the way that we've been speaking.

We know the future is now and again upon us.

But how will it come, and how will it change?

That's what we still have to decide and settle on, but if anything, I'm glad that I'll find out with him. At some point my thoughts must trail off and into nothing, because at some point sleep overcomes me, too, and for a time there's just darkness. But I open my eyes again in the night. I don't know what time it is, just that it's night, and that it's dark, and when I do, I find that he's still there, in my bed, a great deal of humidity and heat in the air and between us, between the places where our skin touches and my arms are wrapped around him. I'm too tired to move or do anything else, so I just close my eyes again and expect to find him gone in the morning, when I wake, like he usually is, and back to his own bed, but when I open my eyes again, and there's light, I see that he's still there. His limbs are still touching mine, and he's even closer now, his body pressed against my body. I watch him. I watch him, just for a moment, like I sometimes do. More light pours through the window that's above us, pours down onto the bed we share, and as he sleeps, I see what the light does, and how it turns his fair skin and hair an even deeper and more beautiful shade of gold than the gods have already made it.

CHAPTER TEN

The rest of the summer passes, and then autumn comes, and Alexandros is even more restless. He's eager to get back to Pella, and he pays less attention to his lessons with Aristoteles, and he sleeps less at night, too. I ask him about this because I'm worried about him, and he gives me an answer he's already given before: sleep makes him feel mortal, he says. It makes him feel vulnerable, and makes him feel like all the others around him that he knows, and not like who he wants to be. I wonder about this and the change in him I've seen as I stand in Aristoteles' study alone because Alexandros is late again, which has become a routine. He left our room after we'd returned from our morning exercises, saying only he needed to go for a walk, and when I offered to come, too, he said he needed to go on his own. I checked the stables before I came and found that Bucephalus wasn't there, so if he's decided to ride instead of walk, then who knows where and how far he's gone. He could be anywhere, I tell Aristoteles, and make my excuses for him, and what's been happening and Alexandros' new absences, but the philosopher just brushes the excuses away.

"It's alright," he tells me.

"He should be here, or at least tell you that he won't be, when he decides he's not going to come."

"He's worried about his future, which he's right to do."

"His future is all that he thinks about, since I've met him."

"And that's why he's Alexandros," Aristoteles tells me, and then winks over the top of the papyrus that he reads. "But you don't give yourself enough credit, Hephaestion. Because it's not *all* that he thinks about."

I know what he's insinuating, and when Olympias insinuated the same, I felt anger, but I sense no malice with Aristoteles; I sense only knowledge, and acceptance, and perhaps even approval, too, I realize.

"You've never asked us about it."

"Asked you about what?"

"Each other, and why we share a room, and spend so much time together."

"I gave you the book, didn't I?"

"The book?" I ask, frowning, not quite understanding.

"You've read the story, and you've read it many times, I would assume, the same as he has."

"The Illiad? Of course. Or heard it spoken."

Aristoteles sets his papers down and then looks at me with different eyes now; his eyes have become serious eyes, darker eyes, stoic and unblinking eyes. "So you realize there is no Achilleus without Patroklos, right? You do understand that, don't you?"

"And you think that I'm him?"

"Do you see yourself differently? Because you know that's how *he* sees you."

"I'm not sure if I see myself at all."

"Why?"

"Because I never stopped to do so, I suppose."

"Perhaps you should, because what is a life, really, if it's not a life examined?"

I pause. Then I nod.

He's right, of course he's right.

And I almost laugh as I think through the rest of it.

"So that means Philippos is Peleus," I say, slowly, putting the analogy together. "Olympias would be Thetis, and that makes you, who . . . *Odysseus*?"

It's his turn to smile now.

"No," he shakes his head.

"Why?"

"It's not the rest of the story that's important, Hephaestion. It's *Alexandros* that's important, just as it was Achilleus that was important, because it's him and his heart that's going to change the world, and it's you that touches his heart. Do you understand what I'm telling you? It's you and you alone, of all that are on this earth that touches the heart that's going to touch and change the world. It's not Philippos, or Olympias, or me, or any of the other Companions, or the girl that he's left back in Pella that he sleeps with sometimes when he's there. It's an orphan prinkipas from an unimportant northern kingdom whom the gods have brought from those mountains and placed directly into his path."

"So you approve, then."

I don't know why this seems important to me, but it does.

"I've had a chance to watch you, these last months, both of you."

"And what do you see when you watch us?"

"I see two bodies, between you, but just one soul."

"That's it?"

"You're so young, Hephaestion," Aristoteles smiles. "You're so very young, and it's beautiful."

"What does that mean? Of course we are, and of course I am."

"It means that most would have to travel continents and generations to find each other, as you have, and to have what it is that you have and what it is I've just described. So what does it matter, Hephaestion, what I think, to answer your previous question? You have the favor of the gods, you both do, of that I'm sure, and as you know, the gods don't give their favor lightly."

"What god?"

"I don't know. That you'll have to find for yourself."

Knock.

There's the sound of knuckles rapping on wood and then Callisthenes opens the door and we both turn to see him as he enters, and when he does, the moment that had been there and just between us is now broken and gone.

Aristoteles smiles and waves him forward from the doorway.

But before Callisthenes reaches us, Aristoteles turns back to me.

"Why don't you take your brown and go find him," he says. "He'll be glad of the company, I think, and unless I'm very mistaken, I don't think there will be many nights like this left for you to be together while you're here. It's a very beautiful place, isn't it? And it's unlike so many of the other places you'll find in the world. Both the place, and also the time."

I look back at him, for another moment.

Callisthenes reaches us, and then I can see him glance between us, wondering what we've been talking about.

Then I finally nod, and I hope Aristoteles can see the gratitude that's in my eyes and feel the thanks that's in my heart as I turn and head towards the door, past Callisthenes and his arms full of papyrus, that he lays on the desk after I pass him, with his own nod of acknowledgement. I get to the door and look back at them, one more time. My soul, his soul, him that I go to find; I finally have the words, and I'll remember this moment. I'll remember this moment and this conversation, I know, for as many breaths as I have left, for all the lengths and distances of as many kingdoms and empires we might explore and cross together, for as many generations that have to come until we'll meet each other again, after this one.

"Chiron."

"Excuse me?"

It's Aristoteles who's spoken, as he looks up from his conversation with Callisthenes. "In your story I wouldn't be Odysseus," he says, "I'd be Chiron, the hermit centaur, who is outcast and alone on the mountain. I detest horses and can't ride them, as you know, but that's who I'd be."

A moment.

Then I smile, and so does he, before he returns to his nephew and the work that's now in front of them. I watch them both, for just another moment, and then as what he's said gathers and settles, becoming a part of me, a very deep and important part, I know, I then turn again, and I finally leave.

I FIND ALEXANDROS SITTING next to Bucephalus, who's grazing on the short and wiry grass that grows wild and ubiquitous around Mieza. They're by a cold and fast-running stream that comes rushing down from Vermio in the distance, and the stream still seems full and swift, even though it's fall now and the snow has all long-ago melted, getting ready to soon come again. It's actually the horse that gives him away, and where he sits, and shows him to me: Bucephalus is black like the night I ride through, but he's also massive, and it's his shadow I first see as it slowly shifts and moves in the darkness. I change the direction of the brown and ride towards them, and when I get there, I swing my leg over the brown's back and jump down to the grass and then drop the reins and let them hang free because I know that with Bucephalus near, the brown won't go very far. It's how it was in Pella, and it's how it is here, too. The brown recognizes Bucephalus when he sees him and makes a small noise—a quick snort and exhale from his nostrils—then moves to stand next to the larger horse there in the darkness, his friend, and push his shoulder against Bucephalus' shoulder to let him know that he's come, and that he's beside him.

I watch the horses, for a moment.

Then I do the same thing, too.

I go to where Alexandros sits on the small rocks near the bank of the stream and looks up at the stars, tracing and retracing the map of both new and old constellations that we've learned and committing the lines and patterns to memory; this hero and that hero, this god and the other one, questions that have answers, and some that don't, just questions, and more questions.

What will my place be, I know he's wondering.

How will he take his place among these stars that watch over us?

I've learned that only those blessed like we've been blessed can see themselves amongst the stars, even just the possibility of it, the potential, whether they actually ever make it there or not. But it's the striving, as he told me, that's where the honor and beauty and life is, and that's of course where the divinity is, too. I sit next to him and let my shoulder push against his shoulder, like our horses have done, next to us, to let him know that I feel him, and that I'm there. He doesn't look at me. It's cold at night in these hills, colder than it gets in Pella, and he left the Akademia at midday and is only dressed in his light chiton and so I reach out and spread the old and worn chlamys that my mother made over both of us. I wrap him in it now, too, along with myself, and when I do, he doesn't shiver anymore, like he did before I came. Neither of us do. We just sit there, wrapped in the cloak that was made by my mother, and made with her love, too, from her heart to her hands and then into this patterned thread.

Silence.

Stars.

Our silence, and our stars.

What of the gods?

"I missed lessons," he finally says.

"Yes," I nod. "You did."

"I'll apologize to Aristoteles tomorrow."

"He didn't seem upset."

"He understands me. Or, at least, I think he does."

"I think he understands you, too. I think he understands both of us."

Alexandros looks down from the sky, and he turns to look at me now, his mis-colored eyes meeting mine there in the darkness and I can tell what they're asking:

What do you mean, Hephaestion?

I've shown you the secrets of my heart, so what are the secrets of yours?

I don't answer.

We sit there, together, the darkness in front of us, behind us, between us, the sky and the stars still above, and even if we don't look at them now, I know that they're still and always there.

"What's going to happen next?" I finally say to him, very quietly, because it seems like I should.

"Our time here is going to end," he speaks quietly, too.

"Yes, it will."

"Yes."

"And then what?"

"War. There's nothing else."

"I was afraid you'd say that."

"Why? It's what we've trained our whole lives for."

"I know."

"But . . . ?"

"But war means—" I think, and then trail off. "I don't know exactly what it means, I suppose, but I think it means the end of something."

"The end of what? For you and me, war is the beginning. It's the beginning of what we've so often spoken and dreamed of together."

"You're right, of course you are. But it's the end of . . . moments like this, maybe."

"How?"

"Because everything will be different, because we'll be different. It won't be this quiet again, it won't be this peaceful, both around or inside of us, and it won't just be me and you, as we are now."

"The world changes, Hephaestion. Every day, the world changes, and it changes us, too."

"*War* changes us," I say, and I'm surprised at how harshly I speak the word, louder, more pronounced, and I don't know why I do. He's right, we've trained for this our whole lives, so why do I feel the way that I do now that it's finally upon us?

Silence.

We're both silent.

"It does," he finally answers, slowly. "But what else can we do?"

"We can remember."

I feel him, next to me, and I smell him when I breathe, the scent familiar in my nostrils, and in my soul. He reaches out and slowly takes my hand, wrapping his fingers gently around and through my fingers, and then when our palms are pressed together and flush against each other, his hand closes over mine. "You're right, Hephaestion," the words come quietly still, slowly, measured. "I suppose, like usual, you're right, and I suppose that's also why you're Hephaestion."

"I don't want to be."

"You don't want to be Hephaestion?"

"I don't want to be right. At least not about this."

"Yes, you do," he smiles as he looks at me. "You always want to be right, and you always are."

"That's a lot of pressure."

"It might be. But it's also why I love you."

"Really?"

"Yes, or at least one of the many reasons."

And there it is.

There is the word, and it's not the first time its been spoken about us, but it's the first it's been spoken between us.

There's more than one word for love in our language; there's the one that Olympias had used, *eros*, when she asked if I loved her son, but the one that Alexandros uses now is different: *agape*. It's a word for love that means more than what she'd asked, and is more than the word she used, too, because it's more than how she thinks, and it's more than what she understands, both her and all the others that see and judge and think they know our secrets and who and what we are.

"You love me?" I finally ask him, still softly.

"Of course I do," he says, very seriously, and squeezes my hand even tighter.

"I love you, too, Alexandros."

"Why?"

I laugh.

I finally laugh, I can't help it.

"Who can answer such a question?" I ask him. "Who can know such things?"

"You."

"No."

"Try."

"I can't."

"Try for me."

"I just know that I do, and that's enough."

Silence.

We sit there.

More silence.

"Yes," he finally nods, slowly, looking up again, looking at me, his mis-matched eyes once again meeting my own. "It most certainly is enough, isn't it?"

It's not a question, and when he speaks, I listen.

When he speaks, I feel.

So do the others.

I take my chlamys from where it rests across both our shoulders and we lay back and I pull the cloak across our chests like a blanket to keep us warm. We push our bodies together, closer. I feel his heart, beating next to my own heart. Then we turn and look up and together now we trace with our fingers the constellations that are already there. Where will we be, among them? What place will we take and which stars will be our stars, and tell our story? What room have the gods found for Alexandros and Hephaestion, two young friends in Macedon, who now know that they love each other.

THE NEWS COMES QUICKER even than Aristoteles expected.

Alexandros and I lay all night under the stars, not ever going to sleep, just laying there and looking up and feeling each other's hearts, holding onto a moment we both know will soon pass and might not ever come again. But as I've said, we will remember it. There will be other moments, I know, there will certainly be other moments that come, but none that will again be quite so innocent, quite so free of care and burden and all the other trappings of the world that's waiting for us outside the olive groves of Mieza and the sanctuary of Aristoteles' new Akademia of learning and knowledge. We're glad that the world will soon come, as we spoke about, but we also aren't, all at the same time. There's not a word for that, I realize. Perhaps there should be. We lay there the whole night together and we think of this, we think of *all* of this, and then when the sun begins to rise and bring hints of new light and warmth, I take my chlamys and fold it away as we each climb up onto our horses and then begin to ride together back towards Mieza, through the still-rising mist of the damp and early mountain morning.

When we get back to the Akademia, Aristoteles is there outside, and he's waiting for us. Callisthenes is with him and by his side, as he was when I left, too, and we see that there's a second letter that's arrived for Alexandros. It's sealed with the Argead Star, also. Alexandros dismounts from Bucephalus, and I do the same, next to him, from the brown, and he goes forward and takes the letter and breaks the seal and quickly scans the contents and what it says. Bucephalus snorts and rubs his great black head against my shoulder as Alexandros reads and I pat his cheek and rub the white ox-head that's marked on his forehead and he snorts again as Alexandros looks up from his letter and meets Aristoteles' small and dark eyes.

"I wish we could have had more time," he says.

"I wish we could have, too," Aristoteles answers him. "But such is the way of the world, isn't it?"

"It doesn't have to be."

"Democracy, philosophy, medicine, ethics. Do not forget these things, Alexandros. Wherever you go, whatever corner of the world your heart and your spirit and your *pothos* brings you to . . . bring these most noble things you've learned here with you, and unite us all, with an appreciation for them, and an appreciation for a just and honest way of living through truth and knowledge, and perhaps most importantly, a greater and truer appreciation for each other, no matter our origins, or our birth, or anything else."

Alexandros breathes.

He looks back at Aristoteles, for the last time, at his teacher, and this our last lesson, here at the Akademia. "Life comes from our parents, and their union that creates us," Alexandros tells Aristoteles, speaking slowly, speaking softly. "But a life well-lived . . . certainly that comes from somewhere else, and so while I may be indebted to my mother and father for living, I will always be indebted to you, Aristoteles of Stagira, and all that we've learned here in Mieza, for living well."

"You give me too much credit."

"I give credit where it's deserved, and I think you might find that the world will follow suit, and do the same thing, too. And how fortunate am I, to live in such a time?" he says, then smiles, wider now. "The time of Aristoteles."

"And how fortunate am I," the philosopher smiles, also, and in the same way, "to live during the time of Alexandros."

"I'm not Alexandros yet."

"You will be," Aristoteles tells him, and then walks forward, away from Callisthenes and some distance from me, too, and he whispers into Alexandros' ear; he cups his hand as he leans close and pitches his voice low so that only they two can hear his words, and then he backs up. I look at Alexandros. I study the look that's on his face, but I can't read it. As I've already said, I know him both more and less than anyone I've ever met and while sometimes his soul is so clear, and so pure, there are also depths to it, layers, corners, and mysteries I don't yet understand.

Will I?

I don't know, I realize.

But such is life, and it goes on.

Then Aristoteles surprises me.

He walks towards where I stand now, and he reaches me, and when he does, he cups his hand and he whispers into my ear, too, and in the same way, so that only we two can hear.

Alexandros watches us.

He watches us, but he doesn't interrupt, and he doesn't ask what's said.

He never will, either.

Is it because he already knows? Or is it something else, and for some other reason?

I don't know.

We leave.

We go back to the room that we share, together.

We find that a servant has already packed all our things and he's mixed them together, not distinguishing between what's mine, and what's his, and for some reason this seems important to me, though I don't think Alexandros even notices because it's simply and just what he expects.

I look at him.

The same golden light pours in from the window above us, just like it did before, when he slept in my bed that night and morning here in Mieza. The light comes and then rests and settles on his skin, on his hair, and I look at him. I think of the word Aristoteles used to describe him, the one that he used to describe what was inside and what would burn and burn and burn until either quenched or extinguished.

Pothos.

Desire, longing, regret, want; the eternal pursuit of the horizon.

Could something such as that be quenched?

No, I know. It can't be. It can only be extinguished.

But the time is now here, and the horizon is now upon us, the one that we have studied and thought and discussed so much: in the hills above Pella, after the lake, while we dried naked and together in the Macedonian sun, all of the early pre-dawn mornings, in the gymnasium, where we trained and fought, the nights in the room that we shared in the palace, where we slept next to each other and dreamed the same dreams, night after night after night. We will now leave Mieza, and we'll leave it different than when we came. It's finally time to explore, I know. It's not time to just look at the horizon anymore, it's time to finally begin our march towards it, together, and discover all we know lays there and in front of us, all we've trained our young lives to be able to march towards and take and make our own, for Macedon, for Greece, for ourselves.

I think of our time here, in Mieza, once more, and I think of our teacher, and what he whispered in my ear.

Temper him, Hephaestion, he'd said, softly.

And what else?

Give him love. Make sure that you always give him love, so that he gives all the rest of us love, too.

I will, teacher.

I promise.

I will do as you ask, for all of us.

CHAPTER ELEVEN

WHEN WE RETURN TO PELLA, we move back into the same room in the palace, and we find that even though nearly two years have passed, the room has remained exactly the same and completely unchanged: it looks as if we'd just left it earlier that morning, and are only returning from training or riding together in the hills. There is one difference, though, that comes after we arrive; the servants bring our things, and when they do, they leave them the way that they'd packed them, which means that they leave them together, all mixed in with each other, and they don't bother separating them. I wonder if Alexandros has told them to do this, or if they've just seen us, and watched us, and decided to do it on their own, because with the way that we live, it's of course fitting and practical. One day he'll wear my chiton, and I'll wear his, the seam higher on my thigh than it is on his thigh because I'm a full head taller than he is, and the next day it'll be the opposite. One day my sandals will be gone and so I'll wear his sandals, and that's how I find out that even though I might be taller than him, his feet are both longer and wider than mine. We begin to blur, both of us, we begin to run together, even more than we already have in Mieza, and before then, when we were here in Pella. I think again of what Aristoteles told me, in his study, in the Akademia.

One soul.

Two bodies.

I smile to myself as I remember his words, the ones I know I'll remember and hold close to my heart. He has a way with words, our teacher, and his reputation is well-earned; his thoughts are simple, but poignant and illuminating of the human condition in a way that's different from anyone else I've ever met.

I'm still young, though.

So who knows who is still out there to meet, what new philosopher we might discover in Athens, or Thebes, or Corinth, or another far and distant land or polis that we might travel to. After we return, though, we also learn that Philippos' wound is worse than we were told. The spear that killed his horse took him high in the leg, near the hip, and tore through a great deal of muscle. He refused medical attention—both on the field, and then after the battle, too—and so the wound became infected and he now walks with a very heavy limp, when he can even walk at all. I see him around the palace, hobbling in the courtyard, across the mosaic-tiled hallways, and he doesn't move like he used to move before, with great strides and purpose; now, he limps on his one good leg while Pausanius walks and supports him on the other side, giving him an arm to hold and steady himself. This must be difficult for a proud and once-strong man, I know, and when I pass them, I nod to Philippos, and then I do the same to Pausanius, but the guard just looks past me and into the distance, as he always does. He does this every time I see them together now, never meeting my eyes, like he did that first day, and I wonder why. I wonder what's happened, and what's changed, because something has, I can tell.

I won't waste time thinking of it, though.

We also learn that upon his return to Pella with his sixth wife, Philippos has decided to take yet another bride, which will be his seventh (and final, too, he says with a great laugh and grin so everyone who hears knows he actually has no intention to stop marrying). The girl's name is Eurydice, and she's just turned sixteen, which means she's even younger than the girl from the north, and is the same age as me and Alexandros. She's the daughter of Attalus, the man who controls all of Lower Macedon, and the ports on the sea there, and is one of Philippos' generals. I assume he's marrying her for pleasure, since there's no territory to gain or loyalty to ensure from someone who's already loyal and Macedonian, but Olympias and Alexandros disagree. They all call Olympias a barbarian, she says—all the Macedonian nobles call her this, behind their hands, behind her back, and they always have—and so by extension, they call her son the same thing, too. Foreigner. Interloper. *Alexandros-barbaros*. The same things they say about me, also, I know, but they don't whisper in such ways about Eurydice, Alexandros tells me. She's one of them, he says, a girl born from one of their great families and not the family of some distant tribe, even if it's the tribe descended of the great Achilleus, and that means something in Pella. So now Attalus and all the rest of his family pray and sacrifice to the gods that their new Macedonian basileia-to-be will bring the basileus a boy-child; they pray that she will bring Philippos a son of pure, undiluted Macedonian blood, because a Macedonian basileus deserves such a thing. There's a rising wave of nationalism, in the face of the impending war against the southern Greeks, seemingly brought on by the abstractness of the thought that what was once just us might now include them, too, and in the days after we return from Mieza, Alexandros spends a great deal of time alone with his mother, discussing this, listening to both her lies and her truths, and wondering what they should do.

I'm nervous, any time he's alone with her.

So instead of sitting in our room and waiting, and letting my thoughts wander, I leave. I go back down to the gymnasium first, and I find Kassandros, Philotas, and Nearchos throwing dice, and I join them. They drink more than I do, and they laugh more and slap each other on the back harder now, too, as I learn men tend to do in the moments and days before they go to war, especially for the first time. And though I join them, and I laugh and drink and slap them on the back, also, I don't feel like one of them anymore, and I realize perhaps I haven't for some time now. Was I ever? I was, I know, and I still am; I'm one of Alexandros' Companions, just the same as they are, but I can see in their eyes that it's different now. Their truth, my truth; their world, *our* world. Alexandros. Me and Alexandros. I can see they feel that's what we've become, and that our circle has split into us, up in the palace, and the rest of them, still down in their rooms off the gymnasium, and even though I'm one of them, I'm also not, too, because I'm more.

Why?

Because I'm more in the eyes of Alexandros.

I've explored much of Pella with him, but there's still so much of the capital I don't know, and so after I leave Kassandros and Philotas and Nearchos at the gymnasium, I enjoy taking the time to slowly discover parts of the city I haven't seen. I find I'm more comfortable in the lower parts, and amongst the people there, who remind me of my people, and so that's where I begin to go more often when Alexandros is away with his mother and so that's also where I meet her. I'm in the agora looking at a large bucket of soaking and marinating olives when it happens. I see that the olives are small and round and very black in color, so I know they must come from the south, where it's warmer, and the soil less rocky, like Aristoteles taught us. *Knowledge for the sake of knowledge.* I smile, remembering the phrase he used to say so often and which is an idea he made it his mission to impart on us, too, his pupils. We never know when the knowledge will be useful, we just know that all knowledge is, and so we will learn, we will strive to learn, as much as we can, always.

"Would you like to try one?" I hear a voice next to me.

I turn towards the voice, and that's when I see her for the first time.

It's a girl that's spoken and I think she seems to be about the same age as I am. She stands there and looks back at me, studying me, with large and perfectly round eyes like the olives she's selling, that are from the south. I don't answer. I don't have the words, which is new for me, a new feeling, and I feel something else unfamiliar, too, deep in my stomach. She waits, and I still don't answer, and then she smiles, knowing what my silence means—and probably the look on my face, too—and so she goes forward and takes one of the olives from the bucket. She holds it out to me, oil slipping from the smooth skin and collecting in her palm as she offers it, then dripping between fingers and to the ground beneath us as I hesitate.

"Go ahead," she says.

I smile.

Or, at least, I try to. I'm not sure what my lips actually do.

"Thank you," I tell her and take the olive from her palm.

I put it in my mouth and slowly, deliberately chew.

"What do you think?" she asks, watching me.

The olive tastes of salt and is flavored with an oil more bitter than I'm used to, I think, and it has the distinct flavor of something that's been exposed to the breeze coming off the sea. Which sea, though? The Aegean, to the east, or the Ionian, to the west, and the sea that's my sea? I don't know.

"It's good," I tell her, as I continue to chew, and then swallow.

"Just good?"

"It's softer than the ones we have here."

"That's because it's from the south," she smiles.

"Where in the south?"

"A town named Firai, in the Peloponnese. It's a half-day's ride west of Sparta, and it's a city that's famous for our dancing. Well, our dancing and our olives, too, of course, as you can taste," she smiles even wider now.

Halfway between the two seas, then.

Right in the middle, between them, in its own bay.

"What brings you all the way here, to Pella?"

"Money. What else?"

I raise my eyebrows, and so she explains.

"My family is in the olive business, as you can see," she tells me, gesturing towards the many large barrels filled with all different types of marinating olives. "My father has two brothers, and while one's stayed in Firai, to continue to sell the family goods at home, the other went to Athens, to sell our olives there in the great city, and my father came here."

"Why? There's more money in the south, and there are more mouths, too."

"Yes, but the olives are better there. Your olives here in the north are too tough, and they're not salty enough, and you use the wrong oil. Try another one. You know that I'm right. You'll try another one of my olives, and then you'll tell me that, too, that I'm right, and that you'll buy some. Perhaps even more than just some," she smiles. "You'll like them so much you might even buy a whole barrel."

"You drive a hard bargain," I laugh.

"I'm my father's daughter," she says, still smiling, then holds out another.

I wait for a moment, then I smile again, too, even wider.

I reach out and take the second olive from her and put it in my mouth and chew again, and she watches me. "You're from the palace, aren't you?" she asks, as I continue to chew, and then swallow.

"No," I shake my head.

"I've seen you walk there. You go past the gate and into the courtyard, and the guards recognize you and don't stop you or ask any questions. They just let you go right in."

"I live there."

"In the palace?"

"Yes."

"But you're not from there?"

"No."

"You'll of course forgive me if I don't understand."

"It's . . . complicated."

"Complicated how?"

I open my mouth, about to explain, but once more, no words come. She smiles again. It seems she knows much about inexperienced boys, boys that have only grown with other boys, and not enough girls, and no sisters, just brothers.

"I haven't seen much of the city," she says, to help me, to continue our conversation. "Perhaps you could show me around, and while we walk, maybe you might tell me?"

"Of course," I nod, feeling something in my stomach again, something strange that I don't often feel.

"Good," she says.

"Good," I say, too.

I can't stop smiling. I want to, but I can't.

And so she takes my hand, and then we go.

WE LEAVE AND WE WALK TOGETHER, back through the city. I ask her name and she tells me it's Helia, like the sun. She also tells me she was only joking about the barrel of olives, but if I did want one, she'd give me a good rate, she adds with a wink and a laugh. I laugh, too, when she does and when she tells me this, and when I do, she knows I'll buy some. I'm a man now, and a warrior, and warriors are paid by the basileus and what better way to spend my first few earned coins, I think, with her hand softly brushing against mine as we walk, our arms at our side, touching each other's as they move with the rhythm of our bodies and strides.

Each time they touch, I feel something.

Excitement. Anticipation. Electricity.

I don't know the city as well as I should, but I do the best I can as a guide in a place where I still think of myself as a foreigner, too, and I show her all the places I know, and the ones I don't? We can discover those together. We keep walking and we keep talking and she asks me about the mountains, and Illyria, and my mother, and younger brother, that I left behind there. "No sister?" she asks, with a smile, and I laugh and tell her no, I don't have a sister. I answer her other questions, too, I answer all of them, and I look at her as we walk, deep into her southern eyes, and I still smile. I can't stop. Why? I don't know. The girls where I'm from are tall, dark, and strong of feature with paler skin, but she's instead lighter, and softer of feature, with darker skin, and she's short, shorter even than Alexandros, and everything about her radiates a beauty of which I don't know enough, though I want to; I very much want to, I want to know more, I want to know so much more. We go past the blacksmith, where I went with Alexandros, the first day that we met. Then we soon come to the gymnasium, and we go past it, too. Leonnatos and Perdiccas are there and standing outside, talking and passing a skin of wine between them, and they look at us, curiously, as we walk past, and I know why, of course. I don't say anything to them, though. I just raise my arm in greeting, and so do they, watching us with raised eyebrows, and we continue on and past them.

"Friends?" she asks, once we're out of ear-shot.

"More," I tell her.

She seems to understand this as she doesn't ask anything further about it as we climb higher into the city, and then we come to the great temple, and the god it was built to honor.

Dionysus.

Olympias' god, and Macedon's god.

Is he Alexandros' god, too?

Helia slips her hand into mine now, as we stand there, in front of the temple. She slips her fingers between my fingers so that they do more than just touch now, as we stand there, and then she moves our hands so they rest against my thigh, just below the hem of my chiton, where there's skin. Electricity. More electricity. We continue on from the temple and we go to the stables. I offer her a horse to ride—any that's there and that she thinks might suit her, I tell her—but she tells me that she doesn't ride very well on her own, that she rides better with others, and so I lead the brown from his stall and expertly tie reins around his head and cheeks in familiar and practiced movements. I lay the loop of worn leather across his mane, like I always do, then I jump up and swing my leg over his back in a single, fluid motion. When I'm there, and in the place where I ride, I reach my hand down and take hers and pull her up after me, so that she sits there, too, in front of me and where I sit.

She smiles and I try not to, again, but I still do. I can feel her in front of me, her body between my legs as I take the reins from the place where they lay. I can feel her between my arms, her back pressed against my stomach and chest, and I can smell her hair as it tickles my nose and neck, under my chin.

We leave the stables and ride through the city.

I don't know where else to take her, and so I go north, into the hills and the mountains and to the place where I go with Alexandros, or at least the place that we used to go, before we left for Mieza. I hold her as we ride, one hand gripping the reins to guide the horse and the other resting across the front of her waist, to hold and protect her, and I hold her especially tight when we come to the river and the brown jumps down the bank and into the water and begins to swim across and Helia lets out a little scream of excitement as he does. The water splashes up and over both of us, and then I smile even wider when the little scream of excitement becomes a laugh and she reaches out and down and feels the cool water that comes to our knees as the horse swims through it. We reach the other side and the brown climbs onto the bank and then out, where he shakes the water from him, and I hold Helia even tighter, so that she doesn't fall, as he shakes, and then we continue. She lets her head roll back and to the side, so it rests gently against my shoulder. I can feel her, and I can feel the sun, too, warm, penetrating, the rays making us perspire so that our skin sticks together, in the places where it touches.

We keep riding and we finally get to the top of the mountain and the lake that before has only been our lake, and I get off the brown, and then help her off, too, after me, holding her in my arms and gently lifting her back down to the grass. She stands there with me and she looks around. She asks what I normally do when I come here to this place, and I tell her that I normally swim in the lake. I think that she's going to hesitate, because I'm a boy, and she's a girl, but she doesn't. She doesn't do anything except take off all her clothes, as if she were Alexandros, and I'm still Hephaestion, and then walk towards the water and go in. Is it cold? I don't know. My eyes are on her. My eyes are on her body;

the curves, the golden skin and hair, all the things I haven't seen or felt in some time, since I've been in Pella.

"Are you coming?" she asks, looking over her shoulder at me.

I uncinch my belt and then take my chiton off, too, so that I'm naked, also, and I follow in after her. I walk behind where she walks, and then when I'm once again next to her, I stand there, behind her, taller than her, and we're together, there in the water, her body in front of mine and my arms wrapped around and holding her.

She can feel me.

I know that she can feel me, pressing against her, and then a breeze comes and she starts to shiver so I wrap my arms tighter and pull her even closer. We stay like that for a moment, and then the breeze passes, and the sun comes again, and we turn and walk back out of the lake. I lead her away from the water and towards where the brown grazes on the short-cropped grass, as he normally does with Bucephalus by his side, but this time he's by himself, and we go to the place where I normally sit with Alexandros, on the bluff, looking out and over all of Macedon, and we sit there together.

I look at her, next to me.

She looks at me.

"Well?" she asks.

"Well, what?" I respond, swallowing.

"Bold on the battlefield, but nowhere else?" she smiles. "Are all you boys the same?"

I still hesitate.

She looks back at me.

Then I move closer, and I close my eyes as my head moves forward, and so does hers, and then they're together, and my lips finally, finally, finally find her lips. I expect her to taste of salt and sea, the same as the olives she sells, but she doesn't; she tastes of honey, I think, sweet and fresh. Is it something she puts on her lips? Or is it her? I don't know. There are still so many mysteries in this world that I don't know. She puts her hand on my chest, as we kiss, feeling it and the muscles that I know are there, and then her lips move away from mine and her hand pushes on me so that I move further down, and then I lay on the ground, rather than sit, and she moves closer. She swings one of her legs over my chest so that she's on top of me, one leg on either side of my body, and she bends her head down, too, and her hair covers my face and tickles my cheeks again as her lips find mine once more and presses against them.

Honey. Sugar.

I kiss her back, in her place on top of me.

She calls me prinkipas.

She leans even lower, and whispers it, into my ear, as I kiss her neck now.

Hephaestion-prinkipas, she breathes. *Prince Hephaestion.*

I swallow and let my head fall back.

"We're closer to the gods here, in the clouds, don't you think?" she whispers.

"Yes," I nod, and I speak quietly, too.

"So let's be gods together, then, while we're with them," she says then moves again, in a different way, while she's on top of me, and that's then when it begins.

I gasp when it does.

I don't want to because I want to seem experienced, but I'm not, and so I do, and I can see that she likes that. Perhaps this is what the gods feel, as she's said; perhaps this is what the gods do, too, and I think of the girl that I knew, down by the docks in Salona, and I think of her because this isn't like it was when we had been together. She had been shy, and younger, and she had waited for me to lead, to guide, to place and show things that I didn't even know myself.

It's not like that with Helia, though. It's not like that being with the sun.

She controls our pleasure.

She controls everything, and so with her, that makes everything different.

It's also better this way, I find.

She guides, and leads, and she brings to me something I've never experienced before.

I can only hope I'm able to do the same for her.

I'm not sure, but I hope.

When it's over, we stop, and we rest, catching our breath as we lay next to each other there on the ground. The sun rises above us, even higher now than it was before, when we were in the lake, this great and powerful thing that brings heat and fire and from which she gets her name. Now I know why, too, because I can feel all those things when I'm with her.

Her hand brushes against mine, and then her arm falls across my stomach, and it rests there as I breathe in deep and powerful breaths, up and down, up and down, up and down.

Then she rolls over and on top of me again.

When the second time is done, we still lay there and rest on the ground, and this time I'm the one that moves and I turn my body so I rest my head gently on her stomach, and we stay like that. We *are* closer to the gods here, aren't we? And maybe Helia was right, and that we're gods, too, even if it's only for a moment, while we're together, and two is temporarily one. One of her hands rests on my cheek as the other moves higher and she gently runs her fingers in little circles through my hair. I've never felt this before, or had someone do it, and I find that I like it and she can feel that I like it. She asks me why I don't have a beard, or why Leonnatos or Perdiccas, who we saw when we passed the barracks, don't have beards, either. We could grow them if we wanted to, she says, still stroking my cheek, my hair, but it's clear that we don't and that we shave and that we do it often—every day, even, she notices—to keep the facial hair away. No boys would do that where she's from, she tells me, and so I tell her it was something started by Alexandros, and that we've followed him.

"Really?" she asks.

"Yes."

"Why?"

"Do you really want to hear about soldiers, and war?" I ask her.

"I'm Greek," she laughs, "and I was born in the Peloponnese, next to Sparta. In fact, most of the boys I grew up with were Spartans. So of course I want to hear about soldiering and war. I might even know more about it than you think."

I smile.

I wonder if she can see it, if she can see my lips, too, as her fingers twist and move and glide through my hair.

So, then, I tell her.

I tell her how Alexandros says that beards can be used against us, in battle, by an opponent grabbing or pulling on it in close quarters, and it's just one of the many things he's thought of during his youth and time at Pella, and the planning and thinking he's done. She nods when she hears this, and I ask her about Sparta and the boys she knew there and she confirms all the things we've heard in the north; she confirms all the myths and legends, and the hardships that are endured and the skills as a soldier and as a man that are created and made because of those hardships and trials. They sound just as fearsome when she describes them as they do in the stories about Xerxes and Thermopylae, and their mighty stand at the hot gates, which happened three generations before ours.

These are the stories I love. I want her to tell more.

She smiles. She won't.

"No more talk of other men," she says, then bends down and kisses me once more, her hair spilling across my face again as she does and then she moves back to her place on top of me, on top of my chest, her legs again on either side of my body, and we make love once more.

It's the same as it was the first two times.

It's intense, passionate, consuming, and I give myself to her, I give as much of myself to her as I can possibly give, so that I can hopefully bring to her even just a small bit of what she's brought and given to me.

I hope that I do.

I wonder, and I hope, but it's just my body that I give to her, though, I know; it's just my body, and my flesh, because my soul? That's something I realize I can't give, because it already has been, to another.

WHEN I GET BACK TO OUR ROOM in the palace, Alexandros is gone, but he soon returns, only a few minutes after I do. He asks about my day after he walks in, and what I did while he was with his mother. Can he tell where I was, and what happened? I don't know because he doesn't usually ask this, but whether he already knows or not, I tell him anyways; I tell him all of it, everything. I tell him about Helia, and how I met her, and where we went, and what we did when we were there. He doesn't react. Perhaps it's my voice, or perhaps it's my words and the way I say them, or perhaps it's because of how he understands sex and that for him, as he's already told me, it's something that makes him feel weak, and mortal, so perhaps he thinks that's how it makes others feel, too. Or maybe it's because of how I've learned he experiences connection between humans, and that true connection for him isn't physical, that true connection is instead something of the mind, and soul, and spirit, which is where we're vulnerable and weak and able to be broken, which also means, in those places where we break, that's where we can be remade, and where two can then be fashioned into one. He's become a strong warrior, with all the training we've done, but this moment lets me know, once again, that his greatest strength is also something else.

I ask him about his own day, after he asks of mine, and he tells me.

He tells me about the worries of his mother in regards to Philippos' new wife, Eurydice, and that the child that will surely soon come from their union will not only be the son of the basileus, but also the grandson of one of Macedon's most prominent nobles, from one of Macedon's most important families. So he'll have the support of the other nobles, and perhaps even the army, too, and so they are now added to all the others, all those who wish to wear the crown that Philippos wears.

Amyntas.
Arrhidaeus.

Attalus, and his daughter.

Enemies everywhere, enemies on all sides.

We go to sleep, and we talk no more of it, and then the next day, Alexandros wakes and leaves again, early in the morning, and so with nothing else to do, I decide to go back to Helia's stall. I walk to the lower part of the city, and then go to the agora again, and I see her, and go to her, but she doesn't have time to go back up to the lake, she tells me. She's curt and only has a few moments to talk, she says, so she pulls me to the side and down an alley she's discovered near where she sells her olives, and we make love again, right there. She pulls me closer to her, against the wall, and then after it's done, we stand for a moment, together, breathing heavily, my skin pressed against her skin, my forehead against her forehead, my sweat mixed with her sweat, and I think we're going to talk, like she said, and like we did before.

But we don't.

She simply adjusts her clothing, back into place and as it was before, and then turns and leaves. She says nothing further; she just goes, leaving me alone.

I breathe in, watching her go.

I breathe in again, and then I breathe out, thinking about what just happened and realizing I don't like it. I don't like it at all.

And that's then when I see them.

I see Aria, first, walking through the agora and holding someone's hand next to her, and then I see the person she's walking with, and the man whose hand she's holding, and it's Amyntas. They go together, between the stalls, looking at the different wares and foods and things that are for sale. They look at the olives, first, and then the spices from Asia, and also the fine silks that have been imported from Egypt with dyes next to them that can turn the silks any color the customer might want, any color the customer can possibly imagine, rather than the typical and traditional bleached white. They look at all these things, and then he leans over, closer, next to her and he whispers something into her ear and she throws her head back and laughs.

She looks at him, up at him.

Then she stands on her toes and pushes her lips up and towards his lips, and they kiss, right there, in the agora, in front of everyone.

They continue on, and through the rest of the stalls.

I watch them as they go, and then I think about what I thought, last night, when I was with Alexandros, and I think of it again.

Enemies.

Enemies everywhere, on all sides; enemies all around.

WHEN I GET BACK TO OUR ROOM, Alexandros is already there this time and sitting on his bed studying a map of southern Greece that's marked with roads and distances and other logistical and military calculations scribbled onto it in black ink. He looks up when I come in, and smiles, and I wonder what's changed his mood, but I don't ask. Instead, I tell him what I saw. I know what it will do to him, and I don't want to hurt him, but I also know that I have to tell him because he needs to know. He's silent for a moment, once he hears, and the smile slowly fades and then leaves, and then after one more moment, he turns and shakes his head and looks down at the map again.

"Did you know that she was with him?" I ask him.

"We were gone for a long time. It was never going to be the same, when we came back."

"I know. But *him*? Of all the people in Pella?"

"She can be with whoever she wants."

"Alexandros..."

Silence.

"May father says that he's ready," Alexandros finally answers, softly.

"What?" I frown.

"He says that he's finally ready to leave, and to go south."

"Do you believe him?"

"No, he can barely walk. But he says it can't wait, and so we'll go anyways."

More silence.

We take that in, both of us.

All that we've trained for, all that we've lived for, at least thus far, together, will now soon be upon us, and I swallow. I also of course take in how and why Alexandros has changed the subject, which answers my question. He may be different than most, but he's still human, too; he's still mortal, and still a young man, which means he still has pride, and pride can be hurt and bruised and trampled. Pride can also, after all those things, then rise again, I know.

"What happened to change your father's mind and force his hand?" I ask, instead of more questions about Aria.

"Some of the farmers in Amphissa have started cultivating land that's supposed to be sacred to Apollo. The Amphictyonic Council has asked Philippos to come and intervene to stop them."

"They've asked him south, with his whole army, to stop some farmers?"

"Yes."

"Which has also given him the excuse he needs."

"Exactly," Alexandros nods, "and the one he's been waiting for. He doesn't need an excuse, not really, after the Athenians broke their oath and defended Perinthos and Byzantios, which are supposed to be ours, but that's the formal reason he'll give for marching south. Demosthenes has already made a speech in Athens calling us barbarians again, and now power-mad, too, on top of that. Power-mad, conquering, land-hungry barbarians who know nothing of the sacred and precious gods and their wishes for freedom and democracy and how we should all either live, or aspire to live."

"Athens pretends they know nothing of conquest, or slavery, when their entire polis is built on it."

"It's of course not the first time a politician has lied," Alexandros says, sideways, finally with a smile on his lips again, which I'm glad to see, "or the first time one has used his lies to manipulate those who listen to him, who want to hear that the world is as he tells them it is, and nothing more, or nothing further and simply that simple."

"And I'm sure it won't be the last time, either."

"No. For there to be prophets, there must also be false-prophets."

"People are fools."

"Some. But there are also still some that have things in them such as this world has never seen, and it's them who will define both who and what we are, and in ways we haven't even yet imagined. And those are the ones we will seek, Hephaestion. We'll seek those lions, and not the other men, the small and scared ones."

"When do we leave?"

"Two days after tomorrow. Philippos has sent word to the generals to prepare the army."

So it will be soon, with barely time to think of what we'll be marching towards and what it might mean and all else that will follow. I look at Alexandros. He still sits on his bed, across from me, and hasn't looked up yet. I sit down, too, on his bed, and move closer to him so that our shoulders are touching, like they so often do, then I reach out and put my arm around him. He waits for a minute. Then he lays his head on my shoulder, next to him. This will be the moment. This will be the last moment of childhood, of youth, and of the way that we grew here and together and away from all that we will now face and endure and become.

This will be our last moment.

Then the moment ends, as moments always do, and Alexandros stands.

I look at him now, above me. "Are you alright?" I ask.

"Of course," he answers, adjusting his chiton, then cinching the belt at his waist even tighter.

He walks towards the door.

"Where are you going?"

He hears me, I know that he does.

But he doesn't answer. He just leaves.

I WAIT FOR ALEXANDROS, but he doesn't come back, not any time during the night, and he's not there when I wake, either. I wait the entire morning for him in our room, and when he doesn't return, I leave and go to the agora on my own to find Helia once more because I know I need to tell her. She has time for me today, she says, when I ask, which means that she has time for more than just the alley, I guess. So we leave and go to the stables again to get the brown and then ride back up into the mountains, and to the lake. We swim again, together, like we did before, naked and hot under the bright and strong Macedonian sun, and then we lay on the grass at the edge of the bluff above the city. She runs her hand through my hair again, in the way that she did before, and that she knows now that I like, her fingers moving in tight little circles, and after we finish with our love, once, twice, and then once more again after that, too, my head rests on her stomach. She doesn't speak, after I tell her what will now come and what we're leaving to go do, and I don't speak, either. I'm glad, because there's no war here, or anything else, and so I just lay there with my head in her lap and her hand on my cheek and we stay like that for some time, watching the sun as it moves above us, finally beginning its slow descent over the mountains in the west, *my* mountains, and then after some time, we stand, without speaking, and after we dress I pull her back up and onto the brown, in front of me, and we ride back down to Pella.

We go through the city.

When we get back to the stables, I put the brown away in his stall, and then I kiss Helia, and tell her goodbye, and that I'll see her one last time tomorrow, before we ride out, and then she leaves, and so do I. She lets her lips linger on mine, before we go, her hand pressed on my chest, my heart, and I wonder about that because she hasn't done it before, and then she turns and heads back down towards the agora and her father and their olives and I begin back up and towards the palace.

I think Alexandros will finally be waiting for me, in our room, when I return.

But he's not.

I wait and I wait, but he doesn't come back that night, and he's not there again the next morning, either, when I wake: his bed remains unused and undisturbed, all of his things exactly where he left them the last time he was there.

There's nothing else for me to do.

So I search for some coins, and then go back into the city.

I walk down past the great Temple of Dionysus, and then continue on, and that's where all the activity is: soldiers construct new sarissas in the street, sharpening the blades on the ends of them until they're polished, deadly, thin, sanding the wooden pikes the blades are attached to until there are no splinters and the wood is completely smooth and strong and ready. They beat the worn and deep dents out of their shields, the dents received from the last campaign in the north they've only just returned from. There's a line outside the blacksmith for those waiting for a new or sharpened xiphos, and some of the men that are waiting are young, like I am, about to experience their first battle, and who are there waiting for their first xiphos. Some of them are not young, too; some are the grizzled veterans of many long and brutal campaigns, Philippos' strong and battle-tested veterans of a thousand northern wars.

I keep walking.

The streets are busy and full, much more so than they usually are.

I go past horses and men, riding and shouting, and women and children, buying food to pack and thread to make fresh chitons and chlamys for travelling, and fighting, doing everything they can to help prepare their men for another campaign of indeterminate length and time and hardship.

Then I come to the agora.

Many of the stalls are empty, and many of the merchants are already gone. Macedon is a kingdom that's dedicated to one thing, and one thing only, and Pella is its capital, its beating heart, and when war comes, the heart of Macedon leaves and travels along with the army; the heart doesn't stay here in the city. So I see that there's no more silk being sold, or dye imported from Egypt; there's no more fish from the Aegean being bartered and traded. I keep walking, then I turn around the corner, and I look towards Helia's stall, where she sold her wares with her father, and I see that she's gone, too. I've brought the coins to buy a barrel of olives from her, as I'd promised, but I see that they're both already gone, along with everything else they'd brought with them, and so now there's no more soft black olives from the south that are being sold in Pella, either. I look, for one more moment, the rest of the world carrying on around me, and perhaps without me, too, as I also feel sometimes, then I put the coins back away, turn in the opposite direction, and head back up and towards the palace and the much-dreamed about future that will now come.

CHAPTER TWELVE

I SIT ON THE BROWN outside the palace, and I hold the reins of Bucephalus, who waits next to me. The three days since I last saw Alexandros have passed, without any further sign of him, and the moment to leave is now upon us. The whole army's gathered. I wait near the other Companions, who are also on their impatient horses, our hands reaching behind us and anxiously gripping and re-gripping the handles of the Kritin broad-swords that we wear across our backs and between our shoulders. We feel the familiar leather that's there, wrapped tightly around metal hilts, and we do this because we know what lies at the end of the road we'll now take, and that the long-waited-for blood will now soon come. We each feel differently, I'm sure. We'll each handle it differently, too, I'm also sure.

How?

I don't know.

But if there's one thing that's certain, it's that we'll soon find out.

Behind where we wait, the rest of the hetairoi cavalry sit their horses, also, with the pezhetairoi foot soldiers behind the hetairoi, and they all wait, just as we do, for the word from Philippos that will send us south and to the future. We're nervous for a different reason, though, we Companions, and the reason isn't death. Death has never brought fear for us, nor had a place in our hearts; it's something else.

"Is he coming?" Philotas asks, from his place next to me, his words just a whisper between us.

I know who and what he's talking about, of course, and it isn't death, or Philippos, it's what all the Companions sit here and wonder.

I don't know the answer, though.

"Of course he's coming," I whisper back, with more confidence than I feel.

"Where's he been the last week?" Kassandros speaks now, louder.

"Why hasn't he been at the gymnasium, or the barracks?" Ptolemaios frowns.

"We've trained our whole lives for this," Leonnatos says. "And now, what, he's just . . . nowhere to be seen?"

"He's *coming*," I tell them.

I say this to Leonnatos, and I say it to all the rest of them, too, with as much strength as I can summon to quiet them with the words I don't want any other to hear. I may not know all of Alexandros, at least not yet, but this much I do know: he wouldn't be late for this unless there was a very good reason.

Behind us, Philippos finally emerges from the palace, with Antipater walking behind him. The basileus comes into the courtyard and heads towards the large, grey stallion that he rides when he's in the capital and that waits for him at the very front of the army, next to Parmenion, who's already mounted and holds the reins of his friend's horse, the same way I do, too. Philippos stands there for a moment, when he gets to the great horse, and I find this strange. What's he waiting for? And then Pausanius quickly comes and bends down to grab Philippos on the shin below the knee and help push him up and onto the stallion's back. This is a first for Philippos, to need assistance like this, I realize, and I also realize the wound to his leg is definitely worse than we've all probably thought, or been led to believe, and not getting better. He sits the horse and winces and shifts uncomfortably with the leg hanging at an unorthodox angle that's not normal for a rider of his skill. Once he's on the stallion, though, Parmenion comes forward to take his place at Philippos' right hand, as strategos, and Attalus comes to take his place on the other side of Philippos, his left, as Pausanius goes to his own horse and jumps up and onto its back and moves to his place behind the basileus. Antipater, who will remain in Pella as regent-basileus while Philippos and the army are away, walks amongst the gathered troops to inspect them. He comes towards us and the hetairoi first, and goes between us, then moves on and past us and to the larger group of pezhetairoi, and once he's gone through all the lines and inspected all the soldiers, he goes to stand across the courtyard from us, by the palace.

"Good?" Philippos asks his friend, his second oldest friend.

There's a moment, and a look between them, the two men.

We have our dreams and our lives, I know, me and Alexandros, and the Companions, but they've had theirs, too, I realize, and this is a culmination of those dreams for them; for Philippos, and Antipater, and Parmenion, who were also young and grew together. This is a culmination of those who had been Companions before we were, and this thing that they most desired—to go south, and conquer all the rest of Greece, together—it's now here, and upon them, and it's upon us, too.

"Perfect," Antipater nods to the basileus.

Then there's another noise in the distance.

I turn to see a rider coming from behind us, from the cavalry, kicking his horse to a trot, and I think it's going to be Alexandros, but it's not: it's a warrior that's broken from amongst the hetairoi and rides towards us, first, then past us, and when he goes by, I see who it is.

Amyntas.

We all watch as he rides past where we sit our horses and he goes to where Philippos is with Parmenion and Attalus and takes his place with them, there at the very front of the army. I look at Philippos, who doesn't seem to register this. I know he does, though, because he registers everything, which means he won't stop Amyntas, or tell him to go back to the rank and file. I've heard the soldiers speak about Amyntas myself, since we've returned—of the boy who was to be basileus before Philippos, and who is now a man himself, in his own right—and they talk about how he's ridden at the basileus' side, and his exploits at Chersonesus, in the campaign against the Thracians. The soldiers all love him, they told me, as he's always the very first among them into battle and he fights with a ferocity that reminds them of Philippos himself, when he was young, and he takes as many women as Philippos used to take after a battle, also, the soldier told me with a wide grin and an un-sly wink.

Soldiers.

Men and the way they talk, when they're alone and without women. I look away.

I glance at Pausanius, who sits on a small, light-colored horse, behind the basileus, and I wonder again about Amyntas and Philippos and how the men speak of them and that's when I finally see Alexandros. He comes from the palace, too, and walks towards the army. He's in full-armor, completely dressed for battle with the bright and multi-pointed Argead star embossed in gold on the front of his breast-plate, and his broad-sword strapped across his back. And then, once I see him, I see who it is that walks with him, next to him, at his side.

Olympias.

Of course.

Philippos turns to look, too, at the commotion, and when he sees her and this spectacle she's created, this entrance for her son, Philippos rolls his eyes and looks away. Cleopatra comes from the palace, also, and Alexandros goes to his sister and hugs her first, kisses her on each cheek, and then whispers something into her ear. I glance at Ptolemaios as Alexandros does this, the same as I did the last time we left, and just the same as before, Ptolemaios doesn't move. A muscle flickers in his cheek again, though, ever so slightly, but he doesn't move. There are no words for him, or from her. He just watches. Olympias stays next to Cleopatra as Alexandros walks towards us and comes to where I wait with his great horse. In one practiced and smooth motion he jumps up and swings his leg easily over the horse's back, and once he's there, he sits tall on Bucephalus. From where he's at now, on the back of his great and wild horse, who is indeed wild—for any that would try to touch or ride him without Alexandros, or perhaps myself, would be thrown in under five seconds—and once he's there, Alexandros sits taller than any other soldier in all the gathered army. From where he's at now, he sits taller than anyone else in Macedon, I know, and very likely all the rest of Greece, too, and he sits taller than even I had remembered.

Heads turn and eyes are drawn to him.

He looks the part: he looks every inch the part, thanks to his great and magnificent horse.

I nod.

Alexandros-prinkipas.

No, I shake my head.

Alexandros-basileus.

Even Amyntas turns and looks as the sun seems to shine a little brighter when Alexandros is among us. Is it a trick of perception, or a generational and divine gift of presence? I don't know, and then there's no more time for thoughts, or anything else, as a loud horn is sounded and Philippos kicks his grey stallion forward. Behind him, the army begins to move, too. The clouds return as we start to leave, and I glance over at Olympias, who stays staring stone-faced at her son; she hasn't looked at her husband once. I wonder the last time she has, or spoken with him, or been to his bed-chamber. There was love there once, I know that there was. Or at least passion, a pure and unbridled passion and obsession. What happened? My eyes move and next to Olympias I see tears on Cleopatra's cheek and I smile at her as we pass, or at least I try to, and she sees me, and she smiles back. Who are her tears for, though? Perhaps they're for more than one. Then, I realize, perhaps they're for none at all, and they're for something else. *Her.* Her place in this world. Perhaps her tears are just that, and they're for her, and for what the world has done, and her unfair place in all this as she's left behind to do nothing except wait.

WE RIDE FOR TWO DAYS, once we leave Pella, then we come to Amphissa, and we stop. These are the fields that are supposed to be sacred because they're the fields that belong to Apollo, and part of being the sacred fields of a powerful god means they must always remain untilled, lest the wrath of that god is risked. The villagers have decided to take the fields over, though, and plant their crops in defiance of the will of the god, and that's the pretense under which Philippos has brought us all south. He's claimed great offense at this, on behalf of Apollo, and the other gods, too, because if one sacred thing can be destroyed, then what about the others? If one sacred law can be flaunted, then are there really any laws at all? He of course doesn't believe this, but he's used it as his reason, and when we come to the tilled fields at dusk, we see that they're unimpressive: a flat and rocky area of land without many crops planted, and nothing much else around them, besides a few low and spaced hills.

The Amphissan farmers scatter, when they see us.

I don't blame them, and I would run, too, if all of a sudden on the horizon and marching towards me and the place where I'd broken the sacred law there was a swirling cloud of dust and then, from that dust, thirty thousand pezhetairoi with polished shields and long, fearsome sarissa glinting sunlight from metal, as if summoned by the mortally-offended Apollo himself. Then along with the thirty thousand pezhetairoi, and in front of them, there's of course the two thousand hetairoi, among which I ride with Alexandros and the rest of the Companions, and all the others of various ages who ride with us as well.

Once the villagers run from the fields, when we appear and they see all this, they don't come back, and neither does anyone else. So we take the fields that we came to take without any battle or incident, and we make our camp there.

The soldiers all get to work raising and staking tents as the sun sinks behind our shoulders, and as soon as camp is struck, and the tents arranged and lifted, we're summoned to a war council: Philippos, Parmenion the strategos, Attalus, Amyntas, another older soldier named Cleitus (who is called "the Black" by his men, I know, but for reasons that I don't yet) and Alexandros, myself, and the rest of the Companions. It's noteworthy for us to be invited to this council, because it's the first time we've been included in any meaningful affairs of war and the basileus. Why have we been invited? If I'm being honest, I'm not really sure, but I think it must have something to do with Aristoteles, and what Phillipos has heard from him about Alexandros, and about us. I look around when we reach Philippos' tent, at the others who have been invited, and I'm surprised to see that Arrhidaeus is there, too, and that he's also dressed in armor with a bright Argead Star on the front, though I imagine it's for tradition and out of respect only, and that he won't be expected to fight.

I see Alexandros look at him curiously, too, and his armor.

Then Philippos, who is in front of us, begins.

"We're in southern Greece now," he tells us, looking at all his generals and everyone that's gathered, and even though he walks with a limp and his body has begun to weaken and betray him, his eyes are as quick and sharp as they've ever been, and his voice is still full, loud, strong. This is what he's wanted, he tells us, what we as Macedonians have worked and trained and innovated for, and now after arriving in the south and making our camp, the first thing that's been done is a letter has been sent to Thebes, asking for a re-affirmation of their allegiance. Athens will have heard of the Macedonian movement south and will have sent a letter to Thebes, also, Philippos tells us, and so now the moment will come: Thebes will have to decide which side they are on, and who they will support, and that will in turn decide if there will be war or peace. Athens already has the support of Achaea, Troezen, Chalcis, Epidaurus, Megara, and Corinth, but without the support of Thebes, they wouldn't dare stand against Macedon.

"And what if they *do* have the support of Thebes?" Cleitus asks.

"Then I suppose it will be war," Philippos looks at him, through his still-good eye, "and we won't have marched all this way just to scare some farmers from these shitty fields," he finishes, and they both smile.

Warriors.

Old warriors.
And old friends, too.
When I see them, do I see future?
I feel as if I should, but I'm not sure that I do.
Why?
Because I'm not from here, I'm not one of them, and perhaps my future lies elsewhere because I have my own people who are not these people.

"What of Sparta?" I hear Alexandros ask, from his place next to me.

Philippos turns from his generals to look at him and he studies his second son with his one still-good eye. "A soldier always recognizes another soldier," Philippos answers, more slowly now. "Cleomenes-basileus has traditionally left us in peace, so I will pay him the same courtesy. The Peloponnese and his polis are his, and will remain so, as long as they stay there. I have no interest in Sparta, or him, or their peninsula."

Alexandros nods.

All the rest of us nod, too, very glad of that.

"Athens is only two days away," I hear another deep and strong voice, and I turn to see Amyntas, at the place where he's moved to stand next to Philippos, which is not lost on me, either. "We could be at their doorstep before they know it, and before Demosthenes has a chance to give another speech and gain more support. We could be there before their letter arrives at Thebes, or the Thebans even have a chance to respond, and we could crush them."

"This isn't just about conquering," Philippos turns towards his nephew now. "We have to rule these people, and their poleis, after we conquer them, so we must do it the right way, and the fair way, otherwise they'll never accept us as rulers and me as basileus."

"They'll never accept us anyways. Every other word out of their mouth is *democracy*," Amyntas spits, almost as if it's the most distasteful thing he can imagine. "They'll accept *no one* as basileus, not anymore, and after what they've allowed themselves to become here in the south."

"Yes, they will."

"How do you know?"

"Because they'll have to, won't they?"

Philippos says this and his eyes flash and for all the roughness he's known for and that I've seen, too, since my time in Pella began, I realize now why he's been able to expand Macedon into the power it's become, and how. Most rulers in our world and of our tribe understand the sword, but he understands the crown, too, and it's all the more shocking when the big, bearded, barrel-chested basileus with the reputation for fighting and drinking and little else is equally adept at diplomacy and politics and reading and inspiring the hearts of men. I've never seen him like this, either, in his element as basileus, and the light that it brings to his dark eyes is something I've only ever seen in one other, and it's because I've seen it in the eyes of his son.

"So it will be, as the basileus has said," Parmenion nods.

"I'll let you know their response, when it comes," Philippos tells us, and then waves his hand in dismissal and to let us know the meeting is over, so we all leave.

Alexandros is closer to the flap and walks out first, and then I follow after, along with the others. Everyone begins to go their separate directions, heading back towards their tents as the sun starts to sink, but Amyntas walks directly towards Alexandros. He stands in front of him, blocking his way, and even with how much Alexandros has grown, Amyntas is still much taller and much stronger, and he's now battle-tested, too. I can see the pale white scars on his arms and legs to prove it, and the arrogance in the smirk on his face. They stand there for a moment, Amyntas posturing, Alexandros simply looking back at him. Then I move to Alexandros' side so he's not alone when he faces this. I look at Amyntas, too, and while he's still bigger and stronger than me, even, it's close, and if I had to wager, I'd bet on myself and my broad-sword against him and his short xiphos.

"Sparta?" Amyntas finally says, as he looks back and forth between us, the smirk plastered on his face getting wider, and then he leans in, closer to Alexandros. "They fuck boys like you in Sparta, little cousin," he speaks louder now, so that the others around can hear. "You do know that, don't you?" he asks.

Alexandros is silent.

Netiher of us answer, we just stare back at him.

"Of course you do," he finishes with a smirk, then nods his head towards me. "That's probably why you want to go, isn't it?"

Then he laughs, loudly, so that all the others can see and hear, too.

There's another moment, another smirk, towards both of us, then he turns and starts to leave. He walks with his loping and arrogant stride back towards where the rest of the men he fights with are building fires and already reaching for their jugs and skins of wine. They've just heard and seen what he's said and done, as Amyntas wanted, and they pat him on the back as he joins them, and they hand him a skin, and he drinks long and deep. He wipes his mouth, then tips the skin back and drinks again, as they all laugh now, too, and cheer for him, and he finishes the skin and tosses it aside and reaches for another.

We stand there, watching. Neither of us move.

I think Alexandros is going to be upset, especially because all the Companions have stopped and watched this, too, behind us, but he isn't. He isn't upset at all. "I thought he would have been a more difficult opponent," he finally says, very simply, and loudly, too, in his own right, and then turns to look at the others, all the rest of the Companions, all of them except me. "I thought he would have been more clever," he says, emphasizing the last word.

"He's strong," Perdiccas warns.

"Being strong is only half a basileus," Alexandros answers. "Haven't we all seen that today?"

I turn and look at the rest of the Companions, who watch Alexandros, and then they nod at his words, and begin to leave, too, back to their tents, to ready themselves for what will now come. Once they're gone, I touch Alexandros on the arm because I know that despite his words and his smile, this has affected him.

"Let's go, too," I say.

He stands there and he stays staring straight ahead, not meeting my eyes, though he reaches up and puts his hand on top of mine, there on his shoulder.

Then he shakes his head. "No," he finally says.

"What?" I ask.

"Not yet. There's something else first."

"What else is there?"

"It's outside of camp."

"Outside of camp where?"

But he doesn't answer and just starts to walk again, and I sigh, and then I do what I always do and follow after him. He walks through the camp, between and past all the tents that are raised now in their neat and ordered rows, and then he finally comes to where Bucephalus waits and is tied next to the brown. I know what he wants, just not where, or what, or how, and so we both ready our horses in silence, bridles tied onto faces, reins on backs and resting in manes, the same as we've done so many times before, then we pull ourselves up and onto them and we begin to ride.

WE LEAVE OUR CAMP and we go south.

The sun sets in the distance to our right as we ride over unfamiliar hills and across unfamiliar streams and fields, and while they might be unfamiliar, they don't look so very different from Pella. The ground is drier and rockier here, and the dirt is a lighter color. The hills are softer and less, too, and the vegetation that's on them more sparse, and where it does grow thick, it grows closer to the ground. And there's more dust. There's definitely more dust, and without the great mountains to break up the horizon, it's also easier in many places to see for great distances.

So this is it, I think, as I look around.

This is what Greece looks like nearly to Attica, to its middle, its center, its heart.

It's not how I'd imagined.

How had I imagined it?

I don't know, just . . . different than this.

I suppose that's what happens when we mythologize, even if the place we do so is where those same myths were born and told and made to come to life.

Or, perhaps even, where they happened.

We keep riding.

I wonder where we're going, but I don't ask, as we continue, hooves pounding across dirt and stone and dust, and then we finally come to a road. Alexandros leaves the dirt and begins to follow it, and I follow him, and after we've gone a short distance, I begin to see people, the first that we've seen since we've left our camp: there are scores of them here on the road, and they're people who look like they've walked and travelled a great distance, and they're heading in the same direction that we are, and then that's when it hits me, and I know both who and what they are.

Pilgrims.

And I know, of course, what it is they've come to see, and I know now what lies at the end of their pilgrimage, because it's the thing I now know lies at the end of ours, too.

Delphi.

The Oracle, the Omphalos.

I smile. Of course.

We keep riding and we gain on the group of pilgrims, and then pass them, and they move to the side as we ride by. We continue on and down the worn path, and then the path begins to rise. We start to climb the hill in front of us, the hill that quickly turns into a low mountain, and the road that we're on begins to circle and double back on itself the higher up the mountain we go and the steeper it becomes. We ride further and further, the road gets even more steep, and then we round a last bend, and that's when we finally see it, rising in front of us.

Alexandros touches Bucephalus on the neck, and he slows.

And when Bucephalus begins to slow, so does the brown.

The horses walk the final distance amongst the scattered pilgrims that are here as we look in front of us and in awe at what we see, the mighty temples that rise through sky and evening mist. First, we look at the Tholos, built with twenty sculpted and ornate Doric columns arranged in a circle and dedicated to Athena and to wisdom; then, we look at the great and steep theater, carved into the side of the mountain, below the wide and long stadium that's been built at the highest point around us. And then after that, we turn our eyes to the greatest of the temples that are there, the Temple of Apollo, and the place where all the pilgrims gather and where inside the Pythia breathes her fumes and then exhales truth and prophecy in turn, and the will of the gods, which is what they've all come for.

And us?

Perhaps that's what we've come for, too.

We slow even more, and then we dismount.

We walk the rest of the way, as it seems we should, out of respect, leading our horses behind us, with pilgrims on either side now and we're just one of their number, just another that's come to hear the wisdom that's given here. The other pilgrims don't look at us. Why would they? They don't know who we are, or why we're here in the south, and what we've come to do. Our accents could give us away, I know, but we don't speak. There's no need. We just look straight ahead and we breathe because that's what all who walk this path and road seem to have settled on and it's a truth and shared truth that's more important than words.

So, we breathe.

And we breathe together, our shoulders gently touching as they do during our important moments and as something that's ours, just ours, and our thoughts and lives and experiences touch, too, when we do, I know.

We continue to climb, even higher, together.

We get closer and we soon reach the temple.

We see there's an arch and entranceway that leads into the building, where all the pilgrims are going, and then we leave the horses outside and we go, too, and I look above the entranceway and that's where I see the famous words that are etched and carved, in small letters, standing watch and guard over the pilgrims and the way inside, the way forward, the generations that have already come and generations that still will.

Know Thyself.

Nothing in Excess.

Be.

We walk underneath the sacred and ancient wisdom that's been there since before time and before us, and that will be there after time, too, and after us, and we go inside along with the rest of the pilgrims. Once we pass the threshold, it becomes strangely cool in the temple, amongst the rock and stone around us, which is wet and damp, and there's a noticeable breeze that passes between the columns, also. We stand there and we look around. The light in the small space is dim, flickering, coming from barely-lit candles that burn soft and low in corners and the pseudo-light is diffused and reflected through the open area and between the people that are there and waiting.

There's a line.

The pilgrims all stand and wait for their turn to go in front of the Pythia, the priestess of Apollo who lives in the temple and brings the words and will of the god that she serves from the heavens and stars down to those here in our world that ask for those words.

Or, at least I think that's where we're going, but we're not.

I move to stand in line, but Alexandros instead reaches and touches me on the shoulder, as I did to him before we left, and pulls me away from the others; he pulls me back and closer towards him, and into the darkness, the flickering light.

"What's the matter?" I ask him.

"Nothing," he speaks quietly.

"Don't you want to hear the words of the god?" I ask. "There's no one here to recognize us, or know who we are, or that we're here."

"I know."

"So isn't that why we came?"

"What?"

"To hear the wisdom of Apollo."

"No."

"Then why?" I ask, but he doesn't answer.

Instead, he looks around, in the darkness.

He looks at the tall columns, at the chipped and sculpted busts of the deities that surround us. "Gods are fathers, and goddesses are mothers," he says, still looking at all the busts, the eyes, the noses, the disapproving looks carved into their faces. "The gods are our parents, but it's not parents who will change the world, Hephaestion. It's not our parents who will shape it in their image, and who will follow and chase the horizon and in some moments perhaps even catch the horizon, and the sun," he says, then turns to look at me. "And do you know why?"

"Why?" I ask, my response just a breath, just a single breath.

"Because it's their children who will do that. It's the *heroes*, the children of the gods who will and change and shape what's around them and what they've been born into. And that's what we are, Hephaestion. We'll never be our parents. We'll never be our fathers, or our mothers, or anything else, neither of us. We'll only ever be their children. We'll only ever be those who change and shape and re-make the world in our own image, because those that have come before us can't do that, and have already failed, simply because we exist."

I recognize what he says, of course I do, I recognize it from the book we read together so often late at night in our room, and so I know now why we're here, and what he wants.

"And what type of hero would you be, Alexandros?" I ask him, my voice still just a whisper.

"Let me show you," he says, then moves closer so he stands in front of me, our chests touching, the crown of his head near the bottom of my nose. "I'll be a hero for you, and you'll be a hero for me," he breathes, his breath mixing with mine, "And together we'll be a light for Greece, and then we'll bring that light we make here out and to the world."

"There's already light in the world."

"Of course there is. But it's not our light."

We're in a corner and no one watches us here because no one knows who we are, as I've said, and so he moves even closer still, his nose touching my chin now, and we breathe, together, we breathe, we just breathe. I can feel his breath as it mixes with mine, that's how close we are, as we exhale, and then we breathe again. There's stone behind us, the cool and sacred stone of the temple, and he pushes me further until my back is against it, and then he tilts his head up, and when he does, mine tilts down until they're even; our faces, our eyes, our lips, next to each other and together.

I look at him, but his eyes are closed.

I feel him, next to me, in front of me, against me.

Then he comes closer still, and he tilts his head up even more, and for the first time, his lips find my lips. This is the first time we've done this, and I don't know what to feel because it's not like it was when I was with Helia, or the girl in Salona, with the house down by the sea and the mother who worked in the palace; it's not like it was with them at all, or with anyone else.

That was *eros*.

So what is this?

Agape, I know.

His lips linger on my lips, staying there for a moment, not moving.

I want to be close to him, like I've always wanted, and that's what I now feel, too, and I'm glad that I do, and that I feel that and I don't feel something else.

Closeness.

Him.

Me.

Us.

Agape.

Then he slowly moves away and takes one step backwards so that we're at arm's length, and he opens his eyes now, and he looks at me. He stares back at me through the flickering and dim candle-light with his twice-colored eyes that penetrate like torches through the darkness of the oracle and the space between us, and that's what I look at: his eyes, his stunning and unique eyes, each with their different color that I know now represent the two dueling natures that are within him, the two parents that he's rejected tonight, that he's rejected in favor of me, and us, and as I look back at him, he breathes a single word, one more word before we go to battle together.

"*Patroklos*," he says, his voice more than a whisper now, stronger.

I look back at him.

Shadows dance across his face and he somehow seems taller, he somehow now seems taller than I know he really is, here in the dark and amongst our love and the gods that are surely watching us and this and everything else that we do.

It's an oath that he's said, that he's whispered, that he's given me.

So I give him my own oath in return.

"*Achilleus*," I say, and my voice is louder now, too.

I want the gods that are in this place to hear it, I want everyone to hear it, and to know it, and so it will be, so it will be, so it will be from this point onward, so it will always be, both now and forever.

WE LEAVE THE TEMPLE and we go back outside.

There are still more pilgrims coming, walking the winding road and through darkness, the end of a great journey for them. We stand to the side from where they arrive and gather and then look back at the temple we just left, the sheer size and beauty and majesty of this wondrous place in the mountains where the gods surely live, too, and we stay there and in their presence for just one more moment. I look back again at all the pilgrims who have come to receive prophecy. We have come, too, but there will be no prophecy for us, as Alexandros has decided, or at least that's what I think.

But I'm wrong.

We turn to head back towards where our horses wait just beyond the entrance, and that's when we hear the words, from behind us. "We receive many basileis here, at the Oracle, but not so many sons of basileis," the low and soft voice says, "and most rare of all, two sons of basileis, and both at the same time."

We pause.

We slowly turn back and towards the temple and see a young girl that's standing there and watching us now, that must have followed us outside, though I don't remember seeing her there before. She's dressed in pure white robes that gather around her shoulder and then fall down beneath her hips, past her knees, almost reaching the ground and her feet which walk upon rock and grass without sandals or anything else. Her hair is bright red, I see, a striking and shocking shade of red, much redder even than Alexandros', and I'd guess she couldn't be more than fourteen years old.

"Who are you?" I hear Alexandros ask, next to me, as she continues to slowly walk towards us, across the rock and grass, and then finally reach where we stand.

"I'm the Pythia," she answers.

"No," Alexandros shakes his head. "The Pythia's inside, giving sulfur-fuelled prophecies to pilgrims and strangers."

"Yes, she is."

"So how could you be her?"

"What makes you so sure there's only one of us?"

I look at Alexandros, and he swallows, and then I look back at her, and I ask my own question. "How do you know who we are?" I ask her.

"You really don't know, Hephaestion-prinkipas?" she smiles now.

"No one calls me that anymore."

"But it's who you are."

"You've never seen us before, have you? Because I don't think I've ever seen you."

"Where?"

"What?"

"Where have you come to?"

"The Oracle at Delphi," I shrug, not understanding, while Alexandros watches.

"And what happens at oracles?"

"Sacrifice."

"And what comes after sacrifice?"

"Prophecy."

"No," she shakes her head. "Not prophecy, Hephaestion-prinkipas. *Truth*. Because at an oracle there's one who can see, one who can see and know more than any other in this world can see or know, because the words that are given to that person are given by gods, and the gods see everything, don't they? And they know everything, too."

Alexandros swallows, next to me.

And so do I; I swallow, too.

"Being the son of a basileus is nothing where we're from. It's not like it is in the east, or in the south. I'm not Hephaestion-prinkipas anymore," I finally say to her, shaking my head, breaking the silence. "There is no word for what I am in Macedon, the same as there is no word for what Alexandros is, either."

"But you're not from Macedon, are you, Hephaestion? Which means that you will be again, though, if you wish to be, in the way that it is in the east, as you say. You know that in your heart. Your kingdom will be yours again, as you've wanted, for so long, your whole life. You will have that, as you've dreamed. But then what?"

"What do you mean?"

"Will you accept?"

"Yes. Of course I will."

"You sound so sure," she says, then her words for me are given and done, and so she turns to Alexandros. She looks him up and down, from his head and eyes all the way to his chest and then past it, past his waist, his hips, his knees, all the way down to his feet, his ankles, his toes, the entirety of him. Then she opens her mouth, and he knows what she's going to do, so he speaks before any words come from her. "No," he whispers.

"It's truth," she says. "So you will hear."

"I don't want to."

"You must."

He looks back at her, then he turns and looks at me.

I have no answer other than to just be there, and with him, as I always have been and always will. She closes her eyes, in front of us, and then when she opens them again and speaks, her voice is different, stronger, full of power and authority in a way it wasn't before: it's a voice that's filled with the divine, a voice that's filled with wisdom and a voice that's filled with stars and gods. *"And now I will tell you the truth,"* she says, in this new and powerful voice. *"Three kings have risen in Persia, and then there is a fourth, who was far richer than all of them, and by his strength and riches, he will have stirred against him the realm of Greece. But then a mighty king shall arise in Greece, who shall rule with great dominion, and do according to his will, and bend all to his will, and once he has risen and set forth, the kingdom that he makes and the kingdom that he leaves shall both be broken and divided, by the four winds above, but not amongst his posterity, nor according to his dominion, for both his kingdoms will be uprooted and given to others besides these."*

Silence.

There are no more words, neither from us, or from her.

Then in front of us the Pythia wobbles on her feet, as if she's about to almost collapse, and I go forward to help her but she waves me away. She doesn't want to be touched, and then her strength begins to return, and she's the young flame-haired girl again, the god now-departing. I look at Alexandros. He stands still, every inch of his body alive and alert and staring back at where the priestess gazes impassively back at him, breathing heavily as she regains her body.

"You have a question?" she asks, reading his eyes, as I have, too.

"What does that mean, what you've said?"

"I don't know."

"The words are from Apollo?"

"No," she shakes her head. "That's why I gave them to you outside his temple."

"So they're yours then?"

"The words aren't mine, either, as none of the words I speak are mine, in this world, just as my life isn't my life, either," she tells us as she looks at us each in turn, her body still weak, exhausted, spent. "These words were first spoken long before me, and long before you, too, son of Pella, and son of Salona, and long before each of you were written in the stars and your names whispered by the gods who live there, which means that they're truth. Prophecy-upon-prophecy, as we say. You've heard them, and you may believe them, or not, because it's words such as these that men and women travel from far and wide to find, and hear, and it's words such as these given at Delphi that turn men and prinkipas into heroes and basileus, from common soldiers into writers of history and shapers of worlds."

She looks at us each one more time.

Her voice is back to normal, how it was before, the god completely departed.

"I will not see you again," she answers. "Once you leave Greece, you won't ever return. That will be your choice, though."

"Is it a wise choice?"

"It's a choice," she says, and then nods, solemnly.

There are now no more moments, or looks, or words, and we watch as she turns and leaves, walking back towards the temple and the pilgrims that are there. We continue to watch and they don't notice her as she moves amongst them, as perhaps we never do when the gods are amongst us and near, and then she finally slips back and inside, between the columns of ancient stone where the words of the one who speaks through her are dutifully given and have been, in some form or the other, since the beginning of time, since the first of us ever looked above and to the stars and asked for reason and answers.

IT'S DARK WHEN WE ARRIVE BACK at the Macedonian camp, but the night is also lit by fires, our fires, and interrupted by the shouts and yells of the men that sit around them and drink and gamble and laugh and fight. The camp is split into young and old, with Philippos, Parmenion, and Attalus around their fires on one side, with the older soldiers and veterans, and there's another side of camp, too, where we see Ptolemaios, Perdiccas, Kassandros, Philotas, Leonnatos, Nearchos, and all the others that are younger and near our age who sit together, the ones for who this will also be a first battle, or second. We dismount from our horses and pages come to take the reins and then we go to the fires where those of the same age as us drink and laugh and tell wild and fantastic stories about all they'll soon do. We sit with the Companions and listen for a moment, as they talk of war and glory, as they have been since we left, many skins of wine ago. We've received our response from Thebes, they tell us, when they see us, almost as an afterthought, and they tell us how it came not very long ago. They tell us Demosthenes himself went from Athens to argue in front of the Theban counsel and it worked and the Theban council has chosen the Athenian side; the Thebans will fight with Athens, their ancient enemy, as they clearly consider us to be an even greater enemy. "So it's true, then," Alexandros says, from his place next to me, almost surprised by what he's heard.

"What's true?" Kassandros asks.

"They really do think us barbarians. It wasn't just rhetoric, and posturing."

"It would seem so," Perdiccas smiles.

"Which also means that very soon they will get to see how barbarians fight," Kassandros laughs, drinking more wine, "and we'll get to see how soft these southern Greeks really are, and have become."

"They defeated the Persians."

"A generation ago. And besides, the only thing softer than a southerner, is an easterner," Philotas tells us, and then laughs.

They all laugh at his words, too.

They all drink more wine, patting each other on the back.

I look at them for a moment, and then I turn and watch to see what Alexandros will do, and as he retreats into his thoughts, I look across and at the fires that are there on the other side of camp. I see Philippos and his generals and counselors and members of the old guard of Macedon around them, and I'm surprised by how calm Philippos seems. I see Amyntas, also, who is bare-chested and wearing no chiton at all, just a loincloth tied at his waist. I see his scarred chest and muscled-shoulders, which he shows to all the world as he drinks more and more and more. I see him, for a moment, but it's Philippos that I watch. There are skins of wine being passed everywhere and between them all but the basileus takes none, which is the first time I've seen that from him. He looks deathly serious, deathly calm. I think of how I saw him at the feast with the Persians, and countless other times at the palace; drunk, and laughing, and looking to drink more, always looking to drink more. I think of how Olympias told me he makes a mockery of Dionysus with his drink, and his sex, but faced with the future he's worked his whole life towards, there's none of that now. Pausanius of Orestis sits next to him and even his deeply beautiful features look serious in a way I haven't seen from him before, an extension of the state of the man that he loves, I suspect, and the moment that has now come, for them, for both of them, together. I feel more eyes on Pausanius, and I'm not surprised to see that they're Philippos' eyes, but then Philippos' eyes move, and I see that they come to rest looking at someone else, and I see that it's me they look back at. No, not at me, I then realize, but next to me.

Alexandros. His son.

Philippos watches as Leonnatos offers another skin of wine to Alexandros but he refuses, just like his father has done, even though Alexandros doesn't know that, and so Leonnatos passes the skin to Ptolemaios instead. Philippos watches this without his eyes changing, but I know what he must be thinking.

Is this my son? Is this him? Is this finally my flesh and blood?

His eyes move.

Now they do shift again, and they find my eyes, and Philippos stares back at me as I sit next to Alexandros, and I look back at him, too.

I don't blink, or look away.

What do his eyes say to me? What do mine say to him?

I don't know.

What does my friend's father think, both of me, and my place next to his son? I'm not sure I'll ever know, because after another moment, Philippos stands and touches Pausanius next to him, lightly, on the thigh, as he rises, and then Pausanius stands, too. Philippos walks away from the fire and back towards the tent, and Pausanius follows after him, and they go inside, together, Philippos first, and then Pausanius after.

The flap shuts.

"He did send a letter to Sparta," I hear Alexandros' voice next to me, and I turn to see him looking at me where I watch his father and the young guard who sleeps with him.

"What?" I ask, frowning.

"Philippos. He did send a letter to Sparta."

"He said that he didn't."

"He lied."

"Are you sure? How do you know?"

"Pausanius told Perdiccas before we left Pella, and Perdiccas told me," he says, and I think that strange because I've never seen Pausanius with anyone but the basileus.

"So why did you ask Philippos the question?"

"So he'd have to answer."

"What did the letter say?"

"He wrote that if the Spartans didn't submit to him then he would bring his invincible army south and to their land and peninsula and destroy their farms, kill their people, and raze their polis."

"That seems rather bold."

"It was. Do you know what their response was?"

"What?"

"If."

I glance at Alexandros and see that he smiles when he says this, when he repeats the Spartan reply.

If.

It's a smile of respect, I know, and boldness.

It's something that Alexandros loves, both are things that he loves.

But it's getting late now, and it's our turn, and so I stand, and when I do, I touch Alexandros on the thigh, also. He nods and then stands, as well, and we leave the fire without saying anything to the other Companions. They're used to this and so they don't say anything to us, either. We walk through the camp, Alexandros beside me, me beside him, then we reach our tent and he goes in first, and I follow after. There are two cots set on either side, pushed against the cloth edges, just like our rooms were set up in Pella and Mieza. He goes to his cot, on the far side of the tent, but I don't go to mine. I go to his with him, and then we both lay down, and I lay there next to him, like we do when we read the Iliad together, our bodies gently touching, only this time there is no book between us. There's just us. There's just us, and silence, and the weight and price of our dreams and ambition. Neither of us speak and we won't. We won't sleep, either. We've each now sworn our oath to the other, the eternal promise of who we'll be in this world in which we live, witnessed only by us and the gods and the one through whom the gods speak and now, tomorrow, the next time the sun rises, we'll ride to war to do both their will, and ours.

CHAPTER THIRTEEN

Our army begins south at dawn, and another great cloud of dust follows along both with and above us. We march through the dry and rolling hills of central Greece, near enough to the same ones Alexandros and I have already gone through, the previous night, and Philippos rides his grey stallion at the front of the army. Next to him are his generals, and then we're behind that, with the rest of the Companions and hetairoi, and the pezhetairoi follow behind us on foot, and that's where the dust comes from. Not the two thousand cavalry that I ride with, along with Alexandros, but the thirty-thousand foot soldiers whose sandaled feet stir up great clouds of southern dirt, the Macedonian veterans with their long sarissa, metal tips glinting in the bright Boeotian sun. Alexandros is quiet as he rides, his eyes scanning the hills in front and around us, looking for some undetermined thing, some yet-unseen but still-familiar place, and so without him to talk to as his eyes scan and search, I retreat into my thoughts again, and I look around, too: we're only a very short ride south of Delphi now, by my calculations from the position of the sun, and it's not long after I make that calculation that I see our scouts riding back towards us. They gallop over rock-covered hills that seem to have been getting lower and softer and with greater distance between them the further we've travelled south and into the heart of Greece. The scouts soon reach us, and when they do, we hear them tell Philippos the moment is now near: they've seen the combined armies of Athens, Thebes, and Corinth, along with the rest of the smaller city-states that march with them, and the armies are close; they're just on the other side of the hills, they say, as they point towards the distance, just a little bit further south now.

"Who else fights with them?" Philippos asks.

"Megara, Achaea, Troezen, Chalcis, and Epidaurus have all joined, as expected. And it looked like Akarnania has come, too, from what we've seen, but we weren't close enough to be sure."

"Anyone else?"

"No, and our spies in Athens have reported there aren't any more that are expected, either."

Philippos nods. "Good," he says.

Then his eyes begin to scan the distance.

I know what they're doing, and of course so does Alexandros; the battle is upon us, and so now Philippos will look for the place that will give our army the greatest advantage or, at the very least, not leave us at a *disadvantage*, which is the same thing Alexandros has been scanning and searching for since we left Amphissa. Philippos waves his hand, not seeing a place he likes, so we keep riding and the army keeps moving behind us, too. I glance at Alexandros again, next to me, but his eyes still analyze terrain, still look straight ahead and then to each side, not at me, carefully making notes and observations, the same as his father's eyes do, too.

He keeps scanning, studying.

And we keep riding.

The road that we're following eventually comes to a fork, and when it does, I see Philippos call the scouts to him again. They confer together and this time I don't hear what they say. I suspect we'll take the fork that leads to the south and east, and further into the heart of Greece, but I'm wrong; I'm surprised when we take the one that leads simply east, and even a little bit north, actually, *away* from Athens and Thebes. Alexandros registers no expression at this news. His eyes just flick this way and that, still taking in the land we travel across, and my eyes take in him, from my place by his side, as they always do. We keep going, and then I see why the choice was made because we soon come to a wide, great, and open area that will work well for our horses and cavalry to be able to ride and charge and for our pezhetairoi to be able to fight, too, in their tight and protective formations and not lose their footing. Besides that, there's also a mountain on one side, enclosing our army into the area so that it can't be flanked or attacked from behind, and another mountain on the other side, doing the same thing there, and between the two peaks and across the great open area there's a shallow and slow-moving river. I see Alexandros raise his head and breathe in. The mountains mean the fighting will be confined to just one front, which makes it perfect for an army with better soldiers, but less of them, which is what we are and have, and the flat and grassy field gives advantage to cavalry, of which we know our hetairoi is the best in the world. Alexandros swallows, and so do I now, because I know what it is that we look at, and what it is that's in front of us: the perfect place for a battle.

Philippos raises his hand, and the army stops marching.

We hear the scouts tell Philippos that the peak to the right is called Mount Thurion, the peak to the left is called Mount Aktion, the river running between them is named Kephisos, and there's a small town that's close, on the other side of the river.

"This is it," I see Philippos nod.

Parmenion nods his agreement, too, as strategos, then the other generals do, also, and so our riders begin to dismount and servants and pages begin to search for even-ground to make our camp. I look around again. I think Alexandros is next to me, but instead I turn to see him walking towards the baggage train as it arrives, after the soldiers. He goes amongst all the things to find the tent that we share and he chooses a place and then sets everything down and begins to raise the tent himself. He measures distances and starts to pound stakes into the ground. I glance at Philippos, who watches this, and then I go to join and help Alexandros. I measure distances with him and I pound stakes, too. The Companions see what we do, and then they come and join us, and when all our tents are raised, we begin to start helping the others with theirs, also. Then the men that sit their horses and stand around us—the regular men, the veterans, from the hetairoi, and the pezhetairoi—they just look at us, and when they see Philippos' son and his Companions, and what they do, they then begin to join, as well. Alexandros and I finish raising a second tent and are about to move on to a third when I see one of the scouts passing and I stop him. Philippos has left with Parmenion, and Attalus stands with Amyntas and watches us, both of them frowning.

"What is it?" the scout asks.

"The village you spoke of earlier, on the other side of the river."

"What about it?"

"What's it called?"

The scout looks back at me, and then at Alexandros, next to me, and the others working in the sun and wiping sweat from their brows; a new way of doing things, perhaps, and soon, maybe, there will be time for many such new ways and new things.

"Chaeronea," the scout says, as he nods.

Then he turns and leaves.

WE SETTLE INTO OUR CAMP and it takes two whole days for Athens, Thebes, and their allies to arrive and take their place across the river from us. Alexandros thinks this is because they don't like where we've chosen to fight, and they want to make us move so that the battle can be somewhere better suited for them, but when they come, they don't seem to mind the location we've picked. This is strange to both of us, because this is their land, and they're the ones with supplies and time and local knowledge, and this is the great battle that will surely shape the next hundred years of this peninsula on which we all reside. And it of course might even shape more than that, too. But when they see where we've chosen, they just begin setting their camp, the same as we did, without trying to pull or push our forces one way or the other, which means they must think we've made a mistake. I'm surprised at their reaction and decision, and I'm also surprised at what I see amongst our own army, too, both while we wait for them, and after they arrive. Our soldiers build more great fires, even during the day, and they start to drink again, also, and early. They drink the whole first day that we're there and waiting, starting when they wake and then ending whenever they pass out and fall asleep, and they drink the whole second day, too, starting again in the morning.

I see this, and I don't understand.

I don't participate in the drinking, and neither does Alexandros, and for the most part we stay in our tent together. We leave occasionally—to bathe in the cold river that flows from the peaks above us, or to eat at one of the fires with the other Companions, who are drunk—but then as soon as we're done with either thing, we return to our tent, and each other. We don't talk much while we're there. We read some, from the Iliad, as we often do, and we polish and sharpen the edges of our broad-swords, but the truth is, our swords have never been sharper and we do it just to keep our hands and minds busy in the face of what is going to soon come.

We don't sleep much, either.

I manage to sleep a little, but Alexandros doesn't even close his eyes during either night before our opponents arrive and it worries me. I ask him about it, after the first night of lying next to him, on the cot that we now share, and knowing that when I wake again in the morning he won't have moved, won't have shifted, won't have even stood or stretched, not even an inch, but he brushes my question away without a response and I won't ask again as I remember what he told me once about the things that make him feel mortal, and why would I want to make him feel that? Why would I want to make him feel that ever, but especially why would I want to make him feel that right now, during the last nights before our first battle?

And then, soon enough, the moment comes.

Even though Alexandros hasn't slept in several days, he still seems alert, on edge, twitchy even, his eyes darting this way and that, which is something I haven't seen since I've known him. I bring a bucket of water to our tent and we each take off our chitons and wash our bodies until they're clean. I don't know why we do this, before a battle, when it's perhaps least important, but we do. Once we're clean, our flesh still raised from the chill of the cold mountain water, we take the razor we've brought and shave with it so that our faces are completely smooth. Then once we've shaved, and we've put our chitons back on, we take our breast-plates from where they rest in the corner of the tent and strap them onto our chests. I do his for him, and he does mine for me, and we don't speak as we dress and arm ourselves. We each help the other with our greaves, too, which will guard our legs as we ride through enemies, and then we take our helmets from where they sit near our bed. We stand there, together. We stand there, and we look at each other. I have one thing to say, one thing I know I *need* to say, though I don't know how he'll react when he hears it. If I don't say it, though, it will live with me forever: the un-said words that have the power to haunt for all the rest of time, and then perhaps even after that, too. "I know what we've said to each other, when we were at the oracle," I tell him, my voice pitched low. "The oath that we made, of who we would each be."

"Achilleus and Patroklos," he nods.

"Yes," I nod, too.

"You've changed your mind?"

"No, it's just . . ."

"It's just what?"

I swallow, gathering myself.

Then I meet his eyes.

"You've become a very good warrior, since we've known each other, and began our training. And while you're Achilleus in the world, and in *my* world, and to me, you're not Achilleus on the battlefield. Not yet."

I look at him.

I study his eyes and expect him to become angry for telling him something that he isn't. "No," he says slowly, and then smiles, he smiles so widely and I'm surprised as it's the first smile I've seen from him in too many days, the first smile since the night under the stars in Mieza, I realize. "I might not be Achilleus on the battlefield, but *you* are, Hephaestion. Or at least you will be. I've never been so sure in my life, and I know no other that's stronger or more skilled with a sword. So stay by my side, and don't go far."

He will be basileus.

I've never been more sure, and I've never been more certain that there was a person put on this earth to change it, to mold it, to bend it to his will and fit it and all of us on it into his golden image. I'm not the most skilled swordsman that will fight today, but he's made me feel like it, and is there a difference? I don't think so. How fortunate am I, I then think, and wonder, to be born into this time, the time of Alexandros-prinkipas. How fortunate am I, I think and wonder, again, to have been brought to him, and to have been put into his path and to have him love me.

"I will," I tell him, and then I nod.

"Do you swear it?" he asks.

"I swear it. Until death, and then beyond. I swear it to you."

"I swear it, too," he tells me, taking my head in his hands and pressing my forehead against his own. "Until death, and then beyond," he whispers.

Then, somewhere, a horn blows.

The moment's now here, and so are we, and so we move apart.

He puts his helmet on, and then I put mine on, too, and after one last look, one last fleeting touch and brushing of hands that hang loose and near our sides, we turn and walk outside the tent. The entire camp is alive with the clanging of steel and rustling of troops and we walk through it all and towards where our horses are waiting. When we reach them, we climb up and onto their backs, and then once we're there, we begin to slowly ride through and around the camp and towards where the lines between the two great armies have begun to form. As we continue and then get there, I see that the hetairoi have begun to position themselves with their backs to the mountains, so that we can't be flanked, but when we reach them, Alexandros gives different orders: he tells them to turn so that we're perpendicular to the peak called Thurion. We're outnumbered by several thousand men, and in doing this, Alexandros has given up the one advantage that we could have had.

"Why?" I ask him, out of earshot of the others.

"So they can't retreat," he tells me.

And he's right.

We'll be more exposed and our numerical disadvantage will be more exploitable, but if we win the day, they'll have nowhere to run; there will be nowhere for them to flee and there will be no protracted campaign with multiple battles and months and years spent fighting and this will all end today, for one way or the other, for Athens and Thebes and their allies, or for us and ours. Above where we sit, the clouds pass, and then sun peeks through. I see Alexandros cock his head to the side and look up, and when he does, the sun shines even brighter. Maybe it's just my imagination again, but I'm not the only one that sees it. "An omen," I hear from over my shoulder, and then turn to see Perdiccas who has spoken and rides towards us with Ptolemaios, Philotas, Kassandros, Nearchos, and Leonnatos next to him. They take their place at our side, their horses breathing heavy, and their riders taking deep, purposeful breaths, too.

They see what Alexandros has done, and they raise their eyebrows.

"Well," Philotas smiles. "One of us isn't going to be leaving here today."

"It'll be them," Ptolemaios looks grim.

"If the gods will it," Nearchos nods.

"They do," Leonnatos frowns. "Of course they do."

"Let's go," Alexandros tells them, cutting the conversation short.

He kicks Bucephalus to a gallop and rides to the left, and we follow after him, together now. We ride behind the whole of the army until we come to the far flank, with the main Macedonian forces gathered to our right, which will be led by Philippos and his generals—Parmenion, Attalus, and the others—and the Kephisos River is there to our left, too, forming a natural obstacle and barrier for any who might try to overtake us on that side. I look at the other forces around us: the hetairoi cavalry, which begin to gather in formation, and the pezhetairoi infantry, and phalanx. They're all hungover from three straight days of drinking and none of them seem too worried about what they're about to face, and I understand, now, why they drink, so that they're numb and don't feel what I'm feeling right now. I don't like the feeling, but I know it's important that I feel it, and so I'm glad that I do. I look at the Athenians, across from us, who line up opposite from Philippos and his pezhetairoi, and even at this distance I can clearly see the nervousness in their movements; I can see the fidgeting, the gripping and re-gripping of swords and shields, the sweat that must be beading on foreheads and rolling down noses and cheeks and chins and chests and backs. I remember what Aristoteles taught us, that these aren't professional soldiers, that they're mostly just common men with common jobs—blacksmiths, shoe-makers, stablehands, merchants, politicians, and yes, even philosophers—and most of them don't train at battle every day, like we do; they train at something else, and only pick up swords when they're forced to, to defend their poleis.

Are they good with them, with their swords?

We'll certainly soon find out, because there are definitely more of them, though the fear in their lines is nowhere to be found in ours and while our men may all be hungover or even still inebriated, I see that they're also confident, calculated, and there's not a single drop of fear anywhere near us, or our camp, or our soldiers.

"Look," Ptolemaios points.

"What?" Kassandros asks.

"There," Leonnatos shields his eyes, against the sun, seeing what Ptolemaios sees.

"The Sacred Band," Perdiccas says as he sees them, too, lining up across from us, and then the rest of us see them, also. This is something that Aristoteles taught us about, even though he didn't often touch on military subjects, and even Philippos has warned us about them; he'd warned all of us two days ago, before the battle had begun. The Sacred Band of Thebes was said to be the greatest fighting force our Greek world had ever known, outside of Sparta, of course. They were one hundred and fifty of the most select and highly-trained soldiers that Thebes had to offer and who, unlike most of the others in front of us that were not full-time soldiers, lived a complete life of war, of drilling and practicing together every day since they were eleven, and then when they went home from the fields and their training, their lives together didn't end, and they were all lovers, too, sleeping with each other every night and bonding themselves in all the earthly ways a soul could be bound to another. Philippos had been held as a hostage in Thebes when he'd been young, and he'd seen them fight, these soldiers who wear bright and tall red crests on their polished helmets, and Philippos even trained with them some, too, during his time there.

We watch as they take their place across from us.

I realize this is who we'll face, and I look at Alexandros next to me.

He knows who they are, and he knows what this means for us, but his expression doesn't change; he doesn't flinch, doesn't blink, doesn't move a single muscle. "What are you thinking?" I ask him, quietly once more, so again it's just us who can hear.

He turns and looks around.

He looks up and down the lines of our gathered army, the lines which are now moving, soldiers stirring, shifting their weight from foot to foot. They stir and shift their weight for a little longer, and then become still. They all take their final positions and grip weapons and close their eyes and whisper prayers to whatever gods they worship and whoever watches over them. Most of the prayers go to the main gods of Greece, but some whisper to lesser-known northern gods, as well, I know, the ones they still speak to and who still live in places like Epirus, and Illyria, and Salona, the gods that my people still make sacrifices to in the hills, and in all the other places that are still wild. I grip the leather reins that I hold even tighter, clenching and unclenching them in my young hands.

"It'll be any moment now," Alexandros tells us.

He speaks louder than I spoke, so that all the Companions can hear, too.

And then, very shortly after his words come, the moment is finally upon us, as Alexandros said it would be, and to our right we see the small and distant figure of Philippos in his gold-trimmed armor with the bright and multi-pointed star of his family on the front of it. We watch as he walks out from the line of pezhetairoi and stands in front of his men, facing them, holding his shield and sarissa, and he speaks. We're too far away to hear his words and exactly what he's saying, but we feel them, or at least I think we do; we feel what he's trying to impart to us, the strength and courage of battle and arms that we were born with and that those philosophers and politicians and mathematicians across from us know nothing about. Maybe those aren't his words after all, I realize, but it's what I feel, and what I believe, and what I want to hear, and so I do. I know it's what Alexandros feels and wants to hear, too, and then with Philippos' speech over, he returns to the Macedonian lines and takes his place in the middle of them where the basileus of Macedon always fights; always first into battle, always first to reach the enemy, always first to draw blood.

There's silence for a moment, as we wait.

It's eerie, strange, with so many men gathered here.

There's one more moment of it, of the silence, one more moment of nothing but these men and their horses, and their steel.

Then a loud horn sounds.

Our pezhetairoi start to advance forward, and so do the troops across from us, but we remain steady. Alexandros moves Bucephalus forward a little bit, so that he's in front of us, where we sit on our horses, and he's in front of all the rest of the hetairoi, too, the same as his father is with the pezhetairoi so he'll also be first into battle. He waits, his eyes trained on the scene across from him as formations begin to take shape, strategy starts to spring into action, and though this is his first time on a battlefield, I realize that what I see in his eyes doesn't seem to be discovery, but rather memory; memory from where, though? Perhaps another life, or another time. I don't know which is true or that I believe, but it doesn't matter because soon there's not much time left for wonder, because soon the lines shift and change, in front of us, and the moment finally comes.

Our moment.

This is what we were born for, and what we've trained for.

"*On my command!*" Alexandros yells as he turns to us, to all of us, his voice strong in a way I haven't yet heard before, in a way that's also perhaps memory, too, and in a way, I realize, that he's had in him all this time. I watch as the Theban forces that were lined across from us begin to pinch inwards, towards the left flank of our pezhetairoi, where our soldiers are most vulnerable, and the Macedonians that are there turn to face their new enemies and a new line is formed. Alexandros sees this, too. It's a stunning lack of discipline from our opponents; it opens two fronts for our phalanx and foot soldiers, which is dangerous for us, but it completely exposes the Thebans to our position and this is what Alexandros has been waiting for; he's been waiting for our enemies to take the bait that was laid for them by his father.

And now they have.

He raises his great broad-sword, and he raises it easily.

"*For Macedon!*" he yells, as loudly as he can, then brings the sword slicing down and through the air. "*And for Greece!*"

That's his signal.

Charge.

We all yell now, too, our unique and new battle-cries.

He kicks Bucephalus to a gallop, and then we do the same, behind him, and we follow and pound after him. We gallop from our position next to the river and fly across the length of great plain in front of us, the ground shaking and trembling as we pick up speed, pace, power, and I struggle to catch him, to take my place at his side as I swore I would, because the brown isn't as fast as Bucephalus, but we will try, we will still try to catch him.

Some of the Thebans see us.

I recognize the red crests on the helmets of the Sacred Band, and they try to rally the others to the danger they now see, but these aren't soldiers that they try to rally, like themselves, and the Athenians and Thebans don't react quickly enough, they don't react nearly quickly enough, and that will now be their end.

We draw our swords as we ride, all of us except Alexandros who already has his drawn and ready. There are two thousand of us and only one hundred of the Sacred Band, only one hundred of their red crested helmets and these soldiers who are only soldiers and lovers and absolutely nothing else.

We're almost to them.

There's fifty paces left.

I raise my sword, high above my head, like my father taught me.

Twenty-five paces.

Closer, closer, closer.

We yell again, and it terrifies them, and us, too.

Ten paces.

I inhale, I hold my breath, and do the others?

I don't know, I don't know anything else but this, and as we get closer those hetairoi that carry the short xyston spears throw them and Thebans fall in front of us and then we're there, and our opponents are in front of me, and us, and then—

Crack.

We smash into their lines and bodies fly as the weight of our horses toss armored men aside that are in our path, and we swing our great broad-swords, and those that threw their xystons draw their swords and swing those, too, and as we do, more bodies fly, lifted in death, and then fall again to the ground in the same way. One member of the Sacred Band brings his shield up to defend himself, and he's used to blocking blows from the short and light xiphos that most Greeks carry, but we're not most Greeks. His eyes go wide as the strength and weight of my broad-sword rips the shield from his arm that must be numb from the force of the blow he's tried to block, and it might even have broken his arm, I know, and then I swing my sword back around. His eyes go even wider at the strength with which I'm able to wield my weapon that's so much heavier than what he's used to, a strength he's never seen before, because I've trained every day of my life for this strength, and then I slice down again, cutting him from his shoulder and into the middle of the chest. I pull my sword back and it catches in flesh, so I flex and strain and pull harder and then it rips free, and when it does, his body slumps to the side and falls to the ground. Blood, fresh across grass.

Death.

A first kill.

I sit on the brown and look down at the body, in shock for a moment and thinking perhaps this deserves ceremony or pause or maybe even something else, but the battle continues around me—metal and steel and death and shouting continue, and are everywhere—and so there's no time for ceremony, or moments, or anything else, and I must continue, as everyone else does, and so I do.

In front of me, I see Alexandros.

He's deep into the enemy lines.

I push the brown after him, knocking away swords and spears that swing and thrust from all directions as best I can, as they come, even though some make it through and cut me on the arms, but I ignore them. I'm almost to him again and that's when I see one of the Sacred Band—he looks young, he looks very young, perhaps not even older than we are—getting closer to Alexandros from behind, near Bucephalus' right thigh, where he can't be seen either by horse or rider.

"*Alexandros!*" I yell.

But the noise from the battle is too much.

I push forward, trying to reach him, but the mass of chaos stops me and there are too many bodies in the way and I won't be able to get to him in time. I watch as the young Theban raises his sword, about to bring it down on Alexandros' unsuspecting back, and I yell again, powerless to do anything but yell and keep yelling, and pushing.

It won't be enough, though.

The sword reaches its apex and then begins its descent, power and skill in the blow, and then—

The Theban screams.

Blood ribbons and plumes through the air as the young Theban's arm is severed, at the elbow, and I look past him to see Ptolemaios holding the broad-sword that's saved Alexandros' life and that he expertly whips back around and down on the Theban's helmet, splitting the helmet in two, as well as what's inside of it, and he ends the Theban's life in an instant or perhaps even less than that.

Ptolemaios sees me.

His helmet is covered in red now, dripping from the top, near the crest, and then down, across his face, his cheeks, his eyes. Alexandros didn't hear me shouting, or see the young Theban that was about to take his life, but someone did.

Ptolemaios nods.

I nod, too.

Then we both turn and rejoin the fighting.

We swing our great broad-swords, together now, and because of our training, our arms don't tire, at least not yet, and more Thebans and Athenians fall. I push my way through the battle until I'm finally back to Alexandros, in the place where I swore I would be, and I breathe easier when I'm by his side again.

"We should push back," I say to him, when I get there. "Towards the others."

But he doesn't hear my words.

He wants to be basileus and he knows that in Macedon the basileus is the one that's bravest and most bold, like his father is, and so that's what he will be, too.

He goes further into the battle, swinging his sword, and I go next to him.

The fighting seems to slow, from what the chaos was like in the beginning, and then I realize it's not the battle that's slowed, it's my mind that has, and perhaps his has, too.

It's still loud, though.

It's still so very loud.

Then I hear another noise, a great cry that goes up, and I turn to look and from my place on the back of the brown, I can see across the battle and towards the pezhetairoi and where Philippos fights with them. The pezhetairoi are pushing back the main forces that are led by the Athenians, and they're breaking them, too. I see in front of me we're doing the same thing, also, that we're striking into the heart of the Thebans, and the Sacred Band, and pushing them back against the mountains that are behind them, and they soon will be there.

And then, once they are, they will be no more.

"*Further!*" I hear Alexandros yell, and I see Bucephalus jump forward.

I squeeze my thighs and bring the brown to a gallop again as we jump and push forward, too, and I ride after them because it's clear now what the outcome of this battle will be, and with victory secure in our grasp, I want to make sure nothing happens to Alexandros during the dying gasps of conflict.

He swings his sword, from high on Bucephalus' back.

Thebans fall.

We get closer to Mount Thurion.

I catch up with him, and I do the same, swinging my sword from the brown's back and fighting off any that try to get near him, near his flank, and then one does and grabs his leg and pulls him from Bucephalus and to the ground where he lands heavily and the wind is knocked from his lungs.

He gulps for air, and he's exposed, vulnerable, on his back.

The Theban raises his sword.

"*No!*" I yell.

The Theban ignores me, of course, but when I yell, Bucephalus rears on his hind legs and one of his front hooves catches the Theban squarely in the face.

How did he learn to do that? Did Alexandros teach him?

I don't know.

Alexandros quickly stands as the Theban falls in a mess of blood and broken bones and death, and Alexandros catches his breath.

There's the sound of horns, in the distance, from the center of the battle.

I watch as Athenians, Thebans, and all the rest put down their weapons.

All around us, they put down their swords and spears, setting them on the ground, and they raise their hands.

Victory.

Surrender.

Alexandros doesn't stop, though. He keeps fighting.

He stands and runs forward and slices through another Theban, a member of the Sacred Band.

Did he hear the horns? He had to have heard them.

I ride after him.

Doesn't he see that they're un-armed?

He must see this, but he doesn't seem to, or it doesn't register, because he keeps fighting. There's another young and unarmed Theban with a dark birthmark across his face and Alexandros races towards him. When he gets there, he runs him through, and I see the young boy's eyes go wide not expecting this as they both fall heavily to the ground in a bloody pile.

The young Theban is dead.

Alexandros isn't, and he rises again.

I run.

I yell.

But Alexandros keeps going.

The next Theban in front of him sees what he's done, and so he quickly reaches down and grabs the spear that he's laid at his feet, in the grass, but it's too late.

Alexandros runs him through, and they both fall again, too.

I'm closer.

Alexandros tries to rise, once more, and tries to keep going, but his sword is stuck, held fast in the chest of the Theban he's just killed.

I'm closer.

He's almost up, almost ready to keep going as he rips his sword free, and I shout again, but he doesn't hear, or doesn't listen, and then I'm there.

I tackle him.

We both fall, but as we do, my momentum takes me past him and he jumps up again and runs at one last Theban who sees him coming and instead of reaching for his weapon, or anything else, the Theban simply closes his eyes and begins to whisper a prayer, his arms raised and palms facing upwards, his face angled high and towards the sun, towards where he hopes his prayer will go, then Alexandros runs him through, too, the same as the others.

I reach him again.

I tackle him to the ground once more and this time I make sure that my weight lands directly on him and when it does he tries to spin, tries to attack me, not recognizing me or knowing who I am, but we've wrestled many times before, and I'm still stronger than he is, so I'm able to pin him to the ground, even as he struggles, and fights back.

"Alexandros," I say his name.

He's covered in dirt, covered in blood.

He still doesn't seem to recognize me, or who I am.

He continues to struggle.

I flex, and strain, and hold him as best I can.

"ALEXANDROS," I say again, louder, and this time he seems to hear me.

He breathes in and then I see his nose twitch and he breathes again after that and I think it must be my scent that triggers something in him, either my scent or the tone of my voice and the inflection in which I say his name with my northern accent, the way that only I do.

"Hephaestion . . . ?" he asks.

"Yes."

"Hephaestion," he says again.

"It's me," I tell him.

And that's when I see the change: I see it come to his eyes, and how they now register this and me, and how he seems to come back and into his body again.

His muscles begin to loosen.

He doesn't fight and struggle anymore.

He looks around.

I see this and know the danger and what has possessed him is now passed, and so I move off him, off his body and the place where I held it to the ground, and then I look around, too.

There are bodies.

There are bodies everywhere; around us, in front of us, every place that we look there are bodies, and more bodies, and there is blood, too, splattered red and slick across all that we can see, and it smells of blood and death everywhere, also.

I see the others.

The Companions.

They gallop towards us with wide and shocked eyes because they've seen what's happened, and what he's done. I make a quick count and they all seem to be there, which brings relief, though Nearchos has blood running down his arm, Kassandros has a long gash across his cheek, and Ptolemaios looks to have a broken and crooked nose. They're all still alive, though.

I look back to Alexandros.

He's shaking now, next to me.

I don't want anyone to see him like this: I don't want anyone to see him like this, or what he's done, so I pick him up and help him to his feet and lead him towards his horse. I turn to Ptolemaios, there with the others, when they reach us. "Take the brown," I tell him, and he nods, understanding.

I go to Bucephalus.

I climb up onto his back, the only other that he'll let ride him besides Alexandros, and then I reach down and grab Alexandros' arm and pull him up after me so that he sits in front of where I sit, like Helia did before, and then, once we're on the horse, I hold Alexandros tightly around the waist and squeeze my legs.

Bucephalus already knows what to do, though.

He starts to gallop and we ride across the battlefield and back towards the camp, and the tent that we share.

We come to it.

I jump off Bucephalus and then pull Alexandros off, too, and I let the horse's reins hang free; he won't leave here, he won't leave Alexandros, he won't leave us.

We go inside.

I carry Alexandros propped against my shoulder, and I lead him towards the basin and water that's there, that we've washed and cleaned ourselves with before the battle.

We stand in front of it again, after the battle now.

I unbuckle his armor, his breast-plate, his greaves, and they all fall to the ground with a loud clang of metal. Then I untie his dirty and blood-stained chiton, and un-cinch the belt at his waist, and these things fall to the ground, too. We're both completely covered in dirt, blood, death, every inch of our skin stained and marked. He stands there and he's naked now and so I use the water in the basin to wash all those things from him. I use the clear and fresh water to try to clean all those things away, just the same as we did before the battle, and I don't know why this is important to me, but it is, and so I do it.

He stares ahead as I wash him.

He stares straight ahead, his eyes blurred, glossed, slowly blinking every five or ten seconds, and then just staring again.

Are they still his eyes?

Is he still who I thought he was, and who I thought I knew?

There's no more blood or dirt on him now, and then once he's clean, he slowly turns and looks at me and the look in his eyes seems as if it's one that's of a child.

If I'm supposed to know what to do next, I don't.

I don't know what to do at all.

So I simply lead him to the bed that we've shared, and he seems grateful for this, and lays down, and when he does, I lay next to him. I'm still bloody, still dirty, still wearing my heavy, stained, and uncomfortable armor, but I lay down and I stay there. I wrap my arms around him again and hold him as close to me as I can hold him, and I don't leave.

I feel him.

I feel his heart, I feel it racing.

We lay there together and the rhythm of his heart gradually begins to slow, and so does his breathing, then they finally both become more steady, until he eventually goes to sleep, and when he does, I'm glad.

I think about what's happened.

I think about all that's happened, and all that I've seen, and felt.

I think about his eyes, as he's stared straight ahead, naked, in front of the basin of water, his two different-colored and slowly blinking eyes. One is light, and one is dark, I know, which I've always known, since the first day I met him.

But, for the first time, I find myself wondering...

Which is his soul?

CHAPTER FOURTEEN

Some time very late in the night, I go to sleep, next to Alexandros, and I don't wake until morning. It's the drums that keep me up. They begin after the sun goes down, and with them also comes the raucous and drunk voices that I hear between drum beats and from around the giant fires that the Macedonians have built once again, but this time they've built their fires with wood gathered from the camp of their enemies which is wood they say seems to burn both brighter and hotter. Whether it does or not—or it's just one of the many myths and stories soldiers believe and tell—they burn all remnants of the Athenians and Thebans ever having been here at this place, letting their baggage and tents and everything else they brought be consumed by flames and, of course, as the flames burn and consume the remnants of their enemies, the victorious Macedonians all get more and more and more drunk.

Some time in the night, though, sleep finally does come, and when I blink my eyes open in the morning, the first thing I do is look next to me, when I feel the empty space that's there.

"You're up?" I hear, and then turn to see Alexandros sitting in the corner.

He's fully dressed in a pressed chiton, leather belt, sandals, and watching me as I rub sleep from my eyes. I blink again, my eyelids heavy. "Yes," I tell him. "I am now."

"Good," he nods. "Philippos has called for us."

"What for?"

"The Athenians and Thebans have come to discuss their surrender."

I look back at him and open my mouth, about to talk, about to speak to him about what's happened because I know that I need to, I know that I need to talk to him about what he's done, but then he quickly stands and walks towards the flap to our tent. He pauses when he gets there. "I'll wait for you outside," he says, and then walks out.

I look down at myself.

I'm still bloody and dirty from the battle, and still wearing my armor, even, which I didn't bother to take off the night before, so I stand and stretch my sore limbs and joints and then reach around and untie my breast-plate. I take it from my body and set it on the ground next to me, then reach down and take off my greaves, too. I pull my dirty and bloody chiton up and over my head, and then use the water from the basin and sponge that's there to clean my bruised skin. Then when I'm clean again, and have washed all the memories and reminders of the day before from me, I find a new chiton in the trunk that we share and wrap it around my body, tying it at the shoulder, cinching my belt tightly at the waist.

When I'm finally cleaned and dressed, I turn to go.

I cross the length of the tent and push the flap outward and then go beyond it. He's standing there waiting for me, as he said he would be, and when he sees me cleaned and dressed, he nods, once, simply, and then turns and we start to walk together, through the camp, on our way to see Philippos and the defeated Greeks.

AS WE WALK THROUGH the Macedonian camp, we pass men that are still drinking and haven't yet been to bed from the night before and it doesn't seem as if they have any intention of going to sleep, either: they still drink, and shout, and wrestle and then when they're done, they pat each other on the back and lift drunken prayers to their great and benevolent and now-victorious gods and goddesses. We walk through them, and all of this, and eventually come to Philippos' tent, where we go past the guard that's outside. It takes a moment for my eyes to adjust from the bright Boeotian sun to the darkness that's inside the tent, but once they do, I see that Philippos stands on one side, with his generals behind him, and Amyntas and Arrhidaeus are there with him, as well.

I look at Philippos.

He's survived the battle and seems relatively unharmed, which is always a question that has to be asked when Macedonians fight, but it's also clear the battle has taken another toll on him and his body.

The flap is pushed open again, and light pours in.

Then through the light, there are two men that come inside and they come to stand in front of us, both still dirtied and bloodied and wearing their armor: one of them is from Athens, and the other is from Thebes. Their heads are bowed when they walk in and take their places, and their heads stay bowed when they speak.

"A great victory, Philippos-basileus," the man from Athens says.

"Yes," Philippos looks back at them, impassively.

"A very great victory indeed," the man from Thebes seems to have a harder time saying this, and I'm silent as they each continue to speak and compliment Philippos on the battle, and his victory over their forces, and how the gods must favor him, and then Philippos waves his hand and tells them the terms of surrender. There will be no tribute paid, Philippos says, and there will also be no traditional exchange of slaves or territory, as the terms that Macedon will ask for are very clear: all the other poleis and kingdoms of Greece, with the exception of Sparta (and I see the hint of a smile from Alexandros when they're mentioned) will become allies of Macedon and they will swear oaths of loyalty to him, Philippos, basileus of Macedon.

I look at the two men who have been sent as ambassadors, and their eyes are wide, because these are very generous terms.

The man from Athens nods. Then the man from Thebes nods, too. *So it will be.*

"No," I hear the single word, and it comes from next to me.

I turn.

So does everyone else.

We all look at Alexandros, who isn't looking at us, but rather looking back at his father and it's Alexandros who is the one who has spoken, and objected.

"No?" Philippos asks, raising his eyebrows.

"The basileus of Macedon," Alexandros says to him.

"What?" Philippos frowns, not understanding. "That's what I said."

"They won't swear loyalty to Philippos," Alexandros tells him, in the same strong and clear voice that he used before battle, the voice made and meant for moments such as this one. "They'll swear loyalty to the basileus of Macedon."

Philippos looks back at his son, and Alexandros meets his eyes, and the younger man doesn't look away; he doesn't shrink, doesn't unsettle, doesn't even blink. I think of the story Alexandros told of Bucephalus, of the last time he challenged his father in public, and I think the same thing is about to happen, and I brace myself for it. I brace myself for the outburst, and the outrage.

I'm wrong, though.

I thought Philippos was going to be angry, but he's not. In fact, he looks more proud of his second son now and in this moment than I think I've ever seen him look before, in all the time I've known him and have been in Pella.

He turns back to the men from Athens and Thebes. "Well," he tells them. "You heard my son."

They look at Philippos, and then they glance at Alexandros next to me, across the tent from where they stand, and they take in this strange young man with the mis-colored eyes and the unreadable look that's on his face.

They have no other choice, so they nod.

"Of course," they each say. "We swear our loyalty to the basileus of Macedon."

"Then there is peace," Philippos finally smiles, too, and his one good eye shines with accomplishment, as the two men bow to him, and then they leave.

He waits until they're gone. Then he turns to us.

"I hear that Demosthenes himself fought," Philippos says to us, when they're out of ear-shot. "I wish I knew what he looked like, so I could have found him."

"Why?" Arrhidaeus asks, his eyebrows raised.

Philippos turns to him, his simple, oldest son. "So I could have killed him," he says, very plainly, as if he's talking about breakfast, or the weather, and to a toddler.

Arrhidaeus reacts.

He almost physically recoils as he hears this because he's not used to such bluntness, I realize, and such blood lust, the way that men are in Macedon, the men that he's grown around. Philippos sees this and smiles again, and laughs, too, which I find strange, and then he claps Arrhidaeus on the back as he waves his other hand, which is the signal for us to leave, and we start to. We all start to go, making our way towards the flap and the exit, but there's one more thing. "You," I hear. "Stay."

I turn back to Philippos, and see that he's looking past me.

He's looking at Alexandros.

I glance towards Amyntas, who sees this, too, and Amyntas doesn't look pleased, but there's nothing he can do and there's no other choice, so he just leaves, and so do we, all of us except Alexandros, who stays behind with his father.

I squint against the bright sun that's even higher now, when I walk back out.

The generals and everyone else begin to disperse and go their separate ways, some heading back to their tents, others to the fires to continue to drink or to start drinking again, for a second day, but I remain outside of Philippos' tent, and wait for Alexandros.

What else would I do?

I look up again at the sun.

I think of how Alexandros had interrupted his father, and what he said, and then I think of Aristoteles and his lesson about the basileus of Macedon and what he told us after his lesson, about the place in which he sees Macedon, and about language, and its importance.

I nod.

He's right, and so it will be, even for a warrior.

Perhaps *especially* for a warrior, and one who would be basileus himself one day.

"You waited."

I turn to see Alexandros coming from the tent, back out, back into the light.

"Of course."

"You didn't have to."

I frown.

We always wait for each other. This isn't lost on me; both this, and how he went outside the tent while I got ready this morning, rather than waiting inside. "What did he want?" I ask instead.

"We're to go to Athens tomorrow."

We start to walk through the camp together, back towards our tent.

"That's expected. A ruler always goes to the place he's conquered after he conquers it, even if the battle was elsewhere."

"No," Alexandros shakes his head. "Philippos isn't going."

"Really?"

"Yes."

"Then who will?"

"Us. Philippos is going back north."

"Us, and who else?"

"No one."

"Not the army, or the generals?"

"They'll go with Philippos."

"*Just us?*" I frown as we walk, not understanding.

"He doesn't want to enter the city like a conqueror, he says. Though he's of course never shied away from that before, so I suspect it's really something else."

"What?"

"He wants them to remain loyal, while he's back in the north, and then in Asia, so he wants them to trust and not fear him. And also," Alexandros smiles now, though I notice it's a forced smile, "he has another wedding to prepare for."

That's right.

We keep walking, past a few of the officer's tents, and we're almost back to our own tent now. We get there. We stand outside.

Silence.

Then the thing I've really wanted to ask.

"He wasn't upset?"

"About what?"

"*The basileus of Macedon.*"

"No, just the opposite."

"Really?"

"He said that he'd never been more proud of me. Actually, what he said was he'd never been proud of me at all, until then."

I look back at Alexandros.

I open my mouth again, about to ask another question, when—

Wham.

I'm tackled to the ground and land heavily in the dirt.

I look up and see Philotas above me, laughing, and the rest of the Companions, too. They've been up drinking like the others and haven't yet been to sleep, and they still smell of wine and dirt and blood and battle. They pull me back to my feet as soon as I land, and now with the business of war finally finished, along with the fighting and the killing, of course, they grab Alexandros, too, and they pull us both with them and towards a giant fire they've built between their tents. There are drums here. There's more wine, and women that must be locals that they somehow were able to find and bring to camp, though how they managed to find them here, I don't know. I guess it's something they've learned and I haven't. There's much in the area of women I still don't know, or understand, and that I've missed, and at times like this, I think I'm glad that I have. Perdiccas puts his arm around me and tells me how they raided the Greek camp and that's where they found all the wine they're drinking and the wood they're burning. "The wood was used to make a pedestal where they erected a bust of Athena," he tells me. "Can you believe that? That's who they brought to a battle."

I frown again. "And you didn't think it unwise to displease her?"

"Don't worry," he tells me, "the bust is safe." And he nods towards the girls who are holding it and raising it in front of their faces as if it's a mask, playing with it, and playing with the men, too. "And besides," he grins, widely now, "who needs wisdom?"

"We all do."

"Not when we have war and strength!" he laughs, and then slaps me on the back again. "Not when we have love, and strength, and wine, and war. Those are our gods, Hephaestion!" he yells. "Those are the gods of Macedon, and the north."

Then he walks away, drinking more wine yet.

He goes to the other side of the fire and laughs with one of the local girls now who holds the bust of Athena, and he raises it in front of his face, too, and when he does, I look at Alexandros as the girl then kisses Philotas, behind the bust. Alexandros has wine now, himself, and he's talking with the others and drinking deeply, making up for lost time while he slept, while we both slept. I need to talk to him, I know that I do, but the moment's gone now again, it's been taken. It's what he wanted, I know, to avoid it, and now it's happened once more, and there's nothing else to do, so instead, I just shake my head and I join them. I drink a skin of wine, and then I drink another, because I don't want to do or think about what I have to, and then when the second skin is gone, I drink one more after that. Once I've had my fill of wine, I switch to mead. Time speeds up and the sun eventually begins to set again, and then disappear. We drink. We drink even more, and it's the first that I've done this, that I've drank this much, and it's also the first that Alexandros has, too, or at least I think it is, because it's the first time he has since I've known him. Who was he before me? I don't know, but perhaps I need to ask.

We go back to our tent.

Two of the girls follow, when we stand, and they come with us.

Why do they come?

We weren't talking to them, and I don't know who they are.

They know who Alexandros is, though, and they want to be close to him, because of who he is, as we'll find that many will want, and so when we reach our tent, we push the flap open and we all go inside, all four of us. I'm not sure what to do once we're there, but it's alright, because they do. They begin to take their clothes off. They stand there, both of them naked, and then they come towards me and Alexandros, and they take our clothes off, too, and so there are soon no clothes left at all and we're all naked and we push the two cots together, the one that's been used, and the one that hasn't, so that together they make one large bed. They lay down, and then we lower ourselves on top of them, me with one, and him with the other, and there's been so much wine I don't remember much of what goes on or what happens next, or what we all do, before we go to sleep, or when in the night they leave, only I know that at some point they do.

There is no pleasure for me.

There is no pleasure because I know I've already failed, though I don't think of it in those terms, at least not yet. I've failed because I never did talk to him about what happened on the battlefield, and I've failed because I allowed it to happen at all, and then even after it has, I've done nothing.

Forgive me.

Please, forgive me.

We had a great victory, a great and deserved victory, and I know I should have done something, said something, made some change in him and between us, but it was so much easier not to. It was so much easier to do nothing, as it so often is, and so that's what I did.

CHAPTER FIFTEEN

A THENS IS A FULL DAY'S RIDE to the south and east, but our trip is even longer because of how hungover everyone is as we sit our horses and head south in the hot and strong southern sun. We stop for fresh water more times than we normally would, and Nearchos throws up in the Kifisos River, not far from Chaeronea. But once we finally do reach the city, later in the day, everything else is forgotten, because to a group of boys from Macedon and the north, Athens is magnificent. In fact, it's more than that; it's so much more. It's massive, and beyond anything we've ever seen before, or dreamt of, and more beautiful, too, and so much more impressive and awe-inspiring than we've imagined, all the times we've heard stories and constructed in our heads what the great city must look like, what it must sound like, what it must smell like and feel like, too, to walk on the wide cobbled streets where heroes and history have walked, past the grand temples built to wisdom and strength, between the buildings where so many that we've read and heard about lived and spoke and fought and loved. How much has been discovered here? How much of history, and our history, began on these streets where we now walk and between these buildings where we now stand?

It's overwhelming.

We also must look strange, and out of place, I realize.

And I know we must look it, because we all certainly feel it.

We keep walking through the streets that wind between the seven hills of the city and look up at the Akropolis in the distance—the akron, the highest point, and highest hill amongst the seven—and the magnificent Parthenon perched on top of it. Every corner and town square has some sort of carving or bust of Athena, the city's patron saint, some near pillars, some etched into walls, and some just standing on their own, and the temples to Athena are all bigger, too; they're all bigger and more ornately carved than any that are in Pella, or anywhere else in the north that I've been or seen, and their temples to Athena dwarf even the Temple of Dionysus that we walk past every day on our way from the palace to the gymnasium. I think about what I felt, the first day that I saw it, what I felt about the sheer size and majesty of it, and now here's more, here's so much more. Is there even more than this, too? I don't know, but as I walk here I understand perhaps a little bit more about life, and what it holds, and the majesty and wonder that can come if it's lived boldly, the way it should be lived.

We continue.

We go to the famous agora.

We walk through all the people that are there and all the stalls, too. There are so many men, women, children, slaves, and servants, all packed together and next to each other in this great city, and while Aristoteles had told us about this, and told us that he estimated there were around two hundred thousand people that lived in Athens, I still didn't think it would be so big and there would be so many. Because there are. The size is near incomprehensible to those who have only seen what we've seen in Illyria, and Macedon, and Pella, in the north and amongst the fields and mountains and smaller villages that dominate our country.

Are we actually barbarians?

Are we, of the northern and more wild tribes, what they in the south have spent so much time saying we are? I don't know, but what I do know is that while there are Greeks in the south, and there are Greeks in the north, we have not built this: we have not built anything even close to this.

But could we?

Could we, if that was our goal, instead of strength and war and conquest?

I don't know. I don't know.

We come to another temple which is also dedicated to Athena, of course, and bigger than all the others, bigger than any other building we've yet passed, and we stop in front of it. We stand there and look at it, all of us with our necks craned, staring and studying the great and carved columns that line the entrance and face the street, taking in the beauty.

"Should we go inside?" Perdiccas asks.

I think of the mask, and of the games they played at Chaeronea, after the battle. I think of strength, first, and then, here in the city that's dedicated to it, I then think of wisdom.

"Have you ever prayed to her?" I ask him, and the others.

I stay looking up at the columns, as they all turn to look at me now. I can feel them, all of their eyes on me.

"What for?" Philotas asks.

"For wisdom, of course."

"I pray for the opposite of that," Leonnatos smiles. "I pray for strength, and the many opportunities to be stronger, and little else. I like my life simple."

"I do, too," Nearchos nods.

"And me," Perdiccas says, also.

"And that's why we won at Chaeronea, right?" Kassandros slaps me on the back, harder than he should. "They might have had wisdom on their side, but we had strength, and such is the way of our world that what we worship triumphs over what they do."

Does it?

I'm not sure that it does.

They all laugh, though, because they're sure.

Well, all of them except Alexandros, who stays silent, because he knows that I'm speaking both *of* and *to* him, and to him alone, as I always do, but he's stayed close to the rest of them and the others and his father and the girls since the battle, so that we wouldn't be alone together and he wouldn't have to hear what he knows I would tell him. The Companions begin to lose interest in the temple and the city and all the rest, and they start making plans to begin drinking again—to drink away their hangovers, they say—and I'm surprised when Alexandros says he'll join them. I will not. I watch as they all leave, heading into the distance and down the cobble-stone streets and back in the direction of the agora. When they're gone, I think of my options, and can't decide what to do, but here I am in this great place for such a short period of time, and so I know I must do something, and more, and so I will.

I look up.

There it is, the Akropolis, and the Parthenon, glittering in the distance, above me, above everything, keeping watch over the city through years, through decades, through so many passing stewards and citizens and so much time.

What has this temple seen?

What voices and dreams has it felt, and heard spoken, and then been realized there within its walls?

That's it, I decide; that's what I'll do.

I will go to find out, and maybe then my wild and northern dreams will be heard amongst all the others that have been heard and dreamed there, too.

I START WALKING BACK towards the agora, like they do, though I take a different route and go *around* the agora, to the southern side, just beneath the Akropolis, and then I go beyond it. I go to the path that smells of either damp or dried pine this time of year, and that leads up and towards the great, rocky outcropping that forms the mighty and towering citadel of sharp and uneven rock above the city and above me, and then I start to climb. I climb up the slope in front of me and breathe heavily as I go, as it's extremely steep, and long, even for one that's in the best of shape, as I am. I keep climbing past the smell of pine that's there until there's only dust, and I finally get to the top, and that's when I see the entirety of the temple in front of me: it's larger and more impressive than anything I've ever seen in my life, and it's so large and impressive I wonder how men and men alone could have built such a thing.

But men and gods together?

Surely that's what has made this, has done the impossible here, because that's what it takes to *do* the impossible, right, men and gods and fate, all intertwined and woven together and working towards one common thing?

I go inside.

It's dark and there are others that are here, too, but not many. There are a few lit candles and the light that comes from the candles is what flickers across the massive gold and ivory statue of Athena that's there in front of me; *Athena Parthenos*, that Aristoteles told us about during one of our lessons in Mieza, and how it had been created by the great sculptor Phidias who also sculpted the statue of Zeus at Olympia, which was one of the wonders of Greece and the world.

My breath becomes uneven, and then stops altogether.

I continue to look and my eyes start at the top of the statue, and the sphinx that's carved onto Athena's helmet, and then the two griffins that are there on either side of it. My eyes tilt further down and I look at the small statue of Nike that she holds in her right hand, and I look at the spear in her other hand and the shield that rests at her feet and serpent that coils and wraps itself around the shield. I wish Aristoteles had taught us more, and of other great things like this; I wish we had more time with him, and his wisdom, there amongst the ancient olives and the cool breeze in Mieza, the imperfect sanctuary that for a time we all shared and was perfect while we did.

The light flickers, and my breath returns.

More people begin to come, and I turn and go back out.

The sun begins to sink, warm and bright in the distance over soft hills and the gentle sea, because it is more gentle here in the south, and the last rays come and begin to touch near where I stand. They come and touch the sea first, and then the countryside, and finally the great Akropolis where I wait for it, where I wait for the light.

I walk to the edge.

I get there and then sit down, and with my feet hanging over the side, I look out and beyond. I think about where I was born, and where I'm from. I think about who I am, and where I now sit, and who I've come here with, to this great city. I'm just a boy from Salona who's now at the very heart of Greece, and the world, in the middle of the greatest city the world's ever seen and known, and it's mine, it's all mine, because he is, and it's our city now, and all the people that we see, whether they know it or not, will swear allegiance to fight for and to serve us because tomorrow they'll swear in our presence to serve the basileus of Macedon.

I think of the battle again.

I think of the battle, and then what happened after, and I know I have a decision to make.

I've prayed to Ares, many times in my life.

I've prayed to Zeus, too, and Apollo, and Hermes, and since I've moved to Pella, I've even tried praying to Dionysus, also, on occasion, as they all do in Pella where he's most strong and most felt and worshipped. He doesn't speak to me, though, in the way that he speaks to the others.

The sun sinks.

It's even lower in the sky now, the light almost gone.

I know what I need, and so for the first time in my life, I close my eyes, just as the light begins to depart, and I now whisper a soft prayer to Athena, too.

ALEXANDROS RETURNS some time in the night. I wake up because when he comes into our room he collapses onto my bed, and next to me, and not on his bed. I move so that our skin doesn't touch, because it's hot, and then the next day, we both rise early to go about our business in Athens, and the reason why we're here. We dress and shave in silence, and then after we do, we meet the rest of the Companions and then leave to go to the ekklesia that will be held—the great gathering of Athenians near another famous hill at the edge of the city, and near the path I took up to the Akropolis—and we all go together. When we finally arrive, we find it's just as Aristoteles had told us and described; we go past the agora again, first, on our way there, which is in the shadow of the Akropolis and the Parthenon perched above, and then we go around and past the Akropolis and on towards the low hill called Pnyx where the ekklesia meets on the raised and level area that sits in the shadow of the much greater one above it. As we round the corner and then reach the hill and ride up it, on the well-worn path, between the tall cypress trees that line it and that smell both sweet and fresh and of ancient pine here, too, we then see the six thousand gathered Athenian men; all Athenian males, once they gain citizenship, are allowed to come to the ekklesia and participate in any decisions that are to be made about the city, and there might be even more than six thousand, now that I begin to count, or at least try to, there are so many who have come to see us and be present for this decision that will affect Athens for the next hundred years, and maybe even more than that, too.

They quiet, when we approach, they all become very quiet.

The hill itself where the ekklesia gathers is sharp and steep with a rocky outcropping at the northern end that forms a natural barrier, and then in addition to that natural barrier, we can see the outline of the engineered one continuing from it, the Themistoclean Wall which is roughly the same height as a grown man. It was something that was built a hundred and fifty years earlier, to keep the Persians out when they made it as far as this city. I can't help but smile. It must have been a lot of work to build it, and it didn't keep the Persians out at all, who burned and razed Athens completely to the ground. There's a new section to it that's also been built, and I realize it must have been built for us, and I smile again because the lesson clearly wasn't learned and the useless wall certainly didn't work to keep us out, either.

We stand in front of the entire gathered assembly.

Then a short and balding man comes forward from that larger group, and he introduces himself.

Demosthenes.

It's the famous orator himself, the one who for the past decade has warned of the rising Macedonian power in the north and has called Philippos and his family and all the rest of us barbarians and not Greek, time and time and time again, and the greatest living threat to them, and their way of life. He holds a cane now, and walks with a slight limp, which is new. I see the Companions near me looking back at him, after he introduces himself, and when they see his cane and limp they smirk at his fresh wound, because they know where he received it, and how, and who gave it to him. I see their looks, and I wonder: why did Philippos send us? Why did he send us, we who are so, so young? I look back to Alexandros and I see that he's stone-faced, and perhaps that's the answer. That's the Alexandros I know, finally, and for the first time since before Chaeronea, I see that Alexandros is himself again, and not the Alexandros I saw after the battle and have seen since then.

Perhaps that's why; perhaps that's exactly why.

Demosthenes stands in front of us.

Another man comes from the assembled Athenians and stands next to him—Demades, the leader of the opposition in the ekklesia—and while they both stand there and all are ready for Demosthenes' famous words that will now come, it's Alexandros who speaks first. "You've stood here, in this very spot, and called my father, and his kingdom, and my home, *barbarian* for more times than I can count," Alexandros says, still stone-faced.

"I have," Demosthenes nods, no use denying what we all know.

"And so what do you say now?"

Demosthenes stands there and looks back at us.

He stands there and looks back at the young men that stand in front of him, measuring both his resolve, and ours, I can see, as he moves and shifts his gaze and stares into Alexandros' twice-colored eyes. "I say that I've stood here and spoken truth," Demosthenes finally answers. "I also say that truth doesn't change anything that's happened, or anything that will."

"No," Alexandros tells him. "It doesn't."

"So what are your father's terms?"

The terms have already been presented, of course, and agreed to, but that's why we're here; to repeat them, in front of all the assembled Athenians and to receive their oaths of support in return. Alexandros has other plans, though.

"Do you still think us barbarians?" he asks instead.

"If I told you differently, I wouldn't have much honor."

"And what about you?" Alexandros asks, nodding towards Demades.

"The people have chosen Demosthenes to speak," Demades says, and he bows his head in deference.

Alexandros looks at him for a moment, and then back at Demosthenes again, next to him, and then he finally turns to all the rest of the people, the whole of the gathered ekklesia. "My father's terms are the swearing of loyalty to the basileus of Macedon," Alexandros says loudly. "He demands loyalty from all people of Athens, as well as all the other poleis that fought with Athens and against us. He also asks for support in both livestock and soldiers, for when we march east. And he has asked for your head, Demosthenes," Alexandros finishes, as he turns back to look at the orator next to him.

There's silence.

Demosthenes swallows.

This last thing of course hadn't been said to him before, or agreed to, and I remain looking at Demades, and the smile that comes and doesn't leave his lips.

"If that's the price for peace, and for Athens to remain as it is . . ." Demosthenes finally stammers, perhaps the first time he's been lost for words here and in front of the ekklesia.

"It's not," Alexandros tells him, his eyes not changing, nor his expression. "I convinced my father we didn't need your head, just your loyalty to Macedon, you above all others whose words sway and move this city."

"That's . . . very generous."

"So there is a deal, then?"

Demosthenes stares back at Alexandros, and the rest of us, for another moment as the breeze that comes brings with it the smell of sweet pine again that drifts over and between us, between all of us that are gathered here at this sacred and important place between the tall and ancient cypress, and then he turns back to the gathered men of the ekklesia.

"All those in favor?" he asks.

Next to him, Demades' hand is the first that's raised.

Then another hand raises, and another, and another still after that. There are more that go up, and then soon all of them do as it is, after all, a very generous offer after such a sound defeat: they will be bled of troops and food, but not having to pay any gold, give any slaves or ransom, or cede land, territory, or the ability to self-govern? That will be seen as a huge victory for all the Athenians that are gathered, and the best possible outcome.

"So we're agreed, then," Alexandros says, nodding, "and there will be peace between all Greeks on this peninsula."

"So be it," Demosthenes says, and then bows.

Demades bows, too, next to him.

It's over, and it's settled.

We turn and begin to walk away, all of us, together, and we've only gone a few paces when we hear Demosthenes' voice, one last time, coming from behind us.

"Alexandros . . ." he says.

And we all pause. We turn back.

"Yes?" he asks, raising an eyebrow.

"Perhaps I was wrong," Demosthenes says, when he has our eyes. "Perhaps I wrong about you, and your father, and Macedon."

Alexandros waits, just for a moment.

Then he smiles.

"No," he says, shaking his head. "No, you weren't."

WE LEAVE ATHENS QUICKLY, right after the ekklesia. I would've liked to have stayed longer and seen more, but we need to get back to Pella before the wedding, as we've been ordered to do. Our horses are saddled and waiting when we return, and when we reach them, we jump up and onto their backs, and then start to ride, heading towards the northern edge of the city and the road that will bring us back north.

I kick the brown to a trot.

I ride so that I'm next to Alexandros again, and Bucephalus.

He looks over at me.

"Well?" he asks, when he sees my eyes.

"Nothing," I say, and shake my head.

He knows me better than that, though.

"What is it?" he asks again.

"Did your father really ask for Demosthenes' head?"

"No. But now Demosthenes knows that he might, and thinks it was me that spared him."

We keep riding.

"So what happens next?" I ask him.

"We go north again, of course."

"Yes, but then what?"

"I suppose that will be up to my father, and how long he wishes to spend in his new marriage bed."

I think of Philippos, and his age, and his leg.

Then I think of Pausanius, and the way that Philippos looks at him.

He won't be in the marriage bed long, I assume, because we always return to the place that heals us, when we need to be healed, and for the basileus, it's not the bed of a child-bride. We keep riding and are just outside the city when we see a grove of low trees, and a man sitting underneath the curved branches. The man is dirty, completely naked, and when Alexandros sees him, he stops one of the Athenians that's going in the opposite direction and asks who the man is.

"That's Diogenes," the Athenian tells us, with distaste in his voice.

I recognize the name.

He's a famous Cynic philosopher and we were told about him by Aristoteles, who recounted stories of his time at Plato's Akademia, while they were both there.

The Athenian continues on, and then so do we.

Alexandros keeps looking at Diogenes, though, and then kicks Bucephalus to a gallop. He starts to ride across the countryside and towards him, and I kick the brown to a gallop, too, and follow after Alexandros. When we get closer, Alexandros slows, and so do I. I ride next to him now, and when I do, he turns to me.

"I'll go the rest of the way alone," he tells me.

I'm confused.

He's never said anything like this to me before, because we've always shared everything, but instead of saying that, or anything else, I simply nod, because things have changed between us, and so I do as he asks and as a different Companion might.

He continues forward, on his own.

I watch from the place between Alexandros, in front of me, and the Companions and the rest of our party, behind, and when he reaches this new and different philosopher, he dismounts. I watch as he drops Bucephalus' reins and the horse stays there with Alexandros, and then Alexandros goes forward to speak with Diogenes. They don't speak for very long, and then once they're finished, and there are no more words, Alexandros walks back to Bucephalus, jumps back up and onto him and then they turn and ride towards us.

When he reaches me, we both sit there, on our horses, and look at each other. There's another look in Alexandros' eyes now; something that I again can't quite read, and I haven't seen or felt before. "What did he say?" I finally ask.

"Nothing," Alexandros answers quickly.

"I saw you speaking. He said something."

Alexandros is silent for a moment, when I say this to him, and he looks down. He stays like this for another moment, his eyes turned away from me. "I can't always be Alexandros," he finally tells me.

"What?" I frown, not understanding.

But he doesn't answer.

Instead, he kicks Bucephalus to a gallop and starts to ride back towards the rest of the group and after another moment of looking back, towards the grove of low trees and the man that sits under the branches there, I turn and join them, too.

We change our course.

Instead of going north and to Macedon, Alexandros now insists that we go west, and back to Chaeronea, first, and when we reach the field, we see that it's still stained red. There are still many men and women here that are collecting all the Greek dead, burying them, burning them, the undignified business that comes *after* war and glory, the things so rarely seen and told in story or song. We pause as we look at all this, and survey all that's in front of us, all that we've done. It's not glory that's here anymore, on this field now; it's just blood and death and the price we've paid—the price we've all paid—and it changes us, as it should. Alexandros calls a Macedonian officer to him and I recognize him as one of Philippos' veterans, a man named Polemon, and Alexandros tells Polemon that he's going to leave him gold.

"Gold?" Polemon asks, not understanding. "For what?"

"To build a monument," Alexandros tells him. "I want you to build something here that will stand for all the rest of time, to give memory to all those who died to bring unity to this peninsula."

"What do you want the monument to be?"

There's nothing for a moment, with Alexandros looking out at the field, at the dead, at those that move amongst them. "A lion," he finally says, then turns to look at me, and only me. "Do you understand now?" he asks.

Then he dismounts from Bucephalus, and starts to walk, away from us.

"What's he talking about?" Ptolemaios says, from his place next to me, frowning and raising his eyebrows as Alexandros goes towards the field of blood.

"Nothing."

"A lion? What does that mean?"

"Let him go."

"That's not what I asked."

"I know, but just let him go," I say again. "Let him be alone."

"Why?"

"Because he is."

They all look at me and they know I understand things about Alexandros that they do not, so after a moment, they just simply nod, and they don't ask any more questions. We sit there and wait. We all sit there on our horses and we wait and watch as Alexandros continues onto the bloody field and walks amongst the dead that are there, amongst the departed, and their ghosts, and he walks alone. I see him stop at a body that I recognize, even from this distance, a young Theban with a dark birthmark on his face and I think about what his mother told me, about the gods that live within him. Why didn't I push him? Why didn't I push him harder, about what he did, and why? Because, I suppose, I'm human, too, and I'm weak in the same way that we all are weak, especially when it comes to those that we love.

Temper him.

I understand now, or at least I think I do, but have I failed?

Is it too late, and have I failed already?

CHAPTER SIXTEEN

WE RETURN TO PELLA, and when we do, we find that a great many things have changed, even during the short time we've been away and in the south. People have heard of Alexandros' exploits from the soldiers who have already come back, and specifically how it was him, Philippos' middle child, who was chosen as the envoy to Athens and thus it is Alexandros, Philippos' middle child, who now so clearly holds the basileus' regard and favor. They've heard about what Alexandros did after the battle, too, but they just smile, and nod, as if it's exactly what a young man and warrior should do. Only a few short months ago, it had been Amyntas, Philippos' nephew, towards whom they smiled and nodded because he held Philippos' regard, which is how fast both fate and favor can change in our world, I realize. And if it changes once in such a fashion, that means it can change again, and in the same way, doesn't it? But how soon and to whom it would go, if it does . . . that's what only time will tell us, and that's what we'll have to wait to find out.

Philippos' leg has seemed to deteriorate even more, after returning from Chaeronea, but he's not allowed it to slow the planning of his wedding. Olympias insists on seeing Alexandros the moment he's arrived back in the city, and when he comes from seeing her, returning to the room we share, his eyes look exhausted as he sits on his bed and sighs, and tells me everything that she's told him; all that she's warned him of, and specifically how she's warned him of Attalus again, who is Eurydice's father and one of Philippos' generals who will now also be his father-in-law. She tells him how Attalus has told all who will listen that his daughter will give the basileus a Macedonian son, a true-born and true-bred Macedonian son for him to leave behind and for all to be proud of before he marches east to liberate the Greeks of Asia Minor that are under Persian rule. And she tells him how Amyntas has told all who will listen that he sleeps with Aria whenever he wants, and that she left Alexandros for a real man, one who doesn't lay with her to hide what he truly is. She is a monster, his mother. His father is, too, in his own way.

Both have made him, and both are inside him.

Which one will win, though? Or will he?

THE DAY OF THE WEDDING soon comes and it's not one that I'm looking forward to. Alexandros and I train with the Companions that morning, down at the gymnasium, like we've done so many mornings before. It feels good to do so again; it feels normal, and I'm glad to be back to our old routine and we smile as we go through our exercises. We laugh, and we joke with each other, enjoying the familiarity, the pattern. We shove each other and playfully wrestle, head-locks, ruffling of hair and pinning each other against sand. Everything's different now, though, because we're warriors now. We've had our first blood and for boys such as we are, that matters. Blood, in our world, and in so many ways, is all that matters.

When we finish training, we leave the gymnasium and walk through the city, and back up to the palace. Alexandros and I walk together, and as we do, everyone we pass nods in deference and respect to the basileus' new-favored son. We get back to the palace, and we go to our room to get prepared and we each use the water from the basin to rinse the dirt from our bodies, and then we shave again. Once we're clean and freshly shaved, we get dressed in silence, in freshly pressed and bleached chitons special for the occasion. We're soon ready. It doesn't take us long. It's not time to leave yet, though, so Alexandros goes to the table in our room where I now see there's a jug of wine, and he pours us each a cup.

"Already?" I ask him, as I take it from his outstretched hand.

"It'll help us get through this," he answers, and he drinks.

We sit there and don't talk much, but we drink together, we each have our first cup, and then we each have another, too. Then soon after our second cups are finished, it's time to go.

We stand.

We straighten our bleached and pressed chitons.

Then we leave, and we walk through the palace, and down to the great Temple of Dionysus, where the ceremony will take place. This is unusual for a Macedonian wedding, to have it at the temple, and it was Attalus' idea to have it here, and in the capital. Why? Because not only is Dionysus the god of wine and ecstasy, but he's also the god of fertility.

The message is not lost on Olympias.

Neither is it lost on her son.

We enter the temple where everyone is already gathered and we stand with the rest of the Companions, near the far wall. Across from us, on the other side of the temple, I see Olympias; she stands amongst all the other wives, and Cleopatra is there with her, too, both of them dressed in white, and when Olympias sees us, she walks in our direction. She leaves the place where she's supposed to stand, with the other wives, and Cleopatra comes along with her. They cross the aisle, and when they do, Alexandros moves so that the place in the center of us is empty, and that's where they come to. The other wives watch them. So do the generals, and the soldiers, and the gathered nobles. I see Amyntas amongst the generals, even though he's not one and doesn't belong there, and he looks shorter to me now than the last time I saw him. I know that can't be, but he still does.

Then there's a noise, and we look back towards the entrance to see Philippos walk into the temple, with his heavy limp, and his new bride next to him.

They slowly come down the aisle that's formed by people on either side, and they approach the temple's simple altar, a large horizontal stone that rests perpendicularly on two other vertical stones. They get closer, and as they do, I see the girl more clearly. I knew that she was young, but this girl is only a child, I realize. How old is she? How old is she really? And who approved this? We had been told that she was sixteen, but she looks younger than that to me, and I know she must to everyone else, then, too.

She holds Philippos' arm, as they walk, and there's fear in her young eyes.

They finally reach the altar, and while the basileus may walk with a more pronounced limp now, than he ever has before, he has a smile on his face, despite the physical pain.

Who is the smile for?

What is it for?

I look to Alexandros, next to me, as he stares across the aisle, and then I look to see who it is that he's staring at.

Attalus.

Watching his daughter, and the basileus.

And the look on Attalus' face? I recognize that look.

Victory. Pure, simple victory.

Philippos and Eurydice stand in front of the priest at the altar, and then Eurydice goes forward, alone, and I see that she carries something in her hand: it's a toy, one of her childhood toys, an old and worn piece of wood that's been carved to look like a small rabbit. She holds it for a moment, clutching it to her chest. Then she bends down and places it at the feet of the priest.

Her sacrifice.

A girl who will now, after tonight, be a girl no longer.

The priest nods as he bends down and picks up the toy, gently placing it on the altar behind him, and then he makes another gesture and a decorated bull is led out from darkness by a young boy and it's moved so that it stands in front of us.

The priest reaches out, and he holds the bull steady, with one hand, as the boy backs away. Then with the other hand, the priest passes an ornate and ceremonial knife to Philippos.

The girl gave her sacrifice, the symbol of her childhood.

Now this is Philippos' sacrifice, a symbol of the strength he'll use to protect her.

Philippos turns and faces the gathered crowd, holding the knife high, for all to see. Then he lowers it, and places it under the bull's throat.

He waits for a moment, for theatrics, and for eyes to settle on him.

Then he flexes and quickly pulls his hand back, in a sawing motion.

The bull lets out a great cry that's then cut short and silenced, as its life rushes down the basileus' hand, wrist, arm, and lands in a great puddle on the mosaic-tiled floor with a splatter that spills across the feet of Philippos, the priest, and also the bride, who closes her eyes and turns away.

The bull stands there.

It turns, to look at Philippos, at his one good eye.

The bull makes one more noise, one more soft and weak noise, in the direction of Philippos, then teeters on its feet and falls to its knees. It stays like that, for a moment, then the great and heavy body sinks all the way to stone, where it then lies still.

Silence.

The priest comes forward.

He bends down and dips the index and middle fingers of his right hand into the blood, then stands again, and walks to the couple.

He wipes the blood on the basileus' brow first.

Strength. Power.

Then he goes to the bride and wipes blood on her brow, too.

Protection. Fertility.

Next to me, I hear Olympias suck in her breath as the priest does this, and I don't know if she makes this sound because she remembers when she stood next to Philippos and was promised to him in the same way, with a vow bound and fortified by the life-blood of the same great sacrifice, or if it's something else.

The priest raises his hands.

He raises them high, up and towards the stars, and the gods.

Then he looks down at us, at all of us that are gathered.

"The gods have blessed this union, and this basileus, *Philippos-Argeadai*," he speaks in a strong and steady voice. "And what the gods have blessed, so shall be."

The crowd cheers.

Everyone that's gathered yells and throws dried fruits and nuts into the air, a Macedonian tradition to bless the new couple with more fertility and happiness.

Then the procession begins.

Attalus comes forward and takes his daughter's hand and puts it into the basileus' hand, and they start to walk again. Well, Philippos shuffles mostly, and unevenly, the priest leading them now, and they walk back in the exact same way, the only difference is that now they crush nuts and dried fruit under their sandaled-feet as they walk.

They leave the temple.

The wives and daughters follow after them, then the generals, and then finally the common soldiers that have been invited to represent the army.

We don't leave, though.

Outside, there's a chariot that waits to bring the basileus and his new bride up to the palace which isn't tradition, but rather a necessity, due to Philippos' leg. The rest of the men and women walk behind the chariot, as it begins the symbolic journey of the new bride, going from the gods at the temple to her new home at the palace.

"I told you," I hear Olympias whisper, once there's no one else left to hear. "Didn't I tell you?"

Alexandros looks at the ground for a moment. I think he won't answer, but then he looks up, and meets her eyes. He's silent, and so is she.

We all watch to see what he'll do.

"We have to go to the feast," he finally says.

"Why?"

"Because he's shown me favor. For once in my life, he's finally shown me favor."

"Just remember what I told you, my young son, my *very* young son," she pauses, then smiles, slowly. "Philippos' favor is the sun, and I've known it once, too, which you sometimes forget, don't you? But just like the sun, which rises in the morning, it also sets and disappears, and the only thing that's left when it does is darkness. You might think yourself favored, and you may be, right now, but he goes to his bed tonight to conceive your replacement in both his favor and the favor of all the others, too. Of that you can have no doubt. So just wait. Just wait, and watch, because it might even be tonight, couldn't it, that he decides to change his mind."

"How?"

"He'll tell you, of course. He'll tell you himself, because he's not clever."

It seems to have gotten colder in the temple.

She turns to me.

"And what of you?" she asks me.

"What of me?" I frown, not understanding.

"Patroklos tried to talk sense into Achilleus," she says, her eyes flashing. "Did he not, after the hero was betrayed by Agamemnon? And so where have you been, Hephaestion? Isn't that the oath you made to each other, and what you swore?"

"Don't bring Hephaestion into this," Alexandros says, next to me.

"Why? Can't he answer for himself? And what about the rest of you?" she asks, then turns to the Companions. "What about the rest of you, my Myrmidons? Can you answer for yourselves, and are you even Myrmidons at all? Don't you want to see my son become basileus?"

"Of course we do," Ptolemaios says, as he steps forward, looking at Cleopatra first, and then Olympias.

"Then *do something* about it," she practically spits at him, at us, at all of us.

Then after she speaks, she turns and leaves.

Cleopatra looks at Ptolemaios, quickly, and then at Alexandros.

"I'll go with her," she tells her brother, then pulls up her chiton so that it doesn't catch around her legs and jogs after their mother.

We watch them go.

There's silence again, then—

"She charges a high price for nine months rent, Alexandros," Kassandros finally says with slurred words, and when we turn to look at him, we see that his eyes are glassy and I know he's been drinking, too, and he's drunk too much.

Alexandros looks at him.

Then he laughs.

He can't help himself. "Some day I'm going to use that, and pretend it was me that thought of it."

"That's no problem," Nearchos smiles, "I don't think Kassandros is going to remember this, so he won't know."

"He's right," Kassandros smiles. "I probably won't."

We all laugh now.

"I need a drink," Perdiccas says.

"Another, don't you mean?" Leonnatos punches his shoulder.

"I think we all could use one," Philotas coughs. "How does anyone deal with these things sober?"

"I don't know," Ptolemaios shakes his head. "Nobody in Macedon ever does, so I suppose that's our answer, and why the gods give us grapes and wine."

"They do, they do," Kassandros answers. "Of course they do. So the feast? All of us?"

"The feast," Philotas nods.

"The feast," we all agree. "The feast."

Fists are pounded against chests, hands are slapped upon backs, more shoulders are punched and hugs given, then we all turn and go up to the palace, together.

THE CANDLES AND LIGHTING ARE LOW, and so are the couches, as they always are. We enter the great hall and there's an area in the far corner, away from the main group, and we sit on the couches there by ourselves. Barely dressed boys and girls come and fill our wine cups, as always, and when they do, we drink, then hold our cups out and they fill them again. In front of us, in the center of the hall, Philippos lays next to his new wife but, as he lays there, even in these first moments, his eyes wander. They turn to Pausanius, who sits amongst the women and wives, who haven't yet been dismissed, and Pausanius looks back at Philippos, too. Philippos wants to go to him, I know, but he won't insult Attalus, or at least I think he won't. Not tonight. All subsequent nights there are no such obligations, of course, as there isn't for any of the many-married men in Pella and Macedon, but there is on the wedding night, when the groom is expected to take the bride to his bed and begin the process of making a child.

I look at Alexandros.

Near us, the other Companions drink their wine and talk to the girls that are around them, and Alexandros drinks his wine, too, more than I've ever seen him drink at a feast, but he ignores the girls that come to him. Instead, he looks at his father, also. He watches with narrowed eyes as Attalus and Amyntas come to sit next to the basileus, and congratulate him, and slap him on the back, and they all drink too much. Philippos is visibly drunk, and laughing along with them, much too loudly, much louder than he normally does, and his laugh echoes through the hall.

I've thought it before, and now I think it again.

Enemies, I think, as I watch them.

Enemies all around.

Alexandros finishes his wine next to me then holds his cup to be refilled again. As soon as it is, he takes another gulp, nearly finishing the whole thing in one drink.

"What are you thinking?" I ask him, with concern.

"That I don't want to be here," he says, as he wipes his mouth.

I look at his eyes.

"Then let's go," I tell him.

"I can't."

"Of course you can."

"It's an insult."

"Since when have you been concered with insults, or decorum? And besides, he's seen us, so he knows we were here, which is enough. There are no rules as to how long you have to stay, he obviously won't remember tomorrow, anyways, and if he does, say you found a girl yourself and left with her. How could Philippos possibly have anything to say against that?"

Alexandros doesn't answer, for a moment, thinking about this.

Then he nods. "You're right," he finally says.

And I am, so we stand.

Alexandros is unsteady, I see, but *only* I can see this because it's only the slightest of tics, only the smallest nuance and difference from the way he normally moves and something no one else but me would be able to pick up on.

I know that I'm right, though, when I see this, and that we need to go.

We start to walk away.

The other Companions look from their wine and girls and raise their eyebrows when they see us, but I just shake my head, and we keep walking. We're almost gone, almost to the great doors and out of the hall, when I hear a voice from behind us: it's a strong voice, coming from near where Philippos lays. "And where are *you* going, Alexandros?" the voice says, and I turn back when I hear it.

So does Alexandros.

I don't want him to, but he does, and I close my eyes briefly to whisper a swift prayer, a prayer to Athena, who I pray to now, before I open them again.

We see Attalus.

He's the one who's spoken and he stands next to where Philippos lies on his couch with Parmenion and Antipater beside him, too, and Eurydice, and then Amyntas also comes to stand near. Alexandros looks at them, then back at me, next to him. He can't say that he's leaving with one of the girls, not now. I don't think he would have, anyways.

"What do you want?" he finally asks Attalus, no hint of wine in his voice.

"You're the son of the basileus, Alexandros, and this is the basileus' wedding! Your father is about to go to his bedchamber with his bride, and I thought you would want to see him off, as is custom," Attalus smiles, then turns and addresses everyone in the hall as he spreads his arms wide. "I thought you would all want to see Philippos-basileus off, as he leaves with his new true-born Macedonian wife, the *first* of his wives to be true-born Macedonian, and on his way to finally make a true-born Macedonian child and heir that we can be proud of here in our kingdom!"

"*True-born*," Alexandros says, his voice rising, the wine coming through now.

"That's right," Attalus answers, as he nods, then turns back to face us.

"So what does that make me?" Alexandros asks, his eyes narrowing.

"The same thing you've always been," Attalus tells him, his words rehearsed, the smile and smirk on his face planned. "The son of a very great ruler, and a used-up barbarian whore."

Silence.

They all wait, everyone gathered in the hall, to see what Alexandros will do.

I wait, too.

I can't intervene.

I can't make this decision for him, and I'm relieved when I see him smile his familiar smile; his small, clever smile, his smile of one in control of his destiny and future, and in control of his anger and temper, too. "You should choose your friends more wisely, Father," Alexandros says. "You never know when they might change their mind and say the same about you."

Everyone laughs.

We turn to leave.

We head towards the door again, at the back of the hall, together, but just as we do—

I see something.

A body.

It streaks past us, quickly, in a blur.

I snap my head to look and in an instant I see that it's Ptolemaios and he's grabbed a xyston spear from a guard who holds it loosely, in surprised fingers, and when Ptolemaios rips it from the guard's hand, he turns and throws it.

"Ptolemaios, no!" I shout, and try to grab him.

But I'm too late.

The xyston sails through the air, twisting, spinning, and then—

Clang.

Philippos, Attalus, and the others duck, and Eurydice shrieks and falls to the floor, too, but the spear sails over them all and bounces harmlessly against a column behind them where it makes a great clattering noise as steel sparks against stone, then falls to the ground.

Philippos is on his feet in an instant.

"Apologize!" he yells.

He's unsteady as he jumps up, and his speech slurred.

I see that Ptolemaios has slipped and fallen, too, heavily and to the floor and in a puddle of spilled wine, and the other Companions have come and are helping him back up through the haze of alcohol, darkness, food, and all other forms of intoxication that the god they worship has brought.

"It's Attalus who should apologize," Alexandros says as he walks forward, to stand between his father and his friend.

He might be able to control his temper, but his loyalty?

Alexandros can stand the insults when they're directed at him, but when they're directed at his friends?

"He nearly killed us!" Philippos yells.

"The spear was nowhere near you," Alexandros replies, in calmer words, but then can't help but add. "And besides, he only did what I should have."

"You little bastard!" Philippos shouts now.

Behind him, Attalus smiles, having finally caused the chaos he wished to have caused and provoked Philippos into publicly using the word he wanted him to use, and all the while Alexandros still stands in front of Ptolemaios, his friend, between him and danger. Alexandros is weaponless as he stands there, unarmed and vulnerable, but he'll protect his Companion, and if anyone ever had any doubt why he's a leader of men and the leader of us, then there is certainly none left now. Philippos goes to take a step—a large step towards his son—but then something happens: his leg seizes up, the wounded one, and when it does...

He slips, and he falls.

He topples from the couch where he had been and lands heavily, on the stone floor, sending a nearby table flying and the wine cups that are on it flip and fall on Philippos, too, spilling more dark red liquid across both him and the mosaic-tiled floor.

He yells in anger, and embarrassment.

He grabs a sword and uses it to help him try to stand, as a sort of crutch, but he slips again as we watch, on the wine and the stone and the hem of his chiton that gets caught under his leg that won't respond in the way it used to when he was young and strong, like we are now, and he knows it. He knows he isn't those things anymore, those things that we are. Is it any surprise that no son follows his father onto the throne of Macedon? Of course it isn't, and I finally understand; in this kingdom, sons aren't heirs, they're threats.

"I'll kill you!" Philippos shouts.

Alexandros walks closer and stands over him, his father.

He's silent for a moment, as he looks down at him, with fire in his own eyes now as he meets Philippos' one good eye.

"If only you could, old man," he says, very calmly, very quietly, this the greatest curse that he knows. And only I, who knows every inch of him, every inch of his body, his mannerisms, his movements, know that he wouldn't have said this if he hadn't started drinking at noon, like the others always do. It's wine that's caused this. Wine, and what else?

Poison.

It's wine mixed with the poison from his mother, the venomous and selfish words that I know still ring in his ears.

Philippos' favor is the sun. It rises, and then it sets, and he goes tonight to conceive your replacement.

Perhaps I haven't given her enough credit. Perhaps I've underestimated her.

"Alexandros..." I say, as I reach out and touch his shoulder.

He brushes my hand away, though, then looks up and around the banquet hall, meeting all the eyes that are there and gathered and that look back at him, especially the eyes of the nobles and generals. "We now control Greece, or at least most of Greece, and the places my father has dared to go," Alexandros tells them, very slowly, insulting Philippos for his decision not to go to Sparta, and the Peloponnese. "This is our time," he continues. "It is no longer the time of Athens, or of Sparta, or Thebes, or Corinth, or anywhere else. It's the time of Macedon, as we all know, and is this the man you'd choose to lead you, to unite all our kingdoms and all our cities and states?" Alexandros holds their eyes, and he keeps looking at those gathered, then he looks down, at his father. "You deserve better," he says, his final words, his final curse. "You all deserve so much better."

In Macedon, basileus' aren't born, they're chosen, and the ones who do that choosing are all the men in this room and he knows they won't forget what they've just seen, and Philippos knows it, too.

"Arrest them!" Philippos shouts from his place on the floor, as he struggles to stand again. "Arrest them all! Every single one of them!"

How did it get to this?

How did it all get to this, and so quickly?

Dionysus.

I look up, and I shake my head, because of course it's Dionysus.

I should have prayed harder to Athena, we all should have.

The guards that are in the banquet hall look confused at first, wondering if the basileus is serious or not, so he screams again. "Now!" he yells, then yells the same thing, again and again, the only thing he can think of. "Now! Now! Arrest them!"

We're unarmed. It's a wedding feast, after all.

The guards grab Ptolemaios first, then head towards the rest of the Companions, at the same time as they come to us, towards me and Alexandros.

They reach out.

They almost grab Alexandros, and they almost grab me, too, but before I know what I'm doing my reflexes and instincts take over and I know I have to do this, so I roughly shove all the guards away, and they fall to the floor.

I may be young, but I'm still the strongest man in this hall.

Perhaps I'm the strongest *because* I'm young.

I'm the best fighter in this hall, too, I know that I am, but we cannot spill any blood here because it's our blood and the blood of those that Alexandros means to rule.

"Come on," I whisper urgently, and grab him and pull him towards the exit.

"No!" he yells.

He tries to struggle against me and back towards where the rest of the Companions fight against the guards, but they're drunk and outnumbered, and only half-clothed, which means they're no match for those that they fight who are none of those things, so they're taken and subdued.

I pull Alexandros harder.

He doesn't want to leave, but we do.

I pull him out into the night as behind us I catch a glimpse of a spear that crashes onto Kassandros' head, shaft and wooden end first, and he falls to the floor in a heap, unconscious, and the same thing happens to the others as they're taken and when I see this, I begin to run, and I pull Alexandros with me, or at least try to, but he stops.

"Come on!" I call to him, as loudly as I dare. "We have to go."

"My mother. We need to get her."

"We can't," I tell him, my words hushed and urgent. "There's no time."

"He'll kill her."

"If Philippos meant to kill her, he'd have already done it, and no amount of distance would stop him. You know that. And besides, she wasn't even there."

He looks torn.

I meet his eyes.

This is important, and I use every ounce of all that I have in me to try to convey that to him, and he seems to understand, and then finally nods.

"Alright," he says.

"Alright," I nod, too.

Then we turn, and we go.

We start to run again and we sprint around the palace, through the gardens, then across the courtyard. Our sandaled-feet pound against the cobble-stoned streets, and we round the familiar corner, near the great temple, and come to the stables.

We go inside.

He quickly goes to Bucephalus, and I go to the brown.

"Which way do we ride?" I hear him ask, as we reach the horses.

"I don't know," I tell him, as I catch my breath. "We just ride," I say. "We just get out of here, out of the city, then figure out what happens next once we're far enough away. Perhaps we send to Aristoteles."

"Epirus."

There's another voice, there in the darkness, behind us, a female voice.

We both turn towards it.

"We go to the Molossians, and my brother. He'll give us sanctuary, and we'll have protection from Philippos there, too, amongst my people."

We both look into the darkness, and then Olympias appears from it.

She walks towards us, calmly, as if she's been expecting this.

Alexandros looks at her, and then back at me, his mouth open. She's still wearing her finest clothes, the ones from the wedding, and has make-up still on her face, though it now looks very incongruous as she stands between bails of hay in this place of dust and leather and horses and men.

Alexandros waits to hear my response. I finally shrug.

It's a direction, at least to start, and as good of one as any.

"We'll go west, then," I say.

"You can ride Bucephalus with me," Alexandros says to his mother, as he moves towards her, to help her up and onto the horse, but she shrugs him away.

Then she smiles.

"You forget, Alexandros," she tells him. "I was born in the mountains, the same as Hephaestion was, and I can ride on my own," she says as she then turns back towards where she came and takes the reins of a great grey stallion that she leads forward. I see that it's a beautiful horse, dark and well-muscled, and its gait steady and even. It's already been bridled with reins hanging loose on its back.

She's ready, and has been waiting for us.

The shouting from the palace gets closer, which means we all know there's no more time left so Alexandros and I bend and jump onto our horses as Olympias stands on a bail of hay and swings her leg over the back of the horse she's chosen, and has been waiting with, waiting because she knew what would happen, waiting because she knew what she'd *made* happen, and then after it did, that we would come. I frown. I recognize the animal, but can't quite place it.

"Whose horse is that?" I ask her.

"Philippos'," she says, and then smiles. "In Macedon, a man that can't keep his horse can't keep his kingdom, either. So that will now be his fate, too."

It changes. So quickly, it all changes.

I look at Alexandros. He looks back at me.

Then without any more time, Olympias kicks Philippos' horse to a gallop, and we do the same with ours, and follow after her, out of the stables. We gallop through the dark streets of the city and away from the palace, then eventually the buildings thin and part, as we get towards the agora, and lower city, and then we leave Pella altogether and there's grass under hooves rather than stone and no light at all except what little comes from stars and moon above. I glance behind me and see Olympias, her ornate and formal peplos trailing in the wind across the back of her horse and behind where she rides, a basileia dressed for a wedding and feast now galloping at break-neck speed through the countryside and away from the city.

And there's something else, too.

It's a look, only a momentary glance on her face, but I see it: the small, secret smile that's on her lips, and I of course recognize it, because it's the same as Alexandros' secret mile.

Where will it lead us?

Where will it lead both of us?

This is the second time I've left a capital and kingdom under cover of darkness, and with a basileus behind that wanted me dead. What does it mean? I don't know, and there's nothing else left except to go, and perhaps find out, so I turn back to the road and continue on, the pounding of hooves becoming rhythmic as we continue to ride away from our home, in silence, plunging further and further into the great and gathering darkness that now surrounds us.

CHAPTER SEVENTEEN

WE RIDE FOR THREE DAYS STRAIGHT, barely taking a break, and also barely speaking ten words amongst us, either in darkness, or when the light comes, in the morning, and during the day. It would be unusual for me and Alexandros, but now it's not just me and Alexandros, and every hill we ride across, every stream we pass, and every mountain we climb, I'm reminded of that when I look and see Olympias riding next to us. How did this happen? I shake my head. I don't know, but it has, and there's nothing else but to continue, so that's what we do.

We arrive in Epirus as the sun is setting.

We're greeted by Olympias' brother, who is also named Alexandros, and he waits outside the Molossian palace and then comes and hugs his sister, first, once we arrive, then Alexandros, his nephew. I'm surprised to see how familiar they are with each other, the two Alexandros', how the older one ruffles the younger's hair as he would do a little brother, and the other Alexandros smiles and laughs and holds my Alexandros at arms-length as he looks him up and down and asks how he's been. I wonder about this later, after we're alone again, and Alexandros tells me of "the other Alexandros," as he calls his uncle, and how it was actually his uncle who had taught him to hunt, and ride, and swing his first sword and all the other things fathers usually teach their sons that Philippos never had time for.

"Why was he in Pella, though?" I ask, not understanding.

"His own father died when he was very young, like yours did," Alexandros tells me. "He was too young to take the throne, so Philippos brought him to Pella."

"There was another that was chosen to rule Epirus?"

"*His* uncle, Arybbas."

"And Arybbas was basileus?"

"Yes, for a time, until Philippos decided he shouldn't be anymore, so he deposed him and installed Alexandros instead, who was loyal to him because he had been raised in Philippos' house, and his sister was Philippos' favored wife."

"And now?"

"Now she's not, and I suppose she'll ask him *not* to be loyal."

And that's exactly what Olympias ends up asking her brother: she wants him to break his alliance with Phillipos, she tells him, barely moments after we arrive and before we've even eaten or drank or had the dust of the road washed from our clothes and skin.

But Alexandros of Epirus refuses.

He tells us that he'll give us sanctuary, all three of us, for as long as we wish to stay with him in Epirus and amongst the Molossians, but he will not make war on the man that saved his life as a child, and then placed him back on his throne.

I see her eyes flash, but she can do nothing else.

She can't force her brother to fight against her husband, and besides, there's no way he could win, either; there's no way an already-conquered Epirus could rise and defeat Macedon, the seat of the newly-formed Greek alliance that includes the entirety of the Greek peninsula and all Hellenic and Greek-speaking people amongst its members, with of course the exception of the Spartans.

We're shown to our rooms.

We walk down a large hallway with mosaic-tiled floors, similar to the floors in the palace at Pella, then the hallway opens to a breathtaking view of the mountains opposite us. We pause for a moment and look out at it. We don't have mountains like this in Macedon, and at the palace there, the great and high-peaked and dramatic kind, and they remind me of something else, also.

Home.

"What is it?" Alexandros asks, next to me, when he sees me looking at them, comfort in the familiarity, for me, in the feeling.

"Nothing," I tell him and shake my head.

We continue.

The servant takes us to the room that we'll share and we walk in and look around: it's larger than the room we had in Pella, and it's set up in nearly the same way, with a washing basin and trunk for our clothes, but instead of two beds, there's only one larger one that's pushed against the far wall underneath a window with a view out to the mountains on the opposite side as the ones we saw from the hallway. "I'll have another bed brought," the servant says quickly, seemingly confused, as if he thinks there's been a mistake, but Alexandros stops him.

"No," Alexandros says. "It's fine as it is."

The servant looks at him and sees that Alexandros is serious, so he nods and walks out, looking curiously at us over his shoulder as he goes.

Then we're alone.

We're finally alone again, and when we are, we both go to the basin and take our chitons off and let them fall to the floor as we splash fresh water onto our skin. We stand there and wash ourselves, and this is when I ask Alexandros more about his uncle, and how they grew together when Alexandros was young, before I came to Pella. I'm curious about this man, his uncle, *the other Alexandros*; I'm curious because he seems more like Alexandros than Olympias, his sister. Our skin is soon clean, and it's not yet late, but the sun's sinking, and we're tired, and there will be more tomorrow, of course—there will be much more tomorrow, trying to figure what to do next, and how to salvage our lives and dreams—so we go to the bed that we'll share and I see a blanket made of fur that's folded and kept at the foot. It's not cold yet, but I know the mountains, and I know *these* mountains, specifically, the northern and western ones, so I know it will be in the night and I pull the fur blanket over us and up to our chests as we lay down. We don't touch at first, as we lay there, together, but then he moves closer, and we do. Our legs, just gently, just ever so slightly brush against each other. He doesn't say anything, and soon his breathing becomes rhythmic, and steady, and we both close our eyes and drift to sleep under fur and next to each other, sharing a warmth that's a world away from everything else and the place we've left, with the peace of the great mountains now surrounding and protecting us.

WE SETTLE INTO LIFE IN EPIRUS, and in the mountains. Each morning we wake and drill with Alexandros of Epirus and his men, to keep ourselves sharp, and after we're done with training, we spend the afternoons much like we did in Pella, too, which means we spend them with each other. We ride from the palace each afternoon and instead of going to places that Alexandros of Epirus has shown us, near the city, we instead go and explore what we don't know, higher in the hills and mountains. We ride between peaks, and we find rivers, and lakes, and all sorts of beautiful places where there are no other people.

Then when the sun begins to sink, we turn and ride back.

Alexandros of Epirus has granted us sanctuary, but he refuses to make war against Philippos, and Olympias becomes more and more restless with every day that passes. She tells him that the soldiers of Macedon would rise up and join him, if they attacked, but Alexandros tells his sister dismissively that her hate of her husband has clouded her judgment, and Alexandros of Epirus is the only one I've heard speak to Olympias in this way, and not cowed before her, and her persuasion. She can't get her brother to budge or change in this judgement, though, and Philippos of course won't budge in his anger, so things just stay as they are.

So, then, she turns her attention elsewhere.

Soon after we arrive, I wake in the middle of the night and see that Alexandros is no longer with me, in our bed, under the furs that protect us from the chill that comes from the mountains. I look for him in our room, but he's not there, either, and so I go back to sleep. When I open my eyes again, the next morning, he's returned.

"Where'd you go?" I ask, as he rubs sleep from his face, next to me.

"What?" he asks.

"In the night. I woke, and you weren't here."

"I went for a walk," he says, then looks away. "I couldn't sleep."

There's no doubt he did go for a walk, and even though I might not know where he went, I know who he went with because it's the only reason he would look away.

His mother.

Olympias.

What does she whisper, out there in darkness, in the night?

I can only guess, but I know that whatever it is, it's poison, like she is.

I think again of Aristoteles, and what he told me, and the charge he gave me. I think of Alexandros, and his mis-colored eyes, and I think of Chaeronea and what happened there, after the battle was over, and more specifically, what I didn't stop from happening after the battle was over.

I have to do something to stop this.

I know that I have to do something, and then it comes to me, like a bolt straight from my youth, from my childhood, from my heart and soul and the boy I used to be, and I begin to plan. I put everything into motion, then when I return, I find Alexandros on the bed in our room, and he looks up when I walk in.

"Where have you been?" he asks.

"There's a place I want to show you," I tell him.

"What place?" he asks.

But I ignore his question.

I just tell him to get ready, and when I see him hesitate, I of course already know why. "She won't mind," I tell him.

"Yes, she will," he says.

"Then she will," I answer, and my words are strong, and so are my eyes, I know. He looks back at me, with just a moment of hesitation, then nods, and once he does, we leave. He doesn't pack anything, he just walks out with me, just as we are, and when we do, I see him glance at his mother's door, the entrance to her chamber, next to ours, his gaze lingering, for one more instant.

I take his hand.

He turns and looks at me.

Our eyes meet, then he finally nods, too, slowly, understanding what I'm doing and even wanting me to, I know, so then we turn and go together, down the hallway, out of the palace and back to the stables so that we can begin our ride to the sea.

WE DON'T TAKE BUCEPHALUS OR THE BROWN, we take two Molossian horses, instead, and make the quarter day's ride to the coast. We ride in silence, each with our own thoughts, and as we get nearer our destination, the mountains begin to thin as we reach the sea. We get to the fishing village that's there and go to the docks. I find the same fisherman I've already found, and he's waiting with his boat, as he said he would be, and when he sees me, he waves. We ride to him and dismount. He takes the reins of our horses and leads them away, leaving us with just the boat, and the sea. Alexandros looks at me, not understanding. I don't tell him, though; I don't tell him anything and instead just go to the boat and get in and then without asking anything, he does the same.

I push off.

I reach over the side and strain and flex and push the wood of the dock again, as firmly as I can, and we drift away from the rocky coast until the current catches and takes us further into the endless blue sea, where the wind picks up, too. I judge the strength and direction of it. I learned how to do this a long time ago, when I was a boy and growing on this sea and in a village not un-like the one we just left, and I make calculations, as I lick my lips and taste the salt that the wind leaves on them and adjust the sails so that the boat changes and turns, also, and takes us in the direction I want.

South.

I see Alexandros watching me, curiously.

"How do you know how to do all this?" he asks.

"You forget, sometimes," I tell him. "I was born on this coast. A little further north, maybe, but boys that are born here learn how to sail before they learn how to ride," I say, and then I smile.

He smiles now, too.

We both know that boys in Greece learn how to ride before they even learn to walk, so he knows that this—the breeze, the boat, the salt, and the water—if I learned how to do this before I learned how to ride, then it's as much a part of me as he is. "You're wild," he says. "Wild like the mountains, and the sea."

I've never thought of it like that before, but perhaps I am.

Perhaps I am wild.

We keep sailing and soon the sun sinks completely and so we sail through night and darkness and there's nothing above but stars. I use them to guide us, as I know how, and the breeze is less now, at night, too, which also means that we go slower. We sit there together in silence and listen to the soft waves as they gently and rhythmically lap against the side of the boat as we continue on and through the starlight. We don't talk much, but Alexandros does ask one thing. "Aren't you going to tell me where we're going?" he says, some time after midnight, but before dawn.

I smile again.

"No," I shake my head.

We keep sailing, and more night passes, though we don't sleep, not at any point, and then soon after the darkness begins to fade, as it always does, the sun starts to rise. There's only a glimmer at first, just a hint of light, a soft glow that begins in the distance off and to our right. Then the glow continues, and grows, and expands, and soon the light begins to return. When it does, I see that there's land that's in front of us: there's a rocky and jagged island that's there and which is what we've been sailing towards and what I've wanted to show him and bring him to see.

He sits up in the boat.

He looks at the island, and then back at me, and he raises his eyebrows.

"What is this place?" he asks.

"It's an island."

"I can see that. Which island?"

I wait for a moment, letting the question linger, letting his words drift and swirl and gather, and then rise, up to the gods, up to the stars.

And then I answer.

"Ithaka," I tell him.

CHAPTER EIGHTEEN

Our boat glides through shallow water and around partially-exposed rocks, which we avoid, then once we're close to the island, we both jump out and into water that's to our thighs and pull the boat up and onto the sand of a small beach that we find in a deserted cove. When the boat is far enough up and onto the sand that it'll be safe from the tide and changing sea levels, we leave it there, and we go to explore the island. I've sailed here before, as a child, but I don't remember much of it, and what I do remember seems to have changed and isn't familiar to me anymore, so I'll see and learn and experience it all over again, the same as he will. There's a small village that's on the far side of the island from where we've landed, and it's that side of the island that's more populated than this one, though there are very few people that live here at all, and so we decide to stay on the side where we've landed and where we're alone. We do go to the other side, though, to see it, and we walk through the small village that's there. We walk in silence and past houses where no one lives anymore, and on streets where very few others walk, and then we see in the distance the ruins of a great building that must have once been a palace, and we go towards it. We get closer and closer, then finally come to the ruins of another thing that was once great and beautiful, but now is no longer. We stop and stand outside of it and take it in, the entirety of it, and all that we both know it used to be.

I know exactly what Alexandros is thinking, because it's what I'm thinking, too.

Is this where the suitors camped?

Is this where they all stayed, when Odysseus was gone those twenty long years, and where they tried to court his wife who remained?

Is that the place where we now stand?

We look around and see how all that's near us, which was once so famous and grand, has turned to nothing more than stone and dust, this place where Odysseus strung his mighty bow and fought with his then-grown son and killed his enemies, and went with his wife back to the great bed he'd carved from a tree.

Is this the place where all those things happened?

I turn and look around us. I look for trees, but I see none.

We duck under the arch of the crumbling doorway and go inside. Our footsteps are quiet as we enter and see that what was once the palace of Ithaka is in complete disarray inside, too, the same as it is outside; it's been completely abandoned, forgotten, left to crumble and be overtaken as we all are, and it's clear that while there were once gods and heroes that lived here, none do anymore. There's nothing. Absolutely nothing. We take it in with silence, the cruelty and unforgiving nature of both time and memory, and it teaches us something. It teaches us both something important. After a few more silent moments with these thoughts and the legends that once lived here, and what it all then has become, we leave and go back out to the courtyard and head back towards the village.

We walk through the village, then towards the fields that are beyond.

We're following the story, the great one, the one we both know so well.

We get to the fields and stand in them and look around and I know we both see the same thing when we stand here; I know we both see Odysseus, the wise one, the clever one, the one that history has remembered, and we see him pretending to be simple and tilling the fields around us with salt rather than seeds. We smile when we see him, and his famous ruse, then we turn and see Palamades. We see him arriving from the sea, coming from his boat and how he comes up to the field here where he takes the crying child from Penelope's arms. She struggles against him, but Palamades' men are there, too, and they hold her, as he takes the baby Telemachus and places him directly in the path of Odysseus' plow. The clever basileus is of course pretending to be mad, but when his son is placed there, Odysseus swerves to not kill him, and his clever game is then a game no more. Palamades calls on Odysseus to honor his oath and sail to Troy, and this is how history is made and a great war is fought, and eventually finished, through the same-type tricks and the power of his mind.

We breathe in; we breathe in this air, his air.

Then we turn.

We leave the field, together, and walk towards the sea.

A slight breeze picks up and then we get there and stand with the wind whipping between us and through our hair, and I feel Alexandros next to me. He inhales again, with purpose, and vision. "Do you see them?" he finally asks, breaking the silence.

I nod, because I do.

Ships.

That's what we see.

Dozens of them, waiting, bobbing in the harbor and on the soft waves.

They're the boats with the sails that carry the insignia of Ithaka, and these are the boats that are ready to start a great journey to foreign waters and foreign lands. These are the boats that are painted and crafted from wind-swept and salt-cured island wood, and these are the boats that will leave this place and *sail, sail, sail,* until they eventually come to the city between two continents, the great city between two great places and times, and what if that city and what it means and stands for is actually more than just that, and it's not a city at all, but a bridge?

And what about us?

Will we be the same as these heroes, the ones we've heard so much about, and will our journey and mistakes be theirs, and repeated, or will they be our own?

Will we be remembered in the same way they're still remembered?

I don't know. I don't know.

It's too much to think about, too much for either of us to take in, so we don't, we just turn, and we leave and go back to the other side of the island.

ON THE FAR SIDE OF THE ISLAND, where there are no villages or people, we go down to the beach and walk through the lapping and salty surf of the clear and azure-tinted waves until we eventually round a bend and find a wide and deep cave where we'll stay. We go inside the cave and take our chitons off and leave them as we then turn and run back out again and down to the beach where we sprint into the water and our summer-tanned bodies dive against the waves. We swim there, together, for as long as we can, then when the sun finally begins to sink, we leave the beach and walk naked on the island amongst the rocky paths to gather the wood we'll need for a fire, and we walk naked because there's no one else here to see or disturb us. We gather what we need and then return to the cave where we pile the wood that we've gathered together, and I spark two stones to bring fire. The spark catches the wood, and then spreads, and as it does, we sit and watch as it all starts to burn. We watch the flames grow, leaping and dancing in unknown and ancient patterns, casting shadows in dark corners and spilling light across where we sit. We still don't bother to put our chitons back on, we just sit there next to the fire and feel our skin tickled by the warmth as the sea-water that was there disappears and all that remains is the salt, just the salt, and our skin, and the fire and light between us.

He looks at me.

"I'm sorry," he says.

I look back at him and know what he means, I know what he apologizes for, what he's finally acknowledging, and I don't say anything. I just look at him, the fire dancing across his mis-colored eyes and I think of his parents again, and what and how they've made him, and what's inside him.

"I'm sorry, too," I finally tell him.

"Sorry for what?" he frowns.

"For not stopping you. That I couldn't do it, and that I wasn't there in time."

"I have darkness in me, I know that I do, and it causes me to stumble, and to fall. But I have light, too, just like we all do, and every day, Hephaestion, *every day*," he says, the emotion rising in his throat, "every day I fight against that darkness, and most days I'm strong enough, and I succeed, and I push it back. But sometimes I don't, and the only thing I know, the only thing that I really know, in all of this, is that when you're with me, I push back more darkness and bring more light to the world. If you're at my side to help make me feel what else is there inside me, and not just the darkness, then the light is so much closer. It's always so much closer, when you are."

I look down at his hand and where he's moved it so that it rests on my hand, and then I think again of the boats, of Odysseus' boats, and where they went when they left this island and the bridge they could have been, rather than the one they destroyed, the bridge that could have spanned continents, people, worlds.

They failed, though, because they brought only death and destruction.

But what about us? What could we bring, and could it be more?

His hand shifts, where it rests on mine, and he moves closer.

I feel him, and I believe again, and there's an electricity of dreams and future that's between us once more like there used to be, when we were young and in Pella and things were simpler and while we've slept together, and next to each other, many times, because we sleep in the same room, this is the first we'll do more than that. His neck bends and he raises his head and his lips find mine again, like they did at Delphi, and his hands are on my chest, my waist, and mine are on his, too. We touch each other, feel each other, and we stay like this for some time before there's then more. I remember what he told me, when we were on the road, on our way to Mieza, and I don't want him to feel that. I know that he has before, but I don't ever want him to feel that again, especially now, but he tells me he won't, and then when it's finished, it's not really finished, is it, it's just begun, and I know that it will *never* be finished, not for all eternity, not for all the rest of time, no matter what else happens and what future comes.

What is distance, or time?

It's nothing compared to this, and to us.

We lay there together on this ancient island of both gods and heroes, and we will be, too, I know. The fire burns lower next to us as time ceases and we lay and hold each other and I'm glad we've come here, to this place, I'm so glad that we've come here and we've walked the paths where they walked before us, and we've swam in the sea where they swam, too, and maybe, just maybe, they even came to this cave that is now our cave. The fire burns even lower and fades, fulfilling the eternal promise of vanished time and passed moments, and as it burns, sleep begins to come, to both of us, but before it does, there's still one more thing, one last thing that's left to be whispered again, in the fading light; a promise, a single word.

"*Patroklos*," he breathes, and I can feel his breath on my skin, his promise tickling and raising the hairs on the back of my neck.

I wait, for a moment, for just one more moment . . .

Then I smile.

I wonder if he can see it, through the darkness, my smile and my lips, and what they do, what they do for him.

"*Achilleus*," I whisper in return.

THE NEXT MORNING, we rise, together.

And as we do, I think of our conversation, and then what happened after, this new discovery and this new thing that's now between us, and I think it will make things more complicated, or at least different, but it doesn't; it instead makes them simpler. Training and the palace and Pella and all else that goes with our former lives is now of the past, and we spend our days exploring the island, every corner of it, and each other. We forget everything else, everything except me, and him, and we run, together, and laugh, and as we do, minutes become hours, hours become days, and days become weeks. Our only job is to look for the food that we'll cook that night and then plan on when and how we'll eat it and who will do what to make sure it's prepared, and I realize as we fall into this rhythm and pattern of nights and days, that we're doing things that adults do: we're eating together, speaking of our time and our days and our dreams, and it's an amazing treasure and gift that we share.

It's a simple existence.

No.

It's *existence*, perhaps as it's meant to be, and for a time, it is, and it's everything, and it's ours, but then things begin to change, as they always seem to do, whether we're the poorest servant or the most favored prinkipas. It begins one afternoon after we've caught three lavraki from the sea and we sit together and clean them on the rocks by the beach, peeling scales away with sharpened stones we've made just for this specific task and then cutting into them through the stomach and throwing guts and innards back into the waves to feed the other fish. I look at Alexandros next to me, at the hint of a beard that's begun to grow on his face since we've been here, and haven't shaved, like we used to do together every morning, and he seems distracted. He's not concentrating on the fish, I see, and the task that's at hand, as he usually does, and he eventually puts the lavraki that he's holding aside, and then stands. He turns and looks back to the east, past the bay where our cave is, and back towards Greece, Epirus, all that we knew before and the lives we previously lived and have now left.

"What do you think he did to them?" Alexandros finally asks.

"Nothing," I tell him, knowing who he's talking and thinking about.

"Really?"

"They're all sons of noble and important families."

"Second and third and fourth sons."

"Our actions at the feast were our own, and not theirs."

"What about Ptolemaios, though?"

"The most he could be accused of is throwing a spear, and let's be honest, he isn't the first at a Macedonian feast, and he certainly won't be the last, either."

"It was Philippos he threw the spear at."

"So?"

"He's basileus."

"Philippos is a warrior first. He'll understand."

Alexandros doesn't answer and just stays staring at the sea, towards the distant coast that we can't see, and the horizon that we've stared at together so many times it's something that's become ritual and gospel. "Every day that we're away is a day that support for Amyntas grows stronger," he finally says.

I know that he's right.

I don't have anything else to say, because I know that he's right, and that it'll be soon now, because it has to be. I keep cleaning the lavraki, knowing that with his words our time here will now be over, and he knows that, too, so when the fish are finally cleaned, we cook them over our flames and we drink some of the wine that we've traded coins for in the village. It's thin and without much flavor, or alcohol, but we drink it anyways because we're thirsty from the salt that's always in the air here and that catches in our throats and dries them. And then, after we've eaten and drank, we go further into the cave, to the place where we sleep, and we lay together, again, the same way we did before, when we first arrived. It's also the last time we will. I don't know how I know this, but I do, and I think Alexandros knows, too. We spend the next three days running through the rocky and uneven fields, climbing the mountains, swimming in the sea and we do nothing else except these things. I insist that we don't, and Alexandros listens, and I insist because soon this will all end, I know. This will all soon end, and we'll need something to remember it by. Not the place, but the time. We'll need something to remember during distant and dark futures in distant and dark lands where all people go when they become older, not just us, of course, but *all* people. And so that's where we'll go, too, I know, because that's where we all go, but right now we're not there, not yet, we're here, on this island that for these past months has been *our* island, and we're together. We run and laugh and climb because we were both made for only one purpose, one solemn and ancient thing, and we too often forget that the future is not yet now, and we're both still just only seventeen.

CHAPTER NINETEEN

WE RETURN TO EPIRUS, and when we do, we learn that there's been word from Pella, and from Philippos. Eurydice has given birth to a child, a small girl that came early, but that's not the real news, which is that he's offered Cleopatra to Alexandros of Epirus in marriage and he's invited the other Alexandros, his son, to come back to Macedon for the ceremony that will take place in the ancient capital of Aigai upon prompt acceptance of his offer. It seems simple, on its surface, but Philippos is smart, I know, and perhaps even smarter than I've given him credit for during the years I've known him: his body is weak and frail now, just a shadow of what he once was as a young man, but it's obvious his mind is still very strong, and still very clear. Cleopatra is valuable to him in cementing allies, everyone knows that, and perhaps even more valuable to him than either of his sons. Daughters of rulers usually are, because they're used to assure the loyalty of who they marry, while all sons do in Macedon is challenge their fathers with their youth and strength and the promise they carry of future and re-wound time. I'm surprised at first, at what Philippos has said and offered, and I see that Alexandros is, too, and then, after I think about it... then, I'm not. Epirus and the Molossians have been strong allies of Macedon while Alexandros of Epirus, who Philippos installed on his throne, has been basileus, but there's also now Olympias' persuasion that has to be taken into account. Philippos can't afford to have an enemy at his direct western border, not even the hint of one, if he plans to march east and keep expanding his kingdom; he can't afford to leave behind *any* enemy, if he plans to do that, and especially not one so close to home.

"I won't accept without your blessing, of course," Alexandros of Epirus says, and I turn to look at him, expecting to find him speaking to his sister, but he's not.

It's Alexandros that he speaks to.

My eyes flick to Olympias, to see how she reacts to this, but she doesn't look at either of them, because I see it's another that she looks at.

Me.

Why?

Of course I know why.

Her eyes don't leave mine, and I know why it's my eyes that they find, because I'm the one that took him from her, spiriting her son away in the night to a distant island for an indeterminate amount of time, her son, her precious son.

Enemies.

Enemies all around.

"Do you care for her?" I hear Alexandros' voice, my Alexandros, and when I turn back to them, I can still feel Olympias' eyes and I can feel her intentions, too.

"I don't know," Alexandros of Epirus tells his nephew. "She was just a baby when I left Pella, barely even born, so I don't really know her."

"She'll make a good basileia. She'll make a better one than anyone I know."

"So you love her, then?"

"She's my sister."

"Not all siblings get along," he says with a smile, and a glance towards his own.

"She's my best friend," Alexandros tells him, as simply as he can.

There's silence as Alexandros of Epirus takes that in, and he looks from his nephew, to his sister again, who's still quiet, still staring at me, then Alexandros of Epirus finally nods and the silence ends.

"So it will be," he says.

My Alexandros nods, too, and moves forward and embraces the other one. "When we came here, it was to an uncle," Alexandros says, then moves away from him. "And now, when we leave, it will be with a brother."

"May the gods will it."

"They do. And they'll favor you, Alexandros. They'll favor both of you."

"What happens now?"

"You send a letter and you accept."

"And then what?" I ask.

"Then we go back," Alexandros says, and turns and looks at me, too. "Then we go back home."

IT TAKES A WEEK FOR US to make the trip from Epirus back to Pella, as there are more riders and baggage that go with us now, and during the trip, I let my thoughts wander. They wander to many things that have happened—to islands and mountains, to caves and flickering fire, and things that have both been said and left unsaid—but when they settle, and I think of Pella, and what we'll return to, I find that it's Ptolemaios that my thoughts settle on. I feel grief. I feel deep, profound grief for him, and sadness. I think of his eyes, the ones that were always so young and hopeful, and I think of her eyes, too, which were the same. I think of the way that she smelled, the first time I met her, in the garden, at the palace, and the way they were together, in secret, when time and night was theirs, just theirs, also in the garden, and they were so alive, and now?

Now that will all be over.

Will they still be alive? Of course they will, but will they really?

It makes me sad, when I think about it, and it does in a way I didn't anticipate, though I always knew it would come to this and she would be given to another and not the one she loves because that's what happens in this world. But does it have to? Is that what Alexandros would tear down, re-make, change and shape in the way that he's been changed and shaped and made, and is a world like that worth the price that will be paid to create and make it real? Because if it's possible, then perhaps the price might be worth it. Perhaps it just might.

"What are you thinking about?" I hear the words come from near my shoulder and I turn to see Alexandros watching me. He'd been riding with his uncle and mother, while I was left with my thoughts, but I see him next to me now.

"Nothing," I tell him, and shake my head.

"It can't be nothing."

I turn and look at Alexandros of Epirus, behind us.

Will he know the bride he rides to already loves another, and has already been loved by another?

If he did know, would he care?

This is the way of basileus and basileia, and so surely Ptolemaios and Cleopatra know that, too, don't they? They know how rulers are crowned and empires made. Of course they do, but there's always hope, and there's the power that hope brings, even if it's only for a moment, for a second, there's still and always the hope that the world could be different for them and that the souls it brings together might be able to *stay* together, regardless of what their parents say, or a basileus, or a basileia, or anyone else.

"Sometimes I wish the world was different than it is," I finally say. "That's all."

"That's *all*?" he smiles.

I smile, too, sadly.

He's not finished, though.

"It *can* be different," he says, softer now.

"I know," I tell him, my voice also pitched low.

"And do you know when it will be different?"

"No."

"When we make it so."

I look back at him, for another moment, as we ride.

I smell mint and thyme again, as clearly and closely as I smelled them the day I met her, in the garden, in the sun, with her lyre.

"What if that's not soon enough?"

"This is the last time," he says, looking at me, into my eyes, knowing now what I'm thinking about. "This is the last time, I swear it," he says, still looking at me. I know he must be thinking about his sister, too, and as much as he loves his uncle, it's not a mystery what he's given his blessing to, and what it will do to the one he cares about more in this world than all save me. I hope his words are truth. I hope his words are truth, and that they're heard by gods, and that our fate will be something else, and so will the fate of all those who come after us, in the world that we'll make, and that it won't be their fate.

WE SOON REACH PELLA and ride through the city. It seems nothing's changed, but then again, as we look around and people look at us as we pass in a way they didn't before, I realize that everything has changed, because we have, and so that means the place we've returned to has changed, too, and it's done so without us. Did time stop when we weren't here? It seems like it should, but of course it hasn't. We keep riding and then round a corner and see the other Companions there and waiting for us, and when they see us, they begin to run. I think they're going to stop, but they don't, and when they reach us they jump and pull us from our horses and they laugh as we all fall to the ground together and I can smell wine and mead but I can also feel their hearts pressed against our hearts and they're full, they're full, they're all so very full and I'm glad of these second and third and fourth sons we've found, because besides being second and third and fourth sons, they're also brothers, too, aren't they?

Yes, they are.

They're our brothers, the ones we weren't born with, but the ones we found, and have now found again.

Alexandros of Epirus raises his eyebrows as Olympias looks away in disgust and displeasure, and it's not just disgust at us, I know, but at a great many things here in the city that we've returned to. We soon climb back onto our horses and we ride the rest of the way through Pella, along the streets, past the agora and houses and temples, and then finally back up to the palace, which will once again now be our home.

We dismount in the courtyard.

We hand the reins of our horses to a servant that comes, and then we see Parmenion, where he stands by the door and waits. We walk towards him. Alexandros of Epirus goes first, and then the three of us follow behind: me, Olympias, and Alexandros of Macedon. "He'll see you two first," Parmenion says, pointing to me and Alexandros of Macedon. "Then he'll see you," he says, pointing to Alexandros of Epirus.

Alexandros turns to look at his mother, who hasn't been mentioned. "And what of Olympias?" he asks.

But Parmenion doesn't answer.

Olympias doesn't say anything, either.

She just walks forward, until she's close to Parmenion, and then when she's there, and to him, she reaches up and touches his cheek. She lets her hand linger, her fingers on his rough skin, his lips, then down to his chin. "Faithful," she says. "So very faithful."

And then, without another look, she turns and leaves.

I think she's going to head back towards her old quarters in the palace—the area where the other wives and women live, near where I first met Cleopatra, in the garden, all those years ago now—but she doesn't, and instead heads back towards the city. I wonder where she'll go, and what she'll do, but then there's no more time for wonder or anything else because there's something more important that waits for us.

The basileus.

Alexandros and I look at each other, and then when Olympias has finally left and disappeared completely between the high-ceilinged buildings, heading towards the great temples and three-storied houses and all else that lays beyond, we then leave Alexandros of Epirus in the courtyard and go inside the palace. Parmenion walks with us and we go down the familiar hallway and towards the familiar door. The walk seems to take longer than it has before, and then we finally come to the door, the entrance to the basileus' office, and I look around. I expect to see Pausanius standing here. I expect to see him keeping watch outside, as he usually does, but he's not in the place where he normally stands; instead, there's a new boy that stands and waits outside. He looks even younger than Pausanius, and his skin is more fair, and it looks softer, too, like he might be from the south.

"Who are you?" I ask him.

"Pausanius, Hephaestion-prinkipas," he speaks quickly, nervously, and I look at him strangely both because of his name, the same as the name of the one who came before him, and because of the word he's used to call me, the one that means nothing here in Macedon.

I frown.

Another boy, another young, foreign boy, and with the exact same name?

I look to Alexandros first, and then to Parmenion, but the strategos just shakes his head and gestures towards the door that he now pulls open.

"He's waiting for you," Parmenion tells us.

I look at the fair-skinned boy that's also called Pausanius, one more time, and then we walk past him, as he bows, and we go inside.

Philippos is waiting.

He's standing behind his great desk when we enter, though when I look closer, I notice he stands nearer the desk than he did before so that he can hold onto the side for support because of the leg that still gives him so much trouble. He stares at us as we come in, turning his head and cocking it up slightly, as Alexandros sometimes does, too, so that it's his good eye that stares at us, the flickering light from the candle near him mixing with the small amount of natural light that sneaks in through the window behind where he waits and I think he's going to look to his son, first, but he doesn't. He looks at me, just as Olympias did, when we returned from Ithaka. "We've stood here together once before, haven't we, Hephaestion of Salona," he finally says.

"Yes," I nod. "We have."

"I wonder," he says. "I wonder if I knew then what I know now, if my answer to you would have been the same."

"I don't know," I tell him.

"I thought you were bold, Hephaestion. I thought you were strong."

"I am."

"Then tell me."

"Your answer would have been the same."

"Why?"

"Because I've served you well."

"I'm basileus. There are many that serve me well."

"Did no one tell you how many I killed at Chaeronea?"

"No."

"I killed more than any other that rode for you."

"Not more than Amyntas."

"Is he the one that told you that?"

Philippos holds my eyes, for another moment, as the candle flicks and cracks and he almost smiles at my answer, the type of boldness and conviction that he likes and respects, I know.

Then he turns to his son.

"Are you going to apologize?" he asks him.

"No," Alexandros says, from his place next to me and without any expression at all.

"Why did you do it?"

"Do what?"

"Betray me."

"It had nothing to do with you, and you know that."

"Then what did it have to do with?"

"Succession."

"That's a very dangerous word to say when I'm still alive, and I'm still basileus."

"One day you won't be."

"And that's the day you think of when you come to my feast and wedding?"

"Yes."

"Why?"

"Because it's the day I always think of."

Philippos stares back at his son with his one good eye and shifts unevenly in place as he holds the desk. I can tell his leg pains him, but I can also tell he's determined to try to not let it slow or weaken him, not in any possible way. I look at him. I look at Alexandros. I realize that this moment is perhaps the closest they've ever been, and strangely, I realize, it's taken this long for a father to see anything of himself in the flesh and blood of his middle son. I've heard that Olympias has told people that Alexandros was born of a god, the same as his ancestor Achilleus was born, and that he's half divine, but it's a lie, of course: Alexandros was born of Philippos, and it's never been more obvious and more clear than it is at this exact moment.

"I didn't think you had it in you," Philippos finally says to him.

"And now?"

"Now I know that you do."

"That's it?"

"Yes, that's it."

"It doesn't bother you?"

"Why would it? It's what I would do, and what I would feel, and as long as the day you dream of and prepare for is a day after I'm gone, then you can fight over my scraps with Amyntas, or Arrhidaeus, or Attalus, or whoever else you want to fight with. And who knows," Philippos shrugs, then smiles, "you might even just win."

"I will."

"I suppose I'll never know. Now send your uncle in."

There's a moment as we stand there, and then Alexandros finally nods, an understanding at last, and so do I, and we turn to leave. We walk back towards the door, and when we almost reach it, Alexandros pauses, and he turns back.

Philippos sees us and raises his eyebrows. "What?" he asks, sharply, not liking his time wasted.

"How long will it be, until you go east?"

"As soon as your sister's married."

"And are we to go with you?"

"Do you really think I'd leave you here to steal my kingdom from under me after all I've just heard?" Philippos asks, and I can see that he's quite serious, that he's deathly serious, and I can also see the change that's come, and the respect.

There's another moment, and then Alexandros finally nods, again, one last time, and we turn and walk out and see Alexandros of Epirus standing there in the hallway, waiting. When Parmenion sees us, he motions for Alexandros of Epirus to go in, after we leave, and the new Pausanius holds the door open for him and once Alexandros is past us and gone, we stand there with Parmenion, alone, and he looks back at us.

"What?" he asks, frowning.

"It was you, wasn't it?" Alexandros says.

"What was me?" Parmenion looks back at him, his eyes giving away nothing.

"You told him to bring us back."

"I told him to leave you to rot in the mountains," Parmenion says, and then turns and leaves. We watch as he walks down the hallway, takes a corner, and finally disappears, back towards the courtyard. Once he's gone, there's silence, as we stand there, we just stand there. I touch Alexandros on the arm and motion for us to go the opposite way, towards our room, and we begin to go in that direction. We start to make the familiar walk, and we smile at the faces we recgonize as they pass us, and they smile back, and nod, just a little, and then we get there, to our room.

We push the door open.

The room is the same and exactly as we left it, which makes me happy in a way and for a reason I can't fully understand or express, and I go to walk inside, to sit down on my bed, but he puts his hand out and stops me.

"No," he says.

"What?"

"No," he shakes his head, repeating the word.

"Why?" I ask, searching his eyes.

He pauses for a moment, looking around at the room, at the familiar things that are in it that no longer seem quite so familiar to him, then he turns and looks behind us, too; he looks back at the hallway, near where we stand, and takes everything in, the porticoes, the courtyard that's in the distance, the entirety of the palace that was once our home, but isn't anymore. We were boys here, as the story said, but we are now no longer boys. "We'll go to your room," he finally tells me, and so we turn, and we do.

WE MOVE INTO THE OLD ROOM that used to be mine, off the gymnasium, the one that was given to me when I first arrived in Pella, and it's slightly smaller than what we'd been used to together at the palace, and when we were at Mieza, and in Epirus, and even the wide and deep cave where we slept during our time on Ithaka. It's big enough, though, because we don't need very much, neither of us do, and also because we won't be here for very long; everywhere in Pella there's the noise of steel being beaten and tempered, the familiar sounds of a city preparing for another war, and that's what our future will be, too, we now know. And while the city prepares for one thing, at the palace, they prepare for something else: a great wedding uniting two important places and allies, and it's something that will come first, before war, and so soon we all leave for Aigai, the ancient and ceremonial capital of Macedon which is where royal weddings always take place, going back years and years, going back decades, going back for many generations of Argeads.

"Why wasn't Philippos' there?" I ask Alexandros, though, before we go, as we stand at the water basin in our room together and wash our faces and shave.

"Why wasn't what there?"

"Why was his wedding here, in Pella, and not in Aigai?"

Alexandros looks at me, then shakes his head, and a welcome smile comes to his lips. "Because it was his seventh one, and I don't think he cared anymore."

I look at Alexandros. He looks back at me.

I shake my head and smile, too, and laugh a little bit as I rinse my face with clean and cold water, and after I do, I stop, and look at him again, next to me, and he stops and looks at me, also. I don't say anything further. After a moment, I go back to the task at hand, continuing to get dressed, reaching for an old chiton, and then my belt, but he stops me.

"What?" I ask him.

"What were you thinking?"

"When?"

"Just now."

"Nothing."

"It wasn't nothing. I can tell."

"It doesn't matter."

"Yes, it does."

I pause as I look back at him, both of us now freshly-shaven, about to put our old chitons on and cinch our belts at the waist before going to the stables.

"You said Aigai is where all royal weddings happen," I finally say.

"Yes."

"So is that where yours will be, too?"

He stands there and looks back at me, in my room, in his room, in our room. "You were with me at Delphi."

"Yes," I nod. "I was."

"You heard what the Pythia said."

"I did."

"So then why would you ask?"

I stand there and look back at him again and I realize that he believes, that he heard the words and the prophecy and that he truly believes.

And since he does, then I will, too.

THE CEREMONY will take place at mid-day.

No one has seen Olympias since we've arrived at Aigai, and we don't know if she'll show up, since it's clear she doesn't approve of the way her youngest has been given to her brother solely for Philippos' dynastic ambitions and security. But her approval doesn't matter, of course, so the wedding will take place regardless of her wishes. Once we arrive, we go to the ancient theater that's halfway up the hill and below where the temples and palace stand, and we look out and across at the great and golden plains in the distance, the planes that reach south until they come to the high and tall-peaked mountain called Olympus, the great mountain of all the great gods. We see the crowd that's already gathered and waiting when we get there, representatives of all the noble Macedonian families from all corners of the kingdom, and there are also a great many southern Greeks that have come north, too; from Athens, and Corinth, and Thebes, and some from the smaller poleis, as well, that are now all our new allies.

I look at them and how they stand together.

The southerners all stand amongst each other, I see, and the Macedonians and other northern Greeks do the same.

Then I turn, and that's when I see Olympias.

She rides up the hill on the great grey stallion she took to Epirus, the one that had belonged to Philippos, and she comes on her own. She approaches the large theater carved into the hill, and when she gets close, she jumps down from the horse and tosses the reins to a servant.

She starts to walk. She doesn't stop.

She doesn't wait for the formal procession, or to enter with her family, or anything else; instead, I watch, along with Alexandros and the others, as she simply goes in by herself and takes a seat on her own. She doesn't sit where the royal family or other wives will sit, or the nobles, or near any of the seats that are reserved for them; she instead goes and sits amongst the common people, as just another woman in the crowd, and I find this strange. I watch Alexandros as he sees her, too, and what she does, but he doesn't speak. He doesn't say anything at all, and I turn and see Philippos arrive, behind us. He comes in a gold-plated chariot up the mountain path with his daughter, Cleopatra, standing on one side of him, and Alexander of Epirus on the other, the man who is to be his brother-in-law and son-in-law both, bound to him through two marriages, such is the importance of the kingdom he rules at Macedon's western border.

Alexander of Epirus smiles and waves to the gathered crowd.

Cleopatra, on the other side of her father, is stone-faced, staring straight ahead and dressed in the traditional white gown with a red veil over her eyes of Greek brides in the north, and after I look at her, I turn and look at Ptolemaios.

He looks away. He doesn't watch. How could he?

The chariot soon reaches us and all three of them dismount, the men first, then Philippos helping his daughter after him, and when they do, I see one more person, also; I see following behind them and on a bright young stallion the blonde and young bodyguard that was outside Philippos' chamber, standing guard at the door, the new and beautiful boy from the south that's also called Pausanius.

I look at him curiously.

On one side of where the basileus has arrived up the mountain, Attalus stands with his daughter, Amyntas, and a few other generals and first-born sons from important families, and they drink. Next to me and Alexandros, and on the other side of the path where Philippos has arrived, the Companions are drinking, too, passing a skin of wine back and forth between them, laughing and slapping each other on the back and getting ready for another wedding they hope won't end like the last one, they joke. Well, that's what they're all joking about except

Ptolemaios, who just pours wine and swallows and looks as if he's been doing so for some time. He stares at the ground as Cleopatra arrives, or to the side, or in any direction besides at the woman that's dressed as I'm sure he's imagined her dressed so many times, but standing at *his* side, and not for her to be given to another.

"Who is this one?" I hear, then turn to see Kassandros looking at Philippos' new bodyguard.

"He's Pausanius, too," I tell him.

"No!" Leonnatos shouts.

"He certainly has a type, doesn't he?" Nearchos says, and then drinks.

"A name is just a coincidence."

"I meant young."

"And blonde, too."

"He swapped boys and didn't even have to learn a new name."

"When he calls out *Pausanius*, which one do you think comes?"

"Both," Philotas scoffs. "He's basileus, and they're children, so of course they both come."

"What happened to the old one," I ask. "The one that was with him before, Pausanius of Orestis?"

"You haven't heard?" Perdiccas raises his eyebrows.

"We've been gone. Heard what?"

Perdiccas opens his mouth to tell me, but then it's too late, because then Philippos walks forward with the same priest that married him and Eurydice, and the priest speaks to us. "The basileus will go in first," he says, raising his voice so that we all can hear. "I'll slaughter the bull, with the basileus at my side, then the bride and groom will enter after the blood, and the rest will follow behind them."

"In what order?" Attalus asks.

"What does it matter?" Philippos says. "Just behind them."

Attalus looks at Amyntas, and his daughter.

All the rest of us nod, and they nod, too.

The ceremony begins.

Philippos starts to walk forward and the younger Pausanius goes with him, as well as five other royal bodyguards, and the priest, so there are seven of them total that go inside. They walk into the amphitheater and across dirt and sand that's been warmed by sun, and when the crowd sees them, they let out a loud and long cheer. They love the man who has expanded their kingdom and made it an empire; they love the man who fights and wins, and brings them pride, and honor, and gold.

Philippos smiles and waves to them in return.

He's a man who has sought praise, and warmed himself in it, as he does now, and so he waves back to them as their basileus and the conquering hero who has expanded their territory ten-fold from what it was during the time of their fathers and grandfathers, and he loves that they love him for this, for what he's done, for all that he's accomplished and all that he still will. We wait behind where he walks and raises his hand, as we were told, and we watch from where we stand and wait as Philippos and the rest continue on and towards the bull that's chained in place at the center of the theater. The chain is attached to a ring in the ground, I see, and the place where they now go has been a place stained by blood for many generations of Argeads that have come here to call upon gods and ancestors to bless unions and families and kingdoms, just the same as they'll call upon them today, through blood given, and blood received.

They finally reach the bull, and then they stop.

The bodyguards spread out in a circle, on all sides of the theater, near where the people sit so that Philippos and the priest stand with the bull alone, as this is business only for gods and kings.

I look at Alexandros, but his eyes are closed. He doesn't watch.

Does he pray?

Or is it something else that he does?

Next to us, the Companions continue to drink and laugh and joke with each other and they don't pay attention to the ritual and sacrifice, none of them except Ptolemaios, of course, who still has his eyes closed, just like Alexandros, but for a different reason, and there's a tear that slips out, I see, a single tear that slips out and down his cheek.

I feel a tear in my own eye, too. For him, for them.

I brush it away, though, before anyone sees, then turn back to the stadium, the basileus, the priest, and the bull. I watch as the priest raises his arms and begins a prayer. He calls upon the gods, to bring them down from their realms and the tall and snow-capped mountain not far from where we stand, he calls to them to witness the sacrifice that will be made and that he'll preside over and then, on the far side of the stadium, in the distance and away from them, I see something else.

There's another guard that comes, a sixth one.

He comes from the far side of the stadium and walks towards them, carrying with him the ancient knife that will be used to spill the bull's blood, the ceremonial blade that's been used for generations and now once again glints in bright Macedonian sun; it's a blade that the priests say has been forged in the mountains north of even the ones where Philippos has conquered, and was forged amongst the wild peaks there by the great Hephaestus himself, my namesake.

I know Hephaestus, and that we share a name, but he's not a god I pray to.

Should I?

I don't know, but what I do know is that this is what I'm thinking as I still look ahead and watch as the guard finally reaches Philippos and the priest and comes to stand close to them. Philippos reaches out to him, to take the ceremonial blade from his hand, but as soon as he does, there's a brief bit of motion between them, a jerked and random movement from both, and then Philippos seems to stop.

He stands there, and doesn't move.

The priest doesn't move, either, and neither does the guard, who brought the weapon.

I squint my eyes.

We're still at a distance, waiting by the path outside the amphitheater before the procession begins and I'm the only one that's watching, or paying any attention, as all the rest drink and pass wine amongst each other, and it's not clear exactly what's happening in front of us, but I know it's something.

Philippos cocks his head, slightly, up and to the side, as he did in his study, only a few days ago, to angle his one good eye towards us and to see us better.

Then his body begins to slump against the guard.

He falls to his knees, first, and I think it's his injured leg that's given out at this most inopportune time, in front of everyone, but then I hear the priest scream, the high-pitched scream of a man who's terrified and has been shaken, and then the priest starts to run, and that's when I know it's not the basileus' leg that's given out.

Alexandros' eyes snap open and he turns towards the noise.

The Companions stop drinking, and they turn, too.

The rest of the people then see, also, in the stadium, and cries go up everywhere; there are so many great cries at what's just happened, from the people who are closer, who can see better, and they all yell, though they can do nothing else except yell as the basileus slumps even further now, all the way to the ground.

He lays there, alone, on the sand.

"No!" I yell, too, and then begin to run.

Alexandros doesn't speak or say anything, but runs next to me, along with the other Companions, and even Amyntas and Attalus run with us, too. I may be bigger and stronger than Alexandros, but because of the weight that comes with my size, he's faster than I am.

He always has been.

He passes me and we both draw our swords, from our backs, as we get closer, Alexandros first, and then me, but it's too late; the guard that's stabbed Philippos has already run from the stadium and out towards the countryside and the mountains, and the new Pausanius, along with the rest of the other bodyguards, have chased after him, out of the arena and towards the hills that surround Aigai, the ancient city, the city of new life, and also, now, the city of death.

We reach Philippos.

Alexandros skids to a halt next to him and takes his head, lifting it up, blood pooling from the wide and gaping wound at his stomach.

"Pater," Alexandros whispers, as he holds Philippos' head in his lap. "Father..."

But it's too late.

Philippos' eyes just stare up at the sky, at the clouds, at the gods who must be there and who must have brought this, too.

There are no last words.

Silence.

There's just silence now, everywhere, a stunned silence, from all who are gathered. We stay like that for a moment, with Alexandros on the ground next to the dead basileus; the dead father, the dead warrior, the dead conqueror and hero.

Even Amyntas is silent, as he looks down at the scene in front of him, the blood that still spills and turns Alexandros' white chiton a very dark shade of red.

After some time, the royal guards return.

I turn when they do, and see that they bring something with them, a body that's slung across the horse that they lead, on foot, and when they get closer, I see the blood-streaked face of the dead man that's slung across the horse's back, and I recognize him.

Pausanius of Orestis.

I breathe in sharply.

The other Pausanius looks heart-broken, tears streaked down his young face as he returns with the guards and comes to look down at Philippos, near us, but not closer than Alexandros, or Cleopatra, who has come to join her brother, still in her wedding dress of course which is now stained red, also, like her veil, and I take them both in for a moment: the first Pausanius, who is now dead, and the second.

Then I turn.

Nearly all of Philippos' family is there with him, even Amyntas, so it's all but one that's missing, and I look through the amphitheater, searching through all the people that are still there and who still look on in disbelief, and anger, and fear, and then I find where Olympias had sat, before Philippos entered the arena, and I see that she's no longer there.

Of course.

I turn and look back down towards where Cleopatra sobs and holds her father, and Alexandros of Epirus stands behind them, next to the other Companions, and Attalus, and Parmenion and Antipater are there, too, with tears in their eyes, also, and we all look down at the body in front of us. I look at the great and gaping wound that I've already seen, the one in Philippos' stomach, the first wound, but when I look again now, I see that there are actually two wounds: there's the great and obvious one to the stomach, but there's also a second, one that's higher, and it's this second one, the smaller but deeper wound that's to the heart, which is the one that's done the most damage, and finally taken the life of Philippos of Macedon.

CHAPTER TWENTY

WE ALL QUICKLY RETURN TO PELLA because a new basileus now needs to be chosen, and when we return, the first thing we hear is crying. It's sobbing, actually, uncontrollable sobbing, and it seems to be everywhere. We hear it when we first reach the courtyard, then it's even louder when we enter the palace, and we learn it's coming from Eurydice, in her chamber, near the other wives. I think it's just grief for her dead husband, at first, the grief of a young girl who's lost someone for the very first time and someone she was only just married to, but then I learn that it's not. It's more than that. She had ridden ahead of us, with Attalus, her father, while we had stayed behind in Aigai to make arrangements for Philippos' body to be brought back to Pella behind us, and she rode as quickly as she could, because when we were all at Aigai, for the wedding, she had left her young daughter with the servants at the palace. When she returned with her father, galloping into the courtyard and jumping off her horse, the servants that she'd left the child with came to her with trembling hands and shaking voices and told her that while she'd been gone the child had died in its sleep. When they told her this, she had collapsed, right there in the courtyard. The child's breath simply gave out, they said, and there was nothing that could have been done and no other explanation; it happens to young children all the time, they had reassured her. I don't believe them, when I hear the story, the same as I'm sure Eurydice doesn't believe them, either.

Attalus reacts differently than his daughter.

Attalus screams and rages at anyone who will listen, but his rage does nothing, because what could it possibly do? It certainly won't bring the dead child back. He knows that but he screams anyways and the look in his eyes eventually turns from anger, to grief, and then perhaps something else.

Fear?

I can hope. I can only hope.

The body of Pausanius of Orestis is also brought back to Pella.

Most who would dare kill a basileus are crucified while they're still living, the highest form of punishment and torture that we know, but some are crucified once they're already dead, too, in a symbolic act to remind everyone of the punishment for regicide and this is what's done to him. We give his body to the pezhetairoi and they take it and pin his hands and feet to a wooden cross with great iron spikes run through bones and already-decaying flesh. I watch as they do this, and so does Alexandros, and we can hear the bones crack as they pound the spikes through his ankles and then we watch as the cross is hung in the middle of the city for all to see, for all to know what happens in Macedon to one who'd dare murder a basileus. The other thing that happens when a basileus is murdered are stories, and whispers begin to spread through Pella faster than the northern wind: stories, rumors, and accusations about what happened, and why, and who might really be responsible, because is a basileus simply murdered by a gilted lover, without help or support from any other? If that were the case, there would be dead kings the length and breadth of the known world.

I think about this myself, and what I've heard, and there's one thing that's stuck with me, one thing I've been curious about in the hours and days since the wedding and murder, so I search for Perdiccas.

I find him near the gymnasium, and when I do, I ask him about what he was going to say to me, before the wedding, and he tells me. It's only a rumor, he says, but while Alexandros and I were gone in Epirus, he'd heard there had been a hunting trip, deep in the mountains north of Pella. Philippos was supposed to go, but in the end, he didn't (probably because of his leg, I assume), and while the basileus had stayed in Pella, some of his guards still went. There was drinking and hunting and then one night there was too much drinking, as there always is, and the hunting turned into hunting of a different type and Attalus had raped Pausanius of Orestis. They say that Attalus had three of his men hold Pausanius down, and despite the guard's screams and pleas, Attalus had taken his pleasure right there, for all to see. He wanted to know what was so special about Pausanius, he'd said, and why the basileus spent so many nights with the guard and away from his daughter, Eurydice, and away from making a son. Pausanius had gone to Philippos after they returned. He asked Philippos for punishment and justice, but the basileus simply waved him away; he was with the younger Pausanius by then, the one from the south, that we'd seen outside his door, and Philippos had no interest in punishing his father-in-law and the second most powerful man in the kingdom. Pausanius of Orestis had returned to Philippos' office, day after day, each time with the same request, but each time Philippos refused to see him, refused to listen to him, refused to do anything to make right the great wrong that had been done.

This is the story I hear from Perdiccas.

Then I hear another from Philotas.

He tells me that he heard Olympias went to the place in the middle of the city where Pausanius was hung, the place Macedonians walk past and look up and curse the flesh of the man who'd murdered their basileus. She'd gone under cover of darkness, Philotas tells me, and the young boy that saw her and told him what he'd seen said she climbed up next to the cross, and Pausanius' broken and decaying body, and whispered something into his un-listening ear. And then, after she'd given her words, she took out a small vial from her chlamys, anointed his forehead with oil from the vial, then kissed him softly, once on each cheek. I don't know if the story is true, or if there was ever any young boy who saw this, because here in the north people tell all kinds of stories, especially when a basileus is murdered, and they also tell stories about those of us who aren't from Macedon, like they are. Do they tell stories about me, too? They must. But the stories about me aren't what are important right now, and the stories about Olympias, whether they're true or not, aren't either. For once, the stories don't matter. The only thing that matters is that the basileus is dead, and now, a new basileus must be chosen.

THIS IS THE MOMENT.

New leaders are selected by acclaim in Macedon, and when the nobles all gather in the great hall to perform this task, they're split, and there's no acclaim that's reached simply by voice alone. There are many contenders for the throne, and several who have at least modest support (Arrhidaeus, Parmenion, Antipater, even Attalus himself are all at least mentioned), but in the end, the army and the people won't choose age, they'll choose youth, and promise, as they always should, so it comes down to Amyntas and Alexandros, as everyone has always known that it would. Amyntas has the support of Attalus and the other wealthy and old families, and Alexandros has his Companions, the second, third, and fourth sons of those families. It's not enough. It's not nearly enough support for Alexandros who seems outnumbered by at least two-to-one, if I had to guess, so attention then turns to Arrhidaeus, the simple brother and oldest son of the last basileus. "Who will you support?" the people ask him, and when they do, Arrhidaeus looks at Amyntas, across from him, and I know what he feels when he looks at him, the cousin who tormented him, for his entire life. I know, because I feel it, too, but about another. Then Arrhidaeus turns and slowly walks to stand next to Alexandros, and me, and the rest of the Companions. That will be his answer. He will support us. It might seem like a small thing for someone like Arrhidaeus to do this, but it's not small; kingdoms and history have been decided by less. There are still nobles who are on the fence, but seeing the two sons of the old basileus standing side-by-side means something to these older men, and while some begin to sway, then join us, their support still doesn't result in a clear majority.

So the decision will go to the army.

Parmenion has all the Macedonian soldiers gather in the hall which means it's packed, as full as it can be, with many more soldiers spilling outside and into the courtyard, and they'll acclaim their next basileus by voice and call, he tells them, as the army does when the nobles are split. Parmenion asks for support for Amyntas, first, and the call goes up amongst the men who have seen him fight, mostly the veterans who have fought with him for years, the ones that were with him through the campaigns in the north, that Alexandros and the rest of us were too young to participate in. Then as their voices fade, Parmenion asks for those that support Alexandros, and there's another call that goes up, mostly amongst those that are younger, those that are more bold and more suited for risk and opportunity, more of the second and third and fourth sons and the sons of those from the lower city: the ones who know Alexandros, and have seen him, and have been near and around him because he's been with and amongst them, too, even though he was the son of the basileus.

The vote is close.

It's definitely close, but my heart sinks when I hear less voices in the second call for Alexandros than I heard in the first for Amyntas.

It happens that quickly, and that simply.

Amyntas will be basileus.

After all this time, and all these dreams, it will have all been for nothing, because it will be Amyntas.

Where will we go?

North.

We'll have to go north, or west, to escape him, because he will undoubtedly see us as a threat and one that he'll want to eliminate, and as quickly as possible.

Parmenion walks forward.

He raises his hands.

Everyone hushes, becomes silent, waiting for him to speak, and then he does, shouting two Greek words as loud as his voice will let him shout.

"*To kratisto!*" he yells.

There's a gasp amongst everyone that's gathered when they hear him, and I smile, I can't help it, because I know what this is; it's the honoring of a final wish.

Who will Philippos' kingdom go to?

To kratisto, as he'd once said. *To the strongest.*

It's what Philippos had always wanted, and now his oldest and closest friend has honored that, and made it so. Amyntas and Attalus aren't pleased, and neither are those that support them, and they come forward and gather around Parmenion and yell and shout. Attalus argues that their acclaim was clearly louder and more, but Parmenion brushes them off and tells him that he heard no such thing, and there was no consensus, so the matter will be decided as Macedonians decide such things, which is by strength. Attalus continues to protest, and so does Amyntas. "You don't wish to fight?" Parmenion finally asks, turning back to them as he asks the question as loudly as he can ask it, so that all will hear.

And when he does, Attalus and Amyntas stop.

Amyntas knows he can't say or agree to anything less than combat now, not if he wants to be basileus, and Attalus knows this, too, because he can't become basileus by ducking a fight and doing so in front of the entire army. So, instead, they just glare with hatred at the strategos, the friend of the old basileus, who is clearly no friend of theirs, and then Amyntas speaks. "So it will be," he says loudly, very loudly, accepting.

All eyes turn now to Alexandros.

And that's how the battle will be set.

"So it will be," Alexandros says, and he speaks loudly, too.

ALEXANDROS RETREATS to the room we share at the gymnasium to get ready, and I go with him, along with the other Companions. They wait on the sand, in the main part of the building, where we used to do our exercises, while I stand in our room with him as he puts on his armor and I beg him to let me fight Amyntas in his place. "No," he tells me, without meeting my eyes, for the hundredth time.

"Why?" I ask again.

"Because I can't be basileus if I don't fight."

"Yes, you can. If Amyntas is dead, if I kill him, then there is no one else."

"There will always be someone else."

"So then I'll kill them, too."

He turns and looks at me, then he smiles, and it's not a sad smile, or anything else. He walks closer and puts his hand on my cheek. "And you would, wouldn't you? But I won't use a champion to fight in my place. That's not our way."

"The army would still accept it as the will of the gods. They would have to, and that the gods have spoken through me."

"Yes," he says. "They're superstitious, and they would accept that. But what of me?"

I realize now what he means, and what he feels.

He wouldn't accept himself, or think himself basileus, if he doesn't do this, and that's perhaps the most important thing. That, perhaps, is the only thing.

What else can I say?

There's no way I can argue with what he's said and feels, and so what else is there, or what else can I do? It's the reason he'll be the leader that he'll be, and so I can do nothing.

I bend down.

I finish tying the straps attached to the greaves on his legs, and then I pick up his breastplate, from where it rests against the wall, the one with the Argead star printed in gold on it. I go to him with it and he spreads his arms so that the armor can be put in place on his chest and I reach around behind him and tie it at the back, securing it where it's placed, and I tie it tightly so it will not fault, will not break, will not leave him exposed and bare. It's the only protection I can give him. My hand lingers when I finish my knot, and my eyes linger, too, near his eyes, and I can feel his breathing on my neck. It's steady. Good.

I back up.

I look at him, and once again meet his mis-colored eyes.

"It's the only way, Hephaestion," he tells me, knowing my thoughts, and what my words would be. "It's the only way, and it was always going to be this."

"I know," I swallow.

"But it's not the end," he says. "This isn't what we've dreamed, or planned, or worked so hard to make real. This is only the beginning of all that."

"I know," I say again.

"Good."

"But just because we know that, it doesn't mean you can be reckless with your life today."

"I won't."

"Because it's my life, too."

"Of course. So what makes you think that I would?"

I think of Chaeronea as he picks up his sword, and I think of the battle, and the aftermath, and I think of Alexandros and what he did. I think of the rage that came and I think of the blood. I think of what I saw in his eyes, the consuming and blinding fire, and I think of the darkness that's in him, the darkness that's there, and next to the light, and gods help me, I pray for it. It's come before, and I pray for it to do the same thing, and to come again now. It's something that's been written about so many times—*sing to me muse, of the rage of Achilleus*—and even if it's not fully understood, we've seen and called it many things and we've called the ones who experience it *heroes*, and *gods*, and we've called them sons of gods, the ones that have that rage and darkness in them and while I might not fully understand what I ask and pray for, I still do. I pray for it to come and to consume him again and make him different and more than he is. I was charged by Aristoteles with one task, one sacred and important thing, and now I stand here in front of Alexandros and I do the opposite of what I promised Aristoteles, and I betray him.

"Keep your sword high," I tell Alexandros, instead of telling him any of this.

"I will."

"I've seen him fight, and while he might have a height advantage, he keeps his blade too low. Remember that, and look for it."

"Anything else?"

"I don't know."

"There's still so much left."

"Yes, there is."

"And so there will be," he says, and meets my eyes.

The sunlight shines through the room and onto his hair and makes it bright and golden again, like it did that morning when I woke up next to him in Mieza, for the first time, so many years ago now. A memory. A distant memory, and a different life, but no matter what life it is, the light always seems to find him. The light always seems drawn to him, and it's here again, and in his eyes now, too, in both of them, reflecting as they look back and into mine, and surely that means something, doesn't it?

"This is it, Hephaestion," he tells me. "This is the day that we're born."

"Yes," I nod, and there are tears in my eyes, and I can't hide or stop them.

He reaches out and wipes them away, and I feel his body tense when he touches my skin.

Have they heard me? Have they heard me already?

How could I have ever doubted?

He reaches down and picks up his shield, which also has the bright and many-pointed Argead star of his family hammered onto it, in bronze and gold, sixteen rays and points exploding from the sun at its center, the sun and light that always seems to search and find him.

There's one more moment, one more moment between us.

Then he turns and we walk out.

WE LEAVE OUR ROOM and head back towards the gymnasium where all the rest of the Companions wait. They sit and look down at the sand, each with their own thoughts, and then when they hear us coming, they look up. They see Alexandros, dressed for war, in his polished armor and with his great broad-sword strapped to his back, and the shield with his family's star on it held tightly in his hand, and they see me behind him, carrying his tall and feathered helmet under my arm. They stand, and then come closer, in front of us, me and Alexandros on one side, and all of them on the other. They look at me first, and I just stare back at them, not saying anything, but they know what this means. It means that I've failed, and that Alexandros will fight. So they turn to look at Alexandros. They stay like this, for a moment, and then Alexandros walks forward. He goes between them, his eyes meeting their eyes, and he nods, and they nod, too, as he touches each of them on the arm, on the wrist, on the shoulder, each individually, and I realize what this is, a sharing and passing of strength to him by those who have supported and made him strong his whole life. And also, this is it, I realize; this is why he'll be basileus, and why he'll be a great basileus. It's not because of gods, and what they do to him, and the favor they either bring or don't bring. It's this. It's the lives he's touched, and the deep and profound connections he's created amongst the friends that have walked with him. Amyntas and the others, they don't have that, do they? They certainly don't have anything close to that. They have no Companions, or anything else; they just have servants, and soldiers, and enemies.

But us?

There is a new generation, and it's all who are standing here together: we are the new Macedon, and the new Greece, and perhaps even the new world, too.

"Ready?" Alexandros asks, softly.

They all nod. They all look at him, and they nod. "Ready," they say, also softly, and echoing their friend.

He walks past them.

I follow behind when he does, and then the rest of the Companions fall in and follow after me. We leave the gymnasium. We start to walk through the city and when we do and pass houses and shops, the people see us and they begin to come out. They come out as we pass—from their homes, their businesses, from wherever they watch—and then I'm surprised to see that they begin to follow us, too, and when they do, I'm surprised to see something else: they're all clean-shaven now, like Alexandros is, like I am, like we all are. It's for him, I realize. It's for him, and for us. The people normally don't participate in the affairs of succession, but these are the people who Alexandros, so different from any other son of any other basileus, has lived amongst and between; these are the people that he's spoken to, that he's walked with, that he knows and who know him.

So they follow us, too.

Is this the first time this has happened in Pella?

Probably. I don't know.

But what I do know is that while the army and nobles might support Amyntas, the people support Alexandros. The people support Philippos' second son, and his Companions, the other second and third and fourth sons with nothing to inherit and everything to prove, just like them. We keep walking, and more put down what they're doing and follow us, some clean-shaven, some not, until we finally come to the edge of town and the ancient stadium that's there and that was built many years and generations ago and is where the battle will be, and where the contested succession will take place.

The army and nobles are already gathered.

They stand on one side of the space, and we then come to stand on the other, across from them.

Parmenion walks forward.

Alexandros looks at me.

I reach out and touch him, and then all the other Companions do the same, too, and after a moment, he's about to walk forward, away from us, and towards Parmenion, but there's one more thing. "The darkness you said you feel inside you," I pitch my voice low, so that only he can hear my words.

"I'll fight with honor," he tells me. "I'll keep it inside, like I promised you."

Then he turns and begins to walk.

From the other side, Amyntas begins to walk, also.

"*Alexandros*..."

He pauses and turns back to me: the sun glints off his shield, off his helmet, off his bright and mis-colored eyes. "What?" he asks.

I wait.

I feel eyes on me, more than just his.

"Don't," I tell him, and I speak louder now, so that all can hear.

He looks at me for one more moment, holding my eyes, too, and perhaps he can now hear my prayer, also, and he doesn't nod, he doesn't blink, he might not even breathe. He doesn't do anything except after one more moment just turn again and keep walking. They each move slowly, Alexandros coming from our side, and Amyntas from theirs, and as they walk, the clouds begin to gather above and cover the once-bright stadium in shadow. They both keep going until they're a few paces from Parmenion, and then they stop: they stand there, not much distance between them, and they glare at each other. "Do you submit to the law of succession of both gods and this kingdom?" Parmenion asks, now that they've reached him, and as he looks between each contender.

Neither answer.

Instead, they nod. They both just nod.

Parmenion turns away and back towards us, the people, on either side. "And do you also pledge to accept the decision of the gods and their will through this contest?" he asks us. "Do you pledge to accept the gods' decision of which of these two sons of Macedon will lead us, their decision of both who will fall, and the other who will rise?"

There are shouts.

There are shouts and the clanging of weapons being pounded against each other, metal on metal, steel on steel as noble, warrior, and city-dweller alike all pledge to listen to what's determined in this age-old rite of succession that's as old as the mountains that surround us, as old as the fields and grass that we stand on.

But me?

I'm not of these mountains, or these fields. I'm from somewhere else, and so instead I bow my head and I think of the gods that live both here, and there. I think of Hephaestus, in the north, my namesake that I do not know or speak to, and I think of Athena, in the south, who I do, and then I think of all the gods of mountains and fields and other things that are in-between, and I call on them. I call on all of them to come now to witness, just as they did before, at Chaeronea, and I call them to make him something else, just like they did then, too. I ask them to make him invincible, to make him a god, as they are, even if it's only for a short time, even if it's only for a moment, only for *this* moment, and there's a price to pay.

Do they hear me?

I don't know.

I hope they do, but I don't know.

In front of us, though, whether they hear me or not, Parmenion begins to walk to the side and away from the combatants to ready the arena for their contest.

A horn sounds.

It's now begun.

They each draw their swords, Amyntas from his waist, and Alexandros from his back, then they begin to circle each other. I can feel the tenseness of all those next to me, the other Companions, and the people, but after my many prayers, I'm overwhelmed by an enormous sense of calm and peace, and I don't feel what they feel.

In front of us, Amyntas makes his move, and he rushes forward.

He swings his smaller xiphos that he still uses but Alexandros dodges to the side and I smile to see his own broad-sword held high, like I told him, and then he comes forward himself and brings the great sword around and crashing down against Amyntas' shield.

The noise is loud, and it echoes between us.

The force of the blow must be painful, and unlike anything Amyntas has ever experienced, I know, or fought against before, because I see his arm falter after the impact and I hear him grunt in pain, even from the distance where we stand. Alexandros sees this, too, and he attacks again and Amyntas defends again with his shield, but he can't hold it steady and the tip of Alexandros' blade drags across the shield and then down and across flesh, too, slicing into muscle near the shoulder of Amyntas' sword-arm as he spins away and red streaks through the air where he just stood.

First blood.

It happens that quickly.

If I've learned anything about battle, in my short life, it's that it always happens that quickly.

They back up.

I squint my eyes and can see Amyntas look down at the wound, judging it, measuring it, then they continue to circle each other once more.

Amyntas sees an opening. He rushes forward again.

He swings his xiphos in another great blow which is the only thing he knows how to do, and Alexandros reads his intention perfectly, and darts to the side, and out of the way, using the quickness and speed that comes with his smaller frame. The rush forward exposes Amyntas once more, also, and Alexandros brings the broad-sword back around in a move that's only possible with a great amount of strength—the strength we've trained for and built, ever since I first arrived—and as the great broad-sword comes around and down in a blinding arc, it crashes against Amyntas' shield again, and there's no mistake this time as I hear him scream and he drops his shield.

He tries to grab it, from the dirt, between them, but Alexandros kicks it away and out of reach.

Above them, the clouds begin to part.

The sun begins to shine, a single ray at first, and then more.

I watch as Amyntas tries to grab his shield again, but Alexandros just kicks it further, and Amyntas' bleeding and broken left arm hangs limp at his side, while his right still holds his short xiphos.

He grips and re-grips it.

Alexandros watches him, calmly. I wonder what he's thinking.

No, I *know* what he's thinking.

Amyntas comes forward once more, and he comes forward heavy, too heavy, and reckless, and he swings. Alexandros easily blocks the blow with his shield, and when Amyntas swings again, Alexandros easily blocks that blow, too.

The same thing happens, again and again.

Do something, I whisper. *This is the moment*, I try to tell him.

The sound of iron and steel clashing against each other fills the stadium, and the fields, and perhaps even the mountains, too, and the Companions along with all the others gathered begin to murmur. The clouds above us part even more than they already have, and the light that's there shifts, gains, expands, and the single beam moves and grows and it now comes to touch Alexandros; it seems to come and linger on him, on his hair again, once more making it a color that's more fair and golden than what it actually is.

The light, the light.

And then . . . that's when it happens.

Maybe it's the light, or the gods, and maybe it's both or either, and maybe I'm wrong and it's something else entirely, or it's just him and him alone, but what happens next is Alexandros springs forward and into action and it's something to behold. It's something for all those watching to behold in wonder and awe, though of course I already have, at Chaeronea, when I saw it and tried to quench it and hide it from the others.

I don't now, though.

Let them see what I've seen, I think; let them know what I know, and here it is, men, women, and children of Macedon, this is what you've helped create, and what you've given to us, to yourself, and to the world. Behold what's in front of us, behold a boy born to lead, a boy born to love and to share that love, a boy touched by gods and prophecy that has come to be basileus of this place, this place where he was born, this place where he now fights, and this place he will soon rule because it's been written by stars and gods and the light that follows him, and perhaps it's even been written by me, too, perhaps there's even a small part that I've written. That is what I've called for, and it's now here, and am I glad that I have, and that it's come?

Yes, I nod, as I watch.

He swings his great sword.

Yes, I am.

Amyntas blocks the blow, but Alexandros swings again.

Amyntas blocks that one, too, but there's another.

And then there's another, and another, and another even after that.

Alexandros doesn't even try to get past Amyntas' guard because he knows that his opponent has worn himself down, and while Amyntas might be bigger, he hasn't trained in the way that we have.

There's more clanging.

There are more sounds of metal that pierce the now-bright afternoon.

Another blow, and another.

Then Alexandros finally swings, and Amyntas parries with his xiphos, but he also falls, the force of the blow pushing him to his knees.

The crowd gasps.

Alexandros is on him, in a moment.

He swings, swings, swings.

The weight of his broad-sword and the power with which he uses it takes its toll on Amyntas, even more than it already has, as Amyntas keeps parrying and blocking the blows, or at least trying to, and Alexandros doesn't do anything else but keep swinging.

Strength, pure strength, no tricks or gimmicks.

Then Amyntas' arm finally collapses under the force of Alexandros' blows, and Alexandros' broad-sword pierces and slices through Amyntas' armor at the shoulder of his right arm and chest, and Amyntas screams again, he screams so loudly that we all hear it and it fills us, and then he drops his sword altogether.

Alexandros punches him in the face.

Once, twice, three times.

They are great blows, but they aren't blows meant to kill.

They're still grappled together on the ground, limbs swinging against limbs, and Alexandros punches again and again and again, not using the blade of his sword, just the hilt, and he bloodies Amyntas' lip, nose, face, blood dripping down and onto his now-darkened chiton and staining it red.

Amyntas is dazed.

And that's when Alexandros stands.

Amyntas is still below him, on the grass, his arms spread at his sides, the blood on his face still dripping, pooling, spilling, mixing with the grass below.

His life now belongs to another, and he knows it.

Alexandros tosses his own shield to the side and reaches to grab Amyntas by the hair, and pull him to his feet.

I don't want to watch this.

I don't want to see him like this.

And while I don't want to see it, it's what I've prayed for, and what he's become, and so I will.

I have to.

I must.

I must see and know what he is, and what I've called, which is what they'll all see now, too.

He pulls Amyntas to his feet by the hair and then they stand there, chest to chest. More blood drips from Amyntas' face, down to his chin, and then underneath his armor and to his stomach and I see Alexandros look at it, at the blood that pools there and at their feet, because they're cousins, after all, and so it's his blood, too.

I listen for his thoughts.

I listen, but I can't hear them.

Who is it that clouds them, and keeps them from me: is it the gods, or is it Alexandros himself?

He reaches out.

He reaches out and he pulls at the straps that hold Amyntas' breast-plate secured to his chest, and Amyntas doesn't stop him as the armor is untied and falls off and to the ground. They then stand there, across from each other, for one more moment, both their chests rising and falling, rising and falling, together, the business of their entire lives now between them.

Why does it have to be like this?

I don't know, but it does. At least right now and in this world it does.

Alexandros raises his great broad-sword and with his own loud scream now he thrusts it forward, in a swift and strong movement, and plunges it into Amyntas' chest, where it goes all the way up to the hilt, the point and half the blade protruding from the other side of his cousin's body, steel glinting in the light that the gods have brought for the one that they favor and follow.

Amyntas doesn't scream. Not this time.

He just stays there, staring, at Alexandros, as more blood begins to pool in his mouth and then eventually his body goes slack, and the life begins to fade and depart from his eyes.

Alexandros rips the sword back and more blood spills across grass, from the wound, and then his cousin falls.

I think he's finished.

But he isn't.

Alexandros raises his sword and brings it down again, and again, and again, and before I know what's happening, I'm running across the distance between us and others are following behind me, not as fast as I am, but they're close, and then I reach him and tackle him from the already-dead and now mutilated body and he raises his sword on me, too, and I don't say anything this time, but then he sees me.

His eyes register.

Through all the blood that covers his armor, his body, his skin and his face, it registers, and he stops.

He lowers his sword now.

He comes back into himself.

I stand.

I slowly pull him to his feet, after me, and then we're both there, standing, and the Companions, and Alexandros of Epirus is there, too, and there's blood on me now, also, as he turns and faces all the others that are gathered. "Amyntas would only be basileus for half of Macedon," he yells to them. "But I will be basileus for *all* Macedon, and Greece, and even more beyond Greece and what is already ours, too," he holds their eyes, looking between them, back and forth. "So who will stand with me? Who will *march* with me?"

Silence.

Slowly, Parmenion walks forward and comes to take his place in front of us, in front of Alexandros.

He looks him over, up and down, up and down.

Then the old strategos nods.

"The gods have spoken," he says, "and they have spoken clearly. I will march with you, Alexandros-basileus, and so will any and all who follow me."

He turns to the army, the ones who sided with Attalus and the others.

Slowly, they begin to murmur, and then one soldier strikes his xiphos against his shield, and then another does the same, and then more do, too, after them.

Soon they all clash weapons against shields, then the others across from them, on our side, join in.

The villagers join in then, also, and so do the Companions.

The noise is deafeaning.

Alexandros raises his arms, his hands, up towards the sky, towards the stars, and I think back to the first moment I met him and the days that followed, all the days we spent in the mountains, in our rooms, and all the things we dreamed of and that we dreamed together during those days. We always seemed to know it would come, that *this* would come, and we were right, because now it's here. I thought it would be different. I thought it would *feel* different. But now that it's here, I don't feel any of what I thought I would.

I look down at the body at my feet.

I look down at the mangled flesh and broken bones of Amyntas-

Argeadai, who only a few short moments ago had the favor of all those who now cheer the man who killed him, the one who would be their new basileus, and they pick Alexandros up and begin to carry him away and back towards the palace to go and celebrate all those things that are in him that I fear, and that they've now seen, as I have; all those dark things that I promised I would keep at bay, but haven't, and so what have I done?

Have I done the right thing?

I shake my head. I don't know, and so I let them.

I let them carry him back to the palace, and the feast that will surely come, and wine, and food, and false promises they'll whisper and fake smiles that won't leave their faces, not for the whole night. I let them go to all this but I don't join them. They all leave together, all except me, and one other, too, I see, and when I turn to find who it is, I see that it's Parmenion that's there and next to me, and I'm not surprised. We stand apart from each other, then he comes closer. He stands next to me and looks down at the body at my feet, too. I have a question. I have a question I've wanted to ask him, ever since we returned from Epirus, and so now I do.

"Why did you tell him not to invite us back?"

He doesn't answer, at least not at first.

We just stand there, in silence, together, for a few more moments.

We both stand there and look down at our feet, each with our own thoughts about what it all might mean, and then he finally does answer, still looking at the body. "My job was to serve Philippos," he tells me, very slowly. "My job was to make him happy, both as his strategos, and as his best friend."

"And his son back in his house wouldn't do that?"

"I knew him, Hephaestion, in the same way that you know Alexandros, which is the way you can only know someone who you've been young with. He wanted to be remembered. That's all he wanted, as all men want, and who speaks of Peleus? Who remembers him? We only speak of his son. We only remember and speak of his great son, so that's why I told Philippos to leave you in the mountains."

My skin raises, on my arms, and on my neck.

It's just the two of us and the understanding that's now between us and the similarity that's there, also, and that I didn't see before, or know. He puts his hand on my shoulder, waits for a moment, then turns and leaves. He begins to walk back towards the palace and he already seems older. It's only been a matter of days, but he already seems older since his friend has died, and I watch as he walks into the distance, until eventually he's gone.

I'm alone.

I stay there on the field with Amyntas, just the two of us, and no one else, and I look down at his body. I expect someone to come back, to return looking for me, or him, but no one does. I look at Amyntas' eyes, like I do Alexandros', but they just stare up and into darkness and I don't hear his thoughts in the way that I hear Alexandros' thoughts. So I'm just left to think and to wonder. I wonder: did he dream the same dreams that we did? I wonder: did he feel the certainty of the same promises that we felt, and kept close to our heart? I wonder: how did he imagine his own end, and was it today, or was it in some distant and great place, as we've imagined ours, in some distant and great time that's far from here and this one?

I don't know.

And now, I'll never know, and neither will anyone else.

I wait for another moment, alone with my thoughts, and what I've done, and then I finally turn and head back towards the city and the others. I'm alone both in and with the darkness that's come, and alone both in and with the shadows, also. I'm alone with the burden of knowing that the innocence and way we once were has now departed, never to return, and all that will be left, both for me and for us, are the dual curses of certain destiny and yet-unrealized greatness.

CHAPTER TWENTY-ONE

I WAS BORN THE SON OF A KING, though I was born without a kingdom to inherit, the same as Alexandros was born, but now he has, though he hasn't inherited his kingdom, he's taken it. He's taken it, and made it his, and he's now basileus of all Macedon, and Greece, and the northern tribes, too, and he's basileus not through blood or birth, he's basileus through strength and strength alone, the thing I've brought from my mountains and home and given to him and added to all the things he already was before me.

But the kingdom that he's won and taken . . . it doesn't last.

In fact, it doesn't even last a day before it crumbles and falls apart.

It's Thebes that breaks their promise first, and then once Thebes does, the northern tribes do, too, and it doesn't surprise me to learn that Kleon is the leader of the splintering and betrayal. He's disloyal and thinks Philippos' death an opportunity for Illyrian sovereignty, and so it doesn't surprise me at all to hear that he's told whoever will listen that he'll never bow or pay tribute to a mere boy, and that Illyrians will never follow one as young as Alexandros anywhere, least of all into battle, or to another continent.

It's a mistake, of course it is.

But it's one that will be made only once, because it's one that *can* be made only once.

That's the trouble that comes from the north.

In the south, the trouble doesn't end up coming from all the poleis, just one. Thebes is the ringleader of the southerners and the first to declare themselves free of Macedonian rule, following Philippos' death, and they try to get others to join them, the same as my uncle has done with the northern tribes. But as far as we can tell, in Pella, no one else joins with Thebes, like they did before. They've all seen our army now, they've seen how we fight, and they've seen Alexandros, too, at Chaeronea, and then after, in Athens, and at the ekklesia. They're better at reading armies and history in Athens than they are in Thebes, and so soon after we hear of Thebes' betrayal, we receive a separate messenger from Athens who says that the ekklesia has met again and Athens intends to honor their word and commitment and reaffirm their allegiance to Alexandros, as the new basileus of Macedon, and all the rest of Greece, too.

Alexandros is silent when he hears this.

He's itching to deal with Thebes because he considers their betrayal to be greater than Kleon's or any of the northern tribes, and as much as he says he wants to go south first, Parmenion convinces him the more prudent action is addressing the problem in the north; they need to consolidate and secure their northern border first, and then go south and into the heart of Greece once more. Alexandros has kept Parmenion as strategos, and I know Parmenion is right, and so do the rest of us. I look at all the gathered men huddled over a map of the peninsula, with Alexandros next to them, and the Companions between and around, on the sides, filling in all the spaces that are left. Youth. That will be what Macedon is now, as we the young have come into power with one of our own, but Alexandros has also kept his father's most trusted friends and generals in their places. The others? The ones that sided with Attalus, and Amyntas? They will have no place and no favor. What will they say? What will they feel, being replaced by us, who for so many of them are the same age as their sons, or even *are* their sons?

I smile when I think about it.

I watch them all together, all the young men that are huddled around

Alexandros, the basileus, *their* basileus, and they love him. This is the future, isn't it? I was worried what they would think after the stadium, but I should have known better, and shouldn't have spared a thought to the desecration of Amyntas and his body because rather than be appalled or taken aback or anything else, they instead love and respect him even more. It's not dishonor that they saw; it was *victory*, just victory.

I think of Aria, in the city.

It's strange that I think of her, but I do, and I wonder what will happen to her.

I've been thought of as Macedonian, for all these years I've lived here, but am I? Am I truly?

No. I am of somewhere else. And I'm beginning to think he might be, too.

I breathe in.

It's time now, it's finally time, and it's all that I've waited for, all that I've trained for, all that I've dreamed of and wanted since I left and first arrived in Pella.

I leave the war council and walk outside.

I stand by myself for a moment and then I hear something behind me and I don't turn because I know it's him. I can feel him, just as he can feel me, and that's of course also the reason he's come. "You knew you would go to Illyria first," I say, once he's there, and next to me, and we're alone. "You knew you wouldn't go south."

"Yes," he nods.

"Then why pretend like you wanted to go to Thebes?"

"So they can think I've listened to them, and they can think I care about their thoughts, and counsel."

"And do you care what they think?"

I know the answer.

Of course he doesn't care about their thoughts: that's why he's Alexandros, and they are who they are, and though he's still young, he's already wise and understands men. He's silent as we stand there. We don't need words. That's something for them, for the others. Then he moves closer to me so that we touch again, his shoulder pressed against mine and his skin softly touching against my skin, there in the heat. "I care what one person thinks," he finally says, speaking slowly, deliberately. "And I've already told him, a long time ago."

"Did you?"

"Yes. Are you ready?"

"I don't know. I'm ready, of course I am. But I also don't know."

"Really?"

"You spend so long thinking about something, and then, when it finally comes? I just don't know. It doesn't feel like I thought it would, I guess."

"Nothing will change," he says, then smiles. "Home is wherever we decide to make it, and family is whoever we choose. And as you know, I choose you, and I think you choose me, too."

"What about blood?"

"What about it?"

"Is it nothing in all this?"

"We spill blood, you and I. That's all it is, and nothing more."

"*Alexandros...*" I begin, but then trail off, and when I do, he nods, and I know he's thinking about his mother, and his father, and so I take him in my arms and he takes me in his, too. He doesn't seem as tall as he did yesterday, in the amphitheater; he doesn't seem very tall at all next to me. He's almost a full head shorter than I am, and he doesn't seem as tall as he does when the gods come and favor him and use him for whatever purpose they've brought and given and injected into his veins, his soul, and so into mine, too, because our souls are one soul, as we've been told. I stay there. I breathe, and so does he. We each hold the other and we breathe. He's who he's always been, but he's also not now, and so I tell him this. I will tell him what he is, and what he is to me, because it's also what he now is to the world. I lean forward, my lips next to his lips, and I whisper.

"*Alexandros...*" I begin again.

"Yes."

But this time, I don't trail off, and I finish.

"*Alexandros-basileus,*" I whisper, so that only he can hear.

TWO DAYS LATER, we gather the army, and then we go north.

We ride to the foothills of the mountains that are there—the same that I crossed, on my way to Pella, all those years ago—but before we begin to cross them again, and head towards Illyria, on the other side, I find two scouts and bring them to me and tell them what I need them to do: I tell them how to go ahead of us and how to sneak into Salona. I tell them how to walk unnoticed through the streets and towards the palace, and then I tell them how to find my mother, and my brother, once they get there, and I tell them what message to bring to them when they do.

They hear me. They nod, and then they leave.

They ride ahead, through the mountains, galloping at a break-neck pace and I watch them for a moment, as we follow the path that they take, but more slowly.

I took this same path on my way to Pella, when I was fifteen, only I follow it now in the opposite direction, and the symbolism isn't lost on me. I ride next to Alexandros now, too, as we ride back towards my home, and as we do, I look around at the forests and mountains that surround us with a mixture of longing and nostalgia. It's a different time of year than when I came—it's late summer, so there's no snow, as there was before—but everything else is exactly the same; the uneven and rock-covered path, the low bridges over rushing streams that lead to deep and wide lakes, the jagged and high-peaked mountains that border and surround everything, the crisp air that's colder and more refreshing than we're used to in the lower country around Pella, the smell of cypress and lavender that grows stronger with every step that we take. It's a very beautiful part of the world, here in the north and the west, but more than that, it's also mine, I realize, which gives it its own type of personal and specific beauty. I allow myself to think about the other life I could have had. I allow myself to think about the other path I could have taken, the one that didn't lead to Pella, and Alexandros, and all that life could have been. I think about these possibilities, and divergences, as we ride through the mountains, and I think about the choices I've made. If I could go back, I'd still choose the same, but we can also still envy and yearn for more than one life, can't we? We can long for more than one path, more than one way and direction to take, as we wander, and make our way through the width and breath of this great and wide world and between and amongst all the souls in it that are living, dying, loving, and crashing together, just like we are.

"There," Alexandros says, from his place next to me.

I shake my head clear of these thoughts and then turn to look at him, and see where he's pointing: in the distance, the scouts I sent ahead to Salona are returning, and ride towards us, and there are two more that ride with them, too, one extra person on each horse. I look at Alexandros, and he looks back at me. Then his lips part, into a wide smile, because he knows what this means. He knows what this means for me, but what I realize is that he also knows what it means for him, too. I heard what he said, back at the palace, in Pella: *we can't choose blood*. But, fortunate am I, that if we could, they are who I would choose. A million times over, and then once again, they are exactly who I would choose.

I quickly kick the brown to a gallop, and he does the same, on Bucephalus, while the army marches and rides behind us as we race along the path and quickly erase the distance between us and those that ride to meet us. We get closer and then we're to them. They dismount before we get there, from where they ride behind the scouts, and then I do, too, as the brown comes to a skidding halt and I jump off, all in one fluid and practiced and urgent movement. I run to them, and when I reach them, I hug her. I hug her first, because of what I've done, and then I hug him, and then both of them together, at the same time. I hold them so close. I can feel their hearts, and I can see their tears. I can see them as they come, wet on my shoulder and the skin of my cheek that's pressed against their cheeks.

"How?" I hear my mother whisper.

And I feel it, too, when she whispers.

I feel the soothing and familiar sensation of the chords in her throat vibrating against my shoulder and I hear the familiar rhythm of her words, the tone, how she says my name, all the things that I know and that I now remember.

I back up.

I look at them.

My mother looks older than she did when I left; the lines on her face are more pronounced with age, and time, and yes, grief, too, which makes the guilt come again. Then I turn and look at my brother. I see that he's taller than he was, but he's not taller than me. At least not yet. He's the same height as Alexandros, I realize, as I embrace him again, and then I move away from them both and hold them at arm's length.

How?

Her question.

How do I explain?

I'm about to try, as best I can, but then I see her eyes shift, and move, and my brother's do, too, and they look behind me.

I smile.

I know why their eyes move, and I know what they see.

They see a great stallion that's been named for the blazing white mark that's on its forehead, and they see a golden-haired young basileus from Greece with mis-colored eyes who swings his leg and jumps to the ground next to us.

He walks towards where we stand.

They see his armor, and his sword, and the way he carries himself, and perhaps they can even feel him, too, in the same way that I feel him.

He gets closer.

He comes to stand next to me, and when he does, his shoulder brushes against my shoulder, in the way that it so often does, and I watch my mother's eyes as she takes this in because now, with this one simple act, she will know. Of course she will know, because a mother always will know.

She looks between us.

"Are you . . . ?"

She looks to me now, and I nod. *Yes*, my eyes tell her. *This is the basileus.*

"I've heard so much about you," Alexandros says to her. "So many stories, and so many wonderful memories."

"We . . ." my brother begins, but then trails off.

"You what?" Alexandros asks, turning his eyes to him.

"We thought he was dead," he finally manages, staring back at Alexandros.

"I know," Alexandros answers, with sympathy in his voice, and understanding, too.

My brother looks back at him.

My mother does, as well.

Then she seems to remember herself and goes to bow in front of him. "*Basileus*," she says.

But when she begins, he stops her.

"No," he says, and she looks at me again, and then back to him. "I was only recently made basileus, but before that I was something else."

"What?" she asks, not understanding, as this isn't normally the way a basileus speaks or acts.

But Alexandros will be no ordinary basileus.

"I was a brother, too, and a son, and since you're Hephaestion's mother, and his brother, I would be yours, also. If you would have me, of course."

My mother looks back and forth, between us, while my brother's eyes are very wide. She recognizes what I recognize, and what I know: that Alexandros has a brother, and a mother, and a father by blood, but he also, for so many reasons, doesn't actually have any of those things. Not really. So she smiles warmly, as a mother would, at her three sons now, standing next to each other, and in front of her.

"Of course," she says.

She comes forward and embraces him as she would if he were her own. Then when they move apart, my brother comes forward, and he hugs Alexandros, too. Alexandros looks back and forth between them, then turns to my brother, looking into his young eyes. "How old are you?" he asks him.

"Fifteen," he says.

"Not old enough," I tell them both.

"Not old enough for what?"

My brother looks back and forth with his mountain eyes that are the same as my mountain eyes, but they're also different, too. They're softer, like he is. He has strength, I can see, or at least the promise of it, and that it will one day come to his frame, but it's not the same type of strength that I have, and it's not the same type that Alexandros has, either. There will be a place for him. There will always be a place for him and other men like him, but it's not the same as our place.

So I don't answer.

Instead, I turn back to our horses, and after Alexandros jumps back up and onto Bucephalus, I help my mother so that she rides behind him, and then I turn to my brother. I help him up and onto the brown, and then I jump up, too, in front of him and take the reins as he holds my waist before we turn and continue on, through the mountains, in front of the army that we lead, to fight for the land of our father and the kingdom and family that neither of us ever meant or wanted to leave.

WE FIND ANOTHER HORSE for my mother, and my brother still rides on the brown with me, so we ride together as a family, away from the others, and as we do, I tell them all that's happened in the years since I've left. I tell them how I knew the blow it would be when they heard that I'd died, but when I tell them why I did it, I see my mother nod, and my brother, too, understanding. I tell them how I met Alexandros and how we've grown together, and I tell them of Pella, and Mieza, and Athens, and Epirus, and Ithaka, and I tell them how Alexandros became basileus. They look at me and ask questions, and when they do, I answer them as best I can. I hear my mother say my name again, when she asks something new, and it's familiar to hear her say it, and comforting. I hear my brother say my name, too, when he asks something, and it breaks my heart because it's almost as if he's forgotten the word; it's almost as if it's something unnatural for him to say, as if his lips and tongue have no practice or familiarity with the syllables and letters.

What have I done?

The only thing I could have.

We keep riding and then soon come to the mountains that are directly above Salona, and we stop. Alexandros sends an envoy to speak with Kleon, and to ask him to come to our camp, to discuss terms of surrender. But Kleon immediately sends back a message calling Alexandros a child, and a coward, and that there will be no words between them and there will be no terms either. Illyria is free, he says, and so is Salona, and they already have a basileus. I see Alexandros smile and shake his head as he hears these words, which he knew would be the words that would come, and so do the rest of the Companions, too, because they know that Kleon hasn't seen them; he hasn't seen them fight, he hasn't seen the hetairoi charge, he hasn't seen the new and fearsome sarissa used by the pezhetairoi, and he hasn't seen our Kritin broad-swords, either.

Pride.

He has pride and arrogance, in equal measure, and he will pay for it, but the blood with which he will pay is my blood, too, because it's the blood of my people. I look at my mother, and my brother. It's *our* blood. It's all of our blood. There is no other way, though, and so it will be, and such is the price of living in a kingdom and allowing oneself to be ruled by a corrupt and power-hungry man such as my uncle. It doesn't matter now, though. In the world that Alexandros and I will make, such men will be destroyed. They will be destroyed, wherever we find them, and then they'll be replaced, and it's fitting that we'll begin with him, the worst among them.

Our army assembles.

We do so as quickly as we can because after our business here in the north, we have more still to do, in the south.

I stand in the tent that I share with Alexandros.

We stand naked and shave our faces together, as we do before every battle, and then once we're done, we begin to dress. We put our chitons on first, and then he helps me with my armor, and I help him with his, the same as we did before Chaeronea, and the same as we'll also do before every battle that we fight together.

We're soon ready.

We leave.

We walk out of the tent and I see my brother standing there waiting for us. He's dressed in old armor himself and carries with him a short, polished, and un-used sword. Alexandros looks at us, and then just at me. I nod to him. He understands. He smiles at my brother and then continues on, by himself, so that we're alone.

When it's just the two of us, my brother tells me he wants to fight.

This is what he's dressed for, and what he's come to do, he says, because he thinks he should, and that it's expected of him. But I can also see in his eyes that he really doesn't want to, and it's not who he is, or what's in his heart; I can see in his eyes that this isn't the type of man that he'll become, and it's certainly not who he is yet, and so I tell him no. I haven't been able to be a big brother for most of his life, but I can change that now.

"Why?" he asks, frowning.

"Because I said so."

"You were the same age as I am when you left and fought."

"No, I didn't."

"What?"

"I didn't fight. I paid the men who found me to tell our uncle that I had fought, and that they'd killed me."

"But you would have, though. If that had been more prudent."

I pause and I look back at him. I won't lie. "Yes," I nod. "I would have."

"Then why shouldn't I?"

"Because you have a brother who's trained his whole life for this, and I didn't have that."

"You'll need every sword you can gather."

I smile. He hasn't seen us fight, either. "No," I tell him. "No, we won't."

"Are you sure?"

"I'm sure," I say again, and he doesn't protest, at least not anymore. What I've told him is truth, but I didn't tell him all the truth, and that there's more, too; I didn't tell him that he's only just returned to my life, and I don't want there to be any chance of him leaving it again, and so soon. I want to be his brother once more. I want to show him what our father showed me, and that he'll then show to his own children, too, when they come, and that they'll then show their children, as well. Because if not him and his children, then who else will there be? I know what I'm taking from him; I know that he's the same age now as I was when I left, and I think of who I was then, and how I would have felt, but my brother's not me. He's not me at all, and so I leave him behind.

He's glad of it, I think.

He's made his case as he thinks he should, and I've said no, so I leave him with our mother and then follow after Alexandros to where he waits on Bucephalus. I jump onto the brown next to him and we ride to the army, and when we get there, I don't stop. I keep riding. I go past the army and then start to gallop, towards the space that's between our soldiers and theirs, and Alexandros gallops after me. "What are you doing?" he yells, as we get closer to the Illyrian lines. "Kleon said there will be no terms or surrender!"

"I know."

"So what are you doing?"

"I want him to see me."

We cross more of the distance and get closer to the Illyrians, to my people, and I see Kleon at his place in the middle of the men. I resent him. I resent him so very much for what he's done, and the blood that has to be spilled here today because of him, and his pride, and I can feel that resentment in my heart as it shifts, changes, and then turns into hate which it really has been all along. He stands with the infantry and they have more men than we've brought, which is perhaps what gives him his confidence, but it's false-confidence and doesn't matter: with the discipline that we have, and our sarrissa and all the other advancements in tactics and weaponry that have been made under Philippos, they won't be able to stand against us. It won't even be close. I stop outside the range of their archers and it must be strange for Kleon to see Alexandros so close to him, and his army, and I know he recognizes him because of his armor and the Argead star that's on it, but me?

He has no eyes for me. At least not yet.

So I raise my sword.

I raise my great broad-sword high into the air, and then I lower it and point the tip at him, across from us, and I see it: I see the moment he looks and recognizes me, and then his mouth goes slack, because how could this be? I make sure he sees my face and my eyes; I make sure he knows what's going to happen today. As I've grown older and matured, I don't know if I've begun to look more like my father, as so many sons do, but in this moment, I hope that I have, and I hope that's who and what he's thinking about, too, my father, his brother, the old basileus.

I don't say anything.

Neither does Alexandros.

We just sit there for a moment longer, on our horses, and then we both turn and gallop back towards our army and their ordered and well-disciplined lines. We reach the Companions and where they sit on their horses, at the head of the hetairoi, and we join them. They all unsheathe their swords now, and then the rest of the army does the same, as a chant begins to go up from the Illyrians across from us, seeing this, which means that the moment is almost upon us.

Alexandros will ride with us, the hetairoi, the same as he did at Chaeronea.

It's tradition that the Macedonian basileus marches with the pezhetairoi, on foot, but Alexandros has trained to be a cavalry officer his entire life and he will do things differently and so Parmenion is at the center of the infantry, and will command them, while Alexandros will still lead us.

He turns to me, next to him.

"These are your people," he says, softly.

"They are," I nod.

"They hold arms against us. They won't be spared."

"Yes, they will," I tell him, and then turn to meet his eyes.

He cocks his head up and to the left, as he tends to do when he's thinking and there's something he hasn't quite grasped, which isn't often, but then he does. I look back at him, and I look back at his eyes and I realize that his hair has changed color once again and perhaps for good: it no longer has the reddish hue it did when I first met him. Now, it's fair, it's always fair, nearly blonde, like the light that shines on him, or is it *because* of the light that shines on him? I don't know, but it most certainly has left its mark on him and who he is, because that's what light does.

He nods.

He nods, just once, because he trusts me.

Then I turn and look up to the sky, to the clouds, to the heavens and the stars that I know are there, the ones under which I was born and grew and that I'm now under once again.

"*Pater*," it's my turn to whisper. "*Father . . .*"

Then in front of us, there's a horn.

And once we hear the horn, the charge begins.

I squeeze my thighs and begin to ride, with Alexandros at my side, and our Companions next to and around us, and as we ride, the ground beneath us begins to tremble and shake. There's the sound of pounding hooves reverberating everywhere as we thunder down and towards the line that's in front of us—not my father's men, or mine, in this moment, but Kleon's men, and *only* Kleon's men—and the distance between us begins to shrink, getting smaller, smaller, smaller, and they get closer, then we're finally to them.

Crack, again.

We crash into them in another great and powerful wave of metal and steel, and then there's blood, too, and there are bodies tossed aside by our horses and the pezhetairoi come behind to fill in the holes that we the hetairoi have made and the Illyrians don't yet realize that these aren't pezhetairoi like they've fought against before, because they've had peace with Macedon for so long.

But they do recognize this now.

And they also recognize their mistake.

The battle doesn't last long.

In fact, it's the shortest battle that any in our army has ever fought, even the veterans and ones who have fought and been in our army since before Philippos. The Illyrians have no cavalry and it's the charge of ours that's broken them—pushed a wide wedge deep and into their lines—and so they all soon drop their swords and surrender. They don't want to be slaughtered, because what would the slaughter be for? Life had been fine as a Macedonian ally, and paying tribute to Pella, and being left in peace, and it will be again, once this is over.

Alexandros raises his arm and the fighting stops.

But it only stops for them. It doesn't stop for me, not yet.

I jump off the brown and push my way through the Illyrians, young and old, who all look at me strangely. I look back at them and can't tell if what I see in their eyes is recognition, or respect, or fear, or something else entirely, and I push past them and through their ranks and towards where I last saw Kleon in the center. The others will be spared, they know that they will, but there's one who won't, and that's who I go to find. The men part in front of me as I walk, and when I get to the center, I look down and see Kleon's body; it lays in the grass at the feet of his generals and he's already dead. His armor has been ripped from his body and there's a fresh and gaping hole in his chest, blood red and sticky and still being pumped from his heart to stain the grass beneath him with its bright color. I look down at him, at his blank eyes staring up, and into the sky. This is something that's been taken from me. I thought this would have been a moment that would have been mine, but it's been taken. "We told him to negotiate before the battle, and then to surrender once it began," one of the generals says, who is young, only a few years older than I am.

"Why didn't he?"

"Because he thought he could win."

"No, he didn't," I shake my head, and then look up again. "And it's your job to convince him of that, Agron," I say to the young general who I recognize from my previous life, and as he looks back at me, I see him recognize me now, too.

"*Hephaestion?*" he asks, barely breathing the word.

It's as if I'm a ghost that's returned, and is now amongst them once more, and which, in so many ways, is exactly what I am.

"Blood didn't have to be spilled," I tell him.

"It did with Kleon. You know that. But now Illyria is yours."

Those three words.

Illyria is yours.

I've waited an entire lifetime to hear them, and now I have, but it's different, and it is because I realize it's not what I want, after all, and it's not what I want because it's not enough. Illyria is Illyria, just as Macedon is Macedon, but there's also more, there's so much more, because there's also the world, too. "Bring your dead and ours," I finally tell Agron. "Well burn them together and then we'll see what Alexandros will do," I say, and then after I'm done, I walk back towards the brown, Illyrian soldiers parting around me, once again, and I know what I see in their eyes now and it is recognition that I see, as I jump back up on my horse and kick him to a gallop, heading away from them and the battlefield, away from the people amongst whom I was born and back towards the ones I now march with and who have made me their own, too.

IT'S THE FIRST TIME we enter a city as conquerors, riding through the streets on horses with an army behind us, and it's strange because the city we enter is *my* city, the place where I was young and where I grew. It's a sight I never thought I'd see, as no young boys ever think they'll see foreign soldiers marching on their streets, but here I am, and even more strangely, I'm one of those soldiers. We enter through the old walls at the eastern end of the city and ride underneath the large and tall-arched stone gate that's there; Alexandros goes first, then me, and then the rest of the Companions and army after that. We pass under the gate and beyond the walls and continue through the middle of town, and I tell Alexandros the way, down the familiar streets I know so well, and people come to greet us. They come out from their houses, and they wave, and smile, and Alexandros smiles, too, when he sees that the adoration is not just for him, but for me, also, because they've heard what the men who fought already know and have told them, that their own son of Salona, Hephaestion, the old basileus' son who they remember from when he was young, has left, and returned a warrior, and a warrior with a conquering army that rides behind him and a warrior that's rid them of Kleon.

They cheer.

They whistle and yell and call my name as we pass.

Hephaestion, Hephaestion, Hephaestion . . .

There's a dark-haired girl in the crowd and she comes forward to where Alexandros rides and reaches up and offers him one of the blue, trumpet-shaped flowers that are so common and grow wild and in great numbers on our hills and in our forests. She offers it to him, where he sits high on Bucephalus' back, and he takes the flower and reaches down as he does and takes her hand, too, and pulls her up and onto Bucephalus' back, along with him, and when he does the people cheer even louder. The basileus of Macedon, riding with a girl from the north, and the basileus is unwed, too? I know that's what they say, and wonder. I smile. Let them. The girl waves and holds Alexandros' waist as they ride and we continue until eventually we make it all the way through the city, and to the palace.

I see the familiar arches, the familiar paint, the worn and cracking stones that I didn't think of as old or worn before I left, but now? Now I've seen more of the world, and so I see differently the palace and place that was once my home. But even though I see it differently, there's comfort here, too; there's comfort in things that don't change.

We dismount in the courtyard.

We hand the reins to two pages that come forward, and then we go inside. Some Illyrian servants follow after us, to offer anything we might need, and the girl that rode with Alexandros follows, too, not wanting to leave the basileus, I know, but he motions for them to wait, and they do, so we go in alone. We walk underneath the arched and carved doorway made of stone, then I turn down the familiar hallway and begin to walk and Alexandros follows after me. I retrace the last steps I took here, the ones I took in darkness and secret when I left, but I'm older now, and I walk them in light when I now walk them again. And I walk them with another at my side. We go further down the hallway and then come first to my brother's old room, which we don't go into, and instead continue on, and finally come to my room. We'll go inside here. I slowly go to the door and push it open, almost scared at what I'll find, and anxious, and when I do, I see that it's been greatly changed; the room is completely different, with someone else living here, a mistress of Kleon, I'd guess, by the women's clothing and make-up and style of decoration, and also the proximity to the basileus' own chambers.

It makes me sad.

It makes my heart sink in a way I didn't realize it would, to see this, and to stand here, and then Alexandros sees this, too, so he reaches out and puts his hand in my hand.

It doesn't matter, really.

The room doesn't matter.

I continue on.

I go further down the hallway and then we finally come to the great chamber, the largest in the entire palace and city, and the one that belongs to the basileus. I don't have many memories here, only bits and pieces from when my father was still alive and lived here with my mother. I see him again. I didn't think that I would, but I do. I see him here, next to the bed, laughing, and I see my mother, too, laughing with him. I see them together. My brother's a baby, on the floor, but I'm not, I'm older, and I run and play with a toy, a carved wooden soldier that my father made for me and I see their smiles as I run and then I jump up and onto the bed with them, and I hear them laugh. All the greatest moments of the earliest and most formative years of my life happened within footsteps of this very spot, this spot where I now stand again. Where *we* now stand.

"It's yours," Alexandros says. "All of it."

"I know."

"Will you stay and keep it?"

I'm silent.

The question he's asked is the one I haven't been able to answer. I thought I could, and I thought I would stay and rule; for so long, I thought I would rule my father's kingdom, as he would have, if he'd lived, but now? Now, I don't know.

"What happens if I do stay?" I finally ask him, very quietly, perhaps the most quiet I've ever spoken.

"You will be basileus, as your father was, and as you've wanted."

"And if I don't?"

"Then we'll continue."

"And we won't come back."

He doesn't answer. He knows the answer, and so do I, which is why I stand here. I look around us again, and at this room that once belonged to my uncle, and to my father, and my mother, and so many generations of my family, both good and bad. It's where I was born and likely where I was conceived, too, I know. Then I turn and look at him, next to me, and I think of all that's happened, all that we've done together, and all that we still could.

This is my home. That will never change.

But what if *I'm* meant to change? What if, like so many others, I'm meant to leave, and to change, because there's something out there that's more, something else that I'm meant for, something that's both bigger and more necessary than just where I began?

"I can't be without you," I finally say to him. "I thought I could once, but I can't."

"I know. And I can't be without you either."

"So where does that leave us?"

"Exactly where we are, exactly where we all are, which is that each of us that's born into this world has a choice to make: either help shape the world that we're born into, or be a part of it."

I'm silent.

I look at the room, in front of us, and then I turn again and look at him.

"My brother is too young to be basileus," I say.

"He won't."

"Then who would?"

"Your mother."

"Until he's of age, of course."

"No," Alexandros shakes his head. "She will rule. She will be basileia until she dies, and then he can rule after her, if the people choose him. Or they might choose another, who knows. That's the new world that we'll build, Hephaestion, and not just here, which is why we leave, too. We go in search of a world that's based on who we are, and not blood, or tradition, or any of the other things that are meant to control and break us. If we let those things define us, then Arrhidaeus would be basileus, I would be nothing at all, and we wouldn't be here, and we wouldn't be together."

Was it ever a choice? Was it ever really a choice for me?

I want to think that it was, because I don't want to think I willingly chose to leave them, and my home, and all that it gave me, but how many have the chance to do what we'll do together? How many have the opportunity to be born into the world, and study it, and then change it, shape it, mold it to the way that they are, and think it should be?

"This is where we'll stay," I tell him.

"What?"

"This room. While we're here, in Salona, this is where we'll stay."

He looks back at me, at my eyes, with his own. "It was your father's?"

"Yes."

"Then it will be ours, too, while we're here."

"Good," I say.

"Good," he answers.

Then he smiles, because he now knows my answer and finally, for the first time since we've arrived, I smile, too. Change will come, as it always does, and it's us, most fortunate, who will bring and shape that change. That's why we'll go. I don't want to. I want to always be as I was when I was here, and I want to be here with him, but that is why we'll go, because we have to.

I TAKE MY BROTHER fishing to tell him what's been decided.

I leave Alexandros behind, at the palace, and I ride to the shore with him and when we get there I give a fisherman a few bronze coins to let us use his boat for the day and then we start to sail. I tell my brother that it won't be him that will be basileus when we leave and I immediately see that he's not angry. He almost seems relieved, actually. I tell him that it's Alexandros' will, and it's part of the new world he aims to create, and that I'm going to help him create. I'm surprised that he doesn't seem alarmed I don't plan on staying. I'm surprised at this, at first, and then I'm not, and I'm sad, because I realize it's not a change for him; it's simply how life has been, and will be again. I've missed so much. I've missed so much, and so I ask him about all these things I've missed, and that I don't know, and I now won't because of the decision I've made, and he tells me. I'm not shocked when I hear that he's not interested in training, or being a warrior, or anything similar to what I was interested in at his age, and instead he tells me of his love of animals, and specifically birds. He tells me about the falcons he trains in the mountains, and the girl that's also from the mountains, that he loves, and he's going to ask to marry him and when he speaks of her, his eyes flash clear and bright, just the same as Alexandros' do when he speaks of the horizon, and the rising sun, and the world that could be there at the end of it all, at the place where the light begins.

My brother looks at me.

He looks at my own eyes and I can tell he's trying to gauge my reaction, and see if I'd give my blessing to this, to his plan of marriage, even young as he is.

I would.

Of course I would.

He might still be young and not yet a man, but as he's also said, he's older than I was when I left for Pella, and I remember what I felt then, and what I was capable of, and besides, love and other affairs of the heart shouldn't wait; they shouldn't ever wait, not for any reason, not even a day, an hour, a minute, a second.

"What do you think mother will say?" he asks, his eyes wide, innocent, hopeful, all the things they should be.

I look back at him.

I wait for a moment, there with him, on the sea, and then I smile.

"I think she's waited for grandkids her whole life," I tell him, "so she'll be the happiest of all of us to hear, because I'm not sure how much hope she has from me in that regard."

"Why?"

I watch him for a moment, the two of us in the boat, together, and then I just smile, and so does he, not understanding his older brother the way that our mother now understands her oldest son. He smiles so wide, from ear to ear, and then I mess up his hair as I think big brothers should do, and we start back to the shore. I ask him to show me his falcons, so after we return the boat to the fisherman, he does. We ride high into the mountains where the great birds live and where the air is colder, thinner, easier to fly, and he shows me how he holds his arm out with food on it—small pieces of meat, he shows me—and they come and land on the leather glove he wears, their talons wrapping around his arm as they sit there and eat, and then just sit there. He pets them, gently, and I walk forward and I do, too, for the first time looking into the eyes of the great birds of prey.

Golden eyes.

Bright, golden eyes.

They look at me for a moment, their eyes darting this way and that, at the stranger that's there, the interloper, then they turn back to my brother, who they know, and one of them gently nibbles at his shoulder, speaking to him, I realize. Then after this is done, and their food is gone, they spread their great wings and flex narrow and strong legs, and with a great push and rush of displaced air, they take off, back to the sky above. We watch as they fly, higher and higher, into the swirling and strong wind. They keep going, and keep climbing, as they get higher yet, over everything, up to the place where there are no mountains, or rivers, or kingdoms, or nations; they fly up and near the clouds, where there's nothing else besides the wind that comes and carries them to whatever far and distant place they might ever wish to go.

THE SUN BEGINS TO SET, and when it does, we return to Salona.

We go to my brother's room instead of mine, where we change our clothes, and wash the salt and dirt from our skin, then once we're cleaned and dressed, we leave for dinner. It's the four of us that will eat together: me, my brother, our mother, and the girl he's going to marry. He's already asked her to marry him, but he now tells our mother, for the first time, after we sit down to eat, and he speaks with nervous words and a shaking voice but he doesn't need to because she's overjoyed, as I told him she would be, and I am, too. I was happy for them before, but the joy increases when I see them together and the happiness that their proximity to the other brings, which is the most beautiful kind of love and happiness. I look at them with envy, and then I don't, because it's something that I know and have, too, I realize, though in a different way. She's not noble, or wealthy; she's just a commoner from the mountains, as he told me, and from a poor family, and she's not particularly good-looking, either. But they're happy. They're so happy together, and I look at them, and then I'm sad again, because I realize that their life will be one I'll never know. I envy them because even though I know love, their love—one that's more peaceful, and more simple—is one I'll never have or enjoy, and for a moment, I feel jealousy. It's not the bad type of jealousy, or the type that's wrong, or filled with regret, but rather it's just the type that's predicated on the curiosity of the second and third and fourth lives we could have had and that we sometimes yearn for when we see those paths followed by another. It's not a desire to switch or change or have those lives, but rather an acknowledgement of what could have been, and that there's happiness and fulfillment and beauty there, too.

Will there be those same things for me, and us?

I don't know.

Dinner ends and my brother and the girl he'll marry stand, and they leave together, holding hands now.

We smile as they go.

Then when they're gone, I'm alone with my mother.

I look at her when we're alone, and I sip my thin Illyrian wine, and she does the same, too, and that's when I tell her what Alexandros has decided: I tell her that Illyria won't have a basileus anymore, but rather a *basileia*, and that it will be her. This is the new world that Alexandros is creating, I tell her, and she'll be a part of it.

She nods, accepting.

"Does it please you?" I ask her.

"I'll do my best."

"Of course," I frown. "But does it please you?"

"Do you love him?"

I look back at her, light from a candle flickering between us.

I've been asked this before, but not recently.

I know that the Companions think this, and wonder, and they want to ask about it but men don't talk to other men in such ways, at least not in Pella, or Macedon, or Illyria. But mothers talk in such ways to their sons. She's just seen my brother, and his happiness, and now she's thinking of me, too, her oldest son, and mine. She uses the same form of the word love I've already used with Alexandros, when we told each other in the mountains how we felt, and it's a different form than she used when talking about my brother; it's the type that's deeper, stronger, more enduring, the type that I feel, and that fills me. And also, the type that will take me from my home.

"Yes," I finally tell her, and then nod, very simply. "I do."

"And so you will follow him?"

"I've told him I will."

"How far?"

"I don't know."

"You won't come back," she says, and it's not a question.

She's met Alexandros, and I came from her, and am part of her, too, and so I know she recognizes in him what I also recognize, which is where we'll go, and what we'll do, or at least where we'll try to go and what we'll try to do. She's always been blessed to be able to read the stars more clearly than the rest of us, and that's perhaps why I look to them so often, whether I can read them or not, simply because *she* could, and so perhaps this is all something she's already known, too, something she's always known, and perhaps that's also why she's not sad, as I am. She's prepared for this moment since I was very young, perhaps even since I was born, and knew that her oldest would not belong to her, or to his brother, or Salona, or Illyria, but instead he would belong to the world. She made me, though. She made me, and gave me to the world, so she will be history, too. Is that what the stars told her? Is that what she's read in them, the stars that I was born under, and that are there next to Alexandros' stars?

It is.

It must be.

She stands and then comes closer.

I can smell her, and I can feel her, and she bends towards where I sit and kisses me on the top of the head and lets her kiss linger. I feel the warmth that comes with it, flowing from her to me, and it's a gift, too, a great gift that I'm perhaps not yet fully prepared to know or understand, what she's doing, and what she's giving, and how, and why. "Blessed are we," she finally says, very slowly. "Blessed are we, who find and are given such as we've found and would give."

"What?" I ask, with a frown, trying to understand her words.

But there won't be any more.

She kisses me again, on the forehead now, and that's what she'll leave me with, and then she turns and goes.

I sit there for a moment longer, in the flickering light.

Then I blow out the candle, and I leave, too.

I WALK DOWN THE LONG and familiar hallway alone.

I'm deep in my thoughts and thinking of the last thing my mother said to me, as I go back to the old basileus' room, which I'll share with Alexandros, and then I get there. I push open the door and as soon as I do, I pause. In front of me is a mess of bare skin and tangled limbs on the great and wide bed, and I see Alexandros first, then the girl he's with, the dark-haired one he pulled up onto Bucephalus' back with him as we rode through the city, and to the palace.

They look up when I enter, and they pause, too.

"Sorry," I say quickly.

I go to turn and leave, and to close the door, but—

"Wait," Alexandros says.

I pause again. I turn and look back.

She looks at me, and so does he.

"Join us," he says, and I realize I'm not interrupting.

I realize they've been *waiting*.

I stand there in the doorway, for one more moment, looking between them before I finally and slowly walk further into the room, as he's asked, closing the door behind me. I continue on and towards them, across the room, my eyes on him, my friend, and then when I'm close to them both, she stands from where she's been on the bed.

I look at her, at her skin, all of it.

"You see?" Alexandros says, with a smile. "She's pale, too, just like you were when you first came to Pella."

My eyes flick to him, and then back to her.

I take her in, and study her: she's older than we are, I realize, by a few years, which I didn't notice before, and she is more pale than the girls in Macedon, and the south, as Alexandros has said, with skin similar to what mine used to be. He stays there in his place on the bed as she comes forward, and he watches us. She comes closer then reaches out and touches me. Her hand goes to my chest, first, and rests there for a moment, doing nothing, then moves underneath my clothes and gently begins to slip my chiton from my shoulders. It falls down, in front of me, and then with practiced fingers she reaches and uncinches my belt from where it's held around my waist and both things then fall to the floor with a soft noise from the belt as the leather hits the ground and my chiton turns into a puddle at our feet.

I stand there, naked, in front of her.

She's naked, too, and so is he, behind her.

I'm cold.

The air is crisper here in the mountains, and it's nearly autumn, as I've said, and it's night now. She can see me shiver so she takes my hand and leads me towards the bed. We get there, and then when we do, she pulls me down with her, down towards her and Alexandros, and the furs that are there, and warmth that's been between them, the warmth that comes when skin touches skin. At first we lay there, and that's it, that's all that we do, but then it begins. She touches me again, and then so does he, and then she touches him, too. We continue and we do more. There is no light here, there are no candles anywhere in the room, so we can't see anything. We feel, we just feel, and we feel each other, all three of us, and neither Alexandros nor I pay attention to the other, we just pay attention to her and the pleasure that's between us. We continue, further, and so does she, and then at some point in the night I drift off and to sleep while they're still awake and with each other, and when I open my eyes again, I see it's still dark, and though she's gone, Alexandros is still there. Of course he is. He's still under the furs with me, next to me, so when I roll over it's his skin that I touch and his golden hair and familiar scent that I smell. I see him watching me, in the darkness, a strange look in his eyes. It must be the middle of the night, or very nearly morning. "Are you alright?" I ask him.

"Yes."

"Then why are you awake?"

"I don't know."

"What are you thinking about?"

"That we have to leave in the morning, and go south."

"No."

"Their oath-breaking can't go without being punished, otherwise others will join them."

"I know."

"But … ?"

"It can wait a day."

"Why?"

"To spend one more here."

"To do what?"

"So I can show you where I grew up."

He doesn't say anything when he hears that, he just looks back at me, then moves closer and into my arms, under the furs, and he breathes, which I know is his answer, and there's more silence, and more darkness, as we both breathe now.

"You were waiting for me, earlier. When you were with her."

"Yes," I feel his chin nod.

"Why?"

More silence.

He looks ahead, and into darkness.

"Do you know how my parents met?"

"No. You never told me."

"It was on the island of Samothraki. He had come from Macedon, and she from Epirus, and they went to the island to be initiated into the same cult and mysteries, which was one of lust and desire. They went, and while they were there, they saw each other, and though the ceremony lasted three days, they never left each other's side, not through the whole thing. Then when it was over, he swore it would never be over, not for them, because of what he felt for her, and so he brought her back to Macedon to be his bride because he said he couldn't ever live without her, that he could never for another moment live without her by his side, and in his bed. It was his lust that did that, Hephaestion, and clouded his judgement. It was both their lusts that did that, and clouded both their judgements, and look what it brought them."

"They made you, and they made Cleopatra. That's not nothing. As difficult as Olympias is, that's still not nothing."

"She wasn't Olympias then. She was called Polyxena, and she only changed her name later, to commemorate Philippos' victories at the Olympic Games."

"Really?"

"Yes. They were in love once, very deeply in love, and that's how it was for many years until they learned their love was really something else."

I'm silent as I take that in.

"What?"

"Just lust, of course, and temporary. So then once that lust departed, as it always does, all that was left for each of them was the seeds of what would be their own destructions. Philippos couldn't be defeated in battle, but he was defeated by himself, and his own weakness of flesh."

I realize what he's saying to me.

So many others have suspected it, and I know he has, too, but here he is next to me and he's saying it out loud. "Are you sure it was her?" I ask him, softly.

"Yes."

"How?"

"Because I'm them. I'm her, and I'm him, too. Or at least I could be, if I let myself."

"I don't understand."

"It's what I would have done."

"No, you wouldn't have."

"I would have wanted to. The only reason I wouldn't have is because of you."

I look back at him, and as I do, I hear Aristoteles again, and I hear the last words he spoke to me.

Temper him. Give him love.

I've tried.

I've tried, as best I can, and I will always try.

"My father conquered all of Greece, which no one before him was able to do, not for two thousand years," Alexandros continues, speaking slowly. "He was going to march to Asia, and he would have if it wasn't for his lust, and what it brought him. It was his lust that ended all his dreams, and his life, and nothing else. And I have that in me, too, because I have him in me. I have *both* of them in me, and I fight against it every day, as I've told you, and some days I lose that fight, but you, Hephaestion," he swallows, then turns and looks at me. "You're what I have that they didn't, and you're the only one I trust to save me from myself, on the days that I lose that battle, because you're the only one that can. You're the only one that can save me from my own flesh and blood, and who I am, and so that's why I waited for you tonight."

I look back at him and think of all he's said.

I think of Pausanius of Orestis, first, and then after I think of him, I think of the younger Pausanius, the one that I met after returning from Epirus, just before Philippos died. Underneath the furs, I shift my body and move even closer to Alexandros, as close as I can, so that my skin presses against his skin as I hold him, the way that we do in the moments when we need to be warmer and closer. I hold him as tightly as I can because I know that he needs it, and now I know why, too, because now I know what he's known all along, since the day it happened, that his father wasn't killed by accident, or jealousy, or a simple lover's quarrel; his father was killed by Olympias, the woman he once loved and gave himself to, and who was the embodiment of his lust and desire, just the same as he was of hers.

CHAPTER TWENTY-TWO

THE NEXT MORNING, we wake early and go in search of my childhood, and a perfect day. We saddle Bucephalus and the brown and ride out of the city with mist still rising, all around us, swirling and spreading near our ankles, and we ride to the mountains. I take him to the top of them, to the very highest peak, where I used to go and climb as a boy, and I tell him that's how I grew strong by climbing these mountains, and when I reached the top, I'd call and hear my voice echo between the peaks. We do the same thing now. I call his name, and he calls mine, and my voice is lower and stronger than it was then, and his voice is low and strong, too, but they both echo just the same as they did when I was a boy. After we leave the peaks, I take him to the great lake, further down and between the mountains, and where my father first taught me how to fish. We swim in the cold and deep waters, and then I show him the river that feeds into the lake, and we get out, and we follow the river. We follow as it twists and winds away from the mountains, flowing swiftly over smooth rock and further into the jagged and sometimes-steep hills, and then we come to my favorite place: it's the place where water pours off high cliffs and forms a pool below. The pool is shallow, so we don't jump from the top of the waterfall, but ride the horses down behind the cliff, and come to the pool in that way, and then when we get there, we ride into it. We ride so that the waterfall is directly above us and crashes down onto our bodies, water cascading and pouring over our heads, and when it does, Alexandros laughs. I reach over and grab him. I tackle him and pull him from Bucephalus and he holds onto me and pulls me from the brown, too, so that we both fall to the water below, where we continue to wrestle as the horses look at us, and then each other, and then move towards the shore where there's seaweed for them to eat. We keep wrestling in the water as the horses eat, shoving each other under, each trying to get the upper-hand and hold the other beneath the surface for longer and longer until we both grow tired and come back to the shore, too, like the horses have done, and we lay on the warm and moss-covered rocks that are there so that we dry.

Then once we're dry, we leave again.

We go more places.

We go away from the mountains and peaks and I show him a dense forest of sweet pines, and then beyond the forest, we find a field that's filled with the blue trumpet-shaped flowers that grow everywhere here, the flowers just like the one the girl gave to him when we entered the city. We sit there, together, in the field of mountain flowers, the horses grazing, as in front of us the sun begins to sink. It goes further and further as we sit there, our shoulders touching, and we watch it.

Then it's time.

We both know that it is.

The sun begins to sink even further, and so we go back to the horses and climb back up and onto them, and then we ride back to Salona. I ask if we should send to see if the girl from the previous night wants to come back, but Alexandros says no, as I know he will, and so we don't, and we just go to bed.

We sleep.

We just sleep, underneath the furs.

Then, too-soon the morning comes, and with it, so does the moment I've been dreading.

WE STAND IN THE COURTYARD and say goodbye to my family, together, because they're his family now, too, even if they only have been for this short time. And while it's goodbye, it's not tearful, because it's the goodbye of a son and brother who was already gone once. I hug my brother first, and for the last time, and I wish him all the happiness I can wish him and I don't ruffle his hair anymore because he stands with the woman that will be his wife and he'll soon be a man, and so that's how I'll treat him. I hug my mother next, and I don't say anything to her because I know I don't need to, because I know she can feel my words with more clarity and truth than I can say them. I thought she would be the only person in the world that would understand me in such a way. How fortunate am I, though, and as she's reminded me, that I've found another because not all of us do, certainly not all of us do. I move away from her after we've held each other, and then Alexandros embraces them both, too, after me, and when he's done, we go to our horses and climb up and onto their backs, one more time, here in Illyria. We look back at my family, below us, and then we look at Salona, too, and it's a final look at both my home and my family. I breathe in and then hold my breath, committing all this to memory: not the sights, but the feelings, which are the things that are stronger than sights or cities or mountains or blood.

I wave to them.

So does Alexandros.

Then we turn and we begin to ride.

This was the first time we've entered a city as conquerors, I realized, when we first came, and now, when we leave, I realize it's also the first time we'll leave a city the same way, never to return or come back again but to still leave ourselves behind when we go; who we were, and the change that comes with being touched by Alexandros and his Companions. We get further away and continue on and through the mountains, all without looking back, not even once, as we've been trained to do, and it breaks my heart, just a little bit, though above us I think I see a great bird of prey looking down and following our path as we ride. Is it one of my brother's falcons, I wonder? I squint my eyes to try to see, but then the bird banks on the wind, flies in the other direction, and soon disappears into one of the many clouds that dot the endless and un-bordered northern sky.

WE RETURN TO PELLA, but when we do, we don't stay long. The first thing we learn when we get there is that Eurydice has taken her own life while we've been away. She's drunk hemlock alone in her bedchamber, and her servants found her the next morning. Alexandros brings the servants that found her to him and he questions them. They tell him that they also found a sword and rope near the empty cup that was on the ground.

It doesn't make sense to me.

It does to him, though, and I see his eyes darken.

His mother asks to see him, also, as soon as we're back in the city.

We're in our old room in the palace when the servant comes and delivers the message, and we're there because even though we've left the gymnasium since Alexandros is now basileus, and come back to the palace, Alexandros has refused to move into the chamber that belonged to his father. I know why now. He looks at the servant when the message is delivered and then shakes his head. He just shakes his head, and I don't envy him. I don't envy Alexandros, having to send this message to Olympias, and I don't envy the servant, the one that will now have to tell her that her son will not see her.

Then as soon as the servant leaves, there's another knock.

I open the door and am surprised when I see Philotas.

Alexandros is surprised, too, and he frowns. "What is it?" he asks.

Philotas has received a request, he tells us, and most strangely, it's come from Attalus, who has asked to see Alexandros, also, the same as his mother has.

We stand there, the three of us.

I think Alexandros' response will be the same as the response he gave to his mother, but I'm surprised when it's not.

"Where is he?" Alexandros asks.

"He said he'll meet us at the great hall."

"Then I suppose we should go and see what he has to say," Alexandros says to our friend, then stands, and we all go, together. We walk through the palace until we eventually come to the great hall that we know so well, the place we've been so many times and where so many important things have happened: the banquet for the Persians, Philippos' wedding feast when we were exiled, and also where it was decided by Parmenion that the next basileus would be chosen by combat, and not by acclaim.

Will a similarly important thing happen here today?

The hall is completely empty now in daytime, light streaming in and past the tall, carved, and ornate columns, and Attalus waits for us alone and in the shadows. When I see him, I realize he's no longer a threat to us, as this once-strong man who controls all of Lower Macedon looks like a shell of his former self. "You wished to see me?" Alexandros says to him, his voice pitched lower and distinct, in a way I haven't heard before and realize is a voice he'll use as basileus, one he's been saving and honing for this specific moment and time.

"Yes," Attalus nods, then takes a step forward.

I move forward when he does, too, my hand going to the sword I wear at my back and his eyes flick to mine for a moment. I see again there's no threat in him, not anymore, as his hand then goes inside his chiton to where he takes a piece of papyrus and hands it to Alexandros.

It's a letter.

Alexandros quickly scans the contents.

When he's done, he hands it to me.

I look down and see that it's from Athens, and from Demosthenes, promising Attalus that he will be basileus of all Macedon if he rises up with his soldiers from Lower Macedon and fights against Alexandros. "I want you to know it was just him, and not the ekklesia, or the polis, or any of the other citizens," Attalus says, as I finish reading, then pass the note on to Philotas.

"And how did you respond?" Alexandros asks him.

"I came here. My response will be when we show up at his doorstep."

"Why?"

"I didn't choose you, or support you. But you were chosen, and so you're ours."

Alexandros meets Attalus' eyes.

He holds them, with his own, and looks into them and into the soul of this man who was his enemy. And while perhaps he still isn't our friend, he's now somewhere between those two things.

Alexandros holds his eyes, for a moment longer.

Then he nods. "So it will be," he says.

And so it will.

WE PREPARE TO GO SOUTH.

Alexandros had announced an investigation into the murder of his father after he had been killed and before we left for Illyria, and he now pronounces the investigation over, and the death caused by a quarrel between lovers, which the people accept because they'd all seen Philippos with Pausanius of Orestis so many times and also knew that Philippos had cast him aside and that men can do terrible things when they're cast aside and told they're less than another. We know the real reason, though, me and Alexandros, and I think there are many more in Pella and beyond who do, too, though they only dare whisper the truth behind their hands and in darkness because they fear her as much as I do, as much as we both do, and they also know what she's capable of.

I'm glad we don't see her.

I'm glad Alexandros chooses this, and that he keeps her away from the palace, and from us. She pulls on him, and the only way to stop that pull is to not let it begin, and so we waste no time. We only stay in Pella for two days: time enough for the soldiers to see their families, play with their children, sleep with their wives, and then it's time to strap our armor back on, climb back astride our horses, and once more ride south to a once-conquered kingdom that needs to be conquered again.

CHAPTER TWENTY-THREE

WE MARCH QUICKER than we ever have before, without stopping, which is something Alexandros insists on, telling us that the energy we exert and sleep that we miss will save lives, and it ends up doing exactly that. When we arrive at Thebes, we catch the Thebans completely unaware. They didn't think we would win in Illyira as quickly as we did, and they also didn't think we would stay in Pella for as short a time as we stayed, and they *of course* didn't think we could march south at the pace which we have and altogether it's a series of massive miscalculations.

When we arrive, we see Theban farmers still outside the walls.

The farmers and their families begin to grab all they can carry and then run when they see us and the thick cloud of dust that travels with our army. They of course know what that dust means, and as we get closer to the city, and the dust begins to gather, and then settle, we watch as they take all they're able to take and hurry inside the great walls and we could have ridden them down and killed them before they'd gotten there—at least the hetairoi could have, those of us on horses—but Alexandros says we won't because we're all Greek so these are our countrymen, too, our brothers. Some of the men protest, but Alexandros tells them that these aren't our enemies, these common folk who are outside the city; our enemies are their leaders, the ones who broke their oaths, and once those leaders are punished and gone, then these are the people who will march to Asia with us in pursuit of the future, in pursuit of a new and even larger world than the one that exists on this continent and peninsula, a world that we will all share, all of us, together.

We choose Perdiccas to send as a messenger.

He rides away from our lines and towards the walls.

The gate opens when he gets near the walls, and a Theban comes out, and Perdiccas speaks with him. Perdiccas offers Alexandros' terms of leaving the city in peace, we know, even if we can't hear his words, as long as the Thebans hand over the oath-breakers and ring-leaders of rebellion, but as we watch, we see that Perdiccas and the Theban don't speak for very long, which we all know can't be good or promising. The Theban then leaves, and goes back inside the city, and the gate closes behind him again and Perdiccas turns and gallops back towards us.

"Well?" Alexandros asks, when he reaches where we wait.

"There will be no peace," Perdiccas shakes his head.

"What did he say?"

"Nothing."

"I saw you talking. He had to have said something."

Perdiccas pauses, and glances at us, the rest that are gathered and watching, then he looks back to Alexandros.

"He laughed, and then gave me his counter-offer," Perdiccas finally says.

"Which was?"

"That if you hand over Parmenion and Hephaestion to be be-headed on the top of their walls, for all to see, then they'll let us leave this field and place in peace."

I frown. Me?

I understand Parmenion, the strategos for both the old basileus and the new, but me along with him?

How do they even know who I am?

It doesn't matter, because it won't be considered, of course, and Alexandros' eyes flick to Parmenion. "Is there any news of the other poleis, or anyone else?"

"There's nothing from Athens, or any other that fought with them at Chaeronea," he says.

"And Sparta?"

"There's been nothing from the Peloponnese, either. There are troops that have moved, but none have left the peninsula, or gone beyond Corinth."

"Then why are the Thebans so bold?" Alexandros asks, and the question hangs there, between us.

It's clear why they are, though.

They don't respect him.

Alexandros waves his hand and all the others bow and leave, and when they do, I stay behind. "Fools," he whispers, under his breath, as soon as they're all gone.

"No," I say, shaking my own head.

"No?"

"Wouldn't we do the same? Even if the greatest army in the world were at our gates, with soldiers numbering more than waves in the Aegean, wouldn't we say the exact same thing, believe the exact same thing, and fight to the death and the very bitter end in the exact same way?"

He looks back at me.

He cocks his head up and to the side, as he does, and the light catches his face more and in a different way and spills jagged and fractured across his features.

"We wouldn't have broken our oaths."

"No," I say, agreeing with him.

"But you're right," he says, and then smiles. "We would fight."

"Yes."

"I'm glad we're not them, though."

"I'm glad, too."

They have insulted him. They have insulted him, and called him a boy, and now they'll pay the price. "I'm glad that we're not them," he says, "and that we're us."

ALEXANDROS ORDERS OUR ARMY closer to the city, or as close as we dare while still remaining out of range of the arrows they can fire from the tops of the walls. But we can't find a way past the walls, so days and weeks pass without much fighting at all. There are a few skirmishes when riders leave the city, the gates quickly opening and closing and the archers above shooting arrows to give cover as we mount our horses and ride after them. Sometimes we catch them, and there's fighting, and sometimes we don't. They're messengers, we assume, travelling again and again to all the other poleis of the south, begging for help against the barbarian tyrants and oppressors that are at their gates, begging for troops, begging for supplies, begging for anything that might save their city and their lives.

But their gamble doesn't pay off because no help comes.

They seem to have an endless supply of food, though, and Alexandros begins to grow restless waiting outside the walls for them to starve. The walls are too high to climb and too strong to breach, so all we can do is wait, and some are better at that than others. The Companions begin to settle in and enjoy themselves, drinking their wine and once again finding local women to come to their fires and tents, and in this way they're content to wait as long as the Thebans are content to wait, which is something Alexandros is unwilling to do. He's stopped drinking wine, there are no women for him, and he stays up all night in our tent, pacing back and forth, unable to sleep. We're better fighters, he tells me, over and over, and we have the stronger army, so why can't we just win? Every night he paces in our tent and asks these questions, even after I've gone to sleep, trying to find answers, and every night he prays, too, asking the gods for their help, which is something I haven't seen him do before, asking them over and over and over again for something to manifest and come that will help show us the way.

And then, after a few weeks, something does come.

Well, not something, but *someone*.

It's late in the afternoon and the Companions sit at one of the fires they've built, and they drink, and talk too loudly, and I sit with them as the sun sets around us and everything's colored a brilliant burnt-orange, a hue and tint that stretches across the uneven fields outside Thebes where we wait. Then I see a rider that approaches, coming across the fields and towards our camp. I see that he comes from the north and I frown because he doesn't ride well, which means he's not a soldier, and so who could it possibly be and coming from that direction? The guards from our camp ride to meet him and I watch as they reach him, and the stranger speaks with them, and then I squint my eyes and recognize him and realize he's no stranger at all. I almost don't recognize him, at first, because it's been so long, and he's far away, and also because this is the exact last place I would ever expect to see him, but here he is.

Callisthenes.

Aristoteles' nephew.

I stand from the fire and go to where he speaks with the guards, a leather case strapped across his back, telling them he needs to see the basileus, but the guards of course don't believe him until I arrive and greet him and then the guards leave and it's just the two of us.

"What are you doing here?" I ask him.

"My uncle sends his greetings," he tells me as he gets off his horse and rubs his legs, his thighs, his lower back, not used to making rides of the distance he's just made.

"Of course," I say, shaking my head, still not understanding. "And that's of course most welcome, but he could have just sent a letter with either of those things. Surely he didn't need to send you all the way here with just his greetings?"

"No, he didn't," Callisthenes tells me, and then meets my eyes. "He's heard of what's happened here, and so he sends something else with me, too."

"And what's that?"

He looks deep into my eyes.

Then he smiles, and when he does, he reminds me of his uncle.

"A way to end this," he tells me.

WE GO TO LOOK FOR ALEXANDROS, and we find him quickly enough, still in our tent where he paces and barely leaves now as he tries to figure what to do about the siege that isn't really a siege, it's just waiting. He looks up when I come in, and then when he sees Callisthenes, behind me, he comes and embraces him, then holds him away and at arm's length, looking him up and down. "Have you grown?" he asks. "You look taller."

"You look well, too, Alexandros-basileus."

"Please," Alexandros slaps Callisthenes on the back. "You've seen me cry, so it's just Alexandros. What brings you to the south?"

"A message, from my uncle. And a gift."

"A gift? What type of gift?"

"The type that brings victory."

Alexandros looks back and forth, between us. He doesn't understand.

I shrug because I don't either, or at least not yet.

"What can possibly bring us victory? The walls are too high and too strong."

"I'll show you," Callisthenes tells him, "but you have to promise something in return."

"Promise to Aristoteles? I've already done that."

"No, promise to me."

"What is it that you want?"

"I want to go with you."

Alexandros looks from Callisthenes, to me, and then back to Callisthenes again. "I don't understand. You want to fight? I can't advise for someone who hasn't trained to do that, but of course there are enough Thebans to kill for any who wants to join, if that's truly what—"

"No."

"Then what?"

"Asia," Callisthenes whispers, and the word slips from his tongue as if it's honey, or nectar, or both mixed together. "Everyone knows that's where you'll go next."

"I thought you were a scientist."

"I am."

"There is no science in conquest. There's just death, and blood."

"Yes, of course. But there's one other thing, too."

"And what's that?"

"*History*," Callistehenes says. "That's the science I've decided to study, and dedicate my life to, the science of the stories that we tell and history, unless I'm very mistaken, Alexandros, just as my uncle saw, history marches with you."

Silence.

Alexandros looks back at him. He cocks his head up and to the side, even though there's no sun here in our tent. "Aristoteles," he asks. "Does he approve?"

"No."

"But you're still here."

"His life is his, and my life is mine."

Alexandros waits, looking back at Callisthenes.

Then he finally nods. "So be it," he tells him.

"Thank you, Alexandros," Callisthenes says, and bows his head, and that's how it's settled: Callisthenes will join us, when we go east, to be the recorder of our journey, however long or short it may be and however important or unimportant, but there's one thing that still comes first, one thing that's still here, and still in front of us, and still needs to be done. "Now what have you brought with you?" I ask and nod to the leather cases that he carries on his back.

"Plans."

"Plans for what?"

"They're designs," he tells us, then takes the case from his back and opens it to take out rolled sheets of papyrus. I look at Alexandros, for a moment, then we both turn and push aside the things that are on the table in our tent and Callisthenes unrolls the papyrus and spreads the sheets across the surface. He puts a sword, a knife, and a helmet on each end to weigh them down and keep them pressed flat, so they don't roll back up on themselves, and we look at them.

They're drawings.

I see lines, sketches, angles, calculations, and many more things I don't quite understand.

"What are they?" I ask.

"Siege engines," he says, pointing at them. "This one is called a catapult, and the other here is a trebuchet."

I look at them again and then I see what they are, what he's showing us, and I also see how they work.

Next to me, Alexandros comes to the same discovery.

"Aristoteles thought of these?" he asks.

"No," Callistehenes says. "They come from Siracusa and an engineer there who designed them for just such a task as this, to take a different impenetrable walled city, there on their peninsula. He gave the plans to my uncle some years ago, when he visited the island, before our time in Mieza."

"And they will work?"

"He wouldn't send me here if they wouldn't."

Silence.

I can see Alexandros, calculating, then he turns to me. "Every soldier we have, Hephaestion," he says, quietly at first, and then louder. "Begin making these engines tonight, with every soldier that we have, and don't stop until they're done."

CHAPTER TWENTY-FOUR

It takes us five days to build the siege engines.

We have to search for a forest, first, and enough wood for us to cut, and when we find one a half day's ride to the north and west, we begin to chop and split the trees that we'll need for the materials to construct the machines. The Thebans find where we are, and that we're away from the main army, and when they do, they launch armed forays against us as we work. There are a few skirmishes, but not much blood is shed. They can't defeat us in open combat, they know, and we know, too, so all they're doing is simply delaying the inevitable.

We soon have enough wood.

Once we do, we go back to our camp, where we hack and saw and fashion the pieces that we've felled together according to the designs that Aristoteles has sent with Callisthenes. Then after a few more days and a few more details and additions of rope, leather, and stone, the engines are finally raised and complete.

We divide the men into groups of five.

We push the newly-constructed engines into position, at a safe distance from the Theban walls, and then each group is in charge of rolling large boulders up and onto the wooden arms that we've created. Once the projectiles are there, we stand back, and then try them for the first time. We cut the rope that holds the arms coiled and down, and once we do, we watch as the arms quickly twist and extend, pulled by the great weight of boulders attached to the other end, and the boulders that we've loaded as projectiles go sailing through the air. In the first volley that we fire, they all miss: some fly over the walls, and we hear screams on the other side, and some fall short and harmlessly into the dirt, and we hear nothing at all. We make calculations and adjust arms and angles, then we try again. We find the range with the second volley and when one of the boulders crashes into the Theban wall, tearing a huge hole where the impact occurs, a great Macedonian cheer goes up. We fire more and more, after the first volley that connects, and a great number of boulders still miss their targets, but some don't; they tear into the walls and it doesn't matter that some of our shots miss, because time is on our side, and there are many large rocks and boulders in these fields and hills.

Callisthenes watches all of this, expressionless.

What is he thinking?

What will he write about this, and about us?

I'm not sure, but I find that I'm curious and I find my eyes turning to him as he watches the siege that goes on for a few days, the boulders that fly through the air and tear more holes in the walls, with many hitting and breaking completely through. And then, once there are enough openings, and a section of wall has completely collapsed, Alexandros orders the army to assemble and to take their positions behind him. Our force divides, with some of us ready to lead the charge through the breach the siege machines have created—the hetairoi first, and then the pezhetairoi behind us, to fill the gaps—and the other group, which will be led by Parmenion, and are all pezhetairoi, will go around to the far side of the city, the northern side. The walls are still intact there, but we've built more machines that are akin to moving towers, and so while the main Theban army defends the breach, where our main army will attack, the walls behind them will be sparsely defended if even defended at all, allowing

Parmenion and his men to jump from the towers to the walls and then down to the city itself. Once they do, and are in the streets and behind them, the Thebans will be surrounded and caught between two forces.

The plan works.

Actually, I'm surprised at how well the plan works.

The catapults stop and so do the rocks and boulders that fly through the air.

And that's when our charge begins.

We gallop across the great field, Alexandros out in front, on Bucephalus, and me next to him, on the brown, and then we reach the breach we've made in the walls and fight our way through it. Soon we're inside. We cut down those that stand in our way, and it's the Theban men that we fight against, as behind them women and children scatter through the streets when they see us. Some of the women come forward and throw themselves at us, and beat at our armor with their fists, and some have small knives, too, but we don't harm them, we just push them away. We harm their husbands, though. We do a great deal of harm to their husbands, and sons, and brothers who swing their swords and meet ours, and then we cut them down, there in their streets, there in front of their houses and temples and families and gods.

It doesn't last long.

The smaller force led by Parmenion is able to jump from our towers to the northern walls, without much resistance, and then they come through the streets, too, and fight their way towards us. They reach where we fight, the Thebans trapped between our two forces and with enemies on all sides of them, everywhere they look. They see this, and when they do, they know it's over and so they throw down their swords and raise their hands.

We lower our swords, too, breathing heavy.

We all turn to look at Alexandros, next to us, covered in dirt and blood and still astride Bucephalus as he surveys another city that's fallen before him, and that he's conquered.

What will he do?

We ride through the streets and this time when we ride it's different than at Salona: there is no cheering, there are no cries of support, no encouraging waves or calls from men and women and children who know our names and smile when they see us because they've just been freed from an evil and unjust ruler.

Instead, there are just looks. Dark and untrusting looks.

And there is also wariness, and distrust, deep anxiety and fear in regards to what will happen next, and it presents a new and unique problem for us; what to do with a conquered people who are unwelcoming.

We go to a great temple, in the middle of the city.

We dismount from our horses, all of us Companions, and soldiers come to hold them as we leave and go up to the temple on foot. We walk past the great pillars that are there and in front of it, and then go inside, and that's where we see a massive open space, and in the open space, a large and tall statue carved from polished marble.

Athena.

Wisdom.

We stand there in silence for a moment, looking up at it, at the features that are carved in her face, the lines in her armor, the intricacies and nuance of the work and skill and craftsmanship that's brought wisdom here and to life. "So what happens now?" Alexandros finally asks, still looking up at her, at the statue, at the god.

The Companions all glance at each other when they hear his question and there's silence for another moment. He's never asked this before, and so bluntly.

Perdiccas finally speaks.

"You've conquered their city. They will swear an oath to you."

"They already did that once, and they broke it."

"No," Kassandros shakes his head. "They swore that oath to your father."

"They didn't. They swore to the basileus of Macedon, and I'm the basileus of Macedon. So if they've broken one oath, what's to say they wouldn't break the next one, too?"

They all look at each other again.

They swallow, really not knowing what will be next.

I do, though.

"There's no other option," Nearchos finally says. "It's an oath, or nothing."

"Yes, there is," Alexandros answers, then brings his eyes from the statue back down and to our friends across from him. "There's always another option."

"What?" Ptolemaios asks, frowning.

I look back at Ptolemaios and study his words, and his intentions. I thought he would have gone in a different direction in action and temperament since Cleopatra's wedding, but he hasn't. He's seemed to bury his feelings and, at least for the time being, this seems to have worked as he's steeled his heart and focused only on things that matter and are at hand, or soon will be, and the things he can contol.

How long will it last? How long will it really last, for any of us?

I don't know.

A broken heart only has a short time until it's either mended, or stays broken forever.

"You've already made up your mind," I say to Alexandros.

"Yes," he nods. "I have."

"And you made it up three years ago, when we first fought them, didn't you? You knew then what they would do, and you knew then, also, what you would do, too."

"They're oath-breakers. I could tell that they alone amongst all the southern Greeks were oath-breakers, and dishonorable, and they alone amongst those who fought against us had no loyalty. They deserve this. They fought with the Persians, when they came, and against the rest of us. So out of anyone on this peninsula, or in this world, they're the ones that deserve this."

"Deserve what?" Perdiccas asks, and the question hangs in the air.

All eyes are on Alexandros, and on me, too, but Alexandros just looks back and now up again at the great statue of wisdom in front of us. I look at the Companions and I think they can see what's in my eyes, and feel what's in my heart because they nod, and then slowly begin to leave, walking out of the temple, back to the streets and the city and the army that waits for us.

Once they're gone, it's just me and him.

Silence. More silence.

"If you knew this would come, then you already know what you'll do."

"Yes," he nods, very quietly, very slowly.

"So why did you ask them? Why did you bring them here and ask what they thought?"

"For the same reason as before. So they feel part of it, and so they feel part of me, too, and what we decide."

I look back at him and I know the gift that I've been given, because while they may not be a part of him, I am. I also feel the great weight of that gift, the burden I will also have to bear and the burden that Aristoteles foretold in his sanctuary of peace and knowledge in the rugged western hills of Macedon. And, I also now realize, he created that sanctuary for just such a moment, and to influence just such a basileus as the one that's here and before me. Alexandros looks down now, from the god, and turns to meet my eyes as my words echo between the pillars and then fade, and when they do, there's nothing left in the stillness but us.

I swallow. So does he.

"We tell each other everything," he finally says.

"Yes."

"So tell me what you're thinking."

"That we don't tell each other everything."

"What have I kept from you?"

"On the road, outside Athens. What did Diogenes say, when you were alone with him?"

He looks back at me again.

Silence.

More silence.

Echoes, and then words fading again, between the pillars.

"He told me he was searching for the bones of my father, but he couldn't distinguish them from the bones of a slave."

"So that's your answer, then? That's what this is about?"

"*Change* is my answer, Hephaestion. My father built this army, and this kingdom, in so many ways, and making them swear another oath that they would just break again is exactly what he would do. He would make them swear another oath, and then he'd go to Asia, and he wouldn't get further than the Hellespont before they'd declare themselves our enemy and it would happen all over, and again, and again, and again, and again after that, and he would never be able to make any difference or make it to any other part of the world because he would never be able to leave this peninsula, not really, and that's why he was Philippos."

"Yes, he was."

"And I'm not."

"But do you want this? Do you want this burden, on your soul? It's a very great price to pay."

"They've been cursed, Hephaestion. Ever since Laius and Chrysippus, they've been cursed."

"It's a city, Alexandros, and these are people. This is not a story. It's not a myth, told to children to teach them a lesson."

"No," he whispers. "Not yet."

I see it.

I see the light that's in him, so often, and I also see the darkness, too, because here it is again, and I think of Aristoteles when I see it, and when I now feel it. I think once more of the charge he gave me, and how this is now a moment in which what I will do will matter, and be remembered, for both of us, and this is perhaps even a moment he foresaw.

He was a studier of history.

And he was a studier of us, too.

So he knows what will happen, and what he's helped create, what we've *both* helped create, and this is the cost we'll pay for our dreams, right here, right now, in front of us, decided under the great and carved statue of wisdom above.

Have we made him proud? Will we make him proud?

"Will you stop me?" Alexandros asks. "Will you tell me that the price is too great?"

"I didn't mean the price for them. I meant the price for us."

"I know."

And so there it is.

May the gods forgive us.

If they were here, would they? If they were here, what would they say, for they'd surely say something because they made us, right? We wait for one more moment, both of us looking up at the statue we've called upon and stood under in criss-crossed shadows, and has she answered us? I don't know. I hope so. We turn and go back outside. I feel a breeze that's picked up, coming from the south now, from the sea, and the Companions are there and so is the army and they're waiting for us. They all stand and wait for word from the basileus, and what he'll decide, and then he does. "Spare the temples," he tells them. "Burn the rest."

WE STAND ON A LOW HILL and watch as the entire city is engulfed in flames. After we leave, soldiers walk through the streets with torches, as Alexandros has ordered, lighting anything they can find and then watching it catch and burn before moving on to the next building. Alexandros and I return to camp, though, and when we get back, Alexandros sees Callisthenes waiting, and he goes to him. He dismounts from Bucephalus and goes to stand in front of him—him first, of all who are there—trying to read his eyes, his thoughts, his emotions, this man who shares his blood with the one whose approval Alexandros perhaps craves and cares about more than any other.

"Do you have anything to say?" Alexandros asks him.

"No," Callisthenes shakes his head.

"Just no?"

"I'm a recorder, Alexandros, nothing more. It's you who are basileus."

Alexandros stands there and looks back at Callisthenes, for another moment, then gives an order for none to disturb him and he goes to his place on the hill, alone, to watch what he's ordered. I know that his command is for all but me, so I go with him, and that's why I stand there, too. Light dances and flickers in front of us, on the horizon, turning it an even brighter shade of orange than it's been before. There are no screams. All the people have been brought from the city, and so they don't burn, only their buildings do: only their homes, their lives, their futures, and their memories.

The flames lick, crack, climb higher into the sky.

So does the smoke, which drifts up and towards the stars.

Will the gods see that smoke? Will they see it, and know what we've done, and will they punish us?

"I built a statue for them and this is how they repayed me," Alexandros finally says. "I gave them every chance to surrender, and honor their oaths, and this is what they chose instead."

"They're just men."

"So?"

"They chose wrong, as men do."

Silence.

Flames, smoke, and silence. More time passes.

"This will live with me, for the rest of my life," he finally says again, and his voice is still soft, no longer the basileus, just the man. "I will carry this with me, Hephaestion, wherever I go."

"Which means that I'll carry it, too."

"It's the price we pay to dream."

"Yes," I say, very slowly. "Perhaps it is."

I turn back to the sight in front of us, and as I do, I know that I've failed.

I've failed him, and I've failed myself, too, and I think I've always known that I would. But perhaps it's also still alright, and it's still as it should be, because if we fail, it doesn't mean anything is over, it simply means that we get up and we try again. We stand there, together, in the night, in the darkness, and we don't move as the city burns in front of us; we don't move until the first rays of light in the morning come, and the buildings in front of us are just ash now that spreads and drifts and floats in the southern Greek wind. I know there will be those that write of this moment, and will remember it different; I know there will be those who are enemies of Alexandros and of me that will say that we killed everyone in the city, and that our army raped and enslaved them, but that's not what happened, or what he did. When morning finally comes, Alexandros leaves the low hill, and so do I, and he sends a messenger to Athens, and to Demades, the man who stood next to Demosthenes at the ekklesia but didn't agree with him. He brings Demades to the great plain where Thebes used to stand and watches as Demades and the other Athenians arrive, and take in what we've done, and the once-great city which is now no more. Demades tells Alexandros after he recovers his speech that Demosthenes acted alone, and didn't have the backing of the ekklesia, or anyone else, and that's why the other Athenians have come, too, to vouch for that, and Alexandros responds by telling Demades that he sent for him to tell him that all the people in front of where we now stand—all those in the Theban camp, who no longer have homes, or lives, or anything else—will now be his problem.

"What am I supposed to do with them?" Demades asks, not understanding.

"Bring them to Athens, make them citizens, or don't, I don't care," Alexandros tells him. "But know that if any of them ever revolt again, or *anyone* on this peninsula does, then it will be you that I'll hold responsible, and it's your city that will burn next."

Demades swallows. He understands. "Is there anything else?"

"Yes. I want Demosthenes' head," Alexandros says, his final word, and then he turns and leaves.

He walks back towards where the army waits, and the page that holds the reins to his great horse, with the brown next to him, as he always is. Alexandros jumps onto Bucephalus and I climb onto the back of the brown, and then he turns to the army. He looks past them, first, towards all the men, women, and children of Thebes that wait to be taken to a new polis because theirs is now gone. Then Alexandros turns from them, and he looks at the army, at his father's army, at his army, at our army.

I hear a word.

It's just one, at first, and it comes from a single, faceless soldier.

Then others hear it, and more pick it up, and they begin to chant, too.

I strain to hear what it is that they say, and then I don't have to, because it grows, and builds, until more and more take it up and soon it's everywhere, all around us, almost shaking the very earth with its strength, its noise, its ubiquity.

Megas, megas, megas . . . Alexandros ó Megas.

This is the moment? This is the moment they choose?

Forgive them.

Gods, forgive them, for they're just men, as I've said.

They keep chanting, and as they do, Alexandros turns and he rides towards me. He comes close so that it's just us two, just us two together, and nothing else, the Companions behind us, and the army behind them, still chanting; louder, louder, louder.

"What is it?" I ask him.

"Promise me we'll never grow old."

I look back at him and I think it's his father he's thinking of again: the great warrior and basileus reduced to a single eye and debilitating limp and the scorn of his many wives and his blood spilled at the hands of one who was only anything and anyone because Philippos was.

"I can't do that," I shake my head.

"Promise me, Hephaestion," he says again, and I see the fire in his eyes.

I think his father is the reason why he asks, and then I realize, it's not; I realize it's something else, because who can possibly live for very long carrying the burden and weight of such things as we'll now carry, and that we've just done?

I look back at him.

I understand now, and I nod, because this can be borne, and perhaps this is why we have just one soul, between us, because we can bear it, together, but not for too long.

"Alright," I tell him. "I promise."

I sit there next to him, on our horses, and as I do, I finally realize, after all that's happened, that this is the price. This is the price the gods demand, the price that they always demand, and it's our happiness and the lives we could have had.

But we will pay the price.

For immortality, and for greatness, we will pay.

CHAPTER TWENTY-FIVE

WE RETURN TO PELLA, but once again we don't stay long, because it's a city that's now no longer our home and hasn't been for some time. I think we both can feel that, because if our journey thus far has shown us one thing, it's this: that home is elusive, and for us to do what we now will, then our home must move, too, because our home, for each of us, has become a person, and not a place. Our home, for each of us, has become each other, and that's what it will always be and what it *must* always be, for all the days that we have left, for all the places that we'll go and conquer and leave pieces of ourselves behind to grow and change and spread and create more homes, more places where all the people of the world will be welcome and brought together and give each other love as we have given love to each other.

That is what we march towards. That is what we'll make.

There are final things to be done, though, while we're still here, and before we leave, and there are final things to be said, too.

Olympias comes to our room.

Or at least she tries to, and I'm surprised when Alexandros locks the door and refuses to see her. She comes again and again, hour after after, but he refuses each time and then eventually puts guards at her chamber door with strict orders to not allow her to leave, not under any circumstances, not to go anywhere, until after we're gone and out of the city.

The plans are all put in place: Antipater will stay behind as regent to hold and rule the kingdom while Alexandros is gone, as he did when we went north, and south, and he'll do the same now when we go east. There's only one direction amongst all we've discussed and planned that hasn't been accounted for, and I'm surprised when Alexandros of Epirus, who's stayed in Pella with Cleopatra while we secured again what Philippos had already conquered, tells us that now things are settled on the peninsula, his eyes have begun to wander, too, and they've begun to wander in a different direction.

"Where?" Alexandros asks him.

"The only place you haven't been, or aren't going," he says, with a smile. "To the west, and the Etruscans and *their* peninsula, on the other side of the Ionian Sea, and the last place I'll be able to expand both your kingdom, and mine. There's a city of Greeks there called Taras, and they've sent and asked for my help in their battle against the Lucanians and another tribe from further north that they call Roman."

"And you will fight for them?"

"I'll fight for us, for Macedon, and for Epirus. You may chase the rising sun, Alexandros, and I might chase the setting sun, but they're both still the sun, right?"

Alexandros nods and embraces his uncle who is now also his brother, too, and three days later Alexandros of Epirus and Cleopatra, who is now Cleopatra-basileia, prepare to leave and go back to their kingdom. We all gather in the courtyard to see them off and my eyes search the others that are gathered until I find Ptolemaios, who stands stone-faced, neither his eyes nor his temperament giving anything away, not anything at all.

I frown. I'm surprised again.

Alexandros says goodbye to his uncle, first, grasping his arm and then embracing him once more, too, and then turns to his sister. He goes to her and I can't hear what he says, as she comes close and he whispers into her ear, but after they embrace, and hold each other, then finally move apart, I can see the tears on both their cheeks. This is his hardest goodbye. This is his only goodbye, really. They stand there together for a few more moments, then she reaches up and wipes one of his tears away, and finally turns from her brother. She starts to walk and comes towards where I stand, until she's right there, and in front of me. I can smell the perfume she wears, the one made of mint and thyme that I remember from the first day we met, and she embraces me, also, and the scent floods my nostrils again, filling my nose and head as she stands on her toes and whispers into my ear, too. "Take care of him, Hephaestion," she tells me, and her words enter and fill me, and I let them. I want them to.

"I will," I nod.

"*Please*," she says, and her voice is different.

"I will," I say again.

"And think of us sometimes?"

I remember Delphi and I hear again the words that we heard when we stood outside the shrine and in front of the Pythia.

Once you leave Greece, you will never return.

We heard the words then, but we both already knew, didn't we?

We both already knew where our futures would lie, even before stone and sulfur and prophecy.

"Always," I tell her, as I nod again, too.

She smiles sadly and when I see her smile, I know that she knows this, also; she knows what I know, and what we both and all now know, but there's nothing that can be done to stop fate and so rather than try, she turns back to her husband, takes his arm, and they leave. She looks over her shoulder as they go, just once, because she hasn't been trained to not look back, like we have, and then she keeps walking. Alexandros and I watch as they go into the city, first, and then through it, getting smaller as they continue on and out of sight. The Companions begin to talk amongst each other once the basileus' sister and her husband have left, and then the Companions all begin to leave, in pairs, heading back towards the gymnasium, and then Alexandros leaves, also, going back into the palace.

Soon they're all gone. All except one.

I make my way towards where Ptolemaios stands, alone, with no one else near us now, or in the courtyard.

There's silence.

He stays there, staring at the horizon, towards where they disappeared.

"She was the daughter of the basileus," he finally says, and then slowly turns to look at me, the only one in Pella now besides Alexandros that knows his secret, the only one that knows *their* secret. "I always knew it would be this way. We both did. But I would've made her immortal, Hephaestion," he says, and his voice is just a whisper now, a small crack amongst the stillness and I see the single tear that's slipped down his cheek. "I would have given her *everything*, and I would have made her immortal."

I think of my own love.

I think of what my life would be if we had been denied or prevented by things beyond our control, unnecessary things that keep us from happiness and our destiny and purpose while we're here on this earth. I see that he holds something in his hand, turning it over and over in his fingers, and I look to see that it's a twig, a small twig, twisted and broken, taken from an olive branch I recognize from a night long ago, a night where there were two lovers in the darkness, slipping away from adults and the world, the skin of the twig now worn and peeled from years of handling and carrying with it the gift and curse of both hope and pain.

"Did you throw the spear at Philippos' wedding to defend her, because Attalus called them both illegitimate?"

"Yes."

"That's the reason all this happened, you know. That's the reason we left, and the reason for the wedding that brought us back, and which made Alexandros basileus."

"I *love her*, Hephaestion. And I know that you, of all that ride with him, knows what that means, and what it does to us, and makes us feel and do," he says, and I can hear the pain in his voice, the pain that he knows I understand. I stand there for another moment as he stares at the empty horizon and the city that's now just gone back to being a city; ignoring his hurt, blind to his plight and all that's just happened and been taken and the way the whole earth has now moved for him, as it once did for me and Alexandros, too, but in a different way and direction. I think of the feast again, and what happened there, and how it was his love for her and what he did that ultimately set in motion the events that would place her in the arms of another.

I reach out and take Ptolemaios' shoulder, and I take it firmly.

I want him to know that he's not alone, not when he's with us, not when he's a part of this, too, and all that's going to come.

"We go to make a new world," I finally tell him.

"So?"

"In the new world we go to make, the one where anything could be possible, perhaps you still might have a chance at immortality yet, for both of you."

THERE'S ONE LAST THING that needs to be done.

Everything is ready for the army to leave, and then the day before we're due to set out, I decide to walk through the palace once more. I go to the basileus' office first, where I met Philippos on the day I arrived in Pella, and I stand in front of the great desk again. I think about who I was then, and what I thought, and felt, and then I think about who I am now. The office belongs to Alexandros, since he's basileus, but when I stand here I will always think of Philippos. I think of his gifts, first, and then I think of his curses, the ones that Alexandros also carries but is determined to fight against and not give into, then I turn to look at the place where Pausanius of Orestis used to stand by the door, in the days of Philippos-basileus. I then leave the office and continue on through the palace and come to the garden where I met Cleopatra, who smelled of thyme and mint then, when I met her, as she still does now. I think of what we spoke of and how she was the first to know who I loved, and who her brother loved, and I stop walking. I can hear the lyre again, the way she played it, and I can hear her voice. It's there, for a moment, and then it fades, as all things fade, and so then once again, when it's gone, I continue. I leave the palace and courtyard and walk into the city. I go past the great Temple of Dionysus, on the same route that Pausanius of Orestis took my first day, then I go past the stables, too, and the blacksmith. Finally, I reach the gymnasium. I go inside. It's empty this afternoon and I walk across the sand that's been mixed with sweat and blood and dreams and all other things that brought us together and defined our lives when we were boys here and together. I look down at my once-pale northern skin that's summer-dark now, like theirs was, when I first saw them, even though it's not summer.

I keep walking and I go to my room.

I expect to find the room empty, too, but it's not; there are things here, a chest of folded chitons, two belts made for waists smaller than mine, a worn stone used to sharpen a blade, and a small carved figure of a girl. Who do these things belong to? I think back again to when I first arrived, and I think of all the moments which have come since, and made me who I am, and have now become gospel as all the small and important moments of our lives do, and then I think of the stars. I think of my stars, that are above us, and I think of his, too, and how blessed am I that they're the same stars? How blessed am I that through fate and gods, my life was chosen and made and placed next to his? That is what I'll get to witness, when we go east, and what I'll get to see: the way the world changes. And most fortunate of all men, I'll get to do it with the one I loved when I was young, and is there any blessing in our lives that's greater? There isn't. I'm a companion and a witness—that is my fate and future and who I am—but my fate and future will also be greater than that, too. My fate and future will be greater than all others save one, because the soul that I shape and that I share will be the one that shapes the world, and we'll shape it and make it as we've been shaped and made, while we were young, and were together, and here, in this very spot; we'll shape it as we've felt, as we've travelled, as we've learned, and wept, and loved, and laughed, and cried, and dreamed, or at least we'll try to do all that, and most certainly we'll die from and during our trying, in some way or the other, as we all do. We will certainly die, either in success or failure, and at some distant time and place from here, when we're no longer as we are now, and will it be enough? I don't know. I believe that it will be, but the truth is I don't know, and truly, truly, truly . . . what else is there? Aristoteles saw a world with Greece at its center, but Alexandros? He doesn't see Macedon, and Greece; he sees only the world. That's his gift. He doesn't see nations, or think in places, he sees and thinks in people. We will march and that's what we'll march towards and others will join us. I know that others will join us, too, and while I don't know how long it might take—it will certainly take longer than our lives, much longer than the sum of our years and days and hours and who we are in this world—but then one day, perhaps, one day, one day . . . one day, maybe we'll all be able to march together, all of us.

I think of my mother, and I think of my brother.

I think of my blood and what I leave and there is a deep and profound ache in my soul for the life with them that could have been, but perhaps there will still be another, one where we can be together, all of us, and grow old, and since there is an ache in my soul, as I think of this, is there one in his, too?

There is.

I know now that there is, because there is one in mine, which means that there's still one thing that's left, just one last thing before we turn east and ride towards the sun, just one last thing before we set out to chase the horizon and the unknown, as we were both born to do.

I THINK THAT ALEXANDROS will be with Parmenion, making last minute preparations with the army and the soldiers, but when I find Parmenion, I see that Alexandros isn't there with him. Parmenion is getting the army ready by himself, preparing for the longest journey and march and time away from our homes and country that any will have yet experienced. When he sees me, he tells me that everything is nearly complete, and that it all will be ready by the next day, when we're due to leave, and he tells me that the Persians know that, too, as he's just received reports of an army gathering near Karia in the Western Satrapies, and he's heard they're under the command there of a mercenary named Memnon.

Could it be, I wonder?

Could it be the same Memnon as the one that saved our lives?

I smile, and I have no doubts, because if there's one thing I've learned in my life thus far, it's this: that history is written long before us, and it lives long after us, and for those of us who can read the stars then sometimes we can get glimpses of it while we're still alive, and still here, on this earth. Armies move as our hearts move, but men? Men move in no strange ways at all.

I think of Memnon again, and the last thing he said to me.

In this great world and grand scheme of gods and stars, and all their plans that have been written and recorded, what is just one boy and his friend?

The world.

Perhaps, as he will now find out, that's the whole world.

"What is it?" Parmenion asks, curious about my smile.

"Nothing," I tell him, as I shake my head, and then I thank him and leave him and the army behind, and I continue on. I search for Alexandros at the barracks, next, because I think he might be getting ready there for the great expedition we're about to undertake, and when I don't find him, I go to the armory after that, in the lower city, where I see Kassandros organizing all the weapons we have and will bring and he tells me Alexandros isn't there, either. I go to the blacksmith after the armory, where Philotas oversees making as many sarissa as possible, because there are of course no sarissa in Asia, and when I find Alexandros isn't there, I turn and go to the agora where I see Philotas. He's with those that buy food and supplies and he's overseeing the purchasing of provisions, enough for the army for at least three months, and when I speak with him, he tells me he hasn't seen Alexandros since the day before last. I go to the temples that are near the palace, and I don't find him there and the priest at the Temple of Dionysus who readies the sacrifice that will be given before our departure tells me he hasn't seen the basileus, either. I search through all the rest of the city, then give up searching, because I don't know where else to go, and so I return to our room and that's where I find him. I walk in and I'm surprised to see him on his bed, because that's the last place I'd think to look for him with so much still to be done before the great moment he's worked his entire life towards, and which is now here.

And when I see him, I frown, because I've never seen him like this.

He lays there and tells me he wants to stay in our room, and on his bed, and I ask him why, but he doesn't answer. He just lays there. I tell him there's something we have to do today, before we leave, and I insist that he comes with me, and when I do, and go to try to pull him from the bed, it seems like he can barely move.

Why? Why is he like this, and why now?

He asks again where we're going, and I don't say.

I just tell him that we have to.

He looks at me strangely when I tell him this because he wonders what I'm talking about, I know, but I still won't tell him, at least not yet. I'll show him because I want him to feel all that I've just felt: it's our last day here in our city, and I've decided that our last day should be the same as our first, and so I take his hand and pull him from the bed and bring him to do the exact same things as we did before, when we were young, all those years ago. We walk down to the gymnasium together, first, which is no longer empty but filled with boys now that are younger than us, and they train the way that we trained, when we were their age, and they're surprised when they see their basileus amongst them. Alexandros just smiles, though, as he seems to come more back to himself here in this place and he tells them to continue on and go about their exercises, the next generation of warriors, the next generation of Companions that we'll leave behind here to train and be better than their fathers. Then we continue on, too, as they resume their exercises, and we go out and to the garden, where we first met.

We stand there, for a moment, in the sun, together.

Then after we leave the garden, we go to the stables.

Alexandros goes to Bucephalus, and I go to the brown, just the same as we did then, and we jump up and onto their backs and start to ride and leave the city. We go north and through the wide and rocky countryside, and then we begin to head up and into the mountains. We climb higher and higher, and go across a familiar stream, our horses leading the way from memory and we, who ride them, not having to lead or guide. We soon reach the top, and the lake, and the horses walk into the water, up to their knees, to eat some of the seaweed and to cool down, but we don't. We leave the horses in the water and walk to our spot on the bluff that looks out over Pella, and Macedon, and all else that there is and that Alexandros now rules, and we sit.

We take it in, all of it, one last time.

We both remember all the times that we were here, and what we dreamed of, and spoke of, and felt, and now?

Now all of that is before us.

"What if we stayed," Alexandros says, from his place next to me, as he still looks out at the horizon. I'm surprised at his question, and surprised to hear his voice small, different, unlike I've ever heard before.

"What do you mean?"

"I've lost everything," he says, and I hear his voice crack now, and I can see the emotion in his eyes. "I've dreamed of this, we both have, of all of this, but it's cost me my mother, my father, my sister..."

"Do you think you're the only one? Because I've lost those things, too."

"So what if we stayed?" he asks again, then turns to look at me. "What if we didn't go east, and we stayed here in Pella, or Pella and Illyria both, like you wanted when you first came, and we ruled what we've already conquered and were happy. We would never lose each other, or anyone else," he says, then swallows, and looks at me. "What if we stayed here, Hephaestion: in our cities, and in our mountains, and beside our sea... just the two of us."

I stare back at him, and everything fades.

I see him as he once was, when we were young, and then I seem him and us as we could be, growing old together, with our family, making new family, laughing, and running, and hunting, and living where we grew.

We would be happy, as he said, I know that we would.

But the world is not made and changed in such ways.

I sit there and look back at him and I've seen one future, so now I ask to see another, and when I do, lightning comes in a way it never has before and I realize something, what Aristoteles meant, all those years ago. I think of the moment after Chaeronea, and when Alexandros defeated Amyntas, and I thought those were the moments and things that lived within Alexandros that Aristoteles wanted me to save him from, and that was how he wanted his pupil tempered, and why he wanted him given love. I only now realize he asked me to give him love so that love would travel with him, wherever he went, because that's the only way he'd keep going, the only way he'd even set out, the only way and reason any of us ever do.

Behind us, a city lays in ruin.

It won't be the last, we both know, and that will be the price.

Aristoteles knew that, too, I now realize; he knew that there would be cities laid waste, and there would be a very terrible price to pay for all this, as there is for any great thing that's done, but the reward would be greater than the price, wouldn't it? The reward would be far greater. Thebes is now gone, never to rise again, from ash, completely wiped off the map of Greece and the world, but what is a map? It's just lines drawn on parchment and in dirt and those lines... those are what we will destroy. Those lines containing nations, separating people and places that say this is you, and that is us, and that's how it is and always will be because that's how it is and always has been. No. That's what we march against, Alexandros and I, and those are the lessons of Aristoteles that we'll bring with us, wherever we go, and that's also what we'll end. There will no longer be Macedon, and Greece, and then the world; now, once we're finally part of it, there will only be the world.

More comes.

I swore that I would never ask Alexandros what Aristoteles said to him, in confidence, before we left, but now his words come to me, too, swift and sure, and so I can only assume that they're needed and they come directly from the gods.

Make the world as it was when you were here.

Of course.

That is our goal, and our duty, and though it will take the sum of our lives, though it will take the entire sum of the rest of each of our lives, we will try. We will try, we will always try, because that's where a wild and golden-haired boy on a great horse once told me that the gods live; not in the stars, where we so often look for them, but in us, when we try, and when we strive, and when we dream.

"Other men stay," I finally say, answering him, my words, my voice, just a whisper now, too.

"And so what do we do?" he asks.

"We leave, and we change."

"I don't want to change."

"We already have. So it's not us that will."

He looks back at me and I meet his mis-colored eyes and I don't know what will be next, the same as he doesn't, but we know the path and what we'll find and make, and we know each other. Then he leans closer and he presses his lips against mine and it's the first time that he's done this in a long time—since Ithaka, I know—and it's not lust, or desire, or meant to be anything else but exactly and precisely what it is: closeness, intimacy, a mixing and filling of souls that are already mixed and filled.

Agape.

Then he turns one last time, to the horizon, our horizon, and when he turns he doesn't look south, and to what we know, but east, and to what we don't, further, further, further, on and towards the path and future that will be ours, the one that we'll take and walk and make, the one that we'll take and walk and make together.

He will set out, I know.

He will set out, and he will change the world.

My job is done.

Alexandros, Hephaestion, and the rest of their Companions crossed the Hellespont in the Spring of 334 BCE with a combined army of Greek, Illyrian, and Thracian soldiers, as well as soldiers from other northern tribes. They conquered the entire Persian Empire, without ever losing a battle, and eventually made it as far East as India and the Ganges River. As the Pythia at Delphi predicted, they never returned to Greece.

The influence of Alexandros ὁ Megas and his accomplishments is vast, with many cities that he founded becoming important cultural centers, but perhaps his most influential accomplishment was his vision for uniting all peoples of East and West, especially with a common spoken language, which would later pave the way for the spread of a new religion that was brought to the world by the son of a carpenter from Nazareth. The New Testament, which tells of Jesus' life, death, and resurrection, would be written in Koine Greek and spread both East and West once it was written, where it could be read and understood by all those in every corner of what had once been Alexandros' great empire.

Alexandros didn't live to see this influence or accomplishment, though. Hephaestion died in October of 324, at the age of 32, and Alexandros, fulfilling his oath to never grow old and not go on without the second half of his soul, died just a few months later, of unknown causes. He was only 33 years old.